Praise for

KISS OF SALVATION

"In his new, riveting murder mystery *Kiss of Salvation*, Waights Taylor Jr. takes readers back to Alabama in the 1940s, a time not unlike our own. With help from a colorful cast of characters, black and white, rich and poor, he offers a fascinating portrait of the American South on the cusp of the civil rights movement. There's electrifying suspense every step of the way, a healthy dose of romance and real compassion of the sort one expects from the author of *Our Southern Home*, his exhilarating non-fiction narrative that readers from Alabama to California have embraced with a vengeance."

—JONAH RASKIN, author of *American Scream: Allen Ginsberg's Howl and the Making of the Beat Generation* and *Rock 'n' Roll Women*

KISS OF SALVATION

A JOE McGRATH AND SAM RUCKER DETECTIVE NOVEL

Also by Waights Taylor Jr.

Non-Fiction

Our Southern Home
Scottsboro to Montgomery to Birmingham
The Transformation of the South in the Twentieth Century (2011)

Alfons Mucha's Slav Epic
An Artist's History of the Slavic People (2008)

Poetry and Fiction

Literary Ramblings
Poems and Short Stories (2010)

Works in Other Publications

This Is What a Feminist Looks Like
The Sitting Room: A Community Library (2014)

Beyond Boundaries
Redwood Writers Anthology (2013)

Healdsburg Alive!
Eight Sonoma County Writers Pay Homage to a Great Northern California Town—Healdsburg Literary Guild (2012)

Love—Poetry Valentines
Healdsburg Literary Guild (2011)

Healdsburg Area Poets from the Hearts
Healdsburg Literary Guild (2010)

Nov. 11, 2014

Dear Marion,
Hope you like murder mysteries.
Love,
Waights

KISS OF SALVATION

A JOE McGRATH AND SAM RUCKER DETECTIVE NOVEL

Waights Taylor Jr.

McCAA BOOKS • SANTA ROSA

McCaa Books
1604 Deer Run
Santa Rosa, CA 95405-7535

This is a work of fiction. Names, characters, places, and incidents are the products of the author's imagination or are used fictitiously. Any resemblance to actual events, locales, or persons, living or dead, is entirely coincidental.

First published in 2014 by McCaa Books, an imprint of McCaa Publications.

LIBRARY OF CONGRESS CONTROL NUMBER: 2014913617
ISBN 978-0-9960695-1-9

Printed in the United States of America
Set in Minion Pro
Cover design by Suzan Reed
Author's photograph by Star Dewar

www.mccaabooks.com

To
LIZ

MAP OF DOWNTOWN AND
SOUTHSIDE BIRMINGHAM

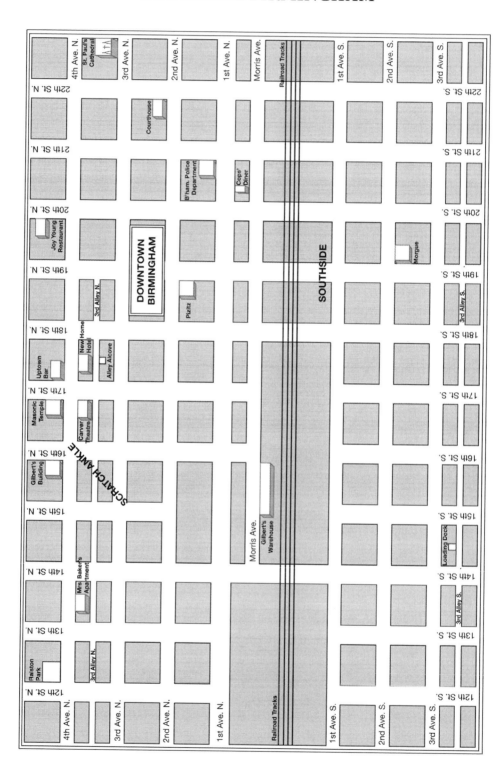

CHAPTER 1

THE BEGINNING

SUNDAY—SEPTEMBER 14, 1947

T HE WEEKEND HAD BEEN QUIET. Joe McGrath liked it that way as he ate breakfast before going to eight o'clock Mass at St. Paul's Cathedral. He had little interest in religion, yet he occasionally yielded to his childhood habit of attending church as if to hedge his bet with God and the hereafter.

Joe felt haggard after another restless night. He seldom slept well since his wife left him seven months ago. He was cleaning up the breakfast table when the phone rang.

"Joe McGrath here."

"You gotta check somethin' out right away, Joe."

"Can't it wait, Chief? I'm just leaving for Mass." Joe didn't expect to get a sympathetic ear to his tepid spiritual needs. He was one of the few Catholics in the department, and most of the cops and the chief considered Catholics a strange religious sect in this predominately Protestant city.

Chief Watson didn't disappoint him. "Nope. You git over to Third Alley North between Seventeenth and Eighteenth in Scratch Ankle. A colored woman's body was found there early this mornin'. Jerry Howard's there now with three men. Coroner's on the way. I want you to take charge."

"Is that all you know?"

"Goddammit, Professor, it was just reported around six. But you know it's busy in the colored part of downtown on Saturday night. There's always lots of partyin' and drinkin' going on. Anyways, get your ass over there and try to clean it up quick and neat."

"What's the big deal, a homicide?"

"No big deal yet. I don't know if it was a homicide. I just don't wants no colored woman's murder or foul play gittin' the big boys in Birmingham riled up. It's been pretty quiet in that part of town lately, and I wanna keep it that way. They expect us to keep a lid on anything that might stir up the darkies. Git movin'.'"

"Okay, Chief. I'll get back to you later today."

"I'll be back home after church and lunch around one or two. Call me on my car radio if somethin' comes up before that."

"Will do. That it?"

"Yep."

Joe hung up, wanting to say, *Yeah, you go to church and lunch while I do the dirty work*, even though he knew this was what he was paid to do.

Joe left the dishes in the sink and performed a ritual he did each day before going to work. He pulled his gun, a Colt Official Police 38, out of its shoulder holster. He loved the feel and heft of the gun in his hand as the shiny bluish carbon steel gleamed at him. He checked that all six chambers were loaded, placed the gun back in the holster, and strapped it to his left shoulder. Joe pocketed his badge, notepad, and pens to complete the standard toolset of his profession. He stuck a pack of Camels in his shirt pocket and put on his tie, coat, and hat.

He was not a sharp dresser. For work, he bought off-the-rack clothing at Pizitz, the city's big, low-price department store. He favored dark colored suits—mostly blacks and grays—white shirts, black shoes with white socks, and simple, unpatterned ties that blended into the dark suits. His one concession to fashion was hats, and today he wore one of his favorites, a seal gray Cavanagh fedora.

Before he left, he phoned the desk officer.

"Birmingham Police Department, Sergeant Donaldson speaking."

"Billy, it's Joe McGrath. I need some info on a call that came in around six o'clock this morning concerning a body found in an alley over in Scratch Ankle."

"Hey, Joe. I just came on duty at seven. Lemme check the log. . . . Yep, here it is. The call was logged at five fifty-eight by Dean Alison. The caller reported a body in the alley behind the New Home Hotel on Fourth Avenue North. The caller was the hotel night clerk, Dave Williams. A guy named Eugene Gould found the body. Jerry Howard and his guys were assigned to follow-up."

"Were Williams and Gould given any instructions?"

"Yep, told to remain in the hotel lobby until the cops arrive."

"Anything else?"

"Nope."

"Thanks, Billy. See you later."

He walked to the curb to get his unmarked police car, although the license plate, an antenna, and a large searchlight mounted on the left front side of the car made the vehicle's use obvious to most people. The brutal late summer heat wave had finally subsided, making the weather tolerable. It was a clear day, or as clear as Birmingham ever got with the iron and steel furnaces blasting smoke into the air day and night.

CHAPTER 2

THE CRIME SCENE

SUNDAY—SEPTEMBER 14, 1947

I<small>T TOOK</small> J<small>OE EIGHT MINUTES</small> to drive downtown on Twentieth Street South through the viaduct that went under the railroad tracks, the vital industrial arteries separating the city's Southside district from Downtown Birmingham. Joe emerged on Twentieth Street North, the main drag in the white business district.

He turned left at Fourth Avenue North and drove past Eighteenth Street North into Scratch Ankle—the accepted, but unmarked, line of demarcation between the white and colored business districts. Whenever Joe came into Scratch Ankle, he visualized the colored men and boys convicted of petty or trumped up crimes who gave the area its name. Until 1928, the state leased the "convict laborers" to the mines, where they were kept in chains and developed itchy welts and bruises on their ankles.

Approaching Seventeenth Street North, Joe saw the New Home Hotel. The alley was blocked by a police car with red lights flashing. A small crowd, mostly colored, stood observing the scene. He looked for signs of a press presence but saw no recognizable reporters. *Good,* he thought, *maybe we can get this off the streets before they get wind of it.*

Joe parked his car across the street from the alley and wrote the time, seven twenty-one, in his notepad. Although he had an excellent memory, experience had taught him that what seemed an unimportant item at the time could later become critical to a case. A few words or a time entry in his notepad could prove to be a useful memory reference.

Joe lit his first Camel of the day. *Goddammit, McGrath. You gotta quit.* He had started smoking again after Mary left him.

Before he entered a possible crime scene, he always reviewed the layout of the area to see if anything caught his eye that might prove to be pertinent in an investigation. He checked out the intersection of Fourth and Seventeenth. The Carver Theatre was on the southwest corner, the Masonic Temple on the northwest corner and the Uptown Bar, a well-known hangout for pimps and prostitutes, on the north-east corner.

Joe then focused his attention to a parking lot on the southeast corner of Fourth and Seventeenth. The chained off lot, about 120 feet deep by 35 feet wide, was in a state of disrepair with numerous weed-filled cracks in the pavement. The one car in the lot appeared to have been there for some time. Adjacent to the lot was the hotel, four stories tall. On the side of the hotel facing the lot, a huge sign had been painted in three lines.

FOR COLORED PEOPLE
NEW HOME
HOTEL

Joe jotted in his notepad, *Why parking lot not used? Busy corner: hotel, Masonic temple, bar, two theaters.* He knew a second colored theater, the Champion, was a few doors east of the hotel.

Near the alley, a young BPD officer he didn't recognize approached him. "Can I help you?"

Joe pulled out his badge. "Homicide Detective Joe McGrath. I'm here to oversee the investigation."

"Sorry, sir. I'm new with the department. I don't know all the senior officers yet."

"That's okay. You're just doing your job. Where's Jerry Howard?"

"Down the alley on the right with the coroner and the body."

"Thanks uh . . . What's your name?"

"Steve Strickland, sir."

"Steve, keep an eye out for any press. Gimme the high sign if you see anyone who even looks like a reporter," Joe said.

"Yes sir."

Joe walked into the alley. Another police car blocked the other end on Eighteenth Street North. The first two buildings to his right, whose fronts would face south on Third Avenue North, had their back areas fenced off. He made a note that, if necessary, he would interview people at the two theaters, the temple, the bar, and the hotel, and have Howard handle the other buildings and businesses near the scene.

The next building faced south on Third Avenue North and was the only building with its back area unfenced. Joe stopped to observe the alcove and the body. The coroner was inspecting the corpse. The woman lay flat on her back with her skirt pulled up over her waist. She had no panties on. Her legs were spread apart in a V, her arms pressing tight against her body. The symmetry of the body position, especially the arms, left the distinct impression that it had been arranged. He could see evidence of trauma around her neck. The ground was devoid of grass and most other vegetation, and the area immediately around her noticeably disturbed, indicating either robust sexual activity or a struggle, or both. Joe scanned the area for panties. None were apparent.

Jerry Howard walked up to Joe. "Hey Joe, I've been expecting you." Jerry was a tall, thin man who always wore a dour expression that belied his good nature.

"Hi Jerry. Sized it up yet?"

"Looks like homicide. It appears she was strangled. Cutter got here about twenty minutes ago with one of his lab guys. He's doing his thing and taking photos. He said the coroner's van is on the way."

"Have you gone over the site carefully?" Joe said.

"We were doing that when Cutter took over."

"Where are the guys who reported the body?"

"They're both in the hotel. Ralph Owens is with them to make sure they don't leave."

"Where are your other officers?"

"One's watching each end of the alley."

"Good. Stick around while I talk with Frank."

Joe avoided stepping on the dirt around the feet of the body and took several steps to Cutler's side. Joe knew Cutler would avoid disturbing the crime scene until both he and homicide finished their initial work.

Dr. Frank Cutler was in his mid forties, short, on the heavy side with a round face that, while chubby like a cherub, most people found attractive. "Cutter," the department's nickname for Frank, was used only when he was out of earshot. He was outgoing and voluble, a fun guy at a party. Observers were always amazed at his dexterity and precision when performing an autopsy, especially considering his pudgy hands.

Joe stared at the body. "Frank, what do you think we have?"

"Oh, hi Joe. It's definitely a homicide. Appears she was either raped or had sex with her likely killer. I'm going to move her to the morgue as soon as you give me the clearance to do so. I want to get her on my table for an extensive exam before any semen gets too old."

"Any idea on time of death?"

"Probably around three this morning. The body temp is ninety-two degrees. The onset of rigor mortis is consistent with my estimate. I'll finalize the time after my full exam."

"That neck abrasion looks pretty bad."

Frank nodded. "I think the killer used a garrote. A quick way to strangle someone. But I gotta examine the neck trauma in the morgue to make sure."

"Isn't it strange the body appears so symmetrical?" Joe said.

"Yeah. The murderer probably arranged it right after he killed her. Lividity indicates the body hasn't been moved. The front of the body is clear. The blood drainage is in the back and buttocks."

"Do you think he's trying to leave some kind of message?"

"I don't know, Joe. That's your job."

"We'll need the body in place for a few minutes to complete a more thorough search."

"Sure, but tell your guys not to touch the body or her clothing."

"Okay, Frank. We'll be through in a few minutes. I don't think your van is here yet."

"It should be along any minute." Removing his gloves, Frank moved away from the body and lit a cigarette.

Joe called to Jerry, motioning for him to come over. "We need to go over this area and the alley as much as possible until Frank's van arrives. I'm sure you noticed her panties are missing."

"I'm not blind," Jerry said.

Joe ignored the dig. "I'll do the area around the body, and you cover the alley. Look carefully for garbage cans or other containers where the killer might have dumped the panties. Also, look over the fences of all the businesses and buildings backing the alley. Note if anything looks interesting, and we can return to those spots after Frank removes her body. Remember, don't disturb the dirt area around her feet; we may be able to get a footprint impression. Let's move. We don't have much time."

"Okay," Jerry said, adding under his breath, "Professor."

Joe paid no attention to the insult. He was used to the chief and others making snide comments behind his back about his religion and education. Once he overheard the chief say to a group of cops, "That goddamn papist professor, he thinks he's so fuckin' smart with his college degrees and hi-falutin' talkin'." And occasionally he heard others use the time-worn epithets of "mackerel snapper" and "rosemary rattler."

Joe knelt beside the body to get a good look at the woman. Attractive, her skin color was soft brown, hair cut short, and probably in her twenties or early thirties. She wore a tight fitting, light blue halter-type top, which even now accentuated her breasts. She wasn't wearing a bra. Her dark blue skirt had been pulled up over her waist. Joe's initial thoughts were substantiated by what he saw. The young woman was likely a prostitute, as Scratch Ankle had a large number of colored pimps and prostitutes who worked the bars, nightclubs, and streets.

Joe combed the ground adjacent to the woman's body to no avail. Other than the disturbed dirt around her body, there were no physical objects or anything else of interest. He turned his attention to the remaining grounds in the alcove with the same results. There was one garbage can and a container in the alcove. The panties were in neither, but he knew it was possible there were no panties since some prostitutes didn't wear them to simplify turning tricks. He made a note to have the crime lab guys bring the two containers back to headquarters. He finished writing his note as the coroner's van pulled up to the alcove.

Frank reappeared. "Joe, my van just arrived. You guys through?"

"Just a sec, let me check with Jerry." Joe looked down the alley and saw Jerry walking back toward him. "Find anything?"

"Nope. We'll get into the fenced off areas in the alley soon," Jerry said.

"Okay."

Joe turned back to Frank. "You can take the body. Give the victim's clothing to the lab guys. Check 'em with a fine-toothed comb."

Frank said, "We've got it. I'll have more for you later today."

"I've got to report to the chief this afternoon. Can you have anything for me before then?"

"I'll try. How do I reach you?"

"Try my home phone first and then my car radio."

"Okay," Frank said, then called to the two technicians, "Bag the body and put it in the van."

"Thanks, Frank." As Joe left the crime scene, he saw young officer Steve by the yellow tape. "Things okay, Steve?"

"Yes sir."

"See anyone that looks like the press?"

"No sir."

"Good. Stay here. Let me know if they show up. I'll be in the hotel."

"Yes sir."

CHAPTER 3

THE INTERVIEWS

SUNDAY—SEPTEMBER 14, 1947

J OE HAD NEVER BEEN IN THE HOTEL LOBBY. He was surprised to see how ornate it was—beautiful oriental carpets, handsome lobby furniture, and an elegant chandelier hung overhead. He approached the clerk behind the check-in counter and held up his police badge. "Are you the guy that called the police about the body in the alley?"

The well-dressed young man said, "No sir, I just came on duty at seven. He's in a meeting room with another colored man." He pointed to a door in the rear of the lobby.

"What time did you arrive at the hotel this morning?"

"About six forty-five. The police were already here."

"How did you get here?"

The clerk's lips quivered. "I rode a bus from my apartment to downtown and then walked here."

Joe smiled at the clerk. "Relax. It's okay. Did you see anything unusual this morning?"

"No sir, it was really slow, even for a Sunday morning."

"Has anyone checked out of the hotel since you arrived?"

"No sir."

"How many guests are still in the hotel?"

"I just checked the register. We have twenty rooms occupied by thirty-five guests. We have seventy-two rooms, but the weekends are slow unless something special's going on."

"We'll want a copy of all the guests' room numbers, their names, addresses, and phone numbers. I'll have an officer pick it up soon. I'd also like you to make a drawing showing where all the rooms on each floor are located. I'll be particularly interested in those guests in the rooms in the back near the alley."

"Yes sir."

"If any guests come down to check out while we're still here, contact an officer. We want to talk with them before they leave."

"Yes sir."

Joe crossed the lobby to the meeting room, knocked, and announced himself in a loud voice. "Homicide Detective Joe McGrath."

The door opened and a cop said, " Hi, Joe. Been waiting for you."

"Ralph, I didn't know you worked with Jerry."

"I don't usually. I swapped days with a regular on his squad. Come on in. I figured we'd see you here soon."

Joe looked across the room at the two colored men sitting side-by-side on a sofa. Joe said quietly, "That Williams and Gould over there?"

"Yep. The boy on the left over yonder is the night clerk, Dave Williams. The other one is Eugene Gould, the colored boy who found the body," Ralph said.

"Let me talk to them alone. Stand guard outside the door and keep everyone out until I finish."

"Okay, Joe."

Joe looked at the two men sitting on the sofa. He could tell they were nervous and unsure what to expect.

"Good morning, I'm Detective Joe McGrath with the Birmingham Police Department." He showed them his badge. "You must be Dave Williams, the hotel night clerk."

Joe offered the men his right hand. The men looked at each other in confusion. It was rare for a white man to initiate a handshake.

"Yes sir, I'm Dave Williams." He stood and shook hands with Joe.

"And you're Eugene Gould, the man who found the body."

"Yes suh, I did." He shook Joe's outstretched hand.

Joe sat down and said, "Sit down guys, I need to ask a few questions. It's all routine stuff when something like this happens. Eugene, let me start with you. Why were you in the alley this morning?"

Joe guessed Eugene Gould's age at between fifty and sixty. He was medium height, appeared to be in good condition with a trim physique, and was dressed in a pair of denim coveralls, standard attire for working class white and colored men. Eugene was pitch black, and the whites of his eyes and ivory white teeth stood out in stark contrast to his dark face.

"Well suh, I works the All Day Diner on Eighteenth. I lives in an apartment on Fifteenth. I works the early shift six days a week. I gets Mondays off. I walks through the alley from my place to the diner."

"What do you do in the diner, Eugene?"

"Oh, I reckon you might call me the handyman. I bus tables, washes the dishes, fixes little things that gets broke."

"About what time were you in the alley?"

"A little after five thirty. I leaves my apartment at five thirty to get to work on time. The boss don't like it when I'm late."

"So, tell me what happened."

"I crossed Seventeenth and went back into the alley, and there she was laying flat on the ground."

"It was still pretty dark, Eugene, and the body's in an alcove where it must have been even darker."

"Yes suh, it was dark—jus' a touch of first light—and I always carry a flashlight. I don't know why, I reckon jus' curiosity, but I always looks into that . . . what'd you call it?"

"Alcove."

"Yes suh, I always looks into that alcove. Maybe it jus' 'cause all the other buildings have the alley fenced off. Anyways, I always slows down and looks in that alcove expecting to see something, like somebody gonna jump me. Never did see nothin' until this mornin'."

"Did you walk into the alcove and take a close look at the body?"

"Yes suh, I did. I turned my flashlight on to get a better look. I could tell it was a woman and things didn't look too good."

"What did you see?"

"Well suh, it wasn't pretty. What I most remembers is her dress being pulled up around her waist and she didn't have no panties on."

"Did you touch the body or pick up anything?'

"Oh, no suh. I knowed it was trouble."

"How did the body appear to you?"

"Suh?"

"How was she lying on the ground?"

"Oh, I sees what you mean. It was kinda funny. She looked like a doll. Her legs were apart and hers arms were right tight to her side, like somebody just laid her down real gentle like."

"Did you recognize the woman, Eugene?"

Eugene paused and looked concerned, as if he didn't want to answer the question. "Yes suh, I did. I thinks I seen her a few times walking the streets at night, if you knows what I mean."

"I know what you mean. Do you know her name?"

"No suh. I only seen her a few times, and I jus' looked at her 'cause she real easy on the eyes."

"Do you know her pimp?"

"No suh, I don't knows that kinda peoples."

"Could it be Charlie Bartlett? He goes by Bongo Drum."

"I heard that name, but I don't knows him."

"What did you do next?"

"I first thought I'd jus' go on my way. Forgit it. Keep my mouth shut. Let someone else take care of it. But she looked so young. I jus' couldn't do that. I didn't wants to go to the diner and tell my boss, so I went to the hotel."

"How long from the time you first saw the body until you went into the hotel?"

"Oh, not more'n five minutes."

"Did you see anyone or any cars before you went into the hotel?"

"No suh."

"So you went into the hotel. What did you do then?"

"I walked right up to this here young man sitting next to me and said, a body of a woman is in the alley behind your hotel."

"Thanks, Eugene. Let's pick it up with you, Dave. Why do you work the night shift?"

"I'm paying my way through Miles College. This job pays well, and I can study since it's usually quiet. I work five nights, Wednesday through Sunday, so I get some catch up time on Mondays and Tuesdays. I just started my senior year."

Joe figured Dave was in his early twenties. He was well-groomed and dressed, well-spoken, about six feet tall, slim, light brown in color, and, but for a harsh look of determination, had a pleasant face.

"Tell me how you reacted and what you did after Eugene told you about the body?"

"My first reaction was disbelief. I asked Eugene if he was sure. He said he was sure and asked if I wanted to see the body. I said no. I took his word for it," Dave said.

"Why didn't you want to see the body to confirm it yourself?"

"I'm not supposed to leave the front desk unless it's an emergency. I believed Eugene. He seemed honest, and I couldn't imagine why he would have made it up."

"And then what?"

"I asked Eugene to tell me what he saw, and he told me the same thing he just told you. I called the police."

"What time was that?"

"I'm not exactly sure, but I think it was about six o'clock."

"What did you tell the police?"

"That a man had just come into the New Home Hotel at 1703 Fourth Avenue North and told me there was a woman's body in the alley behind the hotel. The policeman asked our names, and I gave them to him."

"What did the police officer tell you to do?"

"To stay put in the hotel lobby. He said some police officers would be over shortly to check the situation out."

"What time did the police arrive?"

"It was six twenty-two."

"You sure?"

"Yes sir. I looked at my watch when the officers entered the lobby."

"Dave, did you see or hear anything unusual during the night?"

"No sir, it was a normal Saturday night with street noise from the theater and bar crowds."

"No screams? No sounds from the alley?"

"No sir, nothing that I heard. After closing hours, it was quiet the rest of the night."

"Dave, was anyone else on duty with you last night?"

"No sir. The night maid left at eleven. We don't have a maid on the overnight shift. I handle her stuff if the need arises."

"Did any guests check out before the police got here?"

"No sir, we still have twenty rooms occupied unless one checked out since Eugene and I were sent into this room."

"Did anyone, guests or visitors, come into the hotel after you went on duty and go to any of the rooms in the hotel?"

"Only one registered couple. They returned about eleven thirty, got their key, and went straight to their room."

"Do you know which room they were in and where they had been?"

"Yes sir, they were in Room 304. They told me they just saw *Kiss of Death* at the Carver Theatre."

"Is that room located near the back of the hotel?"

"No sir, it overlooks Fourth Avenue."

"One more question. Why is the parking lot next to the hotel not used?"

Dave looked surprised. "The hotel owns the lot. I've been told there were lots of problems controlling illegal parking. The lot was intended for hotel guests only. But people going to the theaters, the bar, and even the temple would park there. I guess the hotel owners just got tired of fighting it and chained it off."

"Dave, you can go home, and Eugene, you can go to work. I'm gonna send an officer to the diner to check out your story. He'll tell your boss why you were late. Give Officer Owens, who's outside the door, your addresses and phone numbers. If a newspaper reporter tries to interview you, don't say anything or as little as possible. We don't have a good fix on what went on here. That's all," Joe said.

After looking at each other again, as if to coordinate their movements, Dave and Eugene stood up. Joe escorted them to the door, and told Owens to get the hotel register information from the front counter clerk and to interview all guests to learn if they had heard or seen anything suspicious.

Joe went back into the room, sat down, and wrote a few comments in his notepad, adding a note to have Howard check out Eugene's employment at the All Day Diner. He looked up from his notepad just as Steve Strickland rushed into the room. Joe knew what Steve was going to say by the look of excitement on his face.

"Sir, there's a *Birmingham News* reporter out front. He's asking all kinds of questions. I told him I'd get you. He's really pushy."

"That's his job, Steve. Show me where he is."

Once outside, Joe spotted Jack Ritter, the paper's ace investigative reporter, talking to onlookers at the corner. Jack was medium in stature, a little on the plump side, and had a disarming demeanor that served him well during interviews. He always wore his stained felt hat at a jaunty angle.

"Hey, Jack. Out early on a Sunday morning, aren't you?" Joe asked.

Turning, Jack smiled and responded, "No earlier than you, Joe. What's going on here? Your storm troopers' lips are sealed. Are you going to stonewall me too?"

Joe put on a tough face. "Maybe we're still perturbed after the last story you wrote about Birmingham's finest. Let's move away from this crowd. People have keen ears for tidbits, and then it turns into bigger and bigger stories in the retelling."

They stepped over the chain into the parking lot, and Jack said, "I just reported what some of your boys in blue did to quell the last disturbance in Scratch Ankle."

"We haven't had any real problems here in months. We'd like to keep it that way."

"Okay. So what can you tell me?"

"Not much. Frank Cutler and his boys just took the body to the morgue. We might have a report in three or four days."

"Three or four days! What's taking so long? Frank usually moves much faster."

"Come on, it's Sunday. I'm sure Frank wants to go to church and spend the day with his family. I know he'll get started soon."

"So," Jack said in a sarcastic tone, "while we wait for Frank to pray, you gotta give me something."

"I'll tell you what little we know. We have a body. It was found in the alley early this morning, a colored female, about thirty years old."

"Who found her and reported the body?"

"An older colored man found the body, went into the hotel, and the hotel clerk called the police. That's about all I can say at this time."

Jack eyed Joe suspiciously. "Do you think it's a homicide?"

"Don't know. Won't know until Frank completes his examination. Don't make a big deal out of this."

"I'll go easy for a few days. Can I depend on you to call me with the results of the autopsy and Frank's conclusions?"

"Absolutely. I'll tell you what I can."

Jack looked skeptical. "Sounds to me like you're holding back."

"I'll be up front with you, Jack."

"I'll bet."

Joe ignored Jack's sarcasm. "I've got to wrap things up here now. Where are you off to?"

"Oh, I'll mount my white steed and ride around town looking for my next exposé of our city government or police department."

"Good luck with that."

"It's not luck, Joe. In this city, finding interesting things to write about is like picking low hanging fruit off a tree. See you around. If I don't hear from you in a few days, I'll be calling."

"I'm sure you will. See you, Jack."

After Jack drove off, Joe looked around for Jerry Howard and found him in the alley. He filled Howard in on what little he had learned.

As Joe turned to walk to his car, he looked back. "Jerry, go over to the All Day Diner on Eighteenth. Eugene Gould, the colored guy who found the body, works there. Verify that he does. Tell his boss why Eugene was late. Don't reveal a lot of details, just make it clear that Eugene was aiding a police investigation. Call me if anything important comes up."

"Will do, Joe," Jerry said in a laconic voice that expressed his weariness after a long night.

Joe also felt tired. A new case usually gave him a rush of adrenaline, but not today. Getting into his car, he decided to see if he could find Charlie Bartlett.

Joe knew the chief wanted to keep this low key, but he drove away with an ominous feeling in his stomach.

CHAPTER 4

THE HOMICIDE DETECTIVE

JOE McGRATH

"WATCH, JOE AND ADAM. You gotta toss the line sidearm. It's gotta land soft and easy so the bait don't fall off the hooks," Hank said.

Joe and Adam watched as Hank's perfect trout line throw landed in the Little Cahaba River. The three boys were inseparable friends. Hank, a colored boy, was their spiritual leader into the fields and streams surrounding Montevallo, a college town thirty-five miles south of Birmingham. Adam, another white boy, and Joe followed Hank's lead as his faithful acolytes.

"I gotta go home," Joe said. "It's getting late."

He bounded in the front door and shouted, "Mom, I'm home."

"Go clean up. Dad'll be home soon. Uncle Andrew is coming for supper. Have you been on the river with Hank and Adam?"

"Yes, ma'am."

"Then I know you're a mess. Get to it." Elizabeth, Joe's mother, hurried to prepare supper. Joe and his mom had just returned from one of her frequent trips to Boston, her hometown. Joe had been able to go with her since it was summer vacation.

At supper, Elizabeth said, "Peter, I forgot to tell you. I saw some of my Cliffie friends last week. They said to say hello."

She had met Peter in Boston when both were working on graduate degrees: Peter at Boston College's law school, and Elizabeth in

English literature at Radcliffe College. They married after graduation and moved to Montevallo, Peter's hometown, where Joe was born in 1910. Peter became the town's only criminal defense lawyer, who represented white and colored clients with equal vigor, much to the chagrin of many whites in the community. His brother, Andrew was the town's police chief.

"That's nice, honey. You ready for your fall classes?" Peter said.

"Almost. I'm really excited about the new programs," said Elizabeth who taught English literature at Alabama College for Women.

"I know it'll be great. And what did you do today, Joe?" Peter said.

"Hank showed Adam and me how to set a trout line in the river. He's sure good at it."

"I'm glad you've got a friend like Hank. I don't know much about that sort of thing."

"Joe, your dad never took his nose out of a book long enough to bait a hook. But I bet you guys catch some big catfish," Andrew said.

"Thank you, little brother," Peter said, faking a grimace.

"How's the case going, honey?" Elizabeth said.

"Not well. A lot of anger over this one. We'll see. Critical day in court tomorrow," said Peter.

"Don't worry. We'll control the hotheads," Andrew said.

The next morning Peter got up from the breakfast table and kissed Elizabeth. "See you tonight, honey."

Joe walked his dad to the front door and hugged him goodbye.

It was the last time Joe would see his father alive.

ELIZABETH, JOE. I . . . I've got some terrible news. We found Peter. He was murdered."

Thirteen-year-old Joe stared at his mother as if he didn't comprehend what Uncle Andrew had said.

Elizabeth, struggling to speak, murmured, "What happened?"

"We found Peter in the woods west of town. He was shot to death."

Joe started shaking and sobbing. He pounded the chair with his hands and the floor with his feet as if his world was slipping out from under him. He screamed, "You didn't find my father, you found his body. What's wrong with you?"

Elizabeth went to Joe and wrapped her arms around her son. "That's okay, honey. I'm here for you. So is Uncle Andrew."

AFTER PETER'S BODY WAS FOUND, Andrew started to serve as a father figure for his nephew. He knew Joe had led an idyllic life with his family and friends, and that this was going to be a critical time for the boy. Andrew visited Elizabeth one day when he knew Joe was not home.

"Elizabeth, what do you think about Joe becoming involved in the murder investigation? He's smart and inquisitive. I might be wrong, but it might help him deal with the whole situation."

"Andrew, I don't want him hurt any more than he already is."

"I'll watch things closely. If it's not working, we'll stop immediately."

"I'm willing to give it a try. But please keep me informed. He's my little boy, Andrew."

The first time Joe went to his uncle's office to discuss the investigation, Andrew said to him, "Joe, there's some important things about the murder that you need to know. It's gruesome. You'll likely hear about it soon enough. Okay?"

"Yes sir," Joe said.

"Your father's body was found tied to a tree in a remote, wooded area outside of town. He had been brutally beaten before he was killed with a single shot between the eyes. It was as if the killer wanted to be sure he could see it coming."

Joe started to quiver, but quickly composed himself. "I can't wait to get my hands on the bastards that did this. Any suspects yet?"

"No. It might be the Klan, or a disgruntled white or colored client. Maybe a prosecution witness." Andrew smiled. "And I won't tell your mother about your language. I'll keep you in the loop at all times."

Joe accompanied Andrew on investigative trips and interviews, and spent time in his office at the city jail, observing and learning about police work.

Andrew had been right; Joe's sad state of mind and sorrow abated as he became more involved in the investigation. He offered his own theories as to what might have happened, and it proved the start of what became his lifelong interest in police work.

Elizabeth gave Joe her full attention to help him overcome the tragedy and grow up to be a well-rounded, well-educated, open-minded young man. Elizabeth had always worked hard to imbue Joe with her liberal values. Her goal was for him to be like his father: a southern liberal who abhorred bigotry and segregation, yet chose to live and work within its binding restrictions.

Joe was an excellent student, although he had a tough time the year after his father's murder. His grades suffered, but Elizabeth was patient with him and nurtured him through the difficult year.

She also made a point to sit with Joe on most evenings, and they read selections from one of Shakespeare's plays or sonnets.

"Joe, let's continue with *Hamlet*. Hamlet and Ophelia are talking just before the Players start. You read Hamlet's lines. I'll read Ophelia's. Act Three, Scene Two, start at line 107," Elizabeth said.

Elizabeth kept the readings short because she wanted time to discuss Shakespeare's language and meaning with Joe before his interest started to lag. These sessions with his mother and subsequent high school and college classes in Shakespeare left him with a profound knowledge and love for the Bard's works. When Joe was in high school, Elizabeth was able to get permission for him to audit some of her Shakespearean lectures at Alabama College.

Joe loved the lectures, but he really thought it was swell to be the only guy in a class of young women.

JOE, NEAR THE END OF HIS SENIOR YEAR in high school, was studying hard for final exams. He sat in the living room reading Charles Dickens's *Great Expectations*, when he heard the screen door open.

"I saw you in the living room from the street, Joe."

"Hey, Uncle Andrew. Didn't expect you tonight."

"I need to talk to you. Is your mother home?"

"Mom," Joe called toward the kitchen, "Uncle Andrew's here."

Elizabeth came into the living room. "Hi Andrew. Nice to see you. It's been a while."

"Elizabeth, I'd like to talk to Joe alone on the porch."

"Of course. I've got some prep work to do for a class tomorrow."

Joe followed Andrew out the front door. They sat on a porch swing on the balmy spring evening.

"You haven't spent much time working with me on the investigation lately," Andrew said.

"No sir. I've been real busy with school activities."

"I understand and that's good. . . . I need to tell you something that's hard for me to admit." Andrew sat quietly.

Joe tensed up, not sure what to expect. "What is it?"

"You know I've worked tirelessly trying to find whoever it was that murdered your father."

"Yes sir. I know how hard it's been."

"It's been over three years, and we don't have any credible leads. I doubt anything will change. The longer a case goes unsolved, the less likely it will be solved. I'm sorry to have to tell you this."

As Joe's shoulders slumped, he grimaced and slowly rocked back and forth for several minutes making a low, keening sound.

"Joe, don't worry. I'll work on this case 'til the day I die."

Joe rocked for a few more moments. Finally, he looked up at his uncle, tears streaming down his cheeks. "I'm okay, Uncle Andrew. I understand. I appreciate your honesty with me. . . . There's one thing I want you to know."

"What's that, Joe?"

"Someday, I will find the men who murdered Dad. I'm sure more than one man was involved."

Tears came to Andrew's eyes as he reached over and hugged his nephew. The man and the boy cried, clutching each other tightly.

"I'm sure you will, Joe. I'm sure you will," Andrew said in a whisper.

JOE ATTENDED THE UNIVERSITY OF ALABAMA and majored in English literature, much to Elizabeth's delight. His Shakespearean classes were taught by Hugh Stroud, the school's preeminent Shakespearean scholar. Stroud included Joe in a select group of his students that he invited to his home for private readings.

The year Joe started at the university was also the first year of a new criminology major, a field that was just becoming available at a few colleges. In his sophomore year, he started using most of his elective credit hours outside his major to take criminology courses. When he graduated with a Bachelor of Arts in English Literature with Phi

Beta Kappa honors, he had accumulated enough criminology credit hours to claim it as a minor.

After graduation, Joe worked in Tuscaloosa for five years as a high school English literature teacher. His teaching schedule allowed him to continue taking criminology classes at the university, and in 1935, he earned a Bachelor of Science in Criminology. The year ended on a sad note when he had to go home for Andrew's funeral. A heart attack finally ended his search for Paul's killer.

While at the high school, Joe met Mary Firth, who was teaching American history. Joe was immediately attracted to her. She was stunning—five-feet-six-inches tall with an hourglass figure. Her auburn hair cascaded over her shoulders, framing a face seemingly fashioned after a Greek goddess. She was smart, outspoken, and Catholic, although the latter attribute was of little interest to Joe.

Mary was constantly pursued by men, but she was smitten with Joe. He was over six-feet tall with a firm, well-muscled body, and had dark brown hair that was neatly trimmed but for a cowlick on the left front of his hairline. She thought him handsome with his aquiline nose, deep blue eyes, high cheekbones, and square jaw showing off a soft mouth and lips with a moist appeal. She even liked his ears, which were large and seemed the perfect appendages to frame his facial features.

THEY DATED FOR TWO YEARS BEFORE HE PROPOSED. What would prove to be the first fissure in their relationship started while they were dating. Joe soon realized that his girlfriend was a magnet for adoring male eyes. The adoration frequently went beyond just ogling. Mary was used to the constant attention and sexual innuendoes, often explicitly inviting and suggestive. Notwithstanding that she repelled them like most people swat pesky flies, Joe exhibited a personality trait he had never experienced before: irrational jealousy. Paradoxically, because of his looks, Joe experienced much of the same attention from women. He shrugged off the female advances as annoyances, but was unable to see Mary's experiences in the same way.

Initially, Mary laughed at Joe's jealous outbursts, much as she did with the men who approached her. But after they were married, Joe's outbursts became more frequent and virulent.

Mary had wanted to get married in a Catholic church. Joe had agreed, but said he did not attend Mass regularly. They were married in 1935, and their daughter, Jane, was born in 1937. Unlike Mary, Joe had no interest in raising Jane a Catholic. The second fissure in their relationship had been formed.

Joe always knew that he wanted to pursue police work like his Uncle Andrew, and in 1939, he applied and was accepted for an opening with the Birmingham Police Department. Mary knew Joe had earned a criminology degree, but he had never mentioned his longing to work in law enforcement.

When he told her about his job opportunity in Birmingham, her response was quick and direct. "Why do you want to do this? You never talked to me about it. I thought we'd both work in education our entire careers."

"Ever since my father was murdered, I've wanted to. I feel incomplete and unfulfilled teaching. I think police work is my calling."

"Oh, now it's a religious experience?"

Joe shrugged, ignoring Mary's sharp tongue. "No, it's not. You don't understand. I'll never forgive myself if I don't do this."

After days of discussion, Mary reluctantly agreed. It was the start of the third fissure in their relationship.

In late 1939, the family moved to Birmingham and rented a nice house in Southside, and Joe started with the police department. After training, he was assigned to a beat cop position working a tough part of downtown. He became known for his intelligence and work ethic. People in the area he worked also came to like him and trust him, or at least as much as they trusted any cop. As others in the department became aware of his educational background, which was highly unusual in the BPD, some started calling him "Professor."

He applied for an open position in the homicide division in early 1941. He got the promotion largely because of his criminology degree, as several others who applied outranked him in seniority and experience. After four years as an assistant detective, he was promoted to a full homicide detective position.

Joe's new position demanded a tremendous amount of time. He hadn't realized how hard it was on his personal life until the day Mary announced she was leaving him. After that, his work and occasional visits with his daughter became his only salvation.

CHAPTER 5

JOE'S REFLECTION

SUNDAY—SEPTEMBER 14, 1947

As JOE DROVE TO HEADQUARTERS, he realized that his tired and ominous feelings may have more to do with the breakup of his marriage than what he had just observed in the alley. While he knew their marriage had not been going well for some time, he now recognized the signs of trouble that had been present: the incessant demands of his job; Mary's increasing lack of interest in him, including refusal to have sex, and most telling, their almost studied inability to discuss their deteriorating marriage.

Joe's mind drifted back to the night seven months ago when Mary had told him she wanted a separation. He had revisited these moments so often, the evening had become imprinted in his mind.

> *I sat in the living room reading the evening newspaper when Mary came in from the bedroom. Damn, she looked good. I was horny as hell. No sex in months. When I saw her face, I knew trouble was coming.*
>
> *"Joe, I've got something important to talk to you about. Please don't get angry."*
>
> *That placed me on edge. "I guess I can't get anything until you tell me what's on your mind."*
>
> *"I've been thinking about this a lot. You know we haven't been happy for some time. I want a separation."*

"You want what?" My temples started to throb.

"A separation. I think it's best for both of us."

I jumped up and tightly grabbed Mary's shoulders. "It's the math teacher at your school, isn't it? I know it is."

"Let go of me, Joe. You're hurting me."

I released her and slumped into the chair. She rubbed her arms and glared at me with a look of scorn and hate.

"I've told you over and over that there's nothing going on between Mark and me. We're friends. That's all."

I snarled. Beads of sweat formed on my forehead. "Yeah, I'll bet. Is he good in bed?"

"Fuck you, Joe. Your jealousy is out of control. It's one of the reasons our marriage is where it is today. Every time I talk to another man, you go berserk. I can't stand it anymore. I've never had a relationship with another man. Yet, you think I sleep with every guy who says hello to me. It's over, Joe. You don't trust me, and I don't love you."

I tried to calm down. "Please don't do this, Mary. I'm going to change. I promise."

"Sure, just like you changed when you made us quit our good teaching jobs in Tuscaloosa so you could become a cop. And now you think more about your dead father than you do about us."

"Goddamn you, Mary. Leave my father out of this."

"As you wish. Either you move out or I will."

"What about Jane? She'll be shattered."

"She may be for a while. She knows we're not getting along. Children are more resilient than you think."

"So now you're an expert on child behavior as well as jealousy and marriage."

"Sarcasm's not going to help."

My fuse blew. I bellowed in a rage, "Jesus Christ, Mary. You can't do this. I won't allow it."

She laughed at me. "I'll move out tomorrow. You do with the house as you wish."

"Where're you going?"

"My friend Judy has an extra room and bath. We can use it until I make further plans. I'm going to bed. Good night, Joe. I'm truly sorry it's come to this."
I couldn't move. I was numb.

As he turned into the parking lot at headquarters, Joe's thoughts snapped back to the present.

He went straight to the desk officer. "Hello Billy."

"Hey, Joe. How'd it go in the Ankle?"

"Jerry and his guys are wrapping up. Frank Cutler's got the body over at the morgue. We'll see what he comes up with. I need all the records we have on Charlie Bartlett, aka Bongo Drum. I need them pronto. Have someone bring them up to my office."

"Okay Joe. Say, the chief just called and wanted to know what was going on with your investigation. I told him what little I know."

"I'll call him."

"Joe, watch out with Bongo Drum. He's one of the chief's colored cohorts. He keeps the chief informed."

"Yeah, I'll bet he does. Thanks, Billy." Joe knew Bongo Drum would tell the chief what he wanted to hear.

When Joe got to his office, he reviewed the notes he had made at the crime scene. Realizing this was likely to be a tough case, he knew it was time to find a replacement for the sidekick he had lost a few months ago when the guy left the department.

Joe sat with his eyes closed, thinking about next steps. There was a knock on his partially open door. He looked up. "Hey, Danny. C'mon in. So you're in the barrel this weekend in records?"

"Yep, my turn in the rotation. Here's the file on Charlie Bartlett."

"Thanks. That was quick."

"Sergeant Donaldson told me to get my ass in gear and hustle this here file up to you."

Joe smiled at Danny. "Good work."

Danny grinned back at Joe. "Thank you, Detective McGrath."

Joe went through Bartlett's records and noted that he had been jailed six times on prostitution sweeps but was released on bail with no subsequent prosecutions. Joe found his address and phone number, and decided to call him.

A male voice answered. "Hello."

"Can I speak to Charlie Bartlett?" Joe said.

"Yeah, whaddya want?"

"Charlie, it's Detective Joe McGrath with the Birmingham PD."

"I knows who you are, Detective."

"Charlie, a colored woman's body was found this morning in the alley behind the New Home Hotel. No ID. I think she was a prostitute. I need your help."

"Why me? I got nuthin' to do with this stuff. You cops think all these girls works for me."

"Oh, come on, Charlie. You and I know you're one of the kingpins in Scratch Ankle. I need you to come to the morgue and see if you can identify this woman."

"I ain't got time. I'm a busy man."

"Don't make me send some cops to bring you to the morgue."

The phone was silent for a moment. "Okay, I'll come. When?"

Joe looked at his watch. "Noon today at the morgue."

"You're cutting into my church time, but I'll be there."

"Welcome to the club, Charlie. I had to give up my church time too. See you at noon."

Joe hung up and called the morgue.

"Jefferson County Forensic Labs and Morgue. Don speaking."

"Don. Joe McGrath. Let me speak to Dr. Cutler."

"He's performing an autopsy, Detective McGrath."

"Have him call me as soon as possible. It's important. I'm in my office at headquarters."

"Yes sir, I'll be sure he gets the message."

Joe knew the chief would hit the ceiling when he heard that Bongo Drum was called in to identify the body. He decided he would have to know Cutler's findings and Bongo Drum's reaction to the woman's body before he could deal with the chief, so he turned to unfinished paperwork while waiting for Cutler's call.

He had been at the paperwork for almost an hour when the phone rang. He answered it on the first ring. "Joe McGrath here."

"It's Frank, Joe. I just finished the autopsy."

"What can you tell me?"

"Murder by strangulation. A garotte was the weapon. The marks around the neck indicate it was either a piece of rope or wire about a thirty-second to a sixteenth of an inch in diameter. Best estimate of time of death is between three and four o'clock. She had sex recently. A lot of semen in her vagina, but it's hard to say if it represents more than one ejaculation. The sperm were still motile, consistent with sex around my estimate of time of death. If it's the murderer's semen, he's blood type A."

"Any ID or anything found on her person or nearby?" Joe asked.

"Nope."

"Were there any noticeable marks or injuries on her body?"

"A few minor scrapes and bruises, but nothing inconsistent with her having sex lying on firm ground and probably a brief struggle as she was strangled," Frank said.

"Anything else?"

"Nope, that's about it. . . . Oh hell, how could I forget. There is one more thing. When you asked about bruises on her body, I forgot about what I found on her lips. There were minor bruises around and on her lips as if she had been kissed rather violently or passionately. With some people, sex gets pretty rough."

Joe thought about his forced abstinence of late. "I wouldn't know about that. Anything else?"

"Nope, that really is it," Frank said.

Joe looked at his watch; it was eleven ten. "I need another favor. I shoulda called you before I talked to Bongo Drum Bartlett. He's coming to the morgue at noon. I hope he can ID the body. Can one of your guys have it ready for a viewing?"

"Sure. The body's being put on ice. It'll only take a few minutes to get it into the viewing room. I'm leaving shortly, but I'll tell the guys that you're coming."

"Thanks, Frank."

"Be careful with Bongo Drum, Joe. He's one of Watson's boys."

"Goddammit, Frank. You're the second person to remind me of that today. I know. I'll watch it."

"Just trying to help. See you."

Joe left the office at eleven forty for the short drive to the morgue, located in the Southside. If he was late, it would give Bongo Drum an excuse to leave the morgue before he arrived.

CHAPTER 6

THE MORGUE

SUNDAY—SEPTEMBER 14, 1947

T HE COOL AIR AND ANTISEPTIC ODOR, ever present in a morgue, struck Joe as he entered the building. Even so, he couldn't help admiring the new building, which included both the morgue and the city's forensics labs. He knew it was Cutler's pride and joy with a front facade fashioned after a Greek temple with proportions based on the Golden Mean. He had heard some wags call it Birmingham's Parthenon. But the rear of the building, which housed the morgue and crime labs, defied the Greek tradition, concrete block in appearance with no windows.

Joe went to the front desk. "Good morning, Don. Is the body of that woman murdered last night ready for an ID viewing?"

"Hi, Detective McGrath. Yes, Dr. Cutler told me you were coming." Don called someone in the morgue and told him to move the body to the viewing room. He turned to Joe. "It'll be ready in a few minutes. Do you want to come with me?"

"No, I'll join you when my identifying witness arrives." Joe sat down by the front desk to wait for Bongo Drum. He had interviewed Bartlett once a few years before, but he couldn't remember the circumstances except that it wasn't a major incident.

At twelve fifteen, Joe started to worry about a no-show when Bongo Drum walked in with a large, muscular colored man.

Bongo Drum was a short, wiry man, his face narrow and covered with pockmarks. Nattily dressed in beige slacks and a dark brown silk shirt, he wore stylish shoes and a gold chain hung from his front right pocket to his rear pocket. His sidekick wore black slacks and a black cotton shirt. He had bodyguard written all over him.

"Thanks for coming, Charlie."

"As if I had a choice, Detective."

"Oh, you had a choice, and I think you made the right one. The woman's body should be ready for viewing now."

"I hopes we can get this over quickly. Ain't had no troubles in the Ankle lately. I'd likes to keep it that way."

"You and Chief Watson, Charlie."

"The chief's a smart man, Detective. He knows how things works."

"I'm sure he does. We all want peace and quiet."

Bongo Drum looked as if he was going to respond to Joe when Don came out. "Detective McGrath, the body's ready if you are."

"We're ready. Let's go, Charlie. We don't need your escort."

Bongo Drum stared angrily at Joe as he turned to his bodyguard and whispered to him. The guy sat down, and Bongo Drum followed Joe and Don to the viewing room.

Instead of having bodies viewed in the morgue proper, Cutler directed the building's designers to include a separate room for that express purpose. The room, a pastel blue, had walls decorated with copies of paintings by masters such as Degas and Homer, and depicted tranquil, pastoral scenes. The room's lighting was subdued except for a light directly over the viewing table, which could be increased in intensity to give a bright view of the corpse. As thoughtful as Cutler's intentions were to somewhat mitigate the pain and trauma of family members and others asked to ID the body of a possible loved one, the viewing table dominated the room and immediately demanded attention upon entry.

The three men entered the viewing room, and Joe asked Bongo Drum, "Have you been in here before?"

"Twice," replied Bongo Drum.

Turning to Don, Joe said, "Please remove the sheet."

Don pulled the sheet off the woman's head. The three men stood quietly looking at the face.

Joe finally broke the silence. "Do you recognize her, Charlie?"

Charlie continued studying the face. "No, I don't knows whose she is."

Joe looked at Bongo Drum skeptically. "You sure, Charlie?"

"Come on, Detective, I told you I don't knows all these girls whose works the streets. I never seen this girl in all my life."

Joe let out an audible sigh. "Well, have you seen or heard anything in Scratch Ankle that might have led to this?"

Bongo Drum glared at Joe. "I told you I don't knows this girl, and I don't knows nuthin' about what happened here."

"Okay, Charlie. You can go. I'll be in touch if I have more questions."

Charlie abruptly left the viewing room. Joe took a deep breath. "Don, you can put the body back."

"Do you believe him?"

"No, I think he's lying, but I'll let it go for now. I need a copy of the photos taken at the scene and in the morgue. Please have them on my desk at headquarters first thing in the morning."

"Will do, Detective McGrath."

When Joe left, he stood by his car for a few moments thinking about what had transpired and how to deal with it. He had to call the chief and be up front about what he knew and Bongo Drum's involvement at the morgue. He went back to his office.

Joe sat in his office staring at the telephone. He wished he had a better handle on the case before he called the chief. Even with no hard evidence other than the body, he was sure the case was more complicated than it appeared on the surface. He reached for the phone.

"Chief Watson."

"Good afternoon, Chief," Joe said. "I want to bring you up to date on the Scratch Ankle incident."

"Okay. Didya get it wrapped up?"

"No sir," said Joe. He explained the events at the scene including the interviews, the unusual position of the body, and the results of Cutler's autopsy.

"The woman was garroted, Chief."

"Gar-whated?"

"Garroted, she was strangled."

"Speak English! Don't give me that . . . What is it? . . . Frenchy shit."

"Yes sir." He decided it would make the chief only madder if he told him the word was Spanish. Joe then mentioned he had Charlie Bartlett come to the morgue for an identification viewing.

The chief exploded. "You did what? Don't you know Bongo Drum is my main informant in Scratch Ankle? Goddammit, you shoulda checked with me before you called him in."

"Yes sir, I know I should have called you first. But I hoped to get a quick ID of the woman, so I could get closer to wrapping this up. Jack Ritter of the *News* showed up. I put him off for a day or two."

"Jesus, Joe. I told you to keep the fuckin' press out of this."

"Chief, you know I can't control the press, especially someone like Ritter. In fact, I've got to give him a plausible story tomorrow, or he's going to start nosing around until he finds someone who will level with him. And he will find someone. You can bet on that."

"Now listen up, Professor. You don't know shit from shinola. Those colored whores are a dime a dozen, and one more or less ain't gonna make a big difference. She was probably killed by her pimp or one of her tricks. I don't give a shit about finding the creep. Get a quick ID on her so you can find her family, if she has one. Let them have the body for a quick burial. Then you make like an investigation for a while, and the whole thing gonna blow over. You hear me now?"

Joe tried to act contrite. "Yes sir."

"And dammit, Joe, don't you ever go close to Bongo Drum again without my permission."

"Yes sir." Joe's irritation built as he listened to Watson tell him to get a quick ID in one breath and in the next breath tell him to stay away from the man he had used in hopes of achieving that purpose. "Is that it, Chief?" Joe asked.

"Yep, just get it wrapped up. Call me late tomorrow with an update."

"Yes sir." Joe hung up.

AFTER ENDURING THE CHIEF'S TIRADE about contacting Bongo Drum, Joe decided to call it a day. Before he left the office, he jotted two items in his notepad he wanted to do first thing in the morning: (1) Have an officer go through arrest files, look for match with Cutler's headshots; (2) Call Jerry Howard—anything of interest to report?

Joe had an early supper at his favorite diner in Five Points South, one of the nicer Southside shopping areas. The stores in Five Points served most of his needs now that he lived nearby: a dry cleaner, several restaurants, a bank, a movie theater, a bookstore, a small grocery, and two bars. He would have headed straight for his favorite bar, the White Stag, if it hadn't been Sunday. Instead, he stopped at a smoke shop to purchase Sunday's *Birmingham News* as his reading companion while he ate. Joe ordered one of his favorite meals that proved he was a southern boy: fried chicken, mashed potatoes, turnip greens, black-eyed peas, and corn bread, topped off with a cup of coffee and a generous slice of pecan pie.

After supper, Joe dreaded going to his apartment for another night alone, but he was tired. He went home, kicked off his shoes, hung up his coat, shoulder holster, tie and hat, and headed straight for the refrigerator. It was empty except for a few bottles of beer and a quart of milk. He got a beer and had to search around the kitchen for a church key to open the bottle.

Joe settled, his beer in hand, into the apartment's only piece of nice furniture: a large, comfortable chair with an ottoman where he spent many of his leisure hours satisfying his lifelong love of reading. He first scanned the *News*, especially the Sunday summary report of significant police actions and arrests the past week. Joe always reviewed the past week's police activities and arrest logs at headquarters each Monday morning; however, he used the *News* as a pointer toward anything of interest in his casework. He had just about finished his quick scan when an item caught his attention. A white male named Pierce had been arrested the previous Wednesday night in Scratch Ankle on charges of solicitation. The man's name sounded familiar, but Joe couldn't place him. The guy was booked, released on bail, and ordered to appear at a subsequent hearing. Joe tore the short piece out of the paper and put it in his notepad to remind himself to interview the guy. Joe figured the vice squad was performing one of its occasional arrests to demonstrate the department's commitment to controlling prostitution.

Joe put the paper aside, got another beer, and sat down to continue reading a recently purchased book, *I, the Jury*. It was not a book he would normally read; his usual interests were Shakespeare, the classics, and fine novels. He had been reading Volume Five of Marcel

Proust's *Remembrance of Things Past* when he saw *I, the Jury* in his bookstore. He was attracted to the cover and the subject matter: a mystery featuring a tough private eye, sex, drugs, prostitution, and murder. It was the first book by unknown author Mickey Spillane.

As Joe opened the book to his marker, he knew a murder mystery was not the place to look for advice, but it now interested him that the book was about what he had seen and experienced today. The book helped Joe settle down. He knew the case was going to be difficult, especially after the chief chewed him up one side and down the other. He read for well over an hour before falling asleep. He stirred about eleven, took the book to bed, and read until he fell asleep again. He awoke the next morning and felt pretty good, having slept better than usual. A quick shower and breakfast, and he was ready to go to headquarters. He made a note to buy milk, cereal, and beer.

CHAPTER 7

THE CHIEF

ROBERT "BIG BOB" WATSON

BIG BOB WATSON LOVED BASEBALL. From the day he first picked up a mitt, it had been his burning ambition to play professional ball. He never forgot the day in his high school sophomore year when the coach yelled to him from his office.

"Big Bob, git on in here. I gotta talk to you."

Every player in the locker room watched as Big Bob walked into the office. They all knew what was coming.

"Sit down, son," the coach said.

"Yes suh."

"I'm gonna cut you, Big Bob. You sure try hard, but you don't have the arm or the hands to be a good ball player."

Big Bob, at five six, had been tagged with his nickname in his freshman year. At first he disliked the name, but soon wore it as a badge of honor. He hung his head in disappointment. "I wants another chance, Coach."

"Can't do, Big Bob. Look, I heard you call the football games the last two years. You're good. Start doing the baseball games. Besides, the locker room can be tough. I know the other guys rib you a lot."

"I ain't scared of them guys. . . . I'll call the baseball games."

Back in the locker room, he stuffed his belongings and his mitt in his bag. No one said anything until the team bully spoke up. "I reckon this the last time we'll see your sorry ass in here, Big Bob. Shit, we won't miss you. You's the worst second baseman I ever seen. You got hands like meat hooks—"

Before the bully could say another word, Big Bob jumped the guy and started pounding him. The bully was bigger and got on top of him and hit him in the face a few good ones before the coach ran into the room and separated the boys.

Big Bob grabbed his bag and left the locker room with a bloody nose and a black eye, but with his dignity intact. He didn't want to go home, but he had little choice.

His parents were sharecroppers and eked out a meager living working a small parcel for a wealthy landowner near Demopolis. Watson was born in the family home, a large shack by most standards covered with tarpaper and held together by rusted corrugated metal sheets. There was no electricity, and the toilet was an outhouse. Most locals called the family "po' white trash," but learned not say it in front of them unless they wanted a big fight on their hands. The Watsons compensated for their low social and economic status by treating the only group of people lower than themselves in the South's social caste system, coloreds, with extreme racial hatred and prejudice.

Big Bob learned his childhood lessons well and became a rabid bigot. He seldom passed up an opportunity to taunt and harass a colored kid, even if there was no provocation to do so. A poor student in high school, he just met the minimum standards to graduate.

He worked in a paper mill in the Demopolis area for four years, but then moved to Birmingham to seek better employment, taking his pugnacious attitude with him. He had dark hair with a square face that seemed to be yearning for a fight. He was built like a fire hydrant, broad from head to toe. When angry or excited, his face bloated into a crimson balloon. He went to the big city up north with his two trusted attributes: his love and knowledge of baseball, and his racial prejudices.

"OKAY PUDKNUCKERS, PUT THAT THAR PEA in your pocket. Barons win!" Big Bob Watson smiled as he made the final call in another Birmingham Barons game. He was the radio announcer for the city's beloved baseball team. Although he still pined to be a baseball player, he was happy to settle for second best.

His first three years in the city had been tough. The job opportunities weren't as plentiful as he thought they would be. He had to settle for part-time work in a steel mill and a used car lot. He did try to attend most of the Barons home games at Rickwood Field and became buddies with the players and the manager.

At a home game, Watson was seated behind the Barons dugout when the team owner, Patrick Wood, sat beside him. "You're Big Bob Watson, aren't you?"

"Yes suh, Mr. Wood," Watson said, knowing full well that Wood owned the team.

"The guys," Wood said, pointing at the dugout, "tell me you're one of our best fans."

"Yes suh, I loves this team."

"They also say you know the game inside out."

"I played some ball in high school and announced games."

"So you're an announcer," Wood said, looking more carefully at this rough cut young kid. "Have you met our regular announcer, Mel? He's up in the radio booth."

"No suh. I listens to him when I can't make a home game."

"Well, c'mon, I'm gonna introduce you two."

After Wood made the introduction, Watson was allowed to sit in the booth with Mel during games. Watson's best asset, a booming voice, had served him well when he announced high school games. Occasionally, Mel would ask Watson what he thought about a play or the game, and Watson would offer a brief commentary.

One day, as Watson sat in the radio booth prior to a Barons game, Wood rushed in and exclaimed, "Big Bob, Mel just called me. He's real sick. You gotta call the game. Can you do it?"

Without hesitation, Watson replied, "Yes suh, Mr. Wood, I've called 'em afore. I can precede right away."

His voice, knowledge of the game, colorful colloquialisms and malapropisms, and constant stream of poor grammar were an instant hit with the team's fans, most of whom were white, blue collar folks with backgrounds and interests similar to Big Bob's.

After a few games, Mel was out of a job. Over the next few years, Watson's popularity grew enormously in Birmingham and state-wide, as the Barons were the most popular baseball team in the state. The Birmingham Black Barons baseball team also played at Rickwood Field when the white Barons were on the road. Watson didn't announce those games, and it's unlikely he would have if asked because of his strident racial prejudices. Even so, his unique style with the white Barons proved popular with a large colored audience because they loved the game.

STANFORD RAMSEY, ONE OF THE STATE'S WEALTHIEST MEN and Birmingham's principal power broker, sat in his study brooding about his political problems. He had a Barons game on the radio as a background companion. Suddenly his ears perked up.

"What a play, folks. Draper goed high over second base and snagged that thar line drive right outta the sky. That ball was hit like a bullet outta a huntin' rifle. Then he put his foot on second for a douuuu-bbbble play. Innin' over and out. Barons comin' to bat."

Ramsey realized that this was the man to carry his message to the people to further his political agenda.

Before the game was over, he called Patrick Wood.

"Patrick, it's Stanford Ramsey. I was listening to the game and have a business proposition for you."

"Wanna buy my team, Stanford?" Wood said with a laugh.

"Not exactly, but close. I want you to release Big Bob Watson from his contract. I'll compensate you well, say twenty thousand dollars."

"Not interested. He's too popular with the fans."

"This is very important to me, Patrick. Forty thousand dollars."

"What's so important?"

"I'm having a few political tussles that Watson can help me with."

"Yeah, I've heard about your tussles." Wood paused and thought about the substantial amount and Ramsey's power in the community. "You got a deal. How do we proceed?"

"I'll have my lawyer draw up the contract. I'd like to call Watson after the game is over. Will you tell him?"

"Yes. You do know that Big Bob's rough around the edges?"

"Just what I'm looking for," Stanford said.

CHAPTER 8

THE PRINCE

STANFORD RAMSEY

AFTER THE GAME, Ramsey phoned Watson at Rickwood Field. "This is Big Bob. Whatcha want?"

"Hello Robert, this is Stanford Ramsey. Did Patrick Wood tell you I would be calling?"

Watson was flabbergasted as no one ever called him Robert. He knew of Ramsey's wealth and power, and tried to sound more sophisticated. "Yes suh, Mr. Ramsey. Mr. Wood, he told me and said I should listen up to you."

"Robert, I'd like you to join me for dinner at the Downtown Club."

"Yes suh, Mr. Ramsey, I'd be happy to join you."

Ramsey laughed. "Please call me Stanford, Robert. Can you meet me at the club at seven tonight?"

"Yes suh, Mr. uh . . . Stanford." Watson blushed with pride at being on a first name basis with someone like Ramsey.

"Fine. Do you know where the club is, Robert?"

"Yes suh, Stanford." Watson lied.

"Just tell the doorman your name. He'll let you right in."

Watson had to ask Patrick Wood for directions to the club. Wood told him, and added, "Big Bob, listen carefully to what Mr. Ramsey has to say. I strongly suggest you agree to cooperate. He's an important and powerful man."

Although not an elected official, Ramsey led a group of prominent businessmen who controlled the city's political landscapes. Born to wealth, he owned Alabama's largest mining operations, and iron and steel production companies. He earned a law degree at Vanderbilt University, married a wealthy socialite, and spoke in a soft, patrician manner. It was this last trait that had become an obstacle in his political maneuverings.

Ramsey and his business cohorts adamantly opposed President Franklin Roosevelt and his New Deal liberalism. To thwart the New Deal and the unions, Ramsey had been working on a plan to change Birmingham's form of city government to an elected three-person commission. With the new city government system in place, Ramsey was sure he would have *de facto* control of city hall and most key appointments.

Ramsey tried in vain to garner public support for the new system through a series of radio interviews and public speeches. His public pleas fell on deaf ears. His patrician speaking style failed to resonate with Birmingham's voting public, especially blue-collar workers and their families. Ramsey was anathema to this group. A tall man in his fifties, he had all the qualities one would expect of a wealthy, successful businessman. He had a slim build, and dressed in tailor-made suits. He had a full head of dark brown hair with a tint of gray around the edges. He was handsome, his most distinctive facial features being his dark blue eyes and full lips.

A typical Ramsey speech made no sense to the public. His closing remarks in a recent appearance even had his closest supporters laughing behind his back, but they didn't dare suggest he change his style.

> The times are rife with lamentable opposition to my attempts to transform Birmingham's city government into a viable instrument to serve all our citizens with good, sound practices that will thwart the machinations of Franklin Roosevelt and his New Deal zealots. There are those in this city and state who would institute programs undermining our business interests and workers.
>
> Do not heed their mindless pleas, which are intended to mislead and obfuscate the masses. I must dutifully report to you something that grievously concerns me.

There is a cabal amongst us whose duplicity knows no scruples. It includes liberals and Communists who would undermine our southern way of life. Please support these new programs to buttress us all against these malignant forces, or our hallowed culture will disappear in a cataclysmic immolation.

WATSON GOT TO THE DOWNTOWN CLUB a few minutes early, gave the doorman his name, and before he could mention Ramsey, the doorman said, "Go right in, Mr. Watson. Mr. Ramsey is expecting you. The maitre d' will show you to his room."

Confused by what he considered "Frenchy shit," Watson said to the doorman, "Thank you."

He entered into a world he had never experienced. The Downtown Club, Birmingham's exclusive men's club for the city's white elite, had a decor and ambience equaling anything seen in men's supper clubs in New York or London. As Watson stared in awe at the large entry parlor, he saw walls and ceilings paneled in dark mahogany wood. Ornate, but tasteful, chandeliers hung throughout the room. Subdued lighting complemented the demeanor and ambience of the surroundings.

The maitre d' immediately said to Watson, "Good evening, Mr. Watson. Follow me please. I'll show you to Mr. Ramsey's room."

Watson followed him through a large bar area and an even larger dining room. There were small groups of men in both rooms, but they paid no attention to him. At the back of the dining room, there were four doors, and the maitre d' led Watson into a small, private dining room. "Mr. Ramsey, your guest, Mr. Watson, is here."

Ramsey stood up and greeted Watson with his hand extended. "Robert, I'm delighted to meet you at long last. I want to tell you I have been a longtime fan of your excellent radio broadcasts of the Barons games. Please have a seat."

As the maitre d' closed the door, Watson realized the two were in a private room. He said, "Thank you, suh. It's an honor to meet you," as he sat down.

Ramsey sat to Watson's right. "Robert, the honor is all mine. And please, stop calling me sir and Mr. Ramsey." He put his hand lightly on Watson's right arm. "I'm Stanford, and I'm looking forward to us becoming the best of friends. What would you like to drink?"

Watson's chest swelled with pride, and he hoped Ramsey didn't notice because he felt as if the buttons on his shirt might pop off. He had never been treated with such respect by anyone. He answered almost inaudibly, "Bourbon, I reckon."

Ramsey smiled broadly. "Fine choice. My favorite too." He snapped his fingers, and a colored waiter in a tuxedo appeared seemingly out of nowhere. Ramsey said, "William, Mr. Watson and I will have bourbon and water please."

The waiter bowed gracefully. "Yes sir," he said as he turned to Watson. "Good evening, Mr. Watson. I enjoy your radio broadcast of the Barons games."

Watson was taken aback, but didn't show it. He was not used to a colored man talking directly to him. He looked at the man evenly and said simply, "Thank you." He had never had such a polite exchange with a colored man.

"Robert, I've taken the liberty of ordering dinner for both of us. I hope you don't mind. Is a good steak acceptable?"

Watson appeared about to hyperventilate from the fine surroundings and attention and could only mumble, "Yes, Stanford."

"Ah, here's our drinks. Thank you, William. Now Robert, I told the chef to wait a while before preparing our dinner. First, I'd like to get down to business."

Ramsey told Watson about his plans to make Birmingham a bigger and better city by improving its city government, but that he had run into a problem with some of his more liberal opponents who were only interested in their political agenda and not the city's future. He was candid and told Watson how he had tried to speak to Birmingham's masses about the virtues of the proposed government reforms, but he had been unable to connect with the common man.

Getting straight to the main proposition, Ramsey said, "Robert, I want you to become my main spokesman. We'll schedule an ongoing series of public speeches for you in Birmingham and the area. We'll produce a one-hour radio broadcast where you can talk about our new programs, existing city programs, and your beloved Barons. They will listen to you, and by encouraging them to send city hall and the other politicians messages and phone calls of support, we can get our programs going. I'll pay you over twice what you're making now. What do you think?"

Watson's head was spinning. He hardly knew what to say. Feeling completely out of his element, he said, "I don't know much about the city government, Stanford."

Ramsey replied, "Don't worry, we'll teach you what you need to know and say. But remember this, I want you to tell the story the same way you broadcast a Barons game. I love your style of speaking. It will connect with the public. I've been unable to do so, and you're my man to get the job done."

"But you speak so good, Stanford," Watson offered.

"That's the problem, Robert. I speak too well."

After dinner, Ramsey returned to the business at hand. "Robert, what do you think of my proposition?"

Watson now felt both well-fed and well-liquored. He responded to Ramsey as if he had known him for life. "Well Stanford, I'd be right honored and bumbled to works with you."

Ramsey laughed to himself at Watson's awful malapropism. *Oh my God. This is my man.* "Robert, that's great." He handed Watson his business card. "Come to my office Monday morning at ten. We'll start to work."

The Big Bob Radio Hour—knowledgeable locals called the program *The Big Bob and Stanford Radio Hour*—was a resounding success. Watson pushed and cajoled his audiences to support Ramsey's programs and would close with what became a familiar refrain. "Y'all listen up. Big Bob sez, support new city gove'ment."

City hall, and local and state politicians, both New Deal liberals and Ramsey conservatives, were inundated with telegrams, phone calls, and personal visits supporting and demanding the full enactment of Ramsey's grand design. Watson went around town talking about "Stanford and me" as if the men had been close friends for years. Ramsey didn't mind being tied to Big Bob as long as his interests were being served.

Ramsey was able to get his three hand-picked candidates elected as commissioners. He then quietly, but firmly, directed the commission to start selectively replacing key city government positions with men he designated. Birmingham's Machiavellian prince was now in full control and doled out political patronage as he saw fit.

Watson continued his speech schedule and radio program, further solidifying his popularity in the community and the support for Ramsey's agenda. In late 1939, the current Birmingham police chief was scheduled to retire. Ramsey saw a golden opportunity to repay his obligation to Watson as well as have someone who was fiercely loyal in charge of the police department. There was one major problem—Watson had no police education, experience, or training.

When Ramsey first suggested Watson for the job, even the commissioners balked because of his lack of qualifications. Other Birmingham police officers, including Joe McGrath, were much better qualified. It took all of Ramsey's powers of persuasion —both polite and rational, and at times, bullying and irrational— to finally get the commission to agree and make the appointment. Ramsey's actions did not go unnoticed. Jack Ritter of the *News* wrote several scathing articles exposing Watson's glaring shortcomings for the position. The newspaper articles had little impact as the majority of Birmingham's population was now in Ramsey's camp.

In May 1940, at age thirty-six, Big Bob Watson was sworn in. Ramsey directed Watson to immediately start ensuring that key positions in the department were filled with men who would work at his beck and call.

Watson would later wish he had included Joe McGrath as a victim during his initial purge.

CHAPTER 9

THE PARENTS

MONDAY—SEPTEMBER 15, 1947

"GOOD MORNING, SALLY. GOT A KISS FOR ME?"

Sally smiled. "Good morning, Joe. You know I always have a kiss for you."

Joe reached into a bowl of Hershey's Kisses she kept on her desk and took one. "Thanks for the kiss, Sally."

Sally Bowers reminded Joe of his grandmother. She was a pleasant woman, small in stature, who had worked for the BPD for thirty years. She started working as Joe's secretary soon after his promotion to homicide detective two years ago. Joe had been meaning to ask her to go to lunch with him, but time and procrastination kept getting in his way. He knew she was a spinster in her late fifties. She dressed in rather plain, dark dresses and wore her gray hair in a tight bun.

The photos from the morgue were on his desk. Joe found a junior officer in homicide—a young guy named Brendan O'Connor—and told him to look for a match in the arrest records. Joe had no doubts this kid was all Irish: medium height and build, reddish hair, in his twenties, with a light, ruddy complexion scattered with freckles. He had a charming, college-boy-like face that immediately disarmed people who met him. Joe told Brendan to start with the most recent arrests and work backwards.

Joe dialed Jerry Howard's extension.

"Howard."

"Jerry, how'd things go after we split up yesterday?"

"We did the things you asked us to do, Joe. At least the ones we could on a Sunday morning. We searched the cans and all the nooks and crannies in the alley, didn't find anything suspicious. I had 'em bag a few items. They're at the lab, but I don't think they're important. The crime lab guys lifted some prints off a few of the cans if we need them later. I went to the diner. Confirmed that Eugene's worked there for about five years. The owner said he didn't see or hear anything unusual Saturday night. I'll visit the other places you asked me to cover this morning, but I don't expect anybody to be too talkative."

"I suspect you're right about—"

Chief Watson's secretary burst into Joe's office. "Joe, the chief wants to see you now."

"I'll be right with you." Joe returned to his phone conversation with Howard. "Gotta go see the chief. I'll get back to you."

He followed the secretary to the elevator and to the chief's office suite on the top floor. She told Joe to go into the chief's private office.

"Good morning, Chief. You wanted to see me."

Watson growled. "Yeah, sit down. I gotta ID for you on that colored woman."

Joe was surprised, but then he realized what had happened. "Oh."

"Yeah, I talked to Bongo Drum this morning. In fact, he called me. He said he was so upset with the way you treated him that he jus' clammed up. The woman's name is Gloria Phillips. He thinks she lived with her parents out in Ensley."

"Do you think that's her real name or street name?"

Watson was irritated. "I know you think I didn't ask him that, but I did. He's pretty sure it's her real name. Now you git on it and find her parents. Git 'em over to the morgue for a formal ID and git that body outta there and in the ground."

"Yes sir. I'll get right on it."

As Joe left the office, Watson yelled out, "Don't you forget about what I told you about Bongo Drum. He's my darkie, you hear?"

Joe nodded as he closed the door to Watson's office. He went back downstairs thinking to himself, *God, this is not going to be easy.*

He called Jerry Howard back. "Did you talk to Ralph Owens about the hotel guests?"

"Yeah, Ralph interviewed all the guests. They all said they heard and saw nothing. Joe, you know they ain't going to talk to us."

"I know. You and your guys be careful if you come into contact with Bongo Drum or anyone close to him. The chief considers them off-limits. I'll talk to you later today."

Joe located Brendan and gave him Gloria's name and apparent area of residence. He told Brendan to focus his search on that name and let him know as soon as he found anything.

Back in his office, Joe pulled out the phone book and looked up the name Phillips. There was a long list under that name. He checked to see if Gloria was listed, but no such listing existed. Next, he went through each listing and marked those he thought might be in Ensley, a suburb on the western side of the city. Comparing the selected addresses to a large Birmingham street map on his wall, he was able to reduce the list to ten possibilities. A knock on his partially open door broke his concentration.

"Come on in, Brendan. You got anything?"

"Yes sir, Detective McGrath. I think I found the person you're interested in. Her name is Gloria Phillips."

"Sit down, Brendan." He looked through the file. He compared Cutler's facial shots to Gloria's mug shot. Even in a mug shot, Gloria was an attractive woman with a pleasing, girlish smile. There was no doubt the murdered woman was Gloria Phillips. She had been arrested during one of the department's recent sweeps of prostitutes in Scratch Ankle. Her age was listed as twenty-nine, and her home address and phone number matched one of the ten he had found.

"Good job. This is our girl. I'll take it from here." Joe pulled the Pierce newspaper clipping from his notepad and handed it to Brendan. "I've got something else I need you to do. Pull the arrest file on this guy. He was arrested last Wednesday night for solicitation in the Ankle. And see what else you can find out about him. Business or job? Where does he live? If it's not on the arrest report, has he been arrested before? Any social connections, and so forth? If I'm not here, just leave it on my desk."

Brendan read the clipping. "Yes sir."

"One other thing, Brendan. Don't tell anyone that we've got a positive ID on the murder victim. In deference to the parents, I want to talk to them first. We owe them that much."

"Yes, sir, I understand," Brendan said on his way out.

Joe sat mulling over whether to phone or just go out to the house. He decided to drive out to Ensley, not wanting to inform someone about the murder of a child over the telephone. He locked Gloria's file in his desk and left the building.

Although it was only ten thirty, he wanted to get a bite to eat first. He didn't know how long this would take, and he was already hungry. After a cup of okra soup, a ham sandwich, and iced tea, he drove to Ensley. The house was in a colored, working-class neighborhood. He parked a few doors from the house, a small, well-maintained wood frame structure. The front yard was well-kept.

He rang the doorbell and waited, dreading the encounter.

A short, stocky colored woman with gray hair opened the door. She looked surprised to see a white man. "Yes, can I help you?"

"Mrs. Phillips?"

"Yes. I'm Mrs. Phillips."

"My name is Joe McGrath. I'm a detective with the Birmingham Police Department. May I come in?" Joe showed her his police badge.

A look of fear overcame Mrs. Phillips. She stepped back, opening the door to let Joe in. "Is this about my daughter, Gloria?"

"Maybe, ma'am."

Mrs. Phillips could barely utter, "Is she all right?"

Joe knew there was no easy way. "A young woman lost her life last night in Scratch Ankle. We think it may be your daughter."

Mrs. Phillips's knees buckled, and Joe reached to catch her. She screamed, "Albert . . . Albert . . . Albert."

Joe led Mrs. Phillips to the sofa and helped her sit when a tall, colored man with gray hair and a well-trimmed, graying beard came into the room.

"What's the matter, Mabel? Who is this?"

Mabel muttered. "Gloria might be dead."

Albert showed no emotion as he studied Joe.

Joe, wishing he had a better line, repeated, "My name is Joe McGrath, Mr. Phillips. I'm a detective with the Birmingham Police Department." He showed Mr. Phillips his badge.

"What happened?" Albert demanded.

"A young woman was killed in Scratch Ankle last night. It might be your daughter."

Before Albert could speak, Mabel, who was now only whimpering, said, "We know what Gloria did for a living, Mr. McGrath."

"How did the woman die?" Albert said.

Joe couldn't bear to tell them the truth. "The coroner hasn't decided on a cause of death yet."

Albert's shoulders sagged. His rigid facade started to crumble, his face fading from a stoic mask to a grief-stricken tableaux. He stumbled onto the sofa and took Mabel's hands in his. His breathing was labored.

As if she already knew it was her daughter, Mabel finally looked up, her eyes red and watery. "We tried so hard to get her to stop, Mr. McGrath. She went to church. She was a good student. She even went to Miles College for two years. What did we do wrong, Albert?"

Albert squeezed her hands tight and looked at her intently. "We did everything we could, honey. You know as well as I do what happened. It all started after she took up with Bongo Drum and those folks in Scratch Ankle. I could kill 'em all."

Albert turned to Joe, his face a dark scowl. "Who killed her? Was it a white man or colored man?"

"Mr. Phillips, at this point in our investigation, we don't know the answer to either question. We have yet to develop a credible lead or witness. But I'm sure we'll find whoever did it."

Albert stared at Joe. "You cops don't seem to go at it too hard when a colored person is the victim."

Joe was glad the chief wasn't present. "Mr. Phillips, if it's a murder, I promise you that I'll do everything I can to find the murderer."

"What do we do now?" Albert asked.

"I need you to come to the morgue and view the victim. If it is Gloria, state law requires a family member's identification before she can be released to the family. Once that's done, you sign a release form, and she can be picked up by whichever funeral home you designate."

"When do you want us to do this?"

"Ten o'clock tomorrow. If transportation's a problem, I can drive you to the morgue and back."

"I'll drive, Mr. McGrath."

"That's fine. I'll let the morgue know you're coming. I'll be there. Do you know where it is?"

"No."

Joe pulled out his notepad, wrote the address down, tore the page out, and handed it to Albert. "It's in the Southside."

Albert looked at the small piece of paper as if it contained an evil curse and stuck it in his pocket. "Okay, we'll be there at ten tomorrow."

"I'm so sorry to have to come into your home with such news. I'll take my leave now." He nodded to Mabel. "Goodbye, Mrs. Phillips."

Mabel could only nod in return. He returned to the car, wishing at this moment that he was still teaching English literature.

CHAPTER 10

JOE'S NEW SIDEKICK

MONDAY—SEPTEMBER 15, 1947

BACK AT HEADQUARTERS, Joe said to Sally, "I just talked to the woman's parents. They were devastated."

"I'm sure they were, Joe. How hard it must be to tell someone their daughter has been murdered."

"I couldn't tell them. But they knew. I wish there was a way to make it less difficult for them."

"I doubt you ever could. You're a caring man, Joe."

Joe, grateful for Sally's thoughtfulness, said, "Thanks, Sally."

He went into his office, called the morgue, and arranged the viewing for ten o'clock tomorrow. He called Watson's office. The chief was out, so he asked his secretary to tell the chief that Gloria Phillips's parents were coming to the morgue tomorrow to view the body. He called Jerry Howard, but he was also out of the office.

Later that afternoon, he was reading the past week's activity report when Brendan O'Connor walked into Joe's office.

"Did you find much, Brendan?"

"Yes sir. Here's a copy of the complete arrest report." He handed the report to Joe. "A white man, Franklin Pierce, and a colored woman, Angel Dustin, were arrested at the corner of Sixteenth Avenue North and Fifth Street North in Scratch Ankle at eleven thirty last Wednesday night. A patrol car was working the area on the lookout for any activities involving prostitution. They parked on Fifth about one-hundred feet from the corner when they observed Pierce approach Dustin, a woman they thought was a prostitute. After several minutes, they observed the two having a conversation that they thought was a negotiation although there's no mention in their report of any money exchanging hands. One of the officers got out of the car and approached the couple on foot while the other officer drove the car toward the corner. When the officer thought they were about to flee, he yelled at them to halt or he would pull his gun. They stopped before—"

"Sounds like our guy got a bit carried away. Pulling a gun in that situation is absolutely uncalled for," Joe said.

"Yes sir, but he didn't have to. The two halted and the officers interrogated them. They both denied anything illegal was going on. Pierce said he was asking Dustin for directions, and she agreed. The officers didn't believe them, arrested them, and took them to the city jail where they were booked. Dustin on prostitution. Pierce on solicitation. Both were released on separate bonds early Thursday morning."

"What did you learn about Franklin Pierce? I can't place the name, but I've heard it before," Joe said.

Brendan couldn't resist poking a little fun at Joe. "Well sir, this one is not President of the United States." Both men had a good laugh, and Brendan continued, "He's a big shot. Owns Alabama Pipe Company, the biggest producer of iron pipe in the state. They serve most of the state's industrial and municipal needs. They have production facilities in a few other southern states. It's a big business. Pierce lives in Mountain Brook. He's a member of most of the important clubs and organizations in the city."

"What's your background, Brendan?"

"I'm from Mobile. Went to a Jesuit school, Spring Hill College, for three years. Took a two-year sabbatical with Uncle Sam and came back and finished my liberal arts degree. Didn't see much use for it, so I decided to try police work. I joined the department last January."

"Interesting. Did Pierce have any priors?"

"No sir, didn't find any."

"Angel Dustin. I'll bet that's a street name. Did you pull her file?"

"Yes sir. Do you want to go over it?" Brendan said.

"Not in detail now. I'll read it later. Did she have any priors?"

"Four. All for prostitution. One arrest report had an alias listed for her, which might be her real name."

"Do you know who bailed them out?" Joe said.

"A representative of Robert Beauchamp's law firm posted bail for Pierce at two a.m. Someone named Derrick Wilson posted bail for Dustin at seven Thursday morning."

"I think Wilson's the attorney that covers for Bongo Drum Bartlett and his boys and girls. I'm not surprised someone of Pierce's caliber uses Beauchamp. He's considered the best criminal defense attorney in the city and probably the state. Mark my word, Brendan. He'll get Pierce off in nothing flat."

Brendan laughed. "Your word has been marked. On Friday, Beauchamp got an arrest hearing in Superior Court. He asked for a complete dismissal of the solicitation charge since the officers did not overhear the conversation between the two, no money was seen to have exchanged hands, and the two were not observed entering a car or hotel to consummate a presumed sexual transaction. The judge agreed and dismissed the case. Later in the day, the same judge dismissed the prostitution charge against Dustin."

"Good work, Brendan. Especially on Pierce's background and the court hearings. Who are you assigned to in the department now?"

"Basically, I work in records and other odd jobs that come up, mostly paperwork. I guess I'm in training like most new boys."

"How would you like to work with me? You could accompany me on investigations and interviews. I'm sure you'd learn a lot more than just pushing paper around."

"Oh God, that'd be great, Detective McGrath."

"Good. I'll talk to the homicide captain. Leave Dustin's file with me and take Gloria Phillips's file back to records. I'll get back to you as soon as I know something."

"Thanks." After Brendan left the office, Joe called Jack Ritter at the *News*.

"Jack Ritter, *Birmingham Beat*."

Joe smiled as Jack always identified himself by adding the title of his daily column. "Hey Jack. Got a minute?"

"For you, oh esteemed homicide detective, I'm always available for your latest story of murder and mayhem. Got anything for me on Sunday morning's alleyway altercation?"

"A poor alliteration, Jack. I don't want what I'm about to tell you in the paper until Thursday at the earliest. Can do?"

"You're pushing my journalistic principles, Joe. But yes, can do."

"Glad to hear you have some principles, Jack. Comes as a big surprise. The young colored woman's body found in the alley was murdered. Although we have a tentative ID on the woman, her parents will confirm the ID tomorrow morning. I can't give you the woman's name until after her parents ID the body. I can tell you that she is twenty-nine years old and worked the Ankle area as a prostitute. Cutler estimates she was murdered about three o'clock Sunday morning. At this time, we have no credible leads or witnesses."

"Well, that's newsworthy. Birmingham's super sleuth is stumped. What are the parent's names?"

Joe ignored the taunt. "Oh, come on, Jack. I tell you their names, and you'll be on their doorstep before I hang up. You'll get their names and anything else I know tomorrow afternoon or Thursday morning. Leave them alone. They are nice people and quite distraught."

"Okay. What about Franklin Pierce? I read in the police arrest reports that he was busted for solicitation in the Ankle last week. He's a big fish, Joe."

"As I understand it, all charges against Mr. Pierce and the colored woman were dropped in Superior Court hearings last Friday."

"Is Pierce a suspect?"

"Mr. Pierce is not a suspect."

"Joe, you know that some of these gals' best customers are white men, including your boys in blue and some of city hall's finest."

"That's what I hear. We'll follow any credible lead in any direction."

"I'll bet you will. Is that it?"

"For now. I'll call tomorrow or Thursday."

JOE CALLED IT A DAY, got a bite to eat, purchased the three essential items on his grocery list, and headed to his apartment for the night. He opened a beer and got in his chair, but instead of reading the newspaper, he thought to himself, *Oh, how I miss Jane.* He hadn't seen her in three weeks, and now that she lived a hundred miles away, he saw less and less of her.

As much as Joe wished otherwise, he knew where this was going. His mind reeled back to the evening two weeks after he and Mary separated. The old movie played again.

> *Mary had called for the first time since we separated. She had asked if she could come over to talk. I had immediately perked up.*
>
> *She said she'd be over in fifteen minutes. I was ecstatic, thinking she wanted to get back together.*
>
> *I answered the door. God, she looked good. That body and face I'd kill for. I broke into a big smile.*
>
> *"Hi, Joe. Thanks for letting me come over."*
>
> *"Sure. How you doing? You look great."*
>
> *"I'm okay, I guess."*
>
> *She must miss me. "How's Jane?"*
>
> *"She's doing all right. How are you?"*
>
> *"I'm surviving, but I miss you both. This big house is so empty."*
>
> *Mary looked unconcerned. "You're rattling around in here. Why don't you find a small apartment?"*
>
> *My smile faded fast.*
>
> *"Joe, don't look so glum."*
>
> *"What do you want, Mary? Why did you come over?"*
>
> *She looked and checked her manicure. "Jane and I are moving to Huntsville. We'll live with my mother until I find a place. My hometown is a good place for us now."*
>
> *I took a deep breath. It didn't work. I exploded, "Jesus, I thought you were coming over to talk about getting back together. Why are you doing this?"*
>
> *"You know why."*
>
> *"So you just walk away, destroy our family, take our daughter and leave your students in mid-year. What's got into you?"*
>
> *"You. And what choice do I have? I can't deal with your anger and jealousy issues. You need help. Professional help."*
>
> *"Goddammit, if you thought this would make it easier, you're wrong."*
>
> *"It'll be best, Joe. We both need a new start."*

"Yeah, you take our daughter and move a hundred miles away. That's a great new start for me."

"You can come see her anytime you want."

I couldn't think straight. "You think I can just drive up and back to Huntsville at a whim? A murder case just came up. I'm gonna be busy."

"Jane'll be happy to see you whenever you can make it."

"What are you going to do in Huntsville?"

"I'm sure I can find a teaching job, probably part-time initially. I know a lot of people in the school district."

"When are you leaving?"

"This weekend."

"You won't reconsider?"

"No, I've made up my mind. I have to go now. I left Jane with a friend. I'll let you know where we settle down. You know how to get in touch with Mom."

I felt as if a large truck just sideswiped me. I felt dizzy and couldn't focus on anything. "Okay," I mumbled. "Maybe one day I'll understand it all. It seems like a terrible nightmare right now."

Mary said goodbye and left the house.

I punched the door. Almost broke my goddamn hand.

The movie finally ended, but Joe couldn't stop thinking about the conversation and its consequences.

He now knew that he missed Jane much more than he missed Mary. He drove to Huntsville as often as he could to see Jane. However, it soon became apparent that Mary was doing everything she could to turn Jane against him, frequently not even allowing him to see his daughter. He asked Mary to consider a divorce. She refused, saying it was against her beliefs and the dogma of the Catholic Church. Joe knew that Mary was no more a devout Catholic than he was; he was sure it had more to do with maintaining control over Jane.

Exhausted from another brief encounter with his recent past, Joe abandoned his usual nightly reading ritual and went to bed even though he knew he wouldn't sleep well.

CHAPTER 11

THE IDENTIFICATION

TUESDAY—SEPTEMBER 16, 1947

JOE GOT TO THE OFFICE at EIGHT THIRTY FEELING AWFUL. A bad hangover would have been more welcome. He had spent the night tossing and turning with thoughts of Mary and Jane churning in his mind.

He even forgot the Hershey's Kiss routine. "Good morning, Sally."

"Good morning, Joe. No kisses this morning?"

"Tough night. Maybe later for a kiss. I'm going to see the boss."

Dick Oliver, Joe's boss, was from Birmingham money. Joe always approached Dick cautiously, since his political and racial views were opaque. At times, he talked like a southern liberal, but often he would revert to bigoted attitudes matching the chief's and most members of the BPD.

Joe knocked on the captain's door.

"Come in," Oliver said.

"Good morning, Dick. You got a few minutes?"

Dick was a handsome man in his mid-forties and of medium height with blonde hair. When challenged with a tough decision, he had a nervous habit of rubbing his chin or cheek with his left hand while he considered his choices.

"Sure, Joe. Whoa, you all right? You look like shit."

"Yeah, I'm fine. Didn't sleep well last night."

"Get your rest. This is a tough business. What you got on the colored whore killed in the Ankle? The chief keeps asking me."

"I've kept the chief up to date, Dick. I left a message with his secretary yesterday that the deceased woman's parents are coming to the morgue this morning. I'm sure they'll ID her as their daughter."

"That's good. The chief wasn't happy that you called Bongo Drum in here on Sunday. He read me the riot act."

"Yeah, I got the same lecture. I told the chief it wouldn't happen again. I knew they were close, but not that close."

"Yep, strange bedfellows, but the chief trusts him."

"Do you?"

Dick looked annoyed by the question. "If the chief says he's okay, he's okay by me. Joe, the chief wants this murder wrapped up pronto."

"He made that clear to me too. I called Jack Ritter at the *News* and told him what little we know about the woman's murder. I told the chief that I would call Ritter, and he seemed okay with it. You know Ritter will nose around if we don't cooperate with him."

"Just try to keep it low key."

"I will. I came in to ask you to assign Brendan O'Connor to me. I've been without a regular sidekick for over two months. He's a sharp kid. It'd be good experience for him. Investigations, interviews, and things like that."

Dick sat stroking his chin. "Brendan's been here less than a year. I'm not sure he's ready for a change, but I'll let you have him for six months. Then we can talk about his future."

"Thanks. When can he start working with me?"

"Tomorrow. I'll talk to the records folks today."

"I've got to get over to the morgue. The parents will be there at ten."

"Fine, just get it over with."

When Joe arrived at the morgue, Don was at the front desk. "Hi, Don. You ready for the ten o'clock viewing?"

"Yes, Detective McGrath. We'll put the body on the viewing table after the parents arrive. We need to minimize time out of the cooler."

"Is Dr. Cutler in?"

"He's in his office," Don said.

"I'm going to go say hello. Come get me when the parents arrive."

Joe went down the hall to Cutler's office. The door was open. "Good morning, Frank."

"Hey Joe. How's it going?"

"Just great. Another murder. Another viewing," Joe said.

"That's show biz. Say, did you hear about Franklin Pierce?"

"Yeah, he seems to be a hot topic around here," Joe said.

"A hot topic the big boys want to cool off. Pierce is well-connected. He's close friends with Stanford Ramsey. You know what that means."

"Sure do. Do you know Pierce?" Joe said.

"I've met him at a few social functions, but all I really know is—"

Don came into the office. "The Phillips are here."

"Be right there. Talk to you later, Frank."

Joe followed Don to the front lobby. "Hello, Mr. and Mrs. Phillips. Thanks for coming. Please have a seat."

Don left the lobby to see that the body was brought to the viewing room. Joe sat beside the two; they looked as though they had hardly slept. Albert was back in his stoic posture.

"I made arrangements with a funeral home," Albert said.

"Let me explain what we'll do. The victim will be on a long table covered by a sheet in the viewing room. An autopsy had to be performed since—"

Albert asked, "Why?"

"An autopsy is a state requirement in any apparent homicide. The results frequently help us in the initial hours and days of the investigation. We'll just pull the sheet back so you can get a clear view of her face. We need you to verify that she is your daughter. Is that acceptable?"

Albert looked at his wife. She nodded. "Yes sir, that's acceptable," Albert said.

Don came back. "We're ready, Detective McGrath."

When they saw the draped body, Mabel Phillips clutched Albert.

"Would you like to sit down?" Joe asked.

"No," said Albert. "Let's get this over with."

"Don, please pull the sheet down and expose her face."

Mabel and Albert let out anguished screams that would move even the devil to tears. Mabel, struggling to breathe, wailed. Albert's stoic face crumbled. Joe and Don stood behind the couple, prepared to catch them if they fainted. Joe whispered quietly in Albert's ear. "Could you please move closer to be sure that's your daughter."

Albert spoke between gasps. "No . . . need . . . that's . . . Gloria . . . that's . . . our . . . sweet . . . daughter," and arching his head back, yelled, "Oh my God."

Joe asked Don to cover the victim, and said to Mabel and Albert, "Let's go into another room. We're finished here."

He held Mabel on her side opposite Albert, and they allowed him to escort them to the room. As they sat at the table, Don joined them with paperwork in hand. Joe asked Don to explain what was left to be done.

"Mr. and Mrs. Phillips, I am very sorry for your loss. To legally complete the identification of your daughter and release her body to you or your representative, I need you to sign two forms. One verifies your identification and states your relationship to her. The second form gives the coroner's office legal clearance to release her body to you or a representative that you stipulate, a funeral home for example. I'm also required by law to tell you that if anything you stipulate in these forms should prove to be false, you could be subject to prosecution for perjury. Do you understand?"

At the moment, Mabel and Albert looked incapable of understanding anything, let alone the legal requirements. Joe put his hand lightly on Albert's arm. "Do you understand, Mr. Phillips?"

"Yes, that's Gloria. Where do I sign?"

Joe asked Don to guide Albert through the forms, explaining again what was required and where to sign. Don looked at the completed forms. "I know this funeral home, Mr. Phillips. We'll help them in every way possible. Here's a copy of the forms. Please give the release form to the funeral home."

"I will," Albert muttered,

"That's all we need, Mr. Phillips. Are you sure you can drive home? I can arrange for someone to drive you," Joe said.

Albert had recovered somewhat and was more stoic. "I'll be fine, Detective. The funeral home will pick up Gloria this afternoon." He helped Mabel up. "We'll be on our way."

Joe helped the couple to the front door and went back to Cutler's office. "Frank, Don is one fine young man. He was incredibly polite and thoughtful with the Phillips. I suspect they are not used to such treatment from most white people," Joe said.

"I train all my people to treat everyone with equal respect and courtesy. For most that come here, colored and white alike, this is the nearest they ever get to their Maker until their own judgment day. Oh hell, listen to me, I sound like a preacher."

"Sounds pretty good, Frank. I better get going."

"Hey, before you go. When we gonna get together again? Have a beer. Talk about books. You owe me another Shakespearean lesson. How about *Titus Andronicus*? I know nothing about that play."

Joe chuckled ominously at the mention of Shakespeare's bloodiest play. "Yeah, we gotta do that real soon. Wait 'til you hear what Chiron and Demetrius did to Lavinia. It sure as hell resonates with the last few days. See you later."

Joe stopped for a quick lunch at a downtown diner and then drove back to headquarters. He had a must-do task to complete.

At the chief's office suite, Joe told the secretary he needed to see the chief about the woman killed Sunday morning. She hit the intercom switch to the chief's office and said, "Joe McGrath wants to see you."

"Yeah, send him in," and as Joe walked in, the chief barked, "You got the whore's murder wrapped up?"

"The parents just identified the woman's body. It's their daughter. Their funeral home will pick her up this afternoon."

"Good. Now wind down the investigation real quick. Make it like we're following up. It's gonna quiet down real soon."

"Yes sir."

"You hear about Franklin Pierce's arrest?"

"Yes sir, his name's come up several times recently. I thought it might help to talk to him. Maybe he could shed some light on the murder."

Watson erupted. "Goddammit, Professor, don't you go near Franklin Pierce. You do, I'll rip you up one side and down t'other like I did them two cops who arrested him. You understand me?"

Joe knew he had gone too far with Watson. "Yes sir."

Watson's voice dropped to almost a whisper. "Joe, listen up real carefully. Pierce is an important man. He's friends with the most inflexible men in this city including Stanford Ramsey. You knows who Ramsey is, don't you?"

Joe struggled not to laugh at the chief's malaprop. "Yes sir. I've heard a lot about all the influential men and Mr. Ramsey."

Watson didn't bat an eye. "The court dismissed the charge against Pierce. It's all over, and Stanford and me want it to stay that way. You hear?"

"Yes Chief, I understand completely. Is that it?"

Watson broke into a rare smile. "Yep. Good work on gitting those darkies in here so soon and gitting this here thing over with."

"Yes sir." Joe felt a knot in his stomach. He knew "this here thing," as the chief called it, was far from over.

"Close the door on the way out, Joe."

In the hallway, Joe decided to call it a day.

WATSON DIALED HIS PHONE. "Stanford. It's Robert. McGrath jus' left. The whore's parents made the ID. The funeral home will git the body this afternoon."

"That's good. You sure he understands that we want this wrapped up, and he's not to talk to Pierce?"

"Yes, Stanford, he understands."

"Good. You keep McGrath under control or, Robert, it'll be your ass that's in the sling."

CHAPTER 12

THE PARK

TUESDAY—OCTOBER 14, 1947

J EANNIE LEE KNEW SHE SHOULDN'T be out working the Ankle this late at night without her pimp, but she needed the money. Although Black Bronco mistreated her, he did provide protection from weird street people and johns. Things had been slow all month, and she knew Black Bronco had shorted her share of what the johns paid him for her services. *Goddamn*, she thought, *why do he get most all the money? I do all the work.*

At two o'clock, Jeannie, a good-looking woman, well-suited to attracting the attention of men on the prowl, had been on the streets alone for four hours. She had dressed in provocative clothing—a tight-fitting cotton blouse, beige in color and open enough to provide prospective clients a good look at her breasts, and a dark brown cotton skirt slightly flared to facilitate a quickie when necessary.

Jeannie was working Ralston Park at the northeast corner of Fourth Avenue North and Twelfth Street North. She had chosen this spot, away from the busier parts of the Ankle, in hopes of avoiding Black Bronco.

The city didn't maintain the park since it served a colored neighborhood. However, a local colored men's club kept the park immaculate for the families and children in the area. About 200 feet square, the park featured a play area for children with swings, seesaws, a jungle gym, and a sandbox. A small pond with a central fountain was the park's centerpiece. The drinking fountains did not have the usual Colored Only signs on them; apparently, the city fathers and cops couldn't imagine a white person frequenting this park. The back corner of the park in a grove of large trees—a small, unlit grassy area—provided Jeannie and many of her street sisters a secluded spot for their trysts late at night.

On this cool, dry night, Jeannie had hooked only one young colored guy. He said he had five dollars. She reluctantly agreed and led him into the park. She knew it well and went directly to the secluded, grassy area.

She bared her breasts to give the kid a good long look at her nipples, which were large and erect, thanks to the cool evening air. She didn't waste time. She pulled his head down so he could feel and suck her breasts for a few minutes to get him good and hot. Then she dropped his pants to his knees, got on her knees, and gave him a blow job. It took only a few quick sucks, and the kid exploded in her mouth like a Roman candle. She spit his wad onto the grass, always amazed at the sexual potency of young men. The kid pulled up his pants, thanked her, and slunk out of the park, looking ashamed at what he had done. She straightened her clothes and went to a drinking fountain to rinse out her mouth. The entire encounter was over in ten minutes.

Jeannie went back to the corner of Fourth and Twelfth, thinking she would call it a night when she saw him, a white man. She never understood why, but white and colored men walked differently: white guys in a stiff, uptight manner, while colored guys appeared more relaxed and comfortable.

He walked straight toward her, and she thought the night might finally yield a fine catch. He wore a black overcoat and hat. The hat had a huge brim that almost covered the upper half of his head and face. The hat didn't surprise Jeannie; most white guys who came into the Ankle looking for action didn't want to be recognized. That was okay with her as long as they had money.

She put her hands on her hips and thrust them towards him, a provocative pose she used that seldom failed to attract a man's attention.

When he got about ten feet from her, he stopped. "Well girl, what are you doing out here so late?"

"Oh, I reckon I jus' be hangin' around lookin' for some fun. What about you, mistah?" Jeannie said.

"I've had a hard day. Any chance you could help a fellow relax?"

Jeannie affected a small pout. "You got anythin' special in mind, mistah? I's sure I could hep you. I knows a lots of good tricks to makes a man relax."

He smiled and said, "I bet you could. How about we go into that nice, quiet corner in back of the park and see what we can do?"

"Jus' what I had in mind." She decided to push her price way up in hopes that this sucker took the bait. "I do most anythin' you wants for a hundred bucks. Okay?"

He looked around the street and area. "That's fine." As if he knew what the deal would be, he pulled five twenties from his overcoat pocket and handed the bills to Jeannie.

She tried to look nonchalant as she stuck the money into her skirt pocket, more than she usually earned in several days working the streets for hours. She took his hand and led him toward the same secluded spot in the park.

As they went, he kept looking back. Jeannie figured he didn't want to be seen by anyone, especially someone he knew; most of her white tricks were like that. Once in the grove of trees, he checked around again and seemed satisfied that the location was fine.

He smiled at her and took off his overcoat, folded it neatly, and placed it on the ground. He took off his hat, handing it gently as if it were a piece of fine china. He placed the hat on top of the coat, arranging its position carefully. Although there was little light, enough filtered through the trees from the park lamps that Jeannie now got a better look at the man.

About six feet tall, she figured him at around fifty years old. He had a trim body and brown hair. He had a handsome face, except for his blue eyes, which had a hard intensity that initially frightened her. She relaxed when he finally spoke to her.

"Let's lie down here," he said, indicating the spot adjacent to his coat and hat. When he unbuttoned his shirt and took it off, Jeannie took off her blouse and lay on the ground, pulled up her skirt, and spread her legs.

"You got a body like an angel and nice breasts, honey. Tonight, I'm going to make you right with the world." He dropped his pants and underpants to his knees and didn't waste any time mounting her. He already had a full, firm erection.

"Wow, mistuh. You looks like youse ready to go." She was glad since she frequently had to spend a lot of time with older guys getting them good and hard.

Breathing heavy, he said, "Just about." He rubbed his member over her vagina and started to suck on her left breast. He continued rubbing and sucking for several minutes.

Jeannie finally reached down between his legs. "Here, honey, let me put your big boy where it want to be."

He moaned as he entered her and immediately started to push on her like a pile driver. After less than a minute of powerful thrusts, he slowed and kissed her, at first gently, his warm, large lips exciting her. But then he pressed hard on her lips and bared his teeth and bit her around the lips.

She had to push with all her might to get his head up, and she shouted, "Hey, what you doin'? That hurts. No rough stuff, you hear? Come on honey. Jus' fuck me good and hard."

He mumbled, "Yeah," and reached over and pulled something from under his hat.

She knew he was getting close, and in hopes of getting this over with quickly, pleaded, "Fuck me. Fuck me. I wants to feel you come."

He put both of his hands above and on each side of her head and lifted his torso as he panted and pumped even harder. She could tell he was ready to come and heard him groan as he ejaculated.

She felt something tightening around her neck. "Hey, what you do—"

CHAPTER 13

THE INVESTIGATIONS

TUESDAY—OCTOBER 14, 1947

THE INVESTIGATION OF THE SEPTEMBER FOURTEENTH murder had yielded absolutely no leads. Just as the chief had predicted, the attention and interest in the murdered woman had quickly faded. Joe had told Jack Ritter all he had on the case except the woman's body position.

Joe and Jerry Howard had gone to all the businesses, bars, and movie houses near the murder scene. Everyone they had interviewed said nothing or very little. Birmingham coloreds saw no reason to be cooperative with white cops. Just better to keep one's mouth shut.

Only one person had admitted he knew the woman, the bartender at the bar across the street from the New Home Hotel. He had said to Joe, "Yessuh, I seen that girl around but I don't knows nuthin' about her." Joe had known the bartender was putting him off since Bongo Drum and his girls used the bar as their prime meeting place, but he had let it go. Cutler's lab guys had drawn blanks analyzing the samples from the murder scene. End of investigation.

JOE HAD BEEN USING YOUNG BRENDAN O'CONNOR as his sidekick since Dick Oliver gave his approval a month ago. Brendan was bright, attentive, a quick learner, and best of all, he complemented Joe's style:

courteous, intense, and focused. They had worked well together as a team, and Joe was about ready to send him on assignments alone.

Joe shared his office with Brendan, and the two had arrived for work early on Tuesday, October fourteenth. They were discussing current case loads and the day's activities when Joe's phone rang at five after nine.

"Joe McGrath here."

"Joe, it's Billy Donaldson. Just got a call reporting a body in Ralston Park at Fourth and Twelfth in the Ankle. Oliver wants you to cover it."

"Brendan and I are on the way. Send another car with a couple of guys in case we need additional help. Who reported the body?"

"A lady named Jessica Walter. She and her kids were in the park, and one of her kids spotted the body. I got her phone number and address. I told her to wait. I said cops would be there soon."

"Good. Call the chief and the coroner."

"Will do," Billy said and hung up.

"Let's go, Brendan. A body's been reported in Ralston Park."

As he parked, Joe noticed a group of thirty or so people standing around a grove of trees in the back corner of the park.

Brendan looked surprised at the scene. "My gosh, look at all the colored folks. You think we have a problem?"

"I doubt it. This is their neighborhood, and they're curious about what happened."

As a police car approached the park, Joe said, "Brendan, here comes our support. You stay here and talk to them. Tell them to cordon off the entire perimeter of the park. I'll go and get those folks to vacate the park. Interview as many of them as you can before they leave. Ask them if they heard or saw anyone suspicious in this area last night or this morning. You come and join me as soon as you put the other officers to work."

"Okay, Joe."

Joe walked over to the grove of trees, held up his police badge, and shouted, "Folks, please listen up. I'm Detective Joe McGrath with the Birmingham Police Department. I need to have y'all vacate the park so we can conduct an investigation. Thanks for your cooperation. Is there a lady named Jessica Walter here?"

The crowd turned when they heard Joe yell and stared at him with looks of contempt and hostility. Two men in the crowd stepped toward him in a menacing fashion, and he thought he might have been wrong and there might be some trouble. The two men looked at each other and started walking out of the park. The rest of the crowd slowly followed the two men. A small woman of about thirty hesitated at the back of the group and approached Joe.

"I's Jessica Walter."

"Good morning, Mrs. Walter. I'm sorry to have to meet you under these circumstances. Thanks for waiting for us to arrive. Are your kids still here?"

"No suh. A friend come over here and took 'em home. We lives nearby."

"Can you show me the body, please?"

"It's over yonder in them trees. Do I have to look at it again?"

"No ma'am. Just point out the spot, and I'll take a look."

She led Joe to the edge of the grove and pointed into the middle of the trees. He started to enter the grove when Brendan came towards him.

"Joe, I got the other guys working on the perimeter. I talked to a few people, but nobody was helpful. They all say they didn't see or hear anything."

"About what I expected. Brendan, this is Mrs. Walter. She reported the body. Please sit with her on the bench over there. I want to ask her some more questions. I'll be right back."

Joe found a passage through about ten feet of trees to the grassy opening, an oval, twelve to fifteen feet in diameter. When he saw the body laid out on the ground, he immediately knew that his initial misgivings about last month's murder had come to pass.

The body lay facing up, splayed out like an *X* with the arms and legs spread wide at forty-five degree angles to her torso. She was nude except for the area around her waist, where her skirt had been pulled up over her hips. Her blouse and panties laid close to her body.

Joe was careful not to disturb the crime scene. He didn't touch the body, but he got close enough to see her bruised lips and the marks of a garrote around her throat. He also spotted a light-colored blob about eight feet to the right of the body and wrote in his notepad to tell Cutler about it.

He stepped back to the edge of the trees and surveyed the crime scene again, now sure that a sadistic killer was on the loose.

Joe got back to the bench where Brendan and Mrs. Walter sat. "Brendan, go see how the guys on the perimeter are doing. Call the desk officer. Find out when Cutler and his guys will be here. We need them as soon as possible. I'll talk to Mrs. Walter."

"Will do, Joe."

"Mrs. Walter, I do need to ask you a few questions. What time did you and your kids come to the park this morning?"

She sat slowly wringing her hands. "It was—"

"That's okay, Mrs. Walter. Take your time. I know this is hard."

She smiled softly at Joe. "It was 'bout eight thirty. I brings my kids to the park to let 'em play. Ain't much for 'em at our house."

"Yes, this is a lovely park for children. How old are your kids?"

"My boy five and my daughter three."

"Nice ages. I have a ten-year-old daughter. Who found the body and what time?"

"Musta been close to nine. My son run over to the trees there. He likes to hide. Me and sister would play we couldn't find him. But this time, right after he gone in them trees, he comes a runnin' out screamin', 'Mama, mama, they's a naked lady in here.' I didn't know what that boy mean, so I run right over and go into the trees and sees the body. I jus' look real quick; I can tell she dead. I gets the chillun and walks out of the park."

Joe studied Mrs. Walter's face and hands closely. She had relaxed considerably. "What did you do next, Mrs. Walter?"

"I knowed I had to tell somebody, so I went to that gas station," she said, pointing across the street. "I tole the gas man what I seen. He say, 'Well, you bettah call the cops.' He dialed the police number for me. I tole that policeman what I seen and here you are."

"Yes, ma'am, we got here as quick as we could. Did you touch the body or anything around it?"

"Oh, no suh. I wouldn't do that. That disrespect the dead, and I was scared."

"Did you tell anybody else about what you saw?"

"No suh. But that gas man sure couldn't stop talking. He tell everybody that come in the station 'bout it. Pretty soon there were lots of folks in the park. Well, you seen 'em when you got here."

"Yes, ma'am. I saw them. Did any of those folks go in the trees and look at the body?" Joe said.

"Yes suh, a few. I don't knows how many."

Joe decided to wrap it up with a couple more questions. "Do you know if any of them touched the body or took anything?"

"I ain't sure. I couldn't see 'em."

"Did you hear any talk? Things like seeing or hearing something that might be related to the murder."

Mrs. Walter looked confused by Joe's question, and he thought he might have to rephrase it when she said, "No suh, nothing like that. One man I knows who lives close by said it seemed real quiet last night."

"Mrs. Walter, I know you want to get home to your family. We have your address and phone number if we need to talk more. Thanks for your help."

"Yes suh, I wants to get home."

She left the park, and Joe walked over to Brendan and the other two officers. He recognized Steve Strickland.

"Hi, Steve." Joe didn't recognize the other officer. He stuck out his hand. "Hi, I don't believe I know you. I'm Joe McGrath."

"Yes suh, Detective McGrath, I'm Billy Bob Barnes. I mostly works on street patrol. Steve and me was assigned together this mornin'."

"That's good," Joe smiled as he repeated the alliterative name, "Billy Bob Barnes. Glad to have you help us out." Turning to Brendan, he asked, "Is Cutler on the way?"

"Yes sir. I called the desk officer. Dr. Cutler should be here any minute."

Joe stared at the three young officers in a stern manner. He wanted their attention. "That's good. Fellows, we have a serious situation. The MO appears almost identical to the murder last month at Fourth and Seventeenth. I suspect this victim is also a prostitute. I've got to get back to headquarters and talk to Oliver and the chief. Steve, you and Billy Bob maintain a secure perimeter around the park. Don't let any unauthorized people into the park, especially the area around the trees in the back corner. Okay?"

Steve said, "Yes sir."

Billy Bob nodded.

"Brendan, you show Cutler the location of the body. When you take Cutler to the body, check to see if there are any buildings or accesses to the park in that corner. And be sure and tell him I saw a light-colored blob of something about eight to ten feet to the right of the body. His lab guys should collect it for further analysis."

"Okay, will do."

Joe added, "After you get Cutler situated, interview the guy working the gas station across the street. That's where Jessica Walter went to call and report the body. Ask him if he saw or heard anything suspicious and if he's heard any talk. Then work all the businesses and houses along one block in each direction from the park. Finally, if there are any buildings facing the back corner of the park, try to interview anyone in those buildings. Think you can cover all that?"

"I'll sure try, Detective McGrath."

Joe was pleased Brendan addressed him as his superior officer while they were with other officers to avoid talk of favoritism.

"Steve, when Cutler and Brendan finish their work, and the body and other evidence they collect is taken back to the morgue, you and Billy Bob can reopen the park, and the three of you can return to headquarters. No wait. On second thought, ask Cutler if it's all right to reopen the park after he's finished and the body is gone. He may have a reason he wants it secure. If that's the case, you three remain here and call the desk officer. He'll send some guys out to relieve you and then you can come back to headquarters. Make sense?"

"Yes sir," said Steve.

"If the press comes around, especially Jack Ritter, tell them we just opened an investigation into an incident in the park and to call me. I'll talk to you three later today."

As Joe turned to go to his car, he could hear Billy Bob whispering to Steve, "Man, he's thorough. But I hear he's pretty soft on coloreds."

CHAPTER 14

THE DECISION

TUESDAY—OCTOBER 14, 1947

J OE WENT STRAIGHT TO DICK OLIVER'S OFFICE. "Sorry to interrupt,
Dick. You got a minute?"

"Sure do. Billy Donaldson told me you went to Ralston Park.
What's going on?"

"It's serious, Dick. I think we should go talk to the chief."

Dick said, "Okay," and as they rode the elevator, he asked, "What
have we got?"

"I'm pretty sure the victim is a prostitute, and the MO looks just
like the murder last month. This victim was garroted, and the body
was arranged like an *X*. Whoever is killing these women is leaving a
calling card. I don't know what it means, but I'm sure the body positions are saying something. Dick, I think we got a seriously deranged
killer on our hands."

As soon as they entered the chief's office, Watson grimaced at Joe.
"What you got this time, Professor?"

Joe carefully retold all the events from the morning with a detailed
focus on the woman's body position, her bruised lips, and how similar
this murder was to the one last month.

"Chief, I think the guy who murdered these women will strike
again if we can't nail him," Joe said.

"Whaddya think, Dick?" the chief mumbled.

"I'm afraid it adds up, Chief. It sounds real bad."

The chief looked at Joe. "We got any leads?"

"No sir, nothing."

"Well, do ya think it's a colored or white man?"

"I have no idea, Chief. Could go either way. We all know white men are good customers of the women in the Ankle. Hell, I hear that some of our cops and city hall's finest use their services."

Oliver and the chief looked at each other, but said nothing. After a few moments, the chief looked hard at Joe.

"So, what do you suggest we do, Professor. You the one trained in that crima . . . whaddya call it?"

"Criminology, Chief."

"Yeah, that's it. So what do we do?"

"Tough question. I've never experienced anything like this. But I got a couple of ideas. One, will you talk to Bongo Drum and see if he can help us? Maybe he can identify the body unless Cutler—"

The chief cut in. "Yeah, I'll talk to Bongo Drum."

"Thanks, Chief." Joe hesitated. He knew his second suggestion would not go down well with the chief. "Two, we've had problems getting any useful cooperation from the colored community. I'd like to get someone from outside the department to help us."

"Yeah, who?"

"You heard of Sam Rucker? He's a private eye that works in the colored community. He's—"

The chief turned bright red and looked as if he would explode. "You ain't suggesting we use that darkie to work in my police department, are you?"

Joe chose his words carefully. "No sir, not in the department. I'd like to hire him for what he is, a private eye. He's worked in the city for about ten years and has a good reputation. He helped us a couple of years ago in the Yarbo case—the creep who killed a colored store owner. Rucker would work at my direction, assisting me and Brendan O'Connor."

"Joe. I, I, I . . . " The chief had to catch his breath before he could continue. "I can't allow it, Joe. Hell, what would they want next? To be beat cops?"

Joe tried again. "Chief, we need someone like Sam Rucker who can talk to the colored community and do some snooping around that we couldn't get away with."

"Goddammit. Talk to me, Dick," the chief said.

Dick looked uncomfortable as his left hand moved to his cheek. "You're right, Chief. We gotta protect the integrity of the department. The darkies gotta be kept in their place."

Joe frowned, thinking his argument was lost. The chief smiled.

Oliver looked at both men and continued. "But this is a special problem. Like Joe, I don't know exactly what we got here, but it isn't good. Chief, I know Bongo Drum keeps you informed about what's up in the Ankle. But you know he wants to protect his own interest and business. I think as long as Joe directs Rucker, and he works for us as an independent private eye, we can control the situation. Now we gotta keep it quiet. The press and others in the department might get pretty upset."

The chief sat quietly, looking unhappy. "Joe, if I agrees with this, how you gonna do it?"

"Well, first I need to talk to Sam and see if he will consider doing it. He may not want to get involved—"

Reacting as if he hadn't opposed the idea, the chief said, "Whaddya mean? He can't say no to a white man, 'specially a cop."

Joe struggled to keep his composure. "I'm sure Sam will be interested, Chief. We'll have to find a place where we can meet. Probably in Sam's office in the Ankle or maybe an office in a quiet section of town. We obviously can't do it here. We'll—"

"Goddamn right you can't," roared the chief. "That darkie come in this building and you're both out the door."

"Right, Chief. I understand. We'll also need to arrange a way to pay Sam so it doesn't appear on the department's pay records. I could submit my expense reports to you or Dick, show Sam's fees and any other expenses as normal investigation costs. You or Dick approve the expense report. A check gets issued to me for that amount. I pay Sam. To keep the payments even harder to track, the check could be issued from a general account at your disposal."

Dick Oliver laughed. "Jesus Christ, Joe, we're going to have to keep a better eye on you. Sounds like you'd make a good embezzler."

The chief didn't laugh. "Very funny. If we do this, I got an account we can use, but I want Dick to manage it. Think it'll work, Dick?"

"Yeah, I think so. I'm sure there's some rough edges to work out, but we can do it. You okay to go, Chief?"

The chief frowned. "I still don't like it, but I ain't gotta better idea right now. Okay, Joe you talk to Sam about it. Then get back to me and Dick before you sign him up."

"Will do, Chief. I'll try to talk to him as soon as we get this current situation stabilized. I'll keep you up to date on both scores. I better get back to today's murder. Lots of loose ends hanging," Joe said.

"Yeah, you do that. Dick, you stay put. I wanna talk to you."

Joe left the chief's office knowing he would be the subject of their conversation.

THE CHIEF WAITED UNTIL HE WAS SURE JOE WAS GONE. "Dick, I worry about the Professor. Is he too goddamn liberal?"

"Big Bob, Joe's our best homicide detective. Sure he's a little relaxed with colored folks, but we need some of that to get our job done. You know Mr. Ramsey would want our best man on this."

"I'll take care of Stanford. You jus' keep on top of Joe and this here deal. If it blows up, I gonna nail your ass to the wall first. Got it?"

"Don't worry, I'll stay on it and keep you informed."

As soon as Dick was out of his office, the chief called Stanford Ramsey. "Stanford, got something I gotta talk to you about."

"Good morning, Robert. Yes, what is it?"

"Another colored whore killed last night. Looks like the same guy probably did it." He explained the similarities in the two murders and Joe's suggestion to use Sam Rucker.

When Robert finished his explanations, the phone was silent for so long that he finally asked, "Stanford, you there?"

"Yes. I'm thinking about what you told me. Do you think using Rucker makes sense? You know I want these kind of things kept quiet and wrapped up immediately."

Robert cringed. Stanford's tone had changed from collegial to frigid. "Both Joe and Dick Oliver think the murders will continue if we don't find the guy."

"Do we know anything or have any leads?" Stanford said.

"Nope. But we jus' got into the second murder. We'll knows more tomorrow."

"What will we know?" Stanford asked.

Unsure exactly how to respond, Robert said, "Well, maybe the whore's name. Maybe find some evidence at the crime scene."

"Robert, you do your damnedest to control this. I want you to call me whenever anything important occurs. I don't want any surprises. Let me make that very clear. No surprises."

AFTER LEAVING THE CHIEF'S OFFICE, Joe drove back to the murder scene. The body was being loaded into the coroner's van, and he saw Frank Cutler standing next to the van.

"What's it look like to you, Frank?"

"Just like last month, Joe. Time of death around three this morning. I'm pretty sure the light-colored blob is semen. We'll check it in the lab. It's been in the cool air a while, but I think we can test it. And we found a wallet with a driver's license in it. You guys must have missed it. I've bagged it so we can check for prints. I'll let you have it after we examine it."

"Where did you find the wallet?"

"Just beyond the semen blob. It was near the trees in the back of the grove. We almost overlooked it too. It's greenish, blends with the grass and background. One of my techs spotted it while he was collecting the specimen. I'm surprised it wasn't picked up by someone before we arrived."

"You gonna do the autopsy right away?" Joe asked.

Frank motioned to his techs that he was ready to leave. "We'll have it done in a few hours."

"Call this afternoon and tell me what you got. Can you put your techs on the wallet right now? I'd like to get it today."

"Will do," Frank said.

Brendan and the other two officers, Steve and Billy Bob, were removing tape and a few barriers to reopen the park when Joe came up to them.

"Learn anything interesting, Brendan?" Joe said.

"No, nobody's talking. Dr. Cutler did find a wallet. He picked it up with tongs and saw a driver's license in it, but he immediately bagged it for the lab. This might be our break."

"Maybe, but I doubt it. It's too obvious. Too neat. You guys finish this up and come on back to headquarters. Cutler will have autopsy findings and the wallet for us this afternoon. You write up your interviews and observations."

JOE WAS BACK IN HIS OFFICE WRITING NOTES when the phone rang.

"Hi, Joe. It's Frank. Just finished the autopsy. Time of death was about three, as I told you earlier today. Death by strangulation with a garotte. Motile sperm in the vagina. Blood type A. Bruised lips. No other significant bruises. Body's arranged in an X position. You saw it, Joe. Same MO as the murder last month."

"Anything else?"

"She had nine dollars in bills and a few coins in her skirt pocket: one tattered five and four ones all crumpled up. The light-colored blob was semen. It was blood type B. Although speculative, the sperm count appeared low, unlike the sperm in her vagina."

"So the semen on the ground wasn't from the man's semen in her vagina?"

"Can't say for sure. We don't know how many sexual tricks she had recently. We also got a few prints off the wallet. You can have it now."

"Good. I'll send Brendan over to pick it up. Oh, give him two copies of the photos you took of this latest murder victim. I also need two headshot copies of both victims with no BPD markings on them. I gotta show them to someone. Can he pick all that up today?"

"Yes."

"Great. Thanks."

"We aim to please, Joe. You'll have my formal report tomorrow."

When Brendan returned from the park, Joe said, "Go over to the morgue. Cutler's finished with the wallet. Get it and some photos he has."

Two hours later, Brendan returned with the wallet. "It belongs to a guy named Luke Matthew with a Birmingham address. Here are the coroner's photos." Brendan placed an envelope on Joe's desk.

"Do you think he's related to Mark and John?"

Brendan laughed. "Probably. His driver's license birthdate makes him nineteen years old, and he's colored. Lives on the north side, not far from Ralston Park. Got his address and phone number. No priors. I also checked with the juvenile authority. Nothing there either. That's all so far. What do you want to do?"

Joe sighed. "I don't think for a minute this is our guy. But we gotta bring him in and talk to him. In the morning, you go to Matthew's address and bring him in if he's there. If Steve Strickland or Jerry Howard aren't available as support, wait 'til I can be available. Before you leave to get Matthew, sign out with the desk officer. Give him the name and address of the suspect. If you do bring Matthew in, put him in a cell and let him stew. We'll question him together." He pulled a set of the photos from the envelope. "Here. Have someone in records do a file search for a match. I gotta make a private phone call."

JOE HAD MET SAM RUCKER ONCE during the Yarbo trial a few years ago. Sam, working for the family of the victim, had found the critical evidence about the murder that led to a conviction.

Joe found Sam's card in his center desk drawer and dialed the number, not knowing if it was still correct.

"Sam Rucker."

"Sam, this is Joe McGrath, homicide detective with the Birmingham Police Department. Remember me?"

"Of course, Detective McGrath. Glad we nailed the son-of-a-bitch in that trial."

"Me too. Sam, call me Joe. I need some help. Did you hear about the prostitute murdered in the Ankle last month?"

"Yeah. Sounded weird to me."

"It was. We had another murder this morning in the park at Fourth and Twelfth. Same MO. I think we've got a serious problem on our hands. I'd like to meet with you and talk about it."

"Why do you want to talk to me?"

"Sam, you know folks in the Ankle won't talk to police officers. I need your help to work with the community to investigate this thing."

Sam was silent for a moment. "Okay. When and where do you want to meet?"

"Sometime tomorrow in your office," Joe said.

"Fine with me. But you know, every set of colored eyes in the neighborhood will be on you. Then you'll be the talk of the town."

"Damn, you're right. Know any place we can meet?"

"I gotta friend who owns a barbecue joint—Willie's BBQ—fifteen miles north of the city on Highway 31 on the left. You can't miss it, big sign. There's a room we can meet in. Willie will keep his mouth shut. Got damned good barbecue too. Sound okay?"

"Sounds perfect. What time?"

"Nine o'clock work for you? We'll be outta there before the lunch crowd starts coming in," Sam said.

"Yeah, I can do that."

"I'll get there a little early. Set things up. You park in the back. Come in the back door. I'll be waiting."

"Good. Thanks, Sam. See you tomorrow."

SAM HUNG UP THE PHONE, leaned back in his chair, and looked up at the ceiling. *What the hell is going on?* The murder last month remained an unsolved crime, but he knew Big Bob Watson could care less about a colored whore. McGrath's insistence on meeting could be a ploy to involve him in a meaningless investigation in hopes of satisfying the colored community. Or maybe McGrath was shooting straight and wanted to get serious about solving the crime.

Sam called Willie's and arranged the room for the meeting. *This could be very interesting.*

CHAPTER 15

THE PRIVATE EYE

SAM RUCKER

Sam Rucker was raised in a family where religion was the metronome of life. The days of the week and the family's schedule ruled the religious calendar and his father's rigid demands. Reverend Angus Rucker was one of the best-known colored preachers in Alabama. Sam respected and feared his father in equal measures.

"You're a sinner. I'm a sinner. We're all sinners."

The Sunday morning congregation at Birmingham's St. Jude African Methodist Episcopal Church wailed at the admonition.

"The Lord can provide you salvation," intoned Reverend Rucker, using his booming baritone voice to great effect. He was a huge man, well over six feet tall, 250 pounds, not fat, just huge. He loomed over his congregation from the pulpit like the mythical black Jesus.

"Please, sweet Jesus," implored the congregation, underscoring their need with random shouts of "Amen" and "Hallelujah."

"Do you know how to get salvation?" bellowed the reverend.

A woman near the front stood, raised her arms on high. "No, Reverend. Lead us sinners to salvation."

Reverend Rucker smiled at the woman and spoke in a quieter voice. "Let me read from scriptures, Luke 7:37 and 7:38, 'And, behold, a woman in the city, which was a sinner . . . stood at his feet behind him weeping, and began to wash his feet with tears . . . and kissed his feet.' That's the gospel of the Lord."

"Amen! Hallelujah!" rang through the church's rafters.

"Simon the Pharisee observed this woman and thought, 'This man, if he were a prophet, would have known . . . she is a sinner.' Christ said to Simon, 'Her sins, which are many, are forgiven.' And looking at the woman, Christ said, 'Thy faith hath saved thee; go in peace,' " Reverend Rucker said.

The congregation erupted into a litany of "Hallelujah."

Reverend Rucker waved the congregation to silence. "My fellow sinners, Christ forgave this woman, a harlot, not because of her sins, but because of the love she showed him in her heart. She didn't ask for forgiveness. She bestowed her belief and love of Christ on him by washing his feet and kissing them. Humble yourself in front of the Lord. Sinners, kiss your Lord today. It is the kiss of salvation."

Nine-year-old Sam Rucker sat in a pew with his mother and two sisters. His father's sermon confused him. *What was a harlot? How could he kiss the Lord? He had never seen him. If it was so easy to be forgiven, why worry about sinning?*

After church, Sam couldn't play baseball since his father didn't allow physical activity on the Sabbath. Instead, he spent his Sunday afternoons reading. He got his copy of Edgar Allan Poe's works. While he enjoyed the horror stories and poems, the detective stories, "The Murders in the Rue Morgue" and "The Purloined Letter," were his favorites. He read Poe for a while and then found his mother, so she could explain passages he didn't understand.

BORN IN BIRMINGHAM IN 1908, Sam's childhood years were spent in joyous learning. His mother, Rebecca, Sam's touchstone in life, served as a soft counterpoint to his demanding father. Sam thought she was the most beautiful woman in the world. He always noticed that men, colored and white alike, stopped and stared at Rebecca, a tall, stately woman with a regal bearing. She had a chocolate brown face with features seemingly created by a Renaissance artist and dressed well, but simply, in long, dark colored cotton shifts, befitting a pastor's wife. She augmented Sam's elementary school years with home school-ing and nurtured him through his father's harsh religious demands, which left indelible scars on Sam's psyche.

Sam attended Industrial High School, the only colored high school in Birmingham. An outstanding student and athlete, he excelled in football and baseball, and was the valedictorian in his graduating class. He had hoped to study either engineering or medicine in college.

However, his father insisted Sam follow his path into ministry. He dutifully went to a college created by the African Methodist Episcopal Church in South Carolina. Sam graduated with honors with a liberal arts degree. To complete his theological training, he went to an AME Church theological seminary in Ohio. Here he had his first experiences in a world without legal segregation, although racial intolerance and vestiges of segregation were ever present.

A fateful encounter with his father had been building since he reluctantly agreed to pursue ministry. As his first year at the seminary came to an end, he finally accepted that ministry was not his calling. Sam had been reading about the University of Chicago's new curriculum in criminology. He contacted the school, and when they looked at his background and academic achievements, the school eagerly accepted him into the program.

Sam went home to explain his decision to his parents. He told his father he wanted to study criminology, not religion. Rebecca, knowing Angus would explode, tried to convince him that Sam was not being disrespectful.

The conversation came to an end when Sam said, "Dad, I can make a difference in this profession. I can help our people."

"You go to Chicago, Sam, don't ever bother coming back," Angus roared as if calling down damnation on the devil himself.

"Dad, you don't mean that."

"I do. I'll cast you out as Abraham did his son Ishmael."

Sam was conflicted by feelings of anger and hopelessness. "Dad, I'm not going to Chicago to start another religion."

He left the house. It was the last time he saw his father.

WHEN THE UNIVERSITY OF CHICAGO agreed to honor his prior college credits, Sam earned his B.S. in the nascent field of criminology in three years. His mother sent him money on the side, but he had to work at part-time jobs to support himself.

As if the biblical gods weren't through with him, the day after he graduated, his sister Hannah called him. "Sam, it's Hannah."

"Hey, sister. How are you?"

"Sam . . . Dad died last night."

Sam was standing and fell into a chair. He said nothing for a few moments. "What happened?"

"He had a heart attack. He was dead when we got him to a hospital."

"I'll get home as soon as possible."

"Hurry, Sam. Mom needs you. We all need you."

Sam had planned to find work in Chicago. The options seemed endless: the police department, one of the many private investigation firms in the city, a small firm of his own, or even a teaching assistant position at Chicago while he worked on his master's degree. His father's unexpected death had changed everything. He had to return to Birmingham for his father's funeral and to support his family.

St. Jude Church was overflowing with people for Angus's funeral service. Sam delivered the eulogy for the family. He kept his remarks short. After highlighting his father's many achievements, and love of his family and congregation, he closed with what he hoped his mother and sisters would appreciate.

"My father was a religious man to the core of his soul. He loved each one of you as his brothers and sisters. I'll close with the benediction he gave at the end of each of his services.

"Go with God in your hands. Lift your hands high in His praise. Love your family and your fellow man. Amen."

SAM WAS AT A MAJOR CROSSROAD IN HIS LIFE. As much as he wanted to return to Chicago, he realized his life was to be in Birmingham. He had to become the strong male figure in his family. Rebecca was still teaching and planned to retire within the next ten years. His sister, Hannah, had just graduated from Miles College with a degree in education; she planned to follow in her mother's footsteps. His youngest sister, Hosanna, was preparing to enter her second year at Miles, majoring in mathematics.

Finding a job was Sam's first challenge. There were no opportunities in Birmingham for a colored man to use an education in criminology. He found work with a colored newspaper, the *Birmingham*

World, writing a column about crime in the colored community and its ongoing struggle with the predominately racist BPD. He became well-known in the colored community for his candor and advice. Even some in the white community admired his articles, recognizing the city's inequality in criminal justice. However, he was loathed by white politicians, businessmen, and the police department. He received hate mail, usually unsigned, and threatening phone calls.

In 1937, Sam decided it was time to use his education more effectively. He opened an office in the center of the Scratch Ankle business district. It was located on the second floor of an office building. A drugstore was on the ground floor, colored physicians, accountants, and other professionals were located on the upper floors. Sam had two rooms: a reception room off the hallway and his office facing Fifth Avenue North. The frosted glass window on the entry door and the window facing the street read, SAM RUCKER—PRIVATE INVESTIGATOR.

Sam quickly learned that most of his clients were people with life's daily, mundane problems: bad debts and collections, adultery, minor legal disputes, missing loved ones, and runaway children. As pedestrian as he found much of the work, it paid the bills.

However, occasionally a client would come his way that was challenging, meaningful, and rewarding. Most memorable was the case of a white man accused of attempted robbery and the murder of a prominent colored store owner, Grover Alexander. Initially, the DA had been reluctant to try the case; he knew he needed an airtight case to get a jury to seriously consider anything but an acquittal.

CHAPTER 16

THE YARBO AFFAIR

1944

WHEN the murder occurred, two BPD cops in the area heard several gunshots. A minute or two later, the cops saw a man running from the alley behind the buildings where the store was located. They stopped the man. One of the cops recognized him. It was Davie Yarbo, a hood who had been arrested several times for robbery, and assault and battery. Yarbo told the cops he was walking through the alley on his way home. He said he heard gunshots coming from the store and had run in fear. The cops found no weapon on Yarbo, but arrested him because of his past record.

Joe and the crime lab guys were unable to find any concrete evidence tying Yarbo to the crime. No useful fingerprints, the weapon, or any other evidence had been found. Joe got little cooperation from the colored community even though one of their own had been murdered. When it was announced that Yarbo would be released from custody for lack of evidence, the family of the murdered man hired Sam to investigate the case.

SAM HAD BEEN FOLLOWING THE CASE in the newspapers. They reported that the perpetrator had likely entered and exited the store through the rear door facing the alley. The police stated they had thoroughly searched for the gun in the store and all outside areas around the store. Yarbo was described as a short, lean man with extraordinary strength for his size. He had been convicted and jailed twice for robbery, and although a prime suspect in several other burglaries, the evidence proved inconclusive to support a prosecution.

Sam knew finding the weapon was key. He assumed the police had thoroughly searched the store's interior. If Davie Yarbo was the murderer, which Sam thought highly likely, the weapon had to be between the store's back door and the end of the alley where Yarbo was seen and apprehended. The rub was: *Where was the gun?*

He searched the alley several times looking for places the gun might be hidden—garbage cans; weeds and plants; under rocks, door sills, alcoves, and the storm sewer at the end of the alley. He didn't expect to find the gun in any of these obvious spots. *Yes, that was it, too obvious*, he thought. Harking back to his favorite childhood author, Edgar Allan Poe, he remembered Poe's story, "The Purloined Letter." Of course, the gun couldn't be as obvious as Poe's letter because of the gun's size and appearance. But maybe Yarbo put it in a place easily overlooked by zealous cops hunting for the obvious.

Sam went to the store's rear door and stood in the center of the alley. Considering what he had read about Yarbo's strength, he tried to imagine Yarbo running out the door, knowing he had to quickly stash the gun in a place the cops might overlook. Sam looked around the alley, at first seeing nothing unusual. Then he realized that the third building from the street had an interesting architectural feature, a cornice between each of its four floors.

He walked to the near corner of the building to study the cornice between the first and second floors. What looked from a distance as one piece was constructed of two bonded pieces that overlapped, creating a small space. The adjacent building did not extend to the back wall surface of the building with cornices. A metal downspout, about four inches square, on the corner adjacent to the cornice had large brackets every few feet attaching it to the building.

Sam stared at the downspout and cornice. He thought it possible that Yarbo climbed the downspout and stashed the gun. He decided against climbing it himself since the downspout might not hold his body weight.

He hustled home and got a ladder. He propped the ladder up on the wall next to the downspout to shield it from street view. With a flashlight in his hip pocket, he carefully climbed the ladder. He leaned around the building's corner and shined the flashlight into the small space in the cornice. He almost exclaimed aloud, *I'll be damned. There's a gun.*

Concerned that Yarbo might sneak into the alley and retrieve the gun, Sam found a pay phone and called the BPD. He asked to speak to Captain Richard Oliver.

"Captain Oliver."

"Captain Oliver, this is Sam Rucker. I'm a private investigator in—"

"I know who you are, Sam. Whaddya want?"

"Grover Alexander's family hired me to investigate his murder."

"That's our job. You stay out of this."

"I know, Captain Oliver. I'm just trying to help the family. I decided to see if I could find the missing murder weapon."

"So?" Oliver said.

"I searched the alley behind Alexander's store. Another building in the alley has a cornice with an opening at its end. I used a ladder and looked into the opening. I saw a gun in there."

"Did you touch it?"

"No sir. But I'm worried Yarbo may come get it so he can get rid of it. I suggest you send some cops over here to take a look."

"You sure there's a gun there?"

Sam hesitated before answering to ensure his voice didn't sound sarcastic or disrespectful. "Yes sir, there's a gun there unless Yarbo got it in the last five minutes."

"Okay, I'll send Detective McGrath and another man over right away. You stay there by the gun's location."

"Yes sir, I'll be here."

Ten minutes later, Sam watched as two men, one in civvies and one in blue, came toward him in the alley. Sam, confidant the guy in civvies was McGrath, calmly watched for the inevitable reaction from a white man.

Joe obliged and paused, casting a wary eye at Sam's size. "Are you Sam Rucker?"

Sam stared evenly at Joe as the detective drew near, sizing up this cop he had heard so much about. He answered in his soft, deep baritone voice. "Yes, Detective McGrath. I am Sam Rucker."

Joe, still moving cautiously, offered his hand and said, "I've heard a lot about you, Sam. People say you do some good work."

If Joe had ever seen Reverend Rucker, he would have thought he was shaking hands with at a young Angus. Six-feet-four-inches tall, broad in the shoulders and chest tapering to a slim waist, and all held upright and erect by long powerful legs, Sam obviously should not to be trifled with physically. His handsome face had round, sharp features and a strong chin. He wore tan slacks, an off-white dress shirt, a light wool, dark brown sport coat, brown leather shoes, and a brown porkpie hat.

"I try." Sam pointed toward the ladder and the cornice. "The gun's in the space at the end of the cornice. Want to take a look?"

"Yep, that's why we're here. Sam, this is Officer Ralph Owens."

The two men nodded to each other.

As Joe started to climb the ladder, he turned to Sam with a sheepish look. "Oh shit, I forgot my flashlight. You got one?"

Sam cracked a smile and handed his flashlight to Joe. Joe climbed the ladder and pointed the flashlight's beam into the cornice slot.

Joe looked down at Sam. "Yep, there's a gun in here." Turning to Ralph, he said, "Go to the car and get me a camera, some gloves, an evidence bag, and a short, narrow set of tongs."

Ralph returned with the items, climbed the ladder, and handed them to Joe.

Joe took two photos, put on the gloves, carefully extracted the gun, and bagged it. He came down the ladder and handed the camera and bagged gun to Ralph. "Take these over to the crime lab when we get back. Tell them to print the photos and check the gun for fingerprints. Then run a ballistics test and compare it to the bullets we found in Alexander's body."

"Will do, Joe." Ralph said.

Joe turned to Sam. "Nice work. Thanks for calling us. I'm sure you're right about Yarbo. Someday you'll have to tell me how you figured this out. I thought we had combed this area pretty well."

"Thanks." He then handed Joe his business card. "Please call me and let me know the results of the lab test. Alexander's family will ask me where I am in the investigation. I don't want to sound disrespectful, but if I don't hear something from you soon, I'll tell them what I found and what I know."

Joe looked Sam squarely in the eyes. "Don't worry. You'll hear from me. If we're both right about Yarbo, he'll be behind bars soon. If not, we've got more work to do. In the meantime, we all have to keep this under wraps. If Yarbo gets wind of what we know, he'll skip town in a flash. I'll put a tail on him until we get this resolved."

"Good. But I got another idea. Why don't you have a couple of officers tape off the alley and make like they're still searching for the gun around the nooks and crannies along the alley surface. If Yarbo comes to get the gun, especially late at night, he'll figure the cops are still looking for the missing gun."

"You're a smart cookie, Sam. I'll put some men on it as soon as I get back to headquarters."

"See you, Detective McGrath and Officer Owens. And hey, I like chocolate chip. I also like Edgar Allan Poe and 'The Purloined Letter.'"

Back in the police car, Ralph asked Joe, "What the hell that darkie talkin' about? Who's Poe and what's a letter gotta do with it?"

"Like I said, Ralph, he's one smart cookie."

When Joe got back to his office, he sent men to watch the alley. Sam's concern proved correct. Later that night, Yarbo was spotted going toward the alley, but when he saw the tape and the cops, he immediately fled the scene, but not Birmingham. The next day, the lab test results came back positive; the fingerprints were Yarbo's and the gun the murder weapon. A records check revealed that the gun had recently been stolen from a local gun shop.

The cops rearrested Yarbo, and the DA brought him to trial. The prosecution sought a first degree murder conviction. Sam and Joe, the key prosecution witnesses, deftly led the jury through the discovery of the gun and the incriminating lab results. Yarbo's lawyer didn't cross-examine Joe, but asked Sam one question, "Boy, aren't you the one that planted the gun in the cornice?"

Sam ignored the racial slur. "Sir, I found the gun as I testified. And as Detective McGrath testified, it had Yarbo's fingerprints on it and was the weapon that killed Mr. Alexander."

Yarbo's lawyer realized a guilty verdict was likely and saved his best for last. In his closing statement, he offered the jury several improbable alternatives to consider, all wrapped in a hateful appeal to the racial prejudices held by most southern white males.

He first stated that the shooting was not premeditated. "Y'all know white men are honorable and coloreds can't be trusted. Hell, Yarbo's worth more'n two of the darkie that was shot. And if Yarbo shot that darkie, it was in self-defense 'cause that darkie pulled a gun on him."

He then questioned Sam's testimony and motives. "Now, who do you think climbed up that downspout and planted that gun? I'll tell you who it was." He pointed at Sam. "That tall, strong Nigra sittin' right there, not this small, scrawny defendant. Then he called the cops to protect himself."

The defense attorney closed with a searing statement. "Are you gonna let this colored man, this so-called private investigator, get away with this hoax? You heard what this disrespectful Nigra said. He called that colored man Mister, but referred to the white defendant as Yarbo. But hell, what difference does it make? It just one more darkie outta the way. Better off without him."

The prosecution objected to the defense lawyer's last statement. The judge sustained the objection and told the jury to ignore it.

The jury did ignore the defense lawyer's comments, but agreed that the murder was not premeditated and found Yarbo guilty of second degree murder. He was sentenced to twenty years in prison.

Outside of the courtroom, Sam and Joe talked about the trial. Although disappointed the jury rejected the first degree murder charge, they were satisfied Yarbo was at least found guilty by an all-white jury.

Joe, upset about the comments Yarbo's lawyer made in his closing statements, said, "Sam, I'm sorry you had to listen to that crap."

"Happens all the time. You just keep on going. It will change."

Joe looked at Sam quizzically. "You think so?"

"It's coming. Maybe someday we can talk about it."

Sam returned to his day-to-day private investigation work in the colored community. He and Joe's paths did not cross again until Joe called him about the murdered prostitutes.

CHAPTER 17

THE MEETING

WEDNESDAY—OCTOBER 15, 1947

O N WEDNESDAY MORNING, Joe and Brendan went over what needed to be done: get the lab and autopsy reports, and check to see if the file search had found a record matching the latest victim's photo. Joe pulled all the folders on the first murder to share with Sam.

Joe called Dick Oliver and, after filling him in on his planned meeting with Sam, said, "Did the chief call Bongo Drum?"

Dick laughed. "Yeah. He'll go to the morgue later this morning. You're out of hot water on that for now."

"Thanks. Will you call the morgue and let them know?"

"Already have. He'll be there at eleven."

"If Bongo Drum can't ID the victim, we'll have to pull in all the known pimps to view the body."

"Let me know how it goes with Rucker."

"I'll be back later this morning," Joe said.

Before he left the office, he told Sally to have records look for similar past cases in the files and call police departments around the state about such cases.

It was a beautiful, crisp clear day for a drive out of the city. The first hint of fall colors had appeared in the trees with a blue sky and fluffy cumulus clouds. Perfect weather for Alabama's upcoming football game with perennial rival Tennessee at Legion Field this Saturday. Joe had tickets and was eager to go.

He marveled at the beauty of the foliage and sky as he slowly drove north on Highway 31. After about ten miles, he focused his attention to the left side of the road to make sure he didn't miss Willie's BBQ. Sure enough, at about fifteen miles there was Willie's. He parked in the rear.

When Joe opened the back door of Willie's, the sweet smell of cooking meat and savory barbecue sauce overwhelmed his senses. To his surprise, Sam stood in the doorway waiting for him.

"A few minutes early, Detective McGrath. I like that. C'mon in. The coast is clear right now. People come and go here all day."

Sam and Joe shook hands.

Sam led Joe into a small room off the hallway. The room had an octagonal table with eight chairs and a single light hanging over the center of the table. A small table in the corner was stacked with ashtrays and glasses. The room reeked of cigarette and cigar odors.

"I'd get chips, but I don't think you came to play poker."

Joe laughed. "Not today. Smells like it's busy in here."

"Willie runs an honest game, so guys come from all over to play. Have a seat."

They sat side-by-side at the table. They remained silent for a few moments, trying to size each other up and figure out where all this was going.

Joe broke the silence and offered Sam a Camel.

"Thanks, but I don't smoke," Sam said.

"Wish I could say that. Mind if I do?"

"No."

Joe lit up. "Well, I'm not sure where to start. We've got a lot to talk about."

"How about the beginning, Detective McGrath."

"Yeah, that's good. But Sam, please call me Joe."

"Joe, I will when it's just you and me alone. Otherwise, it'll be Detective McGrath."

"Good idea I suppose."

"If you lived on my side of the fence, you'd understand. I use Joe in public, whites and most coloreds would call me uppity."

"Yeah, you're right," said Joe. "I don't live it like you, but I get it. Now, let me show you what we know about the murders. Then we can talk about how best to work together."

"Okay. You want a drink?" Sam asked.

"Maybe later. I'd like to get started."

Joe showed Sam the material he had on the first murder. They spent quite a bit of time on the photos and the autopsy report. He then showed Sam the photos of the second murder victim and said it appeared to be the work of the same murderer. He added that they had not yet identified the second victim.

"Do you know Charlie 'Bongo Drum' Bartlett?" Joe said.

Sam laughed. "Joe, I know Bongo Drum and all his low-life pals."

"He's going to the morgue today. We'll see if he can ID her."

"If he says he can't, he's lying."

Joe told Sam about the wallet, adding that two of his officers were trying to find the person identified in the wallet, a nineteen-year-old colored kid named Luke Matthew, and bring him in for questioning. Joe said he doubted the kid was the murderer. Sam just listened.

Joe finished the review. "Well, what do you think?"

"It looks like the same MO and guy. He's probably a psychopath. Could be white or colored. Let me know what happens with Matthew. The chief will want to nail it on him. Let me take another look at those photos of the two women."

Sam laid the photos side-by-side. Sam studied them carefully for several minutes. "Joe, are you a religious man?"

"Not really. I guess you'd call me a lapsed Catholic."

"I'm not far behind you there. But I think the body positions of the two women are meant to be religious symbols."

"Oh?" Joe said, raising his eyebrows.

"My papa was a preacher and a damn good one. Except he preached all the time—at church, at home, in the car, on our vacations. I got an undergraduate degree from a religious college and a year of seminary training."

"Why did you quit?"

"I finally admitted what I had known for a long time. I didn't want to be a preacher. I went to the University of Chicago and got a criminology degree and here I am."

"I'll be damned. I initially got a degree in English and taught high school while I completed a degree in criminology at the University of Alabama. I think Alabama modeled their program after Chicago's."

"Well, I guess we're a lot alike," Sam said. "Except for the color of our skin."

Sam grabbed a sheet of paper and drew two human figures approximating the body positions of the women with geometric shapes around each one. Then he drew some heavy lines on the shape on the right. He held the paper up for Joe to look at.

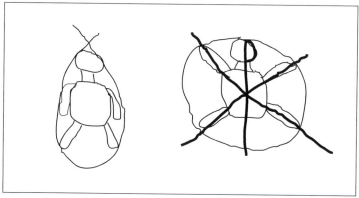

"It was the photo of the second murder that really caught my eye. I'm pretty sure about the figure on the right. The woman's arms and legs are spread like an X. I can't draw well, but you get the idea. It's a simplified depiction of an early Christian symbol called a *chrismon*, the Chi Rho, representing Christ. The Greek chi is represented by the letter X, and rho by P. The X is obvious, and I used half of the woman's head to create the top of the P. See, it seems to fit perfectly."

Sam pointed at the figure on the left. "I'm less sure about the first murder. I think it's another early Christian symbol—the *ichthus*, Greek for *fish*. The shape I drew around the edges of the body works. If I'm right, this guy is a smart, religious psychopath. I can't think of a worse combination."

"Jesus! Sorry, bad choice of words," Joe said. "I could see the second woman's body was in an X, but I didn't know what it meant. It looks obvious now. I'm sure Matthew's not our guy. He wouldn't know about these religious symbols."

"Yep, not likely. If I'm right, whoever it is won't stop. Maybe he'll stop for a while if he thinks we're closing in on him. But he'll resume killing later. Shit, I sound like an expert on psychopaths. We should talk to a psychologist or psychiatrist about this."

Joe nodded. "I'll try to find one at Birmingham's University of Alabama Medical School. Let's talk about how we proceed. I don't have a detailed plan in mind, but I have a few thoughts. Start by interviewing folks in the colored community who might be of help. People who live near the murder scenes, the hotel clerk and the guy who reported the first murder, and local pimps and prostitutes. If they ask, tell them you're doing this for the families of the murdered women. Let's keep our arrangement as secret as possible. We'll meet weekly, more often if necessary, at a place like Willie's. Okay so far?"

"Sounds like a reasonable way to start," Sam said. "I'm sure I can arrange for us to meet here. Willie's a good guy. You gotta day and time in mind?"

"Wanna stay with Wednesday at nine o'clock at Willie's?"

"Okay. I'll talk to Willie before we leave. You wanna meet him?"

"Can he be trusted?"

Sam looked annoyed. "Yes, I've known him a long time. We went to school together. I told him why we were meeting. He wants to help us solve these crimes in any way he can."

"Sure, I'd like to meet him. Don't mean to sound insulting. Just got to be careful."

Sam shrugged. "Okay. What else?"

"Can you start the interviews this week?"

"Yes."

"We need to discuss the business arrangement. Dick Oliver and I had to twist Chief Watson's arm, but he finally agreed. I want to be up front with you. After the chief agreed, I told him we'd find a private place to meet. He then said something to me like, 'Goddamn right you will. That darkie come in my building, you're both out the door.' "

Sam laughed heartily. "Well, the chief's certainly living up to his reputation. Willie's it is. And, what the hell, the chief doesn't know what great barbecue he's missing."

"Hey, how about some barbecue? It smells too good. I didn't have much breakfast."

"Sure. I'll get Willie."

Sam went to the front of the joint and came back with Willie. He was medium height, with a barrel chest and a large stomach that looked as if he loved his own barbecue. Dark black, he wore work coveralls and an apron covered with barbecue sauce. His face was round and jovial.

"Willie, this is Detective Joe McGrath. Joe, this is Willie Colson, the best barbecue man in Alabama."

The two men shook hands. "Good to meet you, Detective McGrath. Hope you and Sam catches that man killin' those colored gals."

"Nice to meet you, Willie. We'll catch him. I'm glad Sam's going to help us. And thanks for letting us meet here."

"Sure. It's quiet now, but you comes back tonight, it'll be rockin'. There's music and dancin' and a lot of good fun."

"Sam tells me you and he go back a long time, school days and all."

Willie looked at Sam and laughed. "Oh yeah, we go way back. I made a high school football hero outta this big fella. We played four years in high school and went undefeated our last two years. Sam was our fullback. I was pullin' guard and got him past the line of scrimmage. Then he jus' runned over anybody got in his way."

Sam patted Willie on the back. "Hell, my grandma coulda run through the holes you opened up. Now you gotta open up some holes for us. We need to meet here every Wednesday at nine o'clock for a while. We need to keep our meetings secret. I'm sure you understand. That okay with you?"

"Sure, Sam. I told you I wants to help. I understand. Ain't no colored cops in Birmingham, last I heared. You wanna keep your meeting secret, you better start early, say seven or eight. Business picks up about ten or eleven and don't usually slow down 'til closin' time."

"Whaddya think, Joe?"

"I think Willie's right. Seven on Wednesday is fine with me. Can we get in that early?"

"I usually gets in about eight," Willie said. "I'll give Sam a key."

Sam was pleased. "Good, that's settled. Thanks, Willie."

Joe added, "Yeah, thanks Willie. Now how about some of that barbecue Sam keeps talking about."

Willie broke into a big grin. "You bet. Got some we just took off'n the pit. What would y'all like? Anything. It's on the house."

"Well, that's mighty kind of you," Joe said. "I'll have pulled pork on white bread and a Coke."

"Can do. How about you, Sam?"

"Same for me."

"Be back soon."

"Let's see, where were we?" Joe said. "Oh, I remember, the business arrangement. We're going to pay you a fair fee for your work. Dick will manage payments at my request. You give me a weekly invoice for your work. I'll give it to Dick, he'll write me a check, and I'll write you a check. All by hand, no mail. The money will come out of an account the chief has for special projects. How much do you charge?"

Sam chuckled. "I see. Special projects, huh? Like work a colored man does for the department on the q.t. You want me to do business by the hour or fixed fee?"

"I want what you consider fair."

"I prefer by the hour."

"What's your hourly rate?"

"I'm gonna give the Birmingham Police Department a good deal. How about four dollars an hour plus expenses?"

"The rate sounds okay to me. What does expenses include?"

"Anything I have to spend to do your work. Things like office supplies, phone calls, gas, meals. I'll itemize it all."

"Okay. I'll have to run it past Dick. You sure it's—"

The door swung open. "Barbecue," yelled Willie.

Willie set a tray on the table with two plates of barbecue, and sides of coleslaw and beans. He served each man a plate and a Coke. "I added a few ribs and sides of slaw and baked beans. You can't eat good barbecue without 'em."

Sam and Joe smiled and said in near unison, "Thanks, Willie."

Willie left the room, and the two men dug in.

"Hot damn, this is great, Sam," Joe said around a mouthful of barbecue. "You weren't kidding me."

"Detective McGrath, I wouldn't pull your leg."

They ate in silence as they savored Willie's food.

Joe popped the last of his pulled pork sandwich into his mouth and took a sip of Coke to wash it down. "Sam, back to the money. You sure that figure works for you?"

"Yeah. I can hear the chief when Oliver talks to him. 'God almighty, we're gonna pay that darkie how much? We don't pays our cops that good.' If there's a problem, let me know. We'll work something out."

"Okay. We'll meet as often as we need to. Here's my card. It's got my direct office number on it, and I wrote my home number on the back. Call me anytime. If anyone but me answers, just hang up. After we get started, I'll probably bring my assistant, Officer Brendan O'Connor, to our meetings. He's a good kid and can be trusted. I have your office phone number. I need your home number."

Sam pulled out his business card, wrote his home number on it.

"Thanks. Anybody live with you that might answer if I call?"

"I'm single," Sam said. He smiled. "Well, not quite. My girlfriend Janice is there often. You can trust her. What about you?"

Joe cast his eyes downward for a few moments. "I live alone. My wife and I separated early this year. I don't have a girlfriend. Maybe one will come along later."

"Sorry to hear that. A guy needs a good girlfriend. It'll happen."

Joe shrugged and looked up. "Yeah, I suppose so."

"It will. Look Joe, we need a signed contract. I trust you. I can't say the same about Chief Watson and many of the officers in the department. Where does that leave me, if all of a sudden, they decide to pull the plug on work and don't pay me for any past due efforts?"

"I don't blame you. Let me talk to Oliver about it. I'll commit to this. If they balk, I'll make good for anything owed you."

Sam looked irritated. "No, I don't want you to do that. If they won't sign a contract, we'll just call it a day. If they balk later, I'll stop working and deal with it myself. You don't need to be involved. I don't want your position jeopardized because of me."

Joe considered Sam's comments. "Look Sam, I'm already out on a limb with the chief on this. If we nail the bastard, there will be no problems. If we don't or screw up, all bets are off. At this point, I'm in it with you, and I hope you're in it with me."

"Joe. I'm in. Where do you want me to start?"

"With the interviews and wherever they lead you. Do you need any of the material I showed you?"

"Yeah. Let me write down the information you have on the people you've interviewed including the names of the first victim's parents. I could also use headshots of the two murdered women. I don't want copies with BPD stamped all over them."

"I thought of that. You keep the two unmarked headshots. They're clean." Joe handed the material back to Sam so he could write down the information he wanted.

"Way ahead of me, Detective."

"I'd like to take your sketch of the body positions. It might come in handy," Joe said.

"Sure. Be my guest."

Joe put the sketch in his briefcase. "Let's exchange home mailing addresses. If we need a faster exchange of material, we'll have to meet at Willie's unless you can think of a closer place."

"Another good idea," Sam said.

"Well, I guess that's it for now. You got any questions?" Joe said.

"Probably, but I can't think of anything right now."

"Call me anytime. We've got to stay close together on this."

"I will. And you call me too. You know you're treading into new territory here Joe. You ready for that?"

"I think so. We'll find out. I gotta get back to headquarters and talk to Dick Oliver. I'll see you next week, if not sooner."

"Okay, Joe. Who knows, maybe our working together will lead to more than just solving these murders."

"Yeah, who knows. I gotta go. I'll say goodbye to Willie."

"Okay, let me get Willie and check the hallway."

Sam got Willie and opened the room's door. "C'mon. It's clear."

"The barbecue was great, Willie. Thanks for your help."

The three men went into the parking lot.

"Joe, you got another car? This car got po-lice written all over it."

Joe looked chagrined. He realized he should have thought about his cop car. "Yeah. I got a forty-two Plymouth Coupe. It's gray. I'll drive it out here from now on."

As Joe backed the car up, he looked out the rolled-down window for clearance and heard Willie ask Sam, "Can you trust him?"

CHAPTER 18

PUPPY DOG

WEDNESDAY—OCTOBER 15, 1947

BACK AT HEADQUARTERS, Joe went straight to the desk officer. "Hi, Billy. How you doing?"

"Hangin' in there, Joe. Hear we got another murdered whore."

"Looks that way. That's why I stopped. Brendan was supposed to sign out when he went to bring a suspect in for questioning."

"He and Jerry Howard left at eight fourteen. They called in a few minutes ago. They're on the way back with a colored kid named Luke Matthew."

"Thanks, Billy. Keep it hangin'."

"Will do, Joe."

He went to Dick Oliver's office.

Dick was spinning a pencil in his hand, looking grim. "Hi, Joe. What's on your mind?"

He told him all about his meeting with Sam. Dick listened quietly until Joe showed him the sketches Sam made of the women. As he explained Sam's theory of the meaning of their body positions, Dick said, "Fuck, I hope he's not right or we've got a lunatic."

Joe replied simply, "Yes," and proceeded with his review.

When Joe was done, Dick said, "I'm okay with the deal. But the chief might not like the hourly rate or the contract requirement."

"You have to convince him. I'm sure Sam's rate includes his overhead costs to maintain his office, his vehicle, and such. Any prudent man would want a contract."

"Yeah, I know. I'll go talk to the chief and let you know what he thinks. Let me show him those sketches."

Joe handed Dick the sketches. "Do you want me to come along?"

"No, I think it's best I talk to him alone. If he blows up, I can handle him better if you're not there. Hang around, I'll let you know what he says as soon as we're done."

"We also got a name out of the wallet found at the crime scene. Brendan and Jerry should be back with the suspect soon. Nineteen-year-old colored kid named Luke Matthew."

Dick's eyes lit up immediately. "Great! The chief will be pleased to hear that. He wants to get this over with."

"I seriously doubt it's the guy. Nineteen-year-old colored kid. It doesn't add up based on the murderer's style. This kid wouldn't know shit about old Christian icons. Hell, most people wouldn't."

"Maybe. How are you going to handle Matthew?"

"I told Brendan to put him in a cell alone. We'll question him together. I'll be the tough guy and Brendan will provide the soft touch. As soon as we finish with him, I'll fill you in."

"I know the chief will push for an arrest on murder one. I have to tell him about it," Dick said.

"I know. Try to hold the chief off until we question the kid and see what we've got."

Dick's eyes turned harsh. "I'll try."

"I'll be in my office."

About forty-five minutes later, Dick came into Joe's office. Dick looked spent, and Joe was sure the chief had nixed the deal.

"He agreed, Joe."

Joe looked surprised. "Great, but you look beat. What happened?"

"Just accept that he agreed. It was like fighting a flamethrower. He pushed back on every issue." Dick handed Sam's drawing to Joe. "I think the sketches convinced him we need Sam's help."

"What did he say?"

"You don't want to know. It's best you work with Sam without the chief's comments. They'll just piss you off. But listen carefully, Joe. The chief made it clear that this deal with Sam better work or your days around here are numbered. Maybe mine too. I'm sticking my neck out for you on this. Don't fuck it up."

Joe, now knowing he faced a more difficult situation than he had hoped, said, "I meet Sam again next Wednesday morning. I'd like to have a contract for him to sign. I also need to tell him how the payment plan will be handled."

"No fucking contract. I didn't even mention it to the chief after his tirade. If I had a better plan, I'd nix Rucker. As we discussed, I'll write the goddamn checks and give them to you for Rucker. Right?"

Tread lightly. This is not going well, Joe thought. "Yes, that's right. I know this is way out of normal channels, but I think it'll work. If it backfires at any point, we can pull the plug with Rucker."

Dick said nothing.

After a pause, Joe said, "I'm gonna tell Brendan and Frank Cutler about Rucker. I need their help on this. But that's it. Just the five of us—you, the chief, Brendan, Frank, and me."

"And Sam Rucker and anybody he tells," Dick said.

"Sam'll keep his mouth shut. You can trust him, Dick."

"You better be right. Don't forget what I said. Don't fuck this up."

JOE WENT BACK TO HIS OFFICE. It was almost eleven. He decided to call Frank Cutler and ask for a psychiatrist recommendation.

"Frank Cutler speaking."

"Hey, Frank. It's Joe. I need your help."

"I'm at your beck and call, flatfoot."

Joe smiled. "I need to talk to the best psychiatrist at the university's med school. I wanna ask him what type of guy would murder colored prostitutes the way these two murders have gone down. Any recommendations?"

"Dr. Wayne Theroux. He's well-known in his field. He's from Chicago. He's real liberal on race issues and had a big run-in with the university board of trustees recently. Late last year—"

"Oh, I remember something about that. What happened?"

"Like I was trying to tell you, he integrated the hospital nursing staff. Things went okay for a while. But the trustees finally jumped all over him. They told him to resegregate the hospital. He reluctantly complied. He knew it was either do it or go. A friend told me Theroux said he would rather stay and fight for change later than run like a dog with his tail between his legs. Anyway, he's your man."

"Can I use your name when I call Theroux?" Joe asked.

"Sure, why not. You might also consider talking to him about your personal life."

"Back off, Frank."

"Just trying to help."

"I know. Thanks."

TWENTY MINUTES LATER, Brendan and Jerry returned. Brendan had a big smile on his face.

"We got him, boss. He's cooling in a cell."

"Good. Jerry, how did our new cop do?"

"He did good, Joe."

"Any problems with Matthew."

"No. Docile as a lamb and scared shitless."

"Jerry, thanks for your help. Brendan and I will question him."

"I hear you doubt he's the murderer," Jerry said.

Joe shot a sharp glance at Brendan. Looking back at Jerry, he said, "I'll make a final judgment after I question him. I do think it's doubtful a nineteen-year-old colored kid did this. Doesn't add up."

"You know the chief wants an arrest and a quick conviction."

"Yeah, so everybody keeps telling me. Don't worry. If I think this kid did it, we'll put the hammer on him."

"Okay. I'll see you guys later."

Brendan sat down with a hangdog look on his face and mumbled, "I guess I shot my mouth off. I was just talking—"

"Damn right, you did. Brendan, we gotta get one thing straight. Everything we talk about is in confidence. When you're talking to others, keep this in the back of your mind: Is this critical and confidential information? It's very important you understand this."

"I do, Joe. It won't happen again. I wasn't thinking when Jerry and I were chatting about Matthew."

"I know. Those moments are when you can be most vulnerable to saying something stupid."

"I understand."

"Good. C'mon, let's get a quick bite before we question Matthew. You been to the cops' diner yet?" Joe said.

"No."

"It's a place just across the street that cops frequent. Good food. Let me have Matthew's wallet." Joe put the wallet in his briefcase along with a drawing he had made of the two religious icons without the bodies.

When they entered the cops' diner, a good-looking waitress called out, "Hey, Big Dick. Table or counter?"

Brendan didn't know who the woman was talking to and was surprised when Joe answered her. "Hey, Helen. Table. My new partner and I need to talk."

"Right over here, handsome. So who's your new puppy dog?"

"Helen, meet Officer Brendan O'Connor."

"Well, Brendan, from now on you're Puppy Dog to me."

Brendan's face put a red light to shame. "Yes, ma'am."

"Puppy Dog, don't you ever call me ma'am again, and we'll get along just fine, you hear."

"Yes, m . . . yes, Helen."

"Whatcha y'all want?"

"Bring Brendan a burger with fries. I'll have a bowl of soup. Two iced tea."

Joe looked at Brendan, who was completely flustered. Joe said, "Helen's got a nickname for all the cops that come in here. Some of 'em, like mine, are pretty raunchy. She's got a good heart and is a lot of fun."

"Well, I guess I'm Puppy Dog." Brendan smiled. "Maybe, I'll grow up and be Top Dog."

"Could be," Joe said.

"You ever been involved in an interrogation, Brendan?"

"No. This'll be my first."

"I thought so. This is how we'll proceed. You keep notes of all my questions and his answers. I'll keep the questions short. Makes it easier for you to keep up. I'll go fast, one question right after another. I find a fast pace pushes the suspect. We can better judge if he's shooting straight with us. Think you can handle that okay?"

"Yeah, I'm sure I can."

Helen served their food.

"If Matthew's not cooperative, we'll work like a tag team. I'll be the bad cop. After an easy start, I'll press harder and harder. We'll sit side-by-side across the table from him. When I nudge you with my knee, I want you to immediately break in. You'll play the good cop. Talk nice and soothing to Matthew. Say something like, 'Luke, it's okay. Detective McGrath is just trying to find out,' and then add whatever seems appropriate. If I nudge you with my knee while you're talking, it means I want you to stop and let me pick it up. I may even cut you off before I nudge you. You don't have to record your comments, but don't ask questions. I'll do all the questioning. Got it?"

"Got it," Brendan said.

"If Luke digs his heels in real hard, I may leave the room for a few minutes. You talk to him as if you're old friends. Just shoot the breeze. Make him understand he's in serious trouble if he doesn't cooperate."

"Okay. I'll do my best."

"Remember, he's just a kid. He's scared to death and has no idea how to handle himself in this situation. Let him know he better level with us or the chief might assign some of his real tough cops to work on him."

Brendan looked surprised. "What would they do?"

"It's not pretty. Whatever it would take to get a confession if that's what the chief told 'em to do."

Brendan grimaced in disbelief. "Jesus, I didn't know—"

"You still got a lot to learn. But we gotta go. We've got work to do." Joe called out, "Hey Helen. We need the check."

She put the check on the table. "Now you come back, Puppy Dog. I'd like to know you a lot better."

As Joe paid the check, he noticed Brendan blushing.

CHAPTER 19

THE INTERROGATION

WEDNESDAY—OCTOBER 15, 1947

BRENDAN BROUGHT MATTHEW into the interrogation room. Joe was in the corner and had arranged the table and three chairs.

"Luke, this is Detective Joe McGrath," Brendan said.

Joe sized Luke up—a slight kid, about five nine, 140 pounds. He had fear written all over his face. His eyes darted about, unsure which way to turn.

Joe spoke in a flat, monotone voice. "Hello, Luke." Joe abruptly pulled the chair out, lifted it slightly, and slammed it to the floor. "You sit here."

Brendan guided Luke toward the chair. He sat down. Joe and Brendan sat on the opposite side of the table.

Joe glared at Luke. "We're gonna ask you some questions. First, we need to know a few things about you. What's your full name?"

Luke's lips quivered as he answered, "Luke Charles Matthew."

"How old are you?"

"Nineteen."

"When were you born?"

"August 14, 1928."

"Where do you live?"

"Birmingham."

"Address?"

"1125 Fourth Avenue North."

"Do you live alone?"

"No suh. I lives with my Momma and Poppa."

"What does your father do?"

"He work for the railroad. He switch cars and stuff like that."

"Does your mother work?"

"Yes suh. She work for some white lady what lives in Southside."

"Did you go to high school?"

"Yes suh."

"What school?"

"Industrial."

"Did you graduate?"

Luke look embarrassed. "No suh. I . . . They expelled me 'bout the end of my sophomore year. I never goed back."

"Why did you get expelled?"

"I done somethin' dumb. I stole some money outta teacher's purse."

"You working now?"

"I's lookin' for a full-time job. I do odd jobs now."

"Like what?"

"Mostly for white folks. Mowing lawns, running errands, stuff."

"Where were you last Monday night?"

Luke looked down at his feet. "I goed to a party at a friend's house in my neighborhood."

"What's your friend's name?"

"Uh . . . " Luke paused as if thinking about what to say.

"C'mon, Luke. Speak up. Can't hear you."

Luke looked up. "Bobby Early."

"What's his address?"

"I don't know the number. He live down the street on Fourth. A couple blocks from my house."

"Can you show us where it is?"

"Yes suh."

"What time did you go to the party?"

"Oh, about nine or ten."

"Who was at the party?"

"Five guys. No girls."

"What were y'all doing?"

"We played some poker. We drank some—" Luke paused.

"Don't worry. We're not gonna arrest you for drinking beer. Is that what you were drinking?" Joe said.

"Yes suh. I was. Some of the guys had some hard stuff."

"How many beers did you drink?"

"Oh, maybe three or four."

"What are the names of the other guys at the party?"

"I only knowed two 'em good. Bobby Early and Jimbo Brown. The other three was called Eddie, Smith, and Rick."

"What time did you leave the party?"

"'Bout two o'clock."

"You sure?"

Luke squirmed. "Yes suh."

"Where did you go after you left the party?"

"I goed right home."

"Did your mother or father hear you come in?"

"No suh. They was asleep. I jus' go to bed."

"You sure you went straight home?"

Luke sat up straight and spoke forcefully. "Yes suh!"

Joe looked at Luke in disbelief, reached into his briefcase, pulled out the wallet, and held it in front of Luke. "Is this your wallet, Luke?"

Luke didn't answer the question. Joe nudged Brendan.

"Luke, you better answer Detective McGrath's questions 'cause something awful happened that night. I'm sure you've got nothing to hide. All you gotta do is tell us the truth. You'll probably be outta here in nothing flat if—" Brendan felt another nudge.

"That's right, Luke. Have you got your wallet?" Joe asked.

Luke sighed. "No suh. I mus' of lost it."

"Any idea where you lost it?"

"No suh. When I got home it was gone."

Joe handed Luke the wallet. "Here, look at this closely, including the driver's license. Is this your wallet?"

Luke looked through the wallet carefully. "Yes suh. This is mine."

"Think one of the guys at the party stole it?"

"I dunno."

"Do you know Ralston Park?"

"Yes suh. It jus' down the street from my house."

"Were you in Ralston Park Monday night or early Tuesday?"

Luke's voice was almost inaudible. "No suh."

Joe jumped out of his chair and stared hard at Luke who almost fall over backwards from fright. Joe stalked out of the room, slamming the door shut.

Luke was quivering.

Brendan smiled at Luke, trying to calm him. "Luke, Detective McGrath is upset 'cause he thinks you're not telling the truth. I know you're scared. Hell, I don't blame you. I would be too. . . . You gonna be all right?"

"I dunno . . . I's afraid . . . What's gonna happen to me?"

"Well, I can tell you what's gonna happen if you don't cooperate with Detective McGrath. I know he sounds tough. But believe me, he won't hurt you. He just wants the truth. You've heard of Chief Watson, haven't you?"

"Yes suh. I hear he pretty hard on colored folks."

"That's right. If the chief decides to have a couple of his favorite officers come in here and work you over, it ain't gonna be pretty. You understand?"

"Yes suh. I think so."

"Just relax, Luke . . . Hey, do you play sports? I played baseball in high school. Shortstop. I wasn't too bad either."

"Yeah, I like baseball. I wish I's playing right now."

"Well maybe someday we—"

Joe came back into the room and quietly sat down. "Okay. Let's try again Luke. Were you in Ralston Park Monday night or early Tuesday morning?"

"Yes . . . yes suh."

"Why did you go in the park?"

Luke fidgeted, staring at his hands. "I's 'shamed to talk 'bout it . . . My Momma and Poppa be real mad if they knowed what I did."

"Tell us what happened, Luke. Everything. Take your time."

Luke took a deep breath as if preparing to dive underwater. "I . . . I left the party 'bout one, not two as I tole you." He paused, expecting to be admonished for lying.

"That's okay. No big deal. Keep going."

Luke looked relieved. The story started to pour out of him as if the dam holding it back had burst. "I walk to my house. Takes only a few minutes. When I get by the front door, I look up the street and see a colored woman. She standing on the corner of the park. I knows right away what she be doing there. Ain't no woman gonna be there at this time of night 'cept for . . . uh . . . you know what I mean?" Luke said.

"Yeah, I know what you mean. Go on."

"So I walks up to the corner to check her out. When I cross the street she ask me what I'm up to. I tell her I jus' left a poker party. She say, 'Have a good time? Win some money?' I tell her I's had fun and won a little money. She say, 'Wanna have some mor' fun?' I ask her what she has in mind. She say, 'We could go back in those trees in the park and mess around. I treat you jus' right for a few bucks.' I never been with a woman before, Mr. Detective. I was scared, but I was interested. She were mighty pretty."

"What did she look like?"

"She look real good. Nice face. Nice smile. Nice body. I could even see most of her nice tits."

"What was she wearing?"

"Oh, this here's hard. I think she had on a light-colored shirt. It was pretty much open in the front so youse could get a good look. Her skirt was dark brown. That's about all I knows."

"What happened after she told you that you two could mess around for a few bucks? You're doing good, Luke. Keep it up."

"I tell her I got five dollars. She don't look too happy 'bout that. She say, 'I gets mor'n that normally. Oh hell, c'mon, let's go behind the trees. Gimme the five dollars.' I pull the five outta my pocket and gives it to her. She stick it in her skirt pocket."

"What did the five look like?"

"Suh? Whatcha mean, look like?"

"Was it a new five dollar bill, an old one, or what?"

"Oh, I see. It was old. Kinda crumpled up. Had a few teared edges."

"Good. Go on."

"We walks back to the trees to a open spot. I never knowed it was there. Things started going fast. She opened her shirt all the way and say, 'You wanna touch and suck my tits?' She take my hands and put 'em on her tits. They felt real good. Then she pull my head down and let me suck on 'em for a bit. Real quick like, she stooped down and pulled my pants down. Before I even knowed what was goin' on, she take my thing and she . . . she . . . uh—"

"Did she give you a blow job?"

"Yes suh, that was it. A blow job. I let go in her mouth almost right away. I jus' couldn't hold on. She stand up and spit my stuff out on the grass. Right there in front of me."

"How did you feel, Luke?"

"I don't rightly know. I mean, sure 'nough it felt good. But then I felt 'shamed 'count of what I done and what I paid her to do. I pulled up my pants, thanked the lady, and goed straight home."

"Did you see her leave the park?"

"No suh. I walked out 'fore she left. I never looked back."

"Do you think your wallet fell out of your pocket while you were with the lady in the trees?"

"Coulda, I don't know. I sawed it was gone when I got home."

"Luke, your wallet was found near the spot the lady spit out your stuff. You sure you don't remember?"

"No suh. I don't remember. But I reckon it did as you say."

Joe pulled out his sketch of the two religious icons and pushed it in front of Luke. "Do you know what these are?"

Luke stared at the sketches for a few moments. "No suh. Never seen nothin' like that."

Joe took the piece of paper and drew a body shape in the Chi Rho icon as Sam Rucker had done. He pushed the paper in front of Luke. "How about this image on the right. Look familiar now?"

Luke looked at the sketch and was thoroughly confused. "No suh. I got no ideas what this all 'bout. Look like you drawed a body I guess."

"The lady you just told us about is dead. She was murdered between one and three Tuesday morning. That's when you say you were with her." Joe stopped to observe Luke's reaction.

The young man started to shake and tears formed in his eyes. "I didn't kill nobody, Mr. Detective. I couldn't do nuttin' like that."

Joe pounded the table and yelled, "Did you kill that woman?"

Luke's body heaved convulsively as he cried. "No . . . no . . . no suh. I didn't kills nobody. I jus' do what I say and goed home to bed."

"Did you see anyone in the park?"

"No suh."

"Did you see anyone near the park?"

"No suh."

"Did you see anyone while you walked home?"

"No suh . . . like I tole you, I went right to bed. . . . I sleep like a baby. I didn't do nuttin'," Luke said.

Joe sat watching him. His tears and shaking slowly subsided. He stared at Joe and Brendan with a blank, unemotional face.

"I'm gonna ask you a few more questions, Luke. Do you remember where you were and what you were doing the night of September thirteenth and the morning of September fourteenth? That was a Saturday and Sunday a month ago. Take your time thinking about it."

Luke wrinkled his brow as if his head hurt. "Oh . . . no suh. I can't 'member for sure. That a long time ago."

"Do you like football?"

Luke seemed to perk up to the abrupt change in the subject of the questions. "Yes suh."

"Do you like the University of Alabama football team?"

"Oh, yes suh. They's my favorite."

"The Saturday after the weekend I asked you about, Alabama played Mississippi Southern at Legion Field and won 34–7. Does that help your memory?"

Luke's eyes lit up, and for the first time, he smiled. "Yes suhhh. Now I 'members. Me and Poppa went to that game. We watch it through the fence. And that weekend afore you asked me 'bout, we was in Greene County visiting my aunt and uncle. Poppa's brother."

"So you were in Greene County on September thirteenth and fourteenth?"

Luke smiled at Joe even broader as if he was a student satisfying a teacher. "Yes suh. We drove down early Saturday mornin' and come back late Sunday afternoon."

"Who can back up your story?"

Luke looked confused. "Well, my Momma and Poppa and aunt and uncle, suh. . . . And some of our friends knowed we goed there."

Joe turned to Brendan. "You get everything down?"

"Yes, I've got it," Brendan said.

"Officer O'Connor will take you back to your cell."

Luke immediately spoke up. "I ain't kill nobody. Why I can't go home?"

"We'll talk again in the morning and then let you go. You sleep on what you've told us. Officer O'Connor, put Luke in his cell and come right back to our office." Joe picked up the wallet and left.

CHAPTER 20

BRENDAN'S CHALLENGES

WEDNESDAY—OCTOBER 15, 1947

W HEN BRENDAN RETURNED TO THE OFFICE, Joe immediately asked, "Well, what do you make of Luke?"

"I don't think he's the killer," Brendan said.

"Why not?"

"He had most of his facts right. At least the ones we know about. If his story about being in Greene County holds up, no way he's the murderer. The two murders gotta be the same guy."

"Yeah, I agree. You musta done a good job while I was out of the room. He opened up like a faucet after I came back in."

"I just let him know what might happen to him if he didn't. He got the picture."

"Ask Sally to type up your notes. We'll get Luke to sign them in the morning. We'll probably release him later."

"Isn't he a suspect? Can we release him?" Brendan said.

"You bet we can. Here's some Cop 101. I bring suspects in all the time to interrogate. Unless the interrogation gives me something I can take to the DA, I gotta release them. Tomorrow morning, I want you to interview Bobby Early and those other guys at the party. Then talk to his parents about their trip to Greene County. If they corroborate Luke's story, we'll release him."

A big grin spread over Joe's face. "I got one more thing you gotta do. You're gonna love it. I want you to get a semen sample from Luke."

Brendan looked stunned. "My God, how'm I gonna do that?"

Joe couldn't help laughing. "Don't worry, you don't have to stroke it for him. Go to the evidence room in the basement. Get a sterile vial with a good, secure cap and a heated container. Take it to Luke and tell him to jack off in the vial. Put it in the heated container and take it to the lab at the morgue. Ask them to see if they can determine if Luke's sample matches the vaginal sample of the murder victim or the semen blob found on the grass. Now that won't be too hard, will it?"

Even Brendan was smiling. "No. I get it. Good idea. I'll do it as soon as I get Sally started on the notes."

"Have her make three copies of the typed notes. I gotta tell Oliver about the interview. He'll tell the chief. I'll see you back here later."

Joe decided to call Frank before he went to see Dick Oliver. As he reached for the phone, it rang. "Joe McGrath here."

"Well Sherlock, I thought you'd be out trying to solve this latest murder. I hear you've got a suspect."

"As I live and breathe, Jack Ritter, my favorite muckraking reporter."

"What's the story, Joe? At the rate you and your buddies are going, there won't be any colored prostitutes breathing soon. Is this the department's latest program to clean up the streets?"

Joe ignored Jack's usual innuendos. "We did have another murder early Tuesday morning in Ralston Park. Haven't been able to ID the victim. We do have a suspect. We'll have more to say about him tomorrow."

"This sounds a lot like the murder last month," Jack said.

"It has some similarities. It's a factor in our investigation."

"Similarities, a factor!" Jack said. He added more calmly, "Joe, I'm not going to let up on this like I did last month. It sounds like it's getting serious. Let me know how it's going tomorrow."

"Okay, Jack. Thanks for your outstanding support and encouragement. Talk to you tomorrow." Joe hung up and called Frank.

"Frank, Brendan will be over shortly with a semen sample from Luke Matthew. I told him to hustle it over to you as soon as he gets it. When we interrogated Luke, he said the woman gave him a blow job and spit his semen on the grass. Can you compare his sample to the others you have and tell if they came from different guys?"

"I'll see what we can do, Joe."

"Thanks. Gotta run." Joe wondered who in the department was feeding Ritter such instantaneous information.

DICK WAS SITTING AT HIS DESK. Joe smiled to himself and thought, *This guy never leaves his office.*

"Hey, Dick. Got a minute?"

"Yeah. Sit down. Bongo Drum identified the Ralston Park murder victim. The jerk wouldn't give the name to Cutler. Said he'd give it to the chief. He did. Her name's Jeannie Lee. Here's her address." Dick handed Joe a piece of paper.

"Sounds like Bongo Drum. We'll check it out tomorrow."

"Good. What about Matthew?"

"Brendan and I just finished questioning him. I'm pretty sure this kid's not the murderer."

"Why?"

Joe explained the interrogation and his conclusions in detail. He added that Brendan would do some interviews tomorrow to verify some of Luke's statements.

"So maybe he's the murderer. We won't know 'til Brendan checks things out, right?" Dick said.

"Yeah, we need that to tie this up with a neat ribbon. But he's not the guy, Dick. It just doesn't fit together."

"Where's Matthew now?"

"We put him back in his cell. We'll probably release him tomorrow morning. I told Brendan to get a semen sample from him so we can compare it to the other semen samples Frank's got in his lab."

"Keep him there. I gotta tell the chief about this right now."

"Yeah, I know. Do you think he'll be okay with how we're handling this?" Joe said.

"We'll see. I'll let you know what he says."

"Will do. Oh, one more thing. Jack Ritter just called me. He already knows we have a suspect. Brendan and I didn't tell him. I think someone in the department is leaking stuff to Ritter."

"Not the first time. If Ritter calls you again, have him call me."

Joe was irritated, but kept calm. "Okay. Can I talk to the chief or the DA? I think they should know everything we have."

"Nope. You work everything through me. If they want to talk to you, I'll let you know. And you and Brendan keep your mouths shut about what's in these notes."

"You're putting me on a tight leash."

"That's the way it is," Dick said.

BRENDAN CAME INTO THE OFFICE with a broad smile. "Well, got a good sample. I immediately took it to the lab. They're gonna test it right away."

Joe chuckled. "You gonna make one mighty fine policeman, Officer Jack Off . . . icer. How're the typed notes coming along?"

"I'll go check." Brendan left the office and returned with three copies of the typed notes along with his originals. He handed Joe a copy.

"Close the door, Brendan." Joe waited as Brendan closed the door, and then looked at him for a long moment. "What I want to talk about now has to be held in complete confidence between the two of us even if you decide not to do it. Can I have your word on that?"

Brendan's face oscillated between concern and fascination. "Sure, Joe. You have my word. I hope you know you can trust me."

"I trust you. . . . You heard of Sam Rucker?"

Brendan looked surprised. "You mean the colored private eye?"

"Yep, that's who I mean. What do you know about him?"

"Not much. I hear he does good work in the colored community."

"Did you work with any colored GIs when you were in the Army?"

"A few. They seemed okay and did a good job. We got along."

Joe leaned forward and looked intently at Brendan. "What do you think has been one of the major problems in our investigation of these two murders?"

Brendan lowered his eyes and plucked a piece of lint off his pants. "The lack of cooperation from the colored people."

"That's right. Even though the two victims are colored, most of 'em won't give us the time of day. What do you think we should do about that?"

Brendan sighed, looking annoyed. "I don't know. Maybe get some help in the colored community?"

Joe nodded. "I've asked Sam Rucker to work with us as part of our team. He helped us solve . . . No, he solved a murder case for us a few years ago. White hood killed a colored shop owner. Sam's work led to a conviction of the white guy. He's respected in the colored community. And he's smart with exceptional analytical skills. What do you think?"

Brendan looked confused. "About what?"

Joe was concerned. *Have I misread Brendan?* "About working together with Sam and me."

"Yeah . . . yeah . . . I guess I can."

"Guess is not good enough, Brendan. You gotta give me your full support on this. Here, let me show you something."

Joe reached in his desk drawer and pulled out the sketch Sam had made of the two women's bodies. He handed the sketch to Brendan. "Sam drew this when I met with him this morning."

As Brendan stared at the sketch, Joe explained the drawings and Sam's theory that the body positions represented Christian religious icons.

Brendan was excited and sat up straight. "Oh my God, I think he's right. I shoulda seen that. Now I remember these icons from a religion class."

Joe laughed. "You're a better Catholic than I am. I never attended Catholic school or took a religious class. I didn't recognize the icons."

"Is Sam a Catholic?"

"He's a Protestant. His father was a famous minister in a Birmingham AME church. Sam's got a college degree. He went to seminary for a year, but decided he didn't want to be a preacher. So he got a criminology degree in Chicago."

"My God, he's better educated than any of the cops I've met . . . Oops, except you, of course," Brendan said.

"Thanks. Now what do you think?"

Brendan was stunned. "Okay, I'm in."

"I've got to be straight with you. You hesitated at first, probably because Sam's colored. Now you're okay with it after you hear how educated and smart Sam is. I need to be sure. It's not going to be easy. We'll need to keep our working relationship with Sam as quiet as possible. The only people who will know are the chief, Oliver, Frank Cutler, and you and me. Eventually, others will find out. It's inevitable.

I hope we have this case wrapped up before that happens. It's also got risks. You know the chief's reputation in the colored community, and most of the cops in the department are bigots or close to it. Then there is the local Klan. Those idiots can get pretty nasty."

"Joe, I'm not a bigot," Brendan said in a raised voice. Lowering his voice, he added, "It's just I've never worked close with a colored person. Well, I did in the Army. I was just surprised. I didn't know what to say."

"I don't think you're a bigot. But we're all tainted. Like me, you were born and raised in the South. Coloreds work for whites, not with them. We'll solve this case with Sam's help. Do I have your full, unqualified support, lips sealed?"

Brendan looked Joe straight in the eye. "Yes. Full support. Unqualified. Lips sealed."

"Good." Joe put one copy of the typed notes in his briefcase. "Go over the notes carefully and make sure Sally got everything right. Gotta go see Oliver before I leave. See you early tomorrow. We gotta lot to do."

"See you, Joe."

As Joe opened the door, he looked back at Brendan. "Hey Brendan, you're gonna like Sam Rucker."

Brendan smiled and nodded.

On his way to Dick's office, Joe thought about his talk with Brendan. *I hope I'm right about Brendan. We can't screw this up. No wiggle room with the chief or most others. Dick's nervous as hell about it too.*

Dick wasn't in. Margaret, his secretary, told Joe that he was still up with the chief. That concerned Joe, but he had to get going.

CHAPTER 21

RUSH TO JUDGMENT

THURSDAY—OCTOBER 16, 1947

Brendan got to work early on Thursday. He needed to get Matthew to sign the typed copy of the interrogation notes and check with the morgue on the results of the semen analysis.

He headed for Luke's cell. He was stunned by what he saw. Luke was lying on his cot. The cot and floor were covered with blood.

Brendan squatted beside Luke's cot. His face was a bloody, pulpy mess. His nose appeared to have been broken, and he was sobbing.

"What happened, Luke?"

Luke curled up in fear.

"It's Brendan O'Connor, Luke. It's okay. What happened?"

Luke could hardly open his eyes. He squinted at Brendan. "Why they do this? I tole you and Mr. Detective everything what happened."

"I know you did. How long did they beat you?"

"A long time. They tole me they gonna keep whippin' me 'til I sign a piece of paper."

"What did the paper say?"

"I dunno. I signed that paper 'fore them po-licemens killed me."

"Did they stop beating you after you signed the paper?"

"Yeah, they stopped. They jus' keep on laughin' and left me alone."

"Did anybody come in here to help you?"

"No suh. I be laying since those two po-lice left."

"Luke, I'm gonna go get Detective McGrath. I'll be right back."

Luke curled up and mumbled, "Yes suh."

As Brendan left the cell area, he said to the cop on duty, "I'm going to get Detective McGrath. Don't let anyone in his cell."

The cop nodded nonchalantly. When Brendan got back to the office, he remembered he had forgotten to get Luke to sign the interrogation notes. *Oh hell*, he thought, *Luke wouldn't have wanted to sign anything else after what just happened. I'll do it later.*

JOE WOKE UP THURSDAY MORNING with a tight knot in the pit of his stomach. He wasn't sure why, but he quickly completed his morning routine and drove to headquarters. He wanted to get Brendan going on the interviews to check out Luke's story.

At the office, he wrote on his notepad the information Oliver gave him on Jeannie Lee, wrote another copy for Brendan, and put it on his desk. He was about to leave for Luke's cell when Brendan ran into the office.

Brendan was drained of his usual ruddy color and his hands were shaking. "Joe, you're not gonna believe what they did to the kid." He collapsed in a chair.

Joe's jaw clenched, but he tried to remain calm. "What happened?"

Brendan had despair written all over his face. "Luke was severely beaten last night. He signed a confession."

"What?" Joe said.

"I went to see Luke right after I arrived this morning." Brendan paused and tried to regain his composure. "He was lying on his cot. The cot and the floor were covered with blood." Brendan explained the rest of his brief conversation with Luke. "It had to be a rigged confession. Right?"

Joe sat at his desk holding his head in his hands during Brendan's explanation. He looked at Brendan and exploded. "Goddammit. Goddammit. Of course, it was a fucking rigged confession. Shoulda known this would happen." Joe calmed down a bit. "Why didn't we let him go last night? Oh fuck, the chief woulda just sent his guys to bring him back in. C'mon, lets go back to his cell."

"Should I bring the interrogation notes? He hasn't signed them."

"No. Don't worry about that now. Let's go," Joe said.

"You were right, I've got a lot to learn."

"Me, too."

As soon as Joe entered Luke's cell, he could see that he was in worse shape than Brendan had described.

Joe turned to the cop who had opened the cell for them. "Jasper, were you on duty last night?"

"Nope. Just came on this morning at seven."

"Why hasn't anyone been in here to help this kid?"

"Nobody told me to do anything."

"Well, I'm telling you now. Call the department doc and tell him we need his help. Then bring me a bucket of warm water and a bunch of clean towels. Pronto!"

Jasper shrugged, as if he could care less. "Okay."

Joe pulled a chair up to Luke's cot. "Luke, it's Detective McGrath. I'm here to help you."

Luke lifted his head and squinted at Joe. "Why y'all do this to me?"

"Officer O'Connor and I didn't do this to you, Luke. Did you recognize the men who beat you?"

"No suh. Never seen 'em. They was po-lice."

"How do you know they were policemen?"

Luke's battered face didn't hide his surprise. "What you mean? They was dressed in po-licemen's clothes."

"Did the cops tell you why they wanted to talk to you?"

"They say they wants to ask me some questions about the colored whore what was killed. I tole 'em I tole Mr. Detective all about it. They say they don't give a shit about what I tole you."

"Did they mention me or Officer Brendan O'Connor by name?"

"I don't 'members your name. I jus' call you Mr. Detective."

"My name is Joe McGrath, Luke. Did they mention us by name?"

"No suh. They say what I jus' tole you. They say they got a piece of paper they wants me to sign. I say I ain't gonna sign no piece of paper."

"Did the cops tell you what was on the paper?"

"They say it was a confession. It say I kill that woman. I say I didn't kill nobody. One of 'em kicked me in the nuts and they starts beating up on me real bad."

"Just a minute, Luke. I gotta talk to Officer O'Connor." Joe motioned for Brendan to follow him out of the cell.

Joe found a quiet corner out of earshot of anyone. "Brendan, I want you to get on two things right away. First, try to do the interviews with Luke's party friends and his parents. I wanna know if we have any corroboration on Luke's story. Second, there's a note on your desk with the name and address of Tuesday's victim. See if you can find any next of kin and get them over to the morgue to ID and claim the body. Be respectful with these folks. Get Strickland or Howard to go with you as support. Don't go alone."

"Okay. What are you going to do with Luke?"

"I don't know, but I'll take care of it. You get busy."

"Right. See you later."

Joe went back in the cell. "Luke, why did you sign the confession?"

"What I gonna do, Mr. Detective? Them mens woulda kill me. They beats on me with fists and a rubber hose. They say they gonna ram this stick up my ass. I was hurting, so I jus' signed the paper."

Joe paused to collect his thoughts when Jasper returned with the warm water and towels. "Doc Weaver is on the way. Here's the water and towels. Want any help?"

"Yeah. Just stand by. We'll see how this goes. Luke, can you stand?"

"I thinks so."Luke struggled to his feet, moaned several times as he straightened up.

"Luke, I'm gonna clean you up a bit. You got a lot of blood caked on your face and shirt. It'll probably hurt some. Let me know if it's too much pain? Okay?"

"Yes suh."

Joe started with Luke's head and face. He tried to be gentle. Luke winced often, but said nothing. Joe had just finished with his head and face when Dr. Weaver walked in.

The doctor was a short, stocky man, in his mid fifties. He reminded Joe of the kind, thoughtful pediatrician he had known as a child.

"This is Luke Matthew, Doctor," Joe said. "We brought him in yesterday for questioning in the Ralston Park murder early Tuesday morning. After I questioned him, I put him in this cell for the night. I intended to release him this morning. When I got in today, he had been severely beaten. I'm cleaning him up. Can you take a look at him and see if he's got any serious injuries?"

Dr. Weaver reached into his medical bag, pulled out surgical gloves, and a few examination tools. "Boy, where do you hurt?"

"I hurts all over, Doctor."

Weaver checked his temperature and blood pressure. "Not bad for what you've experienced. Now I'm gonna feel around your body by pressing here and there. Let me know if it hurts."

"Yes suh."

Weaver started on Luke's face, and commented as he went. "Nose is broken . . . A number of bad bruises and cuts . . . He'll need a few stitches . . . None of the other facial bones are broken . . . Did they hit you on top or side of your head?"

"Don't 'member for sure."

"Lean your head over so I can take a look."

Luke grunted as he bent his neck.

"They whacked you a few times. A few bruises and cuts. Nothing to worry about. Take off your shirt. I want to look at your back and chest."

Luke unbuttoned his shirt, but he couldn't remove it because of the pain in his upper body. Joe and Weaver helped him pull the shirt off his shoulders and arms.

The men were shocked at what they saw. Luke's back was covered with bloody welts about a foot long, as if he had been beaten with a whip. The front of his torso looked as if it had been used as a punching bag. There were some welts, but mostly he was covered with bruises the size of fists.

"Luke, I'm gonna examine the rest of you. It'll probably hurt." Weaver started with his back and then went to his rib cage.

"Oh, that hurt somethin' awful," Luke yelled.

"He's got severely bruised or broken ribs. They'll heal, but it'll take time. I don't think any of his organs are damaged, but only time will tell. I need to get him to the jail infirmary. Jasper, get another officer and you two get him over there right away."

"Yes sir," Jasper said. He left the cell to find assistance.

Doctor Weaver turned to Joe. "You don't need to clean him up. We can do a better job of that at the infirmary. Who did this to him?"

"Two cops apparently came in here last night and beat Luke until he signed a confession. I gotta find out who they are."

"The chief's doing?"

"I don't know," Joe said.

CHAPTER 22

OLIVER'S SUSPICIONS

THURSDAY—OCTOBER 16, 1947

IN HIS OFFICE, Joe found a note from Brendan on his desk. It said that Strickland was going with him to do the follow-up work. He headed for Dick Oliver's office.

Joe burst into Dick's office, and before he could say anything, Dick said, "I've been expecting you."

"Goddammit, Dick. What the fuck is going on?"

"Calm down, Joe."

"Have you seen Luke Matthew this morning?"

"No."

"Two cops beat the shit out of him last night. Forced him to sign a confession."

"Take a seat, Joe. I just left the chief's office. Let's talk."

Joe glared at Dick as he sat down.

"Now listen real carefully," Dick said. "Late yesterday I told the chief about your interrogation of Matthew. He laughed and said, 'That weren't no interrogation.' He called Tommy Langford and Bertie Jackson and told 'em to interrogate Matthew, adding that a confession would do just fine. You know those are two of his favorite guys."

"Yeah, some call them Big Bob's Goon Squad," Joe said, unable to conceal his disgust.

"Better watch what you say, Joe. This morning they told the chief the kid signed a confession. Said the kid attacked them. They tried to constrain him, but he was so violent they had to defend themselves."

"That's bullshit, Dick. I'll bet neither one has one fuckin' bruise or scratch. Christ, they're big bastards. Luke's a scrawny kid. Doc Weaver took him to the infirmary to tend to his injuries. They damn near beat him to death."

Dick looked squarely into Joe's eyes. "You keep this up and you're gonna be in deep shit. The chief's got a suspect. He's got a confession. Hell, he was talking to the DA when I left his office."

"This is not going to stop the murders. The kid's not your man!"

"We'll see about that. It'll be in the DA's hands shortly."

Margaret came in. "Excuse me, Dick. You told me to give you these as soon as I got them." She handed him a big envelope.

Dick opened the envelope, pulled out a stack of papers, and quickly scanned them.

Joe could see that it was the typed notes from Matthew's questioning. "Where did you get those, Dick?"

Dick was irritated. "I sent Margaret down to your office to get any notes you had from your interrogation of Matthew. You should have given these to me, Joe."

"They were just typed up late yesterday and this morning. You would have gotten a copy. Will you give the DA a copy?"

"No! In fact, I want all the copies. You don't have one, do you?"

Joe didn't blink or hesitate. "No, I don't. Fuck, that's like withholding evidence, Dick."

"I'll ignore that."

Joe realized he was skating on thin ice with Dick. "Okay, sorry. A little out of line there."

Dick's expression became almost condescending. "Joe, beside the chief, don't forget the big cheeses in Birmingham. You and I don't want to fuck with them. They're putting a lot of pressure on the chief to resolve these murders. Let things be."

Joe feared he was getting boxed in, but he couldn't resist one more thrust. "I'd like to go ahead and do more work with Sam Rucker."

"Why? This case is all but over," Dick said.

"There'll be more murders. If I'm right, you wanna live with that?"

Dick blushed bright red with anger. "Goddammit Joe, you won't give up. Don't try to lay that shit on me. I do what I have to do to get by. I'm not gonna lead your crusade."

"Dick, I'm not a crusader. Just trying to do my job. I know you don't want a contract. Will you at least help me with Sam's payments?"

Dick put his left hand on his left cheek and rubbed the side of his face in thought. "Joe, I respect your opinion. These notes have some interesting stuff. Here's what I'll do. Submit your expense reports to me. Fold Rucker's fees and expenses in with yours over several expense reports. I'll approve it. You get paid. You pay Rucker. No mention of Rucker. I don't want a traceable record of this deal."

"I think that'll work if Rucker agrees. Thanks."

"You might not thank me later. If any part of this blows, I'll turn my back on you faster than a whirling dervish."

Joe couldn't resist a smile. "Nice image. We'll be careful."

"Good. Keep me up to date on what you and Rucker are up to."

"Joe, right after you left for Dick Oliver's office, Margaret came here and asked for all copies of any notes from your interview with Luke Matthew," Sally said.

"So I just heard from Dick. He has the notes now."

"She wanted any copies Brendan had too. Was it all right to give her the notes?"

"Of course. Dick's the boss."

"What's going on, Joe?"

"Matthew was brutally beaten in his cell last night. He signed a confession. They're going to pin the two murders on him."

Sally turned ashen. "That's awful. That poor young man. I've seen a lot here over the years, but this is the worst."

Joe had never had this type of conversation with Sally. When he was with Mary, he thought of Sally as just an older woman who was his secretary. While he joked with her, he had never confided in her about his views or the details about cases. He wondered how far he should go with her on this. Taking a chance, he asked, "Did either you or Brendan tell Margaret that I have a copy?"

"No," Sally said.

"Good. I'd like both of you to keep it quiet. Is that all right with you? The situation with Luke Matthew is getting out of hand."

"Of course it's all right. I know how things work around here, Joe. And you have my complete support and confidence."

"Thanks, Sally. We gotta talk more later."

Joe sat down in his office thinking about his meeting with Dick Oliver. *I don't really know where Dick is on this. Oh shit, I know where he is. He'll dump me in a flash. He's sure got me boxed in. Gotta call Sam and talk about it.* He told Sally he didn't want to be interrupted. He pulled out Sam's business card and dialed his office number.

"Sam Rucker."

"Sam, it's Joe McGrath."

"What's up, Joe?"

"I need to talk to you today. All hell's broken loose here."

"Yeah, I got a call from Jack Ritter asking me about Luke Matthew."

"What did you tell him?"

"Said I never heard of the guy. He didn't believe me, but so what."

"Christ, how do guys like you and Ritter find stuff out so quick?"

Sam laughed. "You cops. You don't get it. Guys like me and Ritter have contacts all over the city. Hell, Joe, the whole colored community knows what you cops are up to. You couldn't take a shit, we wouldn't know about it. Someone just called me and told me there are two cops at a house on Fourth, a few blocks from Ralston Park. I'll bet you sent them there."

"You win the bet, super sleuth. Can we meet today?" Joe said.

"Sure. When and where?"

"Noon works best for me. Can you think of a place other than Willie's? I'd like a short drive today."

"Noon's okay. Willie's won't work at noon anyway. Too crowded. You comfortable meeting at my house?"

"Sure. But maybe your spy network will spot me?" Joe teased.

"Not if you paint your face black like a minstrel showman."

"Or you sprinkle yourself with talcum powder and come to headquarters. Better yet, wear a white sheet and a cone-shaped white mask. You'll be welcomed with open arms," Joe said with a good laugh.

Sam laughed and then cleared his throat. "Seriously, Joe, have you got my home address?"

"Yeah, I got it."

"Good. Don't park on the street. Turn right just past my house and drive slowly up to the alley so you can see if it's clear. If it's not, just drive around until it's clear. Park in my garage in the alley. There's a door at the far end that goes to the house. I built a covered walkway from the garage to the house back door. Just come in. No one will see you. Sound okay to you?" Sam said.

"Yeah. But you don't need to treat me like a rookie. I know the ropes," Joe said.

"Just being cautious. I'll relax once we work together for a while."

Joe was annoyed. "I guess that's a good idea. I gotta go. Several things to do before I come over to your place. Hang on if I'm late."

"No offense intended, Joe. I'll be here."

Joe hung up and phoned the morgue.

"Hey, Joe. How's it going?"

"Bad morning, Frank. Two of the chief's favorites beat Matthew so badly last night he signed a confession. They've called the DA."

"Christ, it doesn't get any better over there, does it?"

"Nope," Joe said.

"Did you talk to the chief?"

"No."

"Who told you all this?" Frank asked.

"I saw Matthew myself early this morning. Then Dick Oliver told me all the rest. Now I gotta go through Dick to talk to the chief, the DA, or the press. I'm probably not even supposed to be talking to you."

"Did Dick tell you not to talk to me?"

"No. I guess I'm getting paranoid."

"They're putting the muzzle on you, Joe. They want to go after this kid, and they don't want you in the way."

"Yeah, I get all that. I didn't call to cry on your shoulder. Did you or your guys get a chance to look at Matthew's semen sample?"

"Sure did. Interesting result. Matthew is essentially infertile. His sperm count is extremely low compared to the average male. This is less conclusive, but his sperm count is similar to the sperm count in the small amount of moist semen we found on the grass. Both samples are blood type B. And the sperm count in the samples from the two murdered women is high."

"And the blood type is A. So Matthew's not the murderer."

"I didn't say that. Matthew comes along and propositions them. Before trying to fuck them, he strangles them to death. If he fucked them, his sperm would be mixed with the sperm from other tricks the women had the day before they were killed. That makes distinction impossible. To repeat, all I can say is that Matthew is blood type B and appears to be infertile, as is the semen found on the grass."

"Christ, you should be the homicide detective, Frank. So how could a young kid like Matthew be infertile?"

"Multiple possibilities. Birth abnormality somewhere in his reproductive system. Maybe the vas deferens, the ducts that carry sperm from his testicles to the semen, aren't wired correctly. Maybe the mumps after puberty. Take your choice."

"So Matthew testifies at his trial that it's his sperm on the ground. You gotta agree the blood type and sperm count match cast doubt on his guilt, right?"

"Sure. But what Alabama jury is gonna pay much attention to that kinda testimony from a colored defendant?" Frank said.

"If he comes to trial, will you testify?"

"Joe, if I'm called to testify, it'll be by the DA for the prosecution. We'll have to see how everything plays out."

"If the defense called you as a witness, would you testify about Matthew's blood type and sperm count match?"

Frank was silent. "I don't know."

Joe tried not to sound angry. "That's fine, Frank. Thanks for checking the sample. I need to talk to you about something else in confidence. Can you meet me at the White Stag at five today?"

"Sure. I'll have to leave by six. The boss has friends coming over for supper."

"Good. See you then."

Joe hung up, realizing his choices in how to proceed were becoming more and more limited. *Shit, it feels like the day has been going for hours and hours. I have to see what Sam thinks. Christ, I'm getting more dependent on him as the days go on.*

Brendan returned to the office. "Hi, Joe."

"How did it go, Brendan?"

"Not too bad. Matthew's story checks out. And then we—"

"More detail. Fill me in. Start to finish," Joe said.

"First, we went to Bobby Early's house on Fourth. He and his mother were home. His father was at work. I told them there had been a complaint about noise at a party at this house last Monday night. Bobby spoke right up. He said he had a few friends over for a poker party. Said they didn't make much noise, just drank a little bit and played cards. I asked him who was at the party. At first, he didn't want to tell me. I pushed him a little, and he finally reeled off Luke's name and the others Luke mentioned. I asked him what time they left the party. He said most of 'em left about midnight, but that Luke hung around until about one or two. He wasn't exactly sure about the time. I got Jimbo Brown's address. He didn't know the other addresses."

"Well, that matches Luke's story," Joe said.

"Yeah. Then we went to Luke's house. His mother, Addie, was home. She said her husband was at work at the railroad. I told her we had to ask a few questions pertaining to her son. She asked me if Luke was in trouble. I couldn't tell the lady what I had just seen. I told her—"

"I think that was the best way to handle the situation."

"Yeah, I suppose. Sure didn't feel good. Anyway, I told her he was fine and would be home soon. I asked her where the family was on the weekend of September thirteenth and fourteenth. She immediately told me the same story Luke told us. She said she and her husband and Luke had gone to Greene County to see her husband's brother. I asked when they left and returned. Her answer matched what Luke told us. He wasn't in Birmingham when the first victim was killed."

"So it seems. Good work. Any more?" Joe said.

"Yeah, the real hard part. We went to Jeannie Lee's home. Her mother and father were there. Nice folks, but obviously pretty poor. Goddammit, Joe, how often do you have to do this kinda thing?"

"You stay on the force long, Brendan, it occurs way too often. It never gets easy. What happened?"

"A lot of crying and wailing. After they settled down, they agreed to come to the morgue tomorrow at ten."

"You got their names and all that, right?"

Brendan looked offended by the question. "Of course."

"Call Don at the morgue. Give him all the information you have. Ask him to be ready for them tomorrow. You go to the morgue tomorrow and be there with the parents. Help them any way you can."

"Okay. I'll call right now."

"Good work, Brendan. After you left this morning, Dick Oliver sent Margaret over to collect all of Luke's interrogation notes. Before you call Don, I want to talk to you and Sally."

Joe called Sally in.

"Sit down, Sally. I want to talk about Luke's notes."

Sally and Brendan both nodded.

"Dick's our boss, and we have to do as he asks. Now here's the sticky part. I still have a copy of the typed notes, and I want to keep it. Is that a problem for either of you?"

Sally spoke up first. "No, Joe, it's not. Brendan told me how severely that young man was beaten."

Brendan seemed agitated. Joe said, "Brendan?"

"No! No problem. But what's Dick going to do with the notes?"

"Probably sit on them or trash them. They're going to pin these murders on Matthew. The DA's already involved."

Brendan leapt out of his chair. "We gotta do something."

"Cool off. It won't help if we lose our heads. Don't worry, we'll continue to pursue the case with caution. There are a lot of folks, including the chief, who want to see this case closed with a quick conviction."

Brendan sat down, shaking his head.

Joe reviewed what Frank had said about the semen samples and repeated the corroborations Brendan had learned for Sally's benefit.

"Everything we have makes it clear to me that Matthew is not the murderer. Brendan, call the morgue, then write a report on your interviews from this morning. Sally, type it up. Make two copies. I'll keep one. I'll give Dick the other copy and the handwritten report. I'll tell him that's all the material we have on Matthew. I want him to have everything we have. I doubt it, but maybe he'll try to talk the chief out of pursuing this. If Dick or Margaret or anyone asks you if they have all the copies, are you comfortable in answering yes?"

Brendan and Sally looked at each other and nodded vigorously.

"Good. I have an appointment. I should be back by two."

CHAPTER 23

SAM'S HOUSE

THURSDAY—OCTOBER 16, 1947

J OE MADE A BRIEF STOP AT HIS APARTMENT to change clothes and cars. He donned an old pair of denim pants and a tattered plaid shirt he used for yard work at the house he and Mary had lived in before their separation. He put on his scruffy work boots and grabbed his ratty baseball cap. He cranked up his Plymouth, patted the dashboard gently in appreciation when it started, and headed to the north side of the city and Sam's house.

As he neared Sam's neighborhood, he saw mostly well-kept houses with nice yards. A few were in need of major repairs and had overgrown front yards littered with auto parts, kids' toys, and other used equipment. He looked around carefully before he turned into the alley. No one was about, and he felt sure no one had seen him. He parked in Sam's garage and used the breezeway to the back door. He opened it and entered the house without knocking. Sam was waiting just inside the door as he had at Willie's.

"Yes suh, well bless your soul. You come to do some work for this here po' ol' colored boy?"

Joe didn't miss a beat. "No suh, I ain't no worker man. I Burminham po-lice. I come to arrest you for impersonatin' a private eye."

The men laughed and shook hands. "Damn, I shouldn't make fun of my own folks like that. Sometimes, I just can't help it. Any problems getting here?" Sam said.

"Nope. Easy. Just like you said. Nice neighborhood you have here. Sorry I'm late."

"That's okay. C'mon in," Sam said. "We'll sit in the dining room."

Joe followed Sam down the hallway. On his right, he saw the kitchen, painted in contrasting pastel colors, and the appliances appeared new. The dining room had a large table with ten matching chairs. The floors were light brown hardwood accented with oriental rugs. There was an elegant, antique sideboard against the wall, and the room's wallpaper and drapery were perfectly matched and tasteful. The adjacent living room was decorated with fine furniture, lamps, and carpets.

"This is a nice house, Sam. Did you do all of this yourself?"

Sam laughed. "No. My mother and the love of my life, Janice, are responsible for most of it. I just did the heavy lifting, the carpentry, and some remodeling."

"Wow. Beautiful. You and Janice married?"

Sam laughed even harder. "Oh my God, you almost sound like my mother. She's always asking me, 'Sam, when are you going to marry that girl?' I tell her we'll get married when we're both good and ready."

"Oh yeah, I remember. You told me she was your girlfriend when we met at Willie's."

"Lots of folks at the church and some of Momma's friends think we're gonna burn in hell. I know my Dad would agree if he was still alive." Sam's laughter faded to a forlorn expression.

Joe realized it was time to get down to business. "Maybe we should get started. We got a lot to talk about."

Sam appeared relieved. "Sure, sit down. Want some coffee or a Coke?"

"I'll take a Coke. Thanks."

Sam got two Cokes from the kitchen, handed one to Joe, and sat down. "So all hell's broken loose."

"Yep, sure has."

Joe paused to collect his thoughts from the last two days' events. "There's a lot to cover. Let me go through it in order. Then ask me questions."

Sam nodded. Joe reached in his briefcase, got his copy of Matthew's interview notes, and handed the notes to Sam. As Sam scanned them, Joe described the wallet, the identification and arrest of Matthew as a suspect, the interrogation, the brutal beating and subsequent signed confession, his meeting with Dick Oliver, the findings from the semen samples, and the corroborations.

Sam sat quietly, intently focused on everything Joe said, and occasionally shook his head in disgust.

Joe concluded by saying, "Well, do you still want to work with me? It's clear the department bigwigs want to shut me down. I don't know how long I'll have Dick Oliver's tacit support to work with you."

Sam looked long and hard at Joe. "Maybe a more important question—You sure *you* wanna go ahead? If this gets nasty, you could lose a lot more than your job."

"Of course, I don't wanna be a martyr. But fuck, I can't let them fry this kid. That's what they'll do."

"Yeah, I know. But lemme tell you. You make one move to release the information you have about Matthew, those crackers will have you killed in a minute. It might be some of Big Bob's Klan buddies. That Eastview klavern will jump through hoops for him. Or it might be the two who beat the shit outta Matthew. Then they'll turn around and charge a poor, colored drifter with the crime. So then what do we have? Two coloreds who fry and a dead, courageous white homicide detective. And don't forget, a killer's still on the loose strangling a whore to death each month."

"Not much time or room to maneuver," Joe said.

"One month. The two murders were on the same day of the month, the fourteenth. Maybe a coincidence, but I don't think so."

"Yeah, the same date thing is obvious. So, you think the next one'll be on November fourteenth?" Joe said.

"No. I think it'll happen on November twelfth. It's the date of the new moon, or dark moon. So were the September and October dates. The killer wants as much darkness as possible. No moonlight. But I also think there's a weirder connection. Assume we're right about the meaning of the body positions and the religious implications that implies. Witchcraft and some ancients believe the new moon is the time to start new things or even accomplish a major deed. Sure, you can interpret that in many ways. Maybe the killer ties the new moon and his religious beliefs together in a perverse way. Hell, he may even be part of a group with similar beliefs."

"Goddamn, where do you get this stuff? They sure as hell didn't teach it to you at divinity school."

Sam laughed. "No, they sure didn't. I looked in my almanac, since the dates were the same, and learned it was the new moon period. Then I went to the *only*," and after emphasizing the word *only*, added, "colored library in the city and read up on new moon history and stuff."

Joe lowered his head in embarrassment at Sam's mention of the segregated libraries in Birmingham. "That really pissed me off when they closed the libraries to coloreds. They should be open to everyone." He knew that sounded weak. Joe finally realized that he was always at a disadvantage with Sam. Sam was smarter. Sam was managing his life much better. And most pointedly, Sam lived and understood the gross inequities of southern politics and society. Joe decided to change the subject. "Now that's a lot to swallow."

"Swallow it or not, we still have a psychopath on the loose. I'll alert the colored pimps and prostitutes to be very wary between November twelfth and fourteenth. That'll cover both possibilities—new moon or same day of the month."

"You got good contacts with all those people?" Joe said.

Sam sighed. "I know 'em all, Joe. I live with 'em and go to church with a lot of 'em. Can you get the department to increase coverage and surveillance on those dates?"

"I'll talk to Oliver. Can't promise how he or the chief will respond."

"They'll only give it lip service," Sam said.

"Probably. Can you live with the arrangement Oliver will support for now? No contract. I'll bury your fees and expenses in my expense reports. I'll pay you when I get paid."

"Seems I don't have much choice if I want to work with you."

"Yeah. Right now anyway."

Sam rubbed his forehead and scalp in thought. "I'll do it. Can't let them nail this kid. We gotta get moving on our investigation. They'll push this to trial quickly. We've got maybe four to six weeks."

"Hopefully more time. Even if he's found guilty and sentenced to death, there'll be appeals."

"Oh shit, Joe, he'll be found guilty. I don't like saying it, but if another murder occurs in November, the DA may back off."

"Yeah, I've had that thought too. If it happens, I'll talk to Oliver and the chief and tell them I wanna talk to the DA." Joe said.

"If they say no?" Sam asked.

"One hurdle at a time. We'll see. Let's talk about our next steps. I think your interview work in the colored community is top priority. Maybe you'll come up with something I can use on my side of the fence. Sound okay?"

"Sure. I gotta talk to as many of the pimps and prostitutes as I can. I also wanna talk to several colored businessmen. They use their legitimate businesses as a cover. They control a lot of the crime-related activities in the city."

"I know a couple of them myself. Who do you know?"

"No names yet. Got to minimize the risk of work we're doing together getting out."

"Whaddya say if people ask why you wanna interview them?"

"I'll say I've been hired by friends of the murdered women to do some investigative work. Hell, that's almost half true. If they ask who, I'll say that's client confidential."

"Have you interviewed anyone yet?" Joe said.

"Yes. Albert and Mabel Phillips, and Bongo Drum. It was mostly hand holding with the Phillips. They knew what Gloria was doing and that she was working for Bongo Drum, but that's about it. I think Bongo Drum's holding back on me. I'm gonna have to put a little heat on him."

"Can you put a top priority on this?"

"Yeah, I'll get right on it. I'm not being too altruistic here. My business is slow right now. I need the work and money," Sam said.

"Good. Here." Joe handed Sam his notepad. "This is the name and address of the woman killed in Ralston Park. Brendan talked to her parents this morning. They're going to the morgue tomorrow morning to identify and claim the body. Like the Phillips, Brendan said they were devastated and could hardly talk. Frank Cutler gave me the name of a psychiatrist at the university hospital, Dr. Wayne Theroux. Frank says he's a real good guy. The school's board of trustees jumped all over him when he tried to integrate the nursing staffs. Oh, you'll like this. He's from Chicago. I'll call him and try to get an appointment. I'll let you know," Joe said.

"Okay. I heard about the nursing fiasco. Look forward to meeting him. I gotta be straight with you on one thing, Joe. I'm gonna ask Alfred Banks to represent Matthew. That okay with you?"

"I've seen Banks working a few times in court. He's good. Don't tell him about our arrangement or any of the stuff I just told you about Matthew. If he used it in court, Oliver and the chief would suspect I was the leak."

"Joe, as you told me earlier today, you don't have to lead me around like a rookie. You know Matthew will tell Banks about the beating and your interrogation of him. Banks will use it, and some of it will come out."

"I know that. Let's just keep it as tight as we can. I get carried away sometime, Sam. You're no rookie."

"We're both edgy sometime, Joe. We'll be okay. Listen, I gotta tell Janice about us. She works for an insurance company four days a week. She also does work for me in my office. She's got her own place, but we spend a lot of time together. Don't worry, you can trust her. She works with me on almost all my cases."

"Does she do interviews and investigative stuff with you?"

"No. But she's sharp, keeps her month shut, and frequently has some good insights."

"Okay. Let's get to work. By the way, send me your invoices frequently. I need to start spreading your work around on my expense reports." Joe stood up. He was shoving his paper back into his briefcase when the front door opened.

A woman entered the house and called out, "Hi, baby. Why did you park in the street?" When she came into the living room, she turned toward the dining room and saw Joe. Startled, she asked, "Who's that?"

Sam went to her, hugged her, and gave her a kiss. "Hi, honey, I thought you'd be at work until three."

"Got off early today. Who is that, Sam?"

"Janice, this is Joe McGrath. Joe, this is Janice Sellers."

"Hello, Janice. It's nice to meet you," Joe said.

"Nice to meet you, Mr. McGrath. Sam, what are you two talking about? Is there a problem?"

Sam laughed. "No. Joe and I are meeting about some work we're gonna do together. I'll tell you about it later. He's just getting ready to leave. C'mon, Joe. I'll walk out back with you."

"Goodbye, Janice," Joe said.

"Goodbye," Janice said as she watched the men walk toward the rear of the house.

Sam told Joe to wait inside the slightly open back door while he checked to see if the alley was clear. It was, and he called out to Joe, "It's okay."

As Joe got in his car, he said, "Still on for next Wednesday morning at Willie's?"

"Yep. I'll get there a little early to open up."

"Good. I'll bring Brendan with me. Okay with you?"

"If you trust him as I trust Janice, it's fine."

"I do. See you Wednesday. Let's talk sooner if something important comes up."

"Right. Joe, keep an eye on your backside."

Joe nodded.

Sam went back into his house. Janice was waiting in the kitchen for him.

"What's going on, Sam?"

CHAPTER 24

THE REPORT

THURSDAY—OCTOBER 16, 1947

J OE CHANGED CLOTHES AND CARS AT HIS APARTMENT. He got back
to his office at two forty-five.

"Hi, Sally. Is Brendan's report typed up?"

"I'm sorting it out now." She handed him two copies of the typed
report and Brendan's handwritten original. "Joe, records found nothing similar to these murders in our files. The calls to other departments yielded nothing."

"Did Brendan check the typed report?"

"Yes. He said it was okay."

"Good. I'm gonna take 'em to Oliver's office." He winked at Sally
and placed one copy of the typed report in his briefcase next to Luke's
interrogation notes. He removed Luke's wallet from the briefcase.

When Joe got to Dick's office, he wasn't at his desk. Joe smiled to
himself. *Well, I'll be. He does get out after all.*

"Margaret, will Dick be back soon?"

"Hi, Joe. He just went to the restroom. Have a seat in his office."

As soon as Joe sat down, Dick returned.

"Glad you're here," Dick said. "We gotta talk. The DA's going full
blast on Matthew. He's gonna ask Judge Overton to hold a prelimi-
nary hearing on Monday and then call the Grand Jury into a special
session. He wants an indictment. I'm sure Overton will agree."

Joe tried to suppress his smirk. "That'll be a perfunctory session."

"Probably. What you got? You were here waiting," Dick said.

"I talked to Rucker. He'll work with me as you suggested." Joe explained Sam's new moon theory about the two murders and when the next murder might occur.

"Interesting. But pure speculation at this point. I'm not even gonna tell the chief about this. He'll think we're all nuts or moon worshipers."

"Would you suggest to him that we add extra patrols and surveillance on the Ankle streets on November twelve through fourteenth?"

Dick's left hand went up to his chin. "I'll think about it. The chief wants Matthew convicted as soon as possible."

Joe struggled not to explode. *I gotta keep calm with Dick. I piss him off, and I've probably lost the ball game.* "Dick, we need a contingency plan if Matthew's not the guy."

"Look Joe. I'm sticking my neck out letting you work with Rucker. I'll think about it. Got anything else?"

"Yes. Here are all the copies of Brendan's report on his work this morning. And here's Matthew's wallet."

Dick looked at the wallet. "Good. The DA will want this." Dick read the typed pages. "So, you think this exonerates Matthew?"

"No, not necessarily. But it does corroborate key elements of what he told Brendan and me yesterday afternoon."

"Don't you know what the chief would say if I showed him this?"

Joe shrugged his shoulders.

Dick almost yelled at Joe. "He'd say, 'Darkies lie, cheat, and steal. You can't trust a word they say.' " Dick lowered his voice. "Are these all the copies?"

"Yes."

Dick looked dubious. "Okay, if you say so, Joe. Keep me up to date on what you and Rucker are doing."

"Will do. Dick, thanks for letting me work with Rucker. When this is all over, I don't think you'll be disappointed."

BRENDAN WAS IN THE OFFICE WHEN JOE RETURNED. Joe closed the door as he entered.

"Hi, Joe," Brendan said, "how'd it go?"

"I just left Dick's office. The DA's calling the grand jury into session next Monday. He wants a quick indictment. I'm sure he'll get it. Dick's real edgy. I'm sure he thinks I still have a copy of some of Matthew's papers. I'm gonna hide what I have in a safe place."

"Christ, this is gonna make it tough on us to get much done."

"Yep. We'll have to work real cautiously and try not to ruffle Dick's feathers. I met with Sam Rucker at noon. He's gonna interview pimps, prostitutes, and some colored businessmen."

"What do you want me to do?" Brendan said.

"Go to the morgue in the morning and help Jeannie Lee's parents. Then do the follow-up paperwork on the other cases we're working on. Next Wednesday morning at seven, I'm meeting Sam at a barbecue joint north of the city. I want you to join me. Plan to come to my apartment at six."

"Dress as a working stiff. Bring your uniform. We'll change after the meeting. I'll drive my Plymouth."

"Geez, this sounds like a spy novel."

Joe smiled at Brendan's youthful imagination. "I wish you were right. Maybe we wouldn't have two dead women and the wrong man in the slammer. I gotta make a private call. Give me a few minutes."

"Okay. I'll go read my spy novel. Gotta bone up on drop boxes."

Joe looked up the number of the university hospital.

"Dr. Theroux's office. Kathy speaking."

"This is Detective Joe McGrath with the Birmingham Police Department. I'd like to speak to Dr. Theroux."

"Just a moment, Detective McGrath"

"Dr. Theroux."

"Doctor, this is Joe McGrath. I'm a homicide detective with the Birmingham Police Department. Dr. Frank Cutler, the county coroner, gave me your name."

"I've read about you in the newspapers, Detective McGrath."

"I hope it's been mostly flattering."

"I'm sorry to say it's been about the murder and mayhem you're dealing with in our unbalanced city including the recent murders of two Negro prostitutes."

"I like that; unbalanced city. Descriptive. Yet not too pejorative."

"Are you sure you're a cop, Detective McGrath?"

Joe thought to himself: *I'm gonna like this guy.* "Yes sir, sure am. I need to make an appointment with you to talk about a troubling case."

"I see. And what might that case be?"

"I'd rather talk in person. Do you have some time over the next few days? I'd like to explain what we know about the case and get your opinion on the type of person who might commit such a crime."

"What is the crime?" Theroux said.

"Murder, Doctor."

"Of course—homicide equals murder. I set aside two hours at the end of each Friday to work on personal matters—research, writing, the like. I could give you some time then."

"I need to ask if our meeting be held in complete confidence?"

"Detective McGrath, assuming what we talk about is a crime you're investigating, the answer is yes. If not, it depends."

"We fall within the crime bounds. There's one other thing I need to ask you. My colleague is a colored private investigator named Sam Rucker. I would like him to join us in your office. Is that a problem?"

"I know of Sam Rucker. I've read his fine articles in the *Birmingham World*. I've also heard he was a private investigator. Of course, I'd welcome him in my office."

"Good. Can we meet tomorrow at four?"

"Yes, that's fine. I'm on the fifth floor of the hospital, room 515."

"Thank you, Doctor."

Joe hung up and called Sam's home.

"Hello," a female voice said.

"Janice, this is Joe McGrath. Can I speak to Sam, please?"

"Hello, Detective McGrath. I'll get him."

"Hi, Joe. What's up?"

"I got us an appointment with Dr. Wayne Theroux at the university hospital. He'll meet with us tomorrow at four. Can you make it?"

"Yeah."

"His office is on the fifth floor, room 515. Let's drive separately and meet at his office. He's read your articles in the *Birmingham World*."

"My goodness, a well-read white man. I'll be there," Sam said.

"I have to go. Gotta get to the bank before five."

CHAPTER 25

UNEXPECTED CONNECTION

THURSDAY—OCTOBER 16, 1947

J OE WENT STRAIGHT TO HIS BANK IN FIVE POINTS. He got access to his safe deposit box and placed the typed copies of the interrogation notes and the report in it.

Frank wasn't at the White Stag when Joe arrived. He found a quiet table in a corner and sat waiting. The bar in this tony section of Birmingham emulated an English pub. It was decorated in dark wood paneling but well lit so patrons could actually see one another. The bar had a good selection of English beers and a menu with items like bangers and mash, shepherd's pie, and fish and chips.

Frank arrived at ten after five.

"Hi, Constable. How's crime and punishment going in the Magic City?" Frank said.

"Fine, Dr. Cutter. When will you start calling me Inspector Dupin?"

"You've stumped me with that one, oh literary one."

"Edgar Allan Poe character. Sit down, Frank. Want something to eat or drink?"

"I gotta be home no later than six. The wife's throwing a little supper party. I will have a beer."

"Bud okay?"

"Sure."

Joe waved the waitress over and ordered two. "Can I have your complete confidence about our conversation tonight?"

"Sure." Frank grinned. "But only if you don't ask me to assist Brendan in his next jack-off assignment."

"Done," Joe said with a smile. "So Brendan told you, huh?"

"Yep. It's hilarious."

Joe turned serious. "Do you know Sam Rucker?"

"He's that colored private eye, isn't he?"

"Yep, that's the one."

"Don't know him personally. I hear he's a good private eye."

"Yeah, he is. And real smart. He helped us on another case several years ago. I'm sure he can help us find this murderer." Joe told Frank about his recent meeting with Sam, the discussions with Dick Oliver and Chief Watson, and Dick's reluctant agreement to proceed with the arrangement. He showed Frank the religious icon drawings and explained their significance.

Frank reacted to the drawings in much the same way others had. "Holy shit. So that's what those body positions mean."

"Sure looks like it. Makes sense. Frank, I want you to be one of the six people in on this deal. You, me, Sam, Brendan, Dick Oliver, and Chief Watson. It's gotta be on the q.t. Is that—"

Frank looked agitated. "Goddamn right it has to be. If the Klan or any of your other cops find out you're working with a colored private eye, all hell's gonna break loose."

"I know. I've heard it all from Dick and the chief. But are you okay being in the small circle? I want Sam and me to be able to talk to you about forensics and autopsies. If you're not comfortable doing it, all I ask is that you keep your mouth shut."

Frank pursed his lips and furled his brow in thought. "Yeah, I'll do it. But first sign of trouble, and I'll run for cover. I got too much invested in the morgue and my career to go out on a limb too far with you on this. You'll hang alone."

Joe realized he had a reluctant partner. "That'll work. I need your help. Do me one favor. Let me know if you're gonna run for cover."

"Okay. You know, you might be getting in over your head on this case and this deal with Rucker. Maybe you don't give a damn since your personal life is such a fucked up mess."

Joe used his best sarcastic voice. "Thank you, Dr. Psychiatrist. Your analysis is much appreciated."

"Relax, Joe. Just trying to help."

"Yeah, I know. Speaking of psychiatrists, Sam Rucker and I are meeting with Dr. Theroux tomorrow afternoon."

"He'll have no problem dealing with Rucker. He'd love nothing more than to talk to you two do-gooders."

Joe looked surprised. "Is that what you see me as, a do-gooder?"

"Well, that's strong. Shit, you're probably the best cop they got, but you're sure as hell a duck out of water in the department."

Joe changed the subject. "I gotta tell you what else happened today. Brendan followed up on some of what Matthew told us. It checks out. He and his family were out of town the weekend of the first murder."

"Even so there'll be a lot of pressure to nail the kid. Watson and the high mucky-mucks want an end to this," Frank said.

"I know. I heard that loud and clear today. I want an end too, but this kid ain't the guy. His arrest won't stop the murders."

"What do I say? I hope you're right about the kid. I hope you're wrong about the murders. Damn, you don't leave much room, Joe."

"What's new? It's tough."

Looking spent, Frank asked, "Is that all?"

"Yes. Am I asking too much, Frank?"

"You push hard, Joe. I know that's your job and you're a good friend. So still no *Titus Andronicus*?"

Joe smiled. "Not tonight. But I sure owe you big time."

Frank looked at his watch. "Yeah. Gotta get going. Don't want to keep the little woman waiting."

"Thanks, Frank. I'm gonna get a bite to eat here. I'll be in touch."

Joe had a shepherd's pie and another beer.

As he was leaving, an attractive, well-dressed brunette walked in. She appeared to be alone.

Joe nodded at her. "Good evening."

She smiled back at him. "Good evening. You're leaving early."

"I've had a long, hard day. Calling it quits."

"Well, good night. Maybe I'll see you here again soon."

"That would be nice. Good night."

As Joe ambled toward his car, he felt a childish enthusiasm he hadn't experienced in months. He strolled with a skip to his step as a big, Cheshire cat grin spread across his face. *I'll be goddamned. Maybe there is life after Mary. My phoenix just might rise from the ashes.*

CHAPTER 26

SALLY'S STORY

FRIDAY—OCTOBER 17, 1947

J OE ARRIVED AT HIS OFFICE FRIDAY MORNING still feeling giddy about his encounter with the brunette at the White Stag. He planned to go back Friday night in hopes of seeing her again. He decided to dress better today and wore his best suit. It was a stylishly tailored green and brown tweed suit. He wore dark brown shoes and dark olive silk socks instead of his usual white. He topped it off with a matching silk handkerchief and a brown wool Homburg hat.

"Good morning, Sally. Got a kiss for me?"

"Good morning, Joe. You know I always have a kiss for you."

After they completed their morning kiss exchange, Joe asked Sally for messages. Her face lit up in delight. "My, what a lovely suit. No messages." Before Joe could respond, her demeanor turned serious. "Joe, someone searched my desk and files last night."

"How can you tell?"

"I'm a well-organized person, Joe. I maintain all my papers and files in a certain order. A number of items have been moved around, and the papers in the files have been shuffled."

"Is anything missing?"

"Not as far as I can tell."

Joe frowned in disgust. "Lemme take a look in my office."

He was not as well-organized as Sally, but there was a rhyme and reason to where he kept things. He looked in his file cabinets.

It was quickly apparent that someone had rummaged through them. He found his desk in much the same condition. The drawer he had locked yesterday was open. However, it appeared nothing was missing. He called Sally into his office.

"Yep, my desk and files were searched too. Nothing's missing. Don't say anything about this. When Brendan comes in, have him check his desk and files. Tell him not to mention this to anyone."

"Okay. Any idea who might have done this?" Sally said.

"I'm pretty sure I know who is responsible. I wanna leave him wondering whether or not we know. I'm going to see Dick Oliver."

JOE ENTERED OLIVER'S OFFICE WITHOUT KNOCKING.

Dick said, "Mornin', Joe. Say, you look quite dapper. Got a hot date tonight?"

Joe smiled. "Yeah, something like that."

"So, what's on your mind?"

Joe sat down casually and said matter-of-factly, "I wanna fill you in on what we're doing. You asked me to keep you up to date."

Dick looked surprised. "Yeah, I did. But we talked late yesterday. Has anything important happened since then?"

"Nope. But you were so adamant yesterday, I wanted to be sure you were in the loop. Rucker's doing some interviews in the colored community. Brendan's going to the morgue this morning. Jeannie Lee's parents are coming for a viewing. I'm sure it'll be positive. I'll be tying up loose ends on other cases today."

"That's it? Nothing else?" Dick's tone of voice couldn't hide that he expected more.

"No. That covers it. Anything new with the DA?"

"I gave him the wallet. He said it was a important piece of evidence. The prelim hearing and Grand Jury are set for Monday at nine. Joe, you don't have to fill me in on every small step you take."

"Okay, Dick. I'll keep the small stuff to myself."

"Have a good time tonight, Don Juan."

Joe laughed. "Thanks. That'll be part of the small stuff."

"You sure there's nothing else on your mind?"

"Nope. Just an update for you," Joe said as he left Dick's office. *Yep. He had our offices searched.*

When Joe returned, Brendan looked up and said, "Sally told me about the search. The papers in my desk and files were moved around. I don't think anything's missing. Any idea who did this?"

"I'm sure Dick Oliver's responsible. I just talked to him. He was waiting for me to explode. I kept my mouth shut. I want him to stew about it. Did Sally tell you not to talk about the search?"

"Yes."

"Good. They'll watch what we do closely. No surprises, Brendan. We've got to move cautiously and keep our mouths shut."

"What could happen, Joe?"

"You saw what they did to Matthew."

"Christ, they'd do that to us? We're cops."

Joe put his hand on Brendan's shoulder. "They would. If this is too much for you, tell me. I don't want you or anyone else to get hurt."

"No. I'm okay. Fuck, this is a tough business."

"Not what you expected? Listen, time for you to get over to the morgue. Help the Lees if need be. You can handle it."

After Brendan left, Joe went to Sally's desk. "Sally, I'd like to invite you to have lunch with me. We've never had a chance to talk about anything but work." Joe grinned, "And kisses."

Sally played the southern belle for Joe. "Why, Mr. Joe, how could a woman say no to such a handsome young man. Of course, I accept."

"Great. Do you like Chinese food?"

"Oh, yes. I especially enjoy Joy Young."

"Me too. Please call them and reserve a table for noon."

"I'll call right away. Thank you, Joe."

SHORTLY AFTER ELEVEN, BRENDAN returned from the morgue. His face had the haggard look of a much older man. "Goddammit, Joe. It's heart wrenching to watch a mother and father go though this morgue thing. You got any easy assignments?"

"I wish I could say yes. What happened?"

"They ID'd the body as their daughter. The mother fainted, but Don caught her before she fell to the floor."

"What else?"

"Dr. Cutler also came into the room and was supportive. The Lees signed all the papers. When Don asked them who was going to pick up the body, they said they had no money. Dr. Cutler told Don to have the county send a truck over to transport the body to the Lee's church. They said they could handle it from there."

"Good work, Brendan. Why don't you take the rest of the day off. Relax and have some fun this weekend."

"You sure you don't need me?"

"I can handle it. You get outta here."

"Joe, isn't this place delightful? Do you know Joy Young's history?" Sally said.

"No, not really. I just know it's been here as long as I have."

"I like to study Birmingham's history, which is easy, it doesn't go back too far. This is the oldest Chinese restaurant in Birmingham. It was established about thirty years ago by four Cantonese businessmen. I don't know about you, but I think the interior design looks more art deco than Chinese. But I like the colored waiters best. They move like ballet dancers when they serve food."

"Yes, the waiters are great. I'll order. Is that okay?"

"Of course."

After he ordered, Joe said, "Sally, I've been remiss in not asking you to lunch sooner. We been working together almost two years now."

"Don't worry, Joe. I know how busy you are."

"Well, tell me a little about Sally Bowers."

"My goodness, Joe. It embarrasses me to tell you this. I started with the department years ago when you were still a young boy. I started as a file clerk and was later promoted to a secretarial position. I plan to retire when I turn sixty next year."

"Sally, please tell me if this is an inappropriate question. You're an attractive woman. Have you ever been married?"

Looking annoyed, she said, "I'm what society calls a spinster. I find the epithet offensive, yet I've learned to live with it." She paused and began again in a voice that seemed detached from Joe and the surroundings—as if she were talking to herself. She looked down. "I had a love. He was a handsome, dashing young man. Everything a young woman could want. We were to be married in the summer of 1917. We entered World War I in April 1917. My patriotic Harry signed up immediately and was hesitant to continue with the wedding. Not because he didn't love me, but because he didn't want to leave me a widow if he didn't return. His prescience proved correct. He was killed in 1918, only three weeks before the war ended. I was devastated, almost dysfunctional for a while. Soon after, I decided to change jobs in hopes of shielding the pain. I took the job with the department. But it still hurts." Sally looked around as if to figure out where she was.

Joe touched Sally's hand. "I'm so sorry. I had no idea. Forgive—"

Sally smiled. "That's all right."

Two waiters approached with their order.

"Sally, here comes our food. Just as you said, they're pirouetting while they hold the trays over their head like ballet dancers."

"Doesn't this smell good?" Sally said as she looked at the luncheon special Joe had ordered, which included wonton soup, potstickers, sweet and sour shrimp, mixed vegetables, and rice. "Let's enjoy lunch and talk about other things."

They made idle chit-chat about the weather, office gossip, and books they were reading. As they ate their fortune cookies with tea, Sally said, "Joe, I'm troubled by the way Luke Matthew is being treated. You may wonder why I work in such a bigoted environment. I've seen so many cases like young Matthew's. Yet, I sit and do nothing."

"Sally, it's not my place to criticize you or anyone else. I hope you know I don't condone the bigotry in the department. But like you, I choose to continue to work there. I enjoy the challenge of police work."

"I know. That's why I want to tell you something I've never told anyone in the department. If I did, I'm sure I would get fired. I've been making contributions to the NAACP and the ACLU for years. I started soon after the Scottsboro Boys trials began. I became really incensed by the whole affair when one of the young white women, who accused the boys of rape, recanted her testimony. Even then, they were found guilty. When will these injustices stop, Joe?"

"I wish I knew. I'm gonna do everything I can to prove Matthew isn't the murderer. You've already helped with his papers. But I don't want to put you in a position that'll jeopardize your retirement."

"Don't worry. I want to help any way I can."

"Thanks, Sally. I'll let you know what you can do, but we have to be careful. The search of our desks and files is a wake-up call."

CHAPTER 27

THE PSYCHIATRIST

FRIDAY—OCTOBER 17, 1947

JOE HAD ARRIVED AT THE HOSPITAL AHEAD OF SAM. As he stood waiting for an elevator, he saw Sam come into the hospital and heard the white woman behind the reception desk ask him in a condescending voice, "Can I help you?" An elevator came and people started to board. Joe stood aside to observe Sam.

Sam answered the white woman politely. "No, ma'am. I have an appointment with Dr. Theroux."

In disbelief, the woman asked, "What's your name, boy?"

A second elevator appeared, and Joe decided he'd better get on it. He was confident Sam could handle the situation.

Sam turned toward the elevators and said, "I know the way." He knew the main elevators were not segregated since the hospital ignored the city ordinance requiring segregated elevators, arguing that patient and client services might be at risk if the colored employees could not get around the hospital quickly.

Sam rode the elevator to the fifth floor, sensing the sidelong glances and raised eyebrows of the whites. He wanted to laugh in derision at all of them, knowing whites had elevated raised eyebrows to an art form as both a display of social snobbery and racial superiority.

When Sam got to Theroux's waiting room, Joe was sitting reading a magazine. "I see you survived the wicked witch," Joe said.

"All in a day's work, Joe."

"Come in gentlemen. Sit down," Dr. Theroux said. "How can I help you?"

"As I told you on the phone, Dr. Theroux, Sam Rucker and I are working together on a difficult murder case. Only a few people know, and we need to keep our working relationship as confidential as possible. I'm sure you can understand why," Joe said.

Joe thought Wayne Theroux appeared to be straight out of central casting to fill a Hollywood call for a psychiatrist. He was medium height, a bit paunchy around the middle, and about fifty years old. He had a large head of rumpled, graying hair and a well-trimmed salt and pepper beard. His face was roundish, and his skin somewhat splotchy, giving him the appearance of someone who drank too much. He wore a tweed wool suit with an unbuttoned vest. A brick-colored bow tie gave him a decidedly professorial look. He was holding a pipe, which he had the nervous habit of constantly cleaning, reloading with tobacco, and relighting.

"Yes, of course I understand, Detective McGrath. Let me suggest we use first names—Detective, Doctor, Private Investigator are going to get pretty tedious."

Joe and Sam smiled and nodded.

"So what can you tell me about these murders? I assume it's the prostitute murders."

"Correct. I'll start," Joe said. "Sam, you break in if I say something you don't agree with. Hell, just break in if you want to say anything."

Joe reviewed the two murders and what they knew, including Luke Matthew's arrest, beating, and confession. Sam explained his theory on the body positions and the new moon dates. Wayne made a few notes as they talked.

"Occasionally, I get people who ask to interview me because they're writing a thriller or murder mystery," Wayne said. "If I didn't know who you were, I would think this was one of those instances. Obviously, it's not. What specifically would you like to ask me?"

"Wayne, we think it's likely the killer will strike again on November twelfth, the next new moon. Can you give us the profile of a man who might commit these types of murders?" Sam said.

Wayne rubbed his chin thoughtfully. "I've never dealt directly with a person having the type of personality that might commit such crimes. I can tell you right up front that any possible traits I describe to you are difficult to detect. You could pass the killer on the streets every day or meet him in a social setting, and you would not recognize him as the killer. I can explain what little we know about people who commit multiple murders. Would you like to start there?"

"Yes," Sam said.

"Literature is full of persons like this dating back centuries—some think werewolf and vampire myths came into being in medieval times to explain multiple, brutal murders. Of course, in more recent history, the most famous is Jack the Ripper, the Englishman who killed five prostitutes in London in 1888. You know of him, right?"

Both men said yes.

"The Ripper was never identified. All we know today is taken from police reports and the huge interest generated in the case by the press. It was mostly sensational journalism, as our press also does to sell newspapers." Wayne smiled at Sam. "Of course, present company excluded. I've read a number of your articles in the *World*, Sam. Excellent writing. I wish you were still writing for them."

"Thanks," Sam said. "I still write an occasional piece, but I don't have much time for writing now with all my PI work."

"I'll keep an eye out for more articles. Now I don't want to get too pedantic, but let's cover some necessary background to get started. There hasn't—"

Joe cut in. "Wayne, both Sam and I have degrees in criminology. We have studied the profiles of different murderer types, but not too much on this type. I guess because they're so rare."

Wayne look surprised as he reloaded and relit his pipe. "Goodness, I didn't know that. You two certainly don't match my view of men working in Birmingham's law enforcement arena. I'll try to be brief. There hasn't been much academic work done on these types of murderers. And you're right, they are rare. A German psychiatrist, Richard von Krafft-Ebing, published what is still considered the seminal book on the subject of sexual psychopathy just before the Ripper murders. I've read his twelve books, and there's nothing in them that will lead you to the murderer."

Wayne cleared his throat and continued. "Freud followed him and was the founding father of psychoanalysis. One of his central theories was that humans are driven from birth by the desire to acquire and enhance bodily pleasures. I and most of my colleagues are disciples of Freud. Of course, our work has also been influenced by Jung and many others. Most importantly, they added the importance of religion to the human psyche. Oh, before I proceed, let me ask you two a question. Do you know of any other multiple murder cases in Alabama?"

Sam quickly said, "No."

Joe added, "I did have our people research our records and call a few of the larger police departments in the state. Nothing matched what we're dealing with. We're flying blind on this one."

"Well, I'm not sure I can help with your flying skills. Unless you have some specific questions, I don't want to get much deeper into the background weeds. I don't think you want an all-day seminar. Let me list the traits you should consider. But truthfully, some, all, or none may end up matching your guy. We'll start with Freud. Do you gentlemen know of his Oedipus complex?" Wayne said.

"Yes," Joe said.

Sam nodded.

"Good. I'll be brief. In this case, we may have the son attracted to the mother. If a son's mother abuses him either physically, sexually, or emotionally, the child may in later life try to resolve the trauma by mistreating women, usually not his mother. Unless the individual you're looking for is truly psychotic, a 'madman' in lay terms, this Freudian concept is probably the most important thing to keep in mind. You asked for a profile of this man. With Freud's concepts in mind and what you've told me about your investigation, here's my view of the killer's possible characteristics. If Sam's right about the body positions and the new moon, he's likely white, aged thirty to fifty, maybe successful in his business career, and certainly intelligent. Most Birmingham males, Negro or white, wouldn't know anything about the religious icons or new moons. Oh, I admit some might track the moon cycles for various reasons. The religious symbology—"

Sam interrupted Wayne. "There are Negro men in the community who are well-educated and would recognize the icons. But I do agree with you that the murderer is white. Just my hunch at this time. Nothing substantive to go on yet."

"No disrespect intended, Sam. I was speaking of the average male, Negro or white, in our community."

Sam smiled at Wayne. "Understood."

"Where was I? Oh yes, religious symbology adds a fascinating aspect to this puzzle. Religious fanaticism, if that's what it is, could also be a product of childhood trauma. Maybe the murderer became involved in a religious cult or satanic group in adulthood. I could go on, but it gets more and more judgmental and esoteric. Do you have any questions, gentlemen?"

Sam and Joe looked at each other, and Sam gestured with his hand for Joe to answer first. "I understand how difficult it will be to apply what you've told us to our investigation. I think the religious aspects of the murders may be our best entry into this man's world. Have you talked to or interviewed anyone that meets the religious profile you outlined?"

"Joe, just as you want my confidentiality on our talks, which I will agree to, I can't reveal that kind of information about another client or patient. Those talks are equally confidential. But I will tell you that I've never talked to anyone that matches the religious fanaticism I outlined. Any other questions? Sam?"

Sam said, "No. Thank you for a comprehensive review."

"I have one request," Wayne said. "When you arrest a suspect and get a conviction, I would appreciate the opportunity to interview him. If the killer is cooperative, his background and life and the things that led him to do this would be invaluable. It could provide insight into this subject for police and psychiatric evaluations in the future. Will you help me with this?"

"Wayne, when we get to that point, I'll do everything I can to help you," Joe said.

"Thank you. I have to—"

Wayne's secretary stuck her head in the door. "They need your help in room 502. It's an emergency."

"Okay, Kathy. I'll go right away. Gentlemen, it's been a pleasure. I hope it's been helpful." Wayne shook hands with both men and added, "You can remain here as long as you like."

"Thank you, Wayne. We need to talk alone for few minutes then we'll be off. We'll leave separately. We don't want to be seen together."

"I understand. Please let me know how things are going or if you want to meet again." He hurried out of the office.

Joe turned to Sam. "Well, did you learn anything new?"

"Nope, but he did a good job of summarizing what I knew and how difficult it will be to tag this guy. How about you?" Sam said.

"Some of the background stuff was new for me. The summary was familiar. Well, back to work. You want to leave first?"

"Sure. But first, I gotta tell you something," Sam said. "I got a piece of information today, something that may prove interesting. I don't wanna talk about it yet. My source is not trustworthy. He'll say things to get you off his back or just mislead you. I gotta talk to some other guys and see if it adds up."

"Well, you've certainly got my attention. I'll stay tuned."

"Okay. What's up this weekend?"

"I'm going to the Alabama-Tennessee game tomorrow. I may go to Huntsville Sunday to see my daughter. What about you?" Joe said.

"Do it, Joe. You need to see your daughter. Do you good. I'd go to the game if I could get a decent seat. I might listen to it on the radio. Sunday, we go to church and then have a late lunch with our families."

Sam left the building by using the stairs and a side door on the first floor. He wanted to avoid being seen, not because of raised eyebrows, but because the fewer people who saw him in the hospital while Joe was there the better. He now realized he should have used the stairs when he arrived.

Joe left five minutes later. No one gave him a second glance.

CHAPTER 28

THE ENCOUNTER

FRIDAY—OCTOBER 17, 1947

J OE WAS SITTING AT THE BAR IN THE WHITE STAG. It was about six, and he had just started his second beer when she walked in.

She was dressed like a *Harper's Bazaar* model. She was tall, about five feet, nine inches, with a lean figure that exuded femininity and sexuality. He guessed she was in her early thirties. Her brunette hair fell down to the nape of her long neck. Her face was like a Modigliani painting, long and narrow—yet, it fit her tall, lean frame. She was wearing a light gray wool two-piece outfit. The suit jacket, tightly tapered at the waist, buttoned up in the middle but was accented with two rows of buttons on either side on the center row, giving the appearance of a double-breasted jacket. The skirt was tight to her waist and upper hips but flared out gracefully over her legs to mid-calf. She wore light orange gloves and a matching silk scarf.

Joe stepped from his bar stool. "Good evening. Nice to see you again."

"Oh, it's you. Hi, good evening. Are you on your way out again?"

"No. I just got here a short while ago. My name's Joe."

"My name's Diane Lightfoot. I know who you are. Joe McGrath, a homicide detective. My, what a lovely suit."

Joe looked confused. "Thank you. Have we met?" He smiled broadly. "No, not possible. I wouldn't have forgotten."

Diane returned the smile. "No, I've read about you a number of times in the *News*. Occasionally, there's a photo. Jack Ritter often mentions you in his column. He calls you Birmingham's 'super sleuth.'"

"My journalistic nemesis. Actually, Jack's a friend. But you have to watch what you say to him. Can I buy you a drink and a bite to eat?"

"I'd love a drink. I'm meeting friends for dinner in less than an hour, so I'll have to pass on the food."

Joe looked around the room and saw a nice table in the back. As soon as they sat down, a waiter came over with Joe's beer.

"Here's your beer, Joe. What can I get you, Diane?"

She removed her gloves. "I'll have a gin and tonic, please." She looked at Joe with a twinkle in her eye. "Well, it sounds like we're both regulars here. Are you as big a lush as I am?"

"Yes, they have to carry me home every night. Don't tell the chief."

"Oh, my lips are sealed."

"Diane, your unique last name keeps ringing in my head. Where have I heard it?"

Diane blushed. "Oh my goodness. You probably read about my parents in the *News*, especially the society pages if you read them. Daddy's name is Walter Lightfoot. My mother's Cynthia."

"Of course. That's it. I read the Sunday *News* carefully. Now I remember the name. They seem to be in the paper each week. They must be involved in all the high-society stuff in Birmingham."

Diane said, "That's just what it is, Joe, stuff in Birmingham and beyond. My grandfather bought stock in the 1890s in an unknown Atlanta soda fountain drink called Coca-Cola. He later bought more stock from some lawyers in Chattanooga who started Coca-Cola Bottling Company. Every time you put down a nickel for a Coke, the Lightfoots benefit. We're so stinking rich we can't spend it all and don't know what to do with all our free time."

Joe was concerned he had inadvertently opened a wound. "You sound bitter, Diane."

"I know that's how I sound, but that's not the right word. Maybe renegade. It's hard to find a real identity when you grow up surrounded by money and privilege. God, how did I get started on this?"

"I'm sorry. I didn't mean to probe."

"You didn't, Joe. I just let go." She smiled. "Besides, you're the detective. You're probably used to getting things out of people."

Joe laughed. "I wish most of the folks I questioned talked as freely and easily as you do. How do you fill your spare time?"

"I'm interested in fashion and design. I hope to open my own high-end design studio in Birmingham. Right now I work at Maxine's across the street. It's the best women's store for high fashion in the state."

"Your clothes are certainly beautiful. That's a stunning outfit."

Diane giggled and overdid her southern accent. "Why, suh, thank you. You do have excellent taste. I designed this lovely suit myself."

Joe laughed and played along. "Miss Scarlett, you look marvelous."

Diane returned to her usual voice. "I took the job to get some experience. Besides doing some design work, Maxine lets me buy clothes at a significant discount. She gave me this suit and lets me wear others for free. She says I'm good advertising for the store."

"Maxine is sure right about that."

Diane smiled coyly at Joe. "Now don't you ever tell Daddy and Mummy what I just told you. They know I work at the store, but they don't like it. If they knew I got discounts and the occasional free dress, they'd die. I can hear Mummy: 'Darling, Lightfoots do not shop for discounts. That's for the common man. We pay full retail at only the best stores.' And even though Maxine's is the best, she won't set foot in the store because I work there." She laughed uproariously.

Joe also laughed with a joy he hadn't felt in months. "Are you going to the big game tomorrow?" he said.

Diane didn't hesitate, she knew exactly what Joe was asking about. "Oh yes, I'll be there with a few friends. Will you be there?"

Joe tried to sound casual. "Yes, I'm going. I'll be alone this time."

"Perhaps we'll bump into each other." Diane looked at her watch. "I've really enjoyed talking to you, Joe."

"Can I call you? Maybe we could go out to dinner or a movie."

"I'd enjoy that." She reached in her small purse, pulled out her Maxine's business card, and wrote another number on the back. "Here, you can reach me at either number."

"Thanks." Joe pulled out his card and wrote his apartment phone number on it. "I know a lady doesn't call a gentleman, but here's my card anyway."

"Thanks, Joe. You might be surprised. And listen, next time we see each other, we're gonna talk about you, not me."

"It's a deal. Can I walk you to your car?" Joe said.

"No, don't bother. It's just across the street behind Maxine's."

Diane extended her hand to Joe. He took it and let go reluctantly.

Joe ate a light dinner at the White Stag and then went to his apartment for the evening. He sat in his reading chair thinking about Diane. *God, she's lovely. Reminds me of Mary.* That's when it hit him. *I've got to come to grips with my jealousy. Diane must have tons of men friends and suitors. Maybe Frank's right. I should talk to someone.*

He picked up the phone and dialed Mary's mother's home.

"Hello."

"Hi, Mary. It's me."

"Hi, Joe. How are you?"

"I'm fine. I was planning to come up Sunday. Can I see Jane?"

"Yes. What time?"

"Well, I may drive up Saturday night or Sunday morning. If I come Saturday, I'll stay in a hotel. What time are Sunday Masses?"

"Eight and ten," Mary said.

"If it's okay, I'll pick Jane up about quarter to ten, and we'll go to the ten o'clock Mass. Then lunch and maybe a few things around town if the weather holds. I'd bring her back about four."

"Good. She misses you, Joe. You haven't been up here in a while."

"I know. I've been working on a murder case."

"You're always working on a case, Joe."

Joe paused, determined not to get mad. "Well, I'll be there just before ten on Sunday."

"Okay, we'll see you then. Goodbye."

Why do I always feel like shit after a conversation with Mary?

CHAPTER 29

FOOTBALL AND CHURCH

SAT. & SUN.—OCTOBER 18–19, 1947

T HE FOOTBALL GAME WAS A BLUR. Alabama played well and beat Tennessee 10–0. Joe paid scant attention to the game, his mind mostly on Mary and Diane.

His anxiety level rose as he sat in the stadium thinking about the coming encounter with Mary. He always expected to hear something new from Mary that would upset him.

More troubling were his thoughts about Diane. He kept looking for her in the stadium, but that proved fruitless in a crowd of thirty-two thousand. He knew it was irrational—he had just met the woman— yet, pangs of jealousy were crowding his thoughts. While still in the stadium, Joe pledged to himself that he would call Dr. Theroux next week to schedule an appointment to discuss his personal life.

He drove to Huntsville after the game, had supper, and spent the night in a local hotel. He arrived at Mrs. Firth's house at nine fifty Sunday morning. Both Mary and Jane opened the door. They were both dressed for church, Mary in a pale green wool suit and Jane in a dark blue frock. Joe recognized both outfits.

Jane jumped into Joe's arms and squealed, "Daddy!"

"Hi, honey. I've missed you so," Joe said. "Good morning, Mary," he added.

Mary looked annoyed. "Joe, the two of you better get going. Mass starts soon. I went to an early Mass."

It had been over four months since Joe had been in a church. Being in church made him feel trapped, but he noticed Jane was engaged in all aspects of the service. When the time came, Jane didn't hesitate to go forward to receive Communion.

When she returned to the pew, she whispered to Joe, "Daddy, why didn't you take Communion?"

He offered a lame excuse. "I haven't been to Confession."

Jane looked at Joe disapprovingly, but said nothing.

As they were leaving the church, a man approached them. "Hello, Jane. Did you enjoy Mass today?"

Jane smiled. "Hi, Mr. Flemming. Yes I did. This is my father."

"Good morning. I'm Jeffrey Flemming."

As Joe did so often in his work, he quickly looked the man over. He was of medium build and height, had a pleasing but not handsome face, and wore a well-tailored charcoal gray wool suit.

Joe had a sense the man was the first of several new things he would experience on this visit. "Hi, I'm Joe McGrath." The two men shook hands. "Sorry, Jane and I have to get going. We're having lunch together. Nice to meet you, Mr. Flemming."

Back in the car, Joe asked, "Jane, who was that?"

"That's Mom's new friend. He's nice, isn't he?"

Joe tried to look sincere. "Yes. Where would you like to go for lunch, honey?"

Jane looked at Joe sadly. "I wish we could go to Britling Cafeteria. It's so nice, and I could always order what I wanted."

Joe knew Britling was Jane's favorite place to eat in Birmingham, a local chain that had raised cafeteria-self-service style to an enjoyable dining experience with its good food, service, and pricing in a nice restaurant setting.

"Me too. But there's no Britling in Huntsville. I bet we can find a nice cafeteria here."

Joe stopped at a gas station, and the attendant suggested a place nearby. It was a small diner with a six-stool counter and five tables covered with brown paper for tablecloths. Joe thought, *Should have known better than to ask a gas station attendant*, but since it looked clean, they ordered fried chicken, mashed potatoes, and greens. After they ate, Joe asked Jane, "Well, that was pretty good, right?"

Jane was adamant. "Yes, but it was not Britling."

"Honey, when you come to Birmingham for Thanksgiving or Christmas, I promise I'll take you to Britling as often as you want."

Their next stop was a large city park with a lake. They rented a paddle-wheel boat and cruised the lake. Later in the afternoon, they went to an ice cream parlor and shared a big banana split.

Joe drove around in the countryside before taking Jane home. They talked about school and Jane's new friends. Jane asked Joe several times when he and Mommy were going to get back together again. At first, he tried to be circumspect. "Honey, Mom and Dad have a lot of things to talk about before that happens."

But after Jane's fourth inquiry, Joe said, "Jane, I don't think Mom and Dad will ever get back together. We both love you very much and will always be here for you." Jane became silent, and Joe took her back to her grandmother's house.

Joe hugged Jane, not wanting to let go. "Goodbye, honey. I'll come back and see you soon."

"Jane, I'm gonna walk Daddy to his car," Mary said. "Joe, I have a couple of things I need to tell you."

Joe thought to himself: *Oh god, here it comes.* "Yes, what is it?"

"I've met someone. We just started dating. I met him at the church."

Joe tried to act nonchalant. "That's good. I think I just met him. Jeffrey Flemming?"

Surprised, Mary said, "Yes, that's him. Did Jane tell you?"

"Nope. He came up to say hello to Jane, and we met. So you're going to church regularly again?"

"Yes. I thought it'd be good for Jane and me, what with all the changes. I do find it helpful. And I missed the church."

Joe couldn't resist saying, "Yeah, helped you find another guy."

Mary responded calmly. "No, that's not so. The two are completely unrelated. We had been going to church months before I met him. I planned to tell you before Jane happened to mention him. Sorry it happened this way."

"You said you had two things to tell me."

"Yes. I want Jane and me more involved with the church. And maybe someday, I'll want to remarry in the church. So I had a talk with our parish priest last week about the possibility of an annulment. I told him about our marriage. At first, he said it was unlikely since we had been married for such a long time and had a child. Then I told him you didn't want Jane going to a Catholic school. He said that changed everything and that I should file for an annulment."

Joe laughed sarcastically. "So I'm the heavy again. Did you tell him about my jealous outbursts?"

"No, of course not. Joe, don't you see? This would be better for us both. We'd have to get a civil divorce first. I know I was adamantly against it when you first mentioned it. But with an annulment, our marriage never existed—we were never married in the eyes of the church. It would improve and simplify our lives."

"You've really been thinking a lot about this. What about Jane?"

"She's still our daughter, Joe. Nothing changes that, legally or with the church."

"I suppose. I gotta go. I'll think about it. Thanks for telling me."

Joe turned away.

Mary called out, "Will you start the civil proceedings?"

Joe jumped into his car and drove off abruptly. He looked in his rear view mirror and saw Mary slowly going back to the house.

He felt a sense of sadness and emptiness, wondering when things would change. He didn't realize that Mary felt the same way.

EVERY TIME SAM WENT TO SUNDAY SERVICES at St. Jude AME Church, he was overwhelmed with a sense of guilt over his last personal encounter with his father when Reverend Rucker disowned him. As he sat with his family in their assigned pew, he could see his father's huge image towering over the congregation.

The guilt feeling and image faded when the current pastor came to the pulpit. Reverend Stockton was a short man with a jovial face and the demeanor of a teddy bear. He lovingly embraced his congregation and made Sam smile. His sermons were short and to the point.

Sam was surprised when Stockton said, "Brothers and sisters, I wanna talk to y'all this morning about some terrible events in our community. Early last Tuesday mornin' a second young lady was brutally murdered in downtown Birmingham. The first young lady was murdered last month. It's no secret these ladies made their livin' on the streets sellin' their bodies, where they paid the ultimate price for their sins. But remember what the Bible, Matthew 21:31, tells us Jesus said to the chief priests in the temple: 'And the harlots go into the kingdom of God before you.' Now please join me in a minute of silent prayer. Forgive these two women in your heart and ask God to accept them into his holy heaven." Reverend Stockton and the congregation bowed their heads in prayer.

The reverend lifted his head and continued in his usual low-key manner, "Amen. One other thing, brothers and sisters. I know the Birmingham police are not to be trusted. But if any of you saw or heard anything that might be related to these murders, please report it to the police. If you're concerned how the police might treat you, come talk to me. Praise the Lord."

Sam was pleased to hear the reverend's message, and he smiled at the word "harlots." It reminded him of his youth when he first heard the word used in one of his father's sermons. Then it hit him. In the same sermon, his father had used the phrase the "kiss of salvation." *My god*, he thought, *that's what those bruises were on the dead women's lips. The killer kissed them violently as an act of salvation.*

After the service, most gathered in the church's social hall to visit and exchange pleasantries. The businessman Sam most wanted to interview about the murders also attended St. Jude. He hoped to see him to arrange an appointment, but the guy appeared to have skipped church today.

Sam and Janice, his mother Rebecca, and his sisters and their husbands went to Birmingham's finest colored restaurant for a mid-afternoon dinner. They had been there well over an hour and were ordering desserts when Marcus arrived.

Marcus Gilbert was the wealthiest and most powerful colored businessman in the city. The restaurant owner greeted him and his party as royalty and escorted them to a large, reserved table in the center of the room, where they would be on display for all to see. His party included his wife and three sons, two business associates, and two large, beefy men who were his bodyguards.

Marcus owned a number of legitimate businesses—a funeral parlor, a bank, and several automobile dealerships and gas stations—that served the colored community well and enhanced his reputation with all of Birmingham. But add in the monies from the illicit activities he controlled—prostitution, gambling, bootlegging, predatory lending—and he was among the wealthiest men in Birmingham of any color. As Stanford Ramsey dispensed political patronage to run his political machine, Marcus dispensed monetary patronage to garner support from city hall, the police, and the white power establishment. His payoffs to the police and city hall employees were so regular that they became accustomed and beholden to him for their standard of living.

Marcus hadn't finished high school, and he had started working in Birmingham's steel mills at sixteen. He soon understood that money was to be made by opening small businesses to serve the city's expanding, but poor, colored community. His efforts grew rapidly to the empire he controlled today.

He was medium height and his thin, taut frame from his steel mill days had prospered as well as his bank account. He was now a rotund, fat man. His round face was benign and friendly unless he felt challenged. Then his large eyes would instantly penetrate one's space with an icy, cruel stare. He dressed well in the latest and best men's suits available. To accentuate his power and status, he always wore a gold tie pin featuring a large diamond, matching diamond cuff links, and a huge diamond ring. His persona and appearance said, "I'm important. Don't fuck with me."

Although Sam knew Marcus well, he waited until his party was comfortably settled before he approached him. Marcus saw him coming toward his table and stood up.

"Well, I be damned. If it ain't the city's best, cleanest private eye. What you on my tail for now, Sam?"

Sam laughed, ignoring Marcus's "cleanest" barb. He refused to take Marcus's money. "Hey, Marcus. Yep, I hear you been up to no good."

"I jus' doin' what I do best. Making a little money here and yonder. How y'all doin'?" Marcus said motioning over to Sam's table.

"We're all doing well. Mom's still teaching, but she'll probably retire soon. Y'all doing okay?" Sam said to the entire table.

Marcus answered for them all. "We be doin' good. Sorry we missed church today. But what I's miss most is your daddy's sermons. He was sumthin' else."

"Yeah, I miss him too. Marcus, I need to talk to you. Can I come over to your office tomorrow?"

Marcus eyed Sam with a steely caution. "I ain't in no trouble now, am I?"

Sam laughed. "Hell no. You know you can't do anything wrong. I need your help with a problem I'm having."

"Well, in that case, I's glad to hep. Not tomorrow. How's Tuesday 'bout eleven?"

"That'll work. I'll see you then. Thanks."

"Say hello to your mama and sisters," Marcus said as he nodded and waved at them.

AFTER SAM GOT HOME SUNDAY EVENING, he found his seldom-used Bible. It took him a while, but he finally found the passages in the Book of Luke pertaining to his father's use of the "kiss of salvation." He read it carefully, wanting to be sure he had interpreted it correctly.

The kiss of salvation. Damn. We've got a madman on our hands.

CHAPTER 30

THE GRAND JURY

MONDAY—OCTOBER 20, 1947

"Good morning, Sally. Oh, do I need a kiss after the weekend," Joe said when he arrived in the office on Monday.

"Good morning, Joe. You know I always have an extra special kiss for you on Monday."

Joe took a Hershey's Kiss from the bowl on her desk. "Thanks for the kiss, Sally. Did you have a nice weekend?"

"Yes, I saw a movie Saturday night—*Gentleman's Agreement.*"

"I've heard good things about it. What did you think?"

"Excellent. Starred Gregory Peck and Dorothy McGuire. It's set in New York City. It's about anti-Semitism. I think it's good enough for an Oscar."

"Sounds interesting. I'll have to catch it. We have enough anti-Semitism around here to tell that story."

"True. Joe, after you left the office Friday, Jack Ritter called. When I told him you had left for the day, he asked to speak to Dick Oliver so I transferred him. Did you read his *Birmingham Beat* column in the Sunday *News*?" Sally said.

"No, didn't have time to read the paper yesterday. I got back from Huntsville last night. Spent time with my daughter Jane. She's doing—"

"Oh, I hope everything's okay. Are Jane and Mary doing well?"

"Jane's doing fine. Did our favorite critic rake us over the coals?"

"I brought a copy in. Here, I think you should read it."

"That bad, huh?" Joe took the copy into his office. He groaned and then exclaimed, "Goddamn!"

Ritter's column detailed the recent murder and the arrest of Luke Matthew. Joe was particularly angry about one paragraph.

> Homicide Captain Richard Oliver told the *Beat* that the diligent work of Homicide Detective Joe McGrath and his young sidekick, Officer Brendan O'Connor, led to the arrest of Luke Matthew. Oliver added that their excellent work was responsible for Matthew's subsequent confession as the murderer of two colored prostitutes recently. The *Beat* has always considered McGrath the top homicide detective in the department. He continues to show his ability to solve the city's most difficult murder cases.

I gotta call Sam and make sure he knows about this. He realized that Oliver had used Ritter to box him in. Now he would be the hero to whites and the villain to coloreds for Matthew's arrest.

Joe stormed out of his office without so much as a glance at Sally and called out, "I'm going to Oliver's office."

"Where's Dick?" Joe asked Margaret.

"He's gone to the courthouse, Joe. Lance Roberts wants him there as a witness in Matthew's prelim and Grand Jury hearings."

"What time does it start?"

"At nine, in about twenty minutes."

Joe hustled to the courtroom. Dick Oliver sat in the first row behind the bar and District Attorney Lance Roberts at the prosecution's table.

Luke Matthew sat at the defendant's table. Joe was glad to see the colored lawyer, Alfred Banks, sitting next to Luke—Sam had obviously talked to Banks about representing Luke. As Joe approached Dick's seat, Luke turned and looked at him. He was dressed in nice slacks and a white shirt, no tie. Although his face still showed some swelling, and the sutures Doc Weaver had applied were evident, Joe was surprised to see how much better Luke looked. A colored couple sat behind Luke. They appeared to be in their forties. Joe figured they were Luke's parents.

Jack Ritter and two other reporters were at the press table. Grand Jury members were seated in the jury box. Except for court personnel, the remainder of the courtroom was empty.

Joe sat next to Oliver, who smiled at Joe. Joe returned the smile with a grimace and whispered, "Thanks for all the crap you fed Ritter."

Dick put on his best paternalistic expression. "Meant every word I said. You guys did a great job. The chief was pleased."

Joe couldn't help raising his voice. "Bullshit. You're trying to lock my hands. I can't—"

Lance Roberts spun around, scowling at the men. "Keep it down."

Judge Overton came into the courtroom. The bailiff called the court to order. Roberts opened by entering Matthew's confession as his prime argument for a Grand Jury indictment. Defense attorney Banks objected on the grounds that the confession had been coerced from Matthew, adding that his client had been brutally beaten. Overton overruled the objection and asked Roberts if he had any witnesses to call.

Roberts said, "I have only one witness. I can call Homicide Captain Richard Oliver to corroborate the confession."

"That's not necessary. I'm prepared to hand this over to the Grand Jury for consideration." Turning to the jury, Overton said, "Gentlemen, District Attorney Roberts will join you with any witnesses he plans to call. Consider what he presents, ask any questions, and decide whether to return an indictment or a no bill. I must remind you and all who participate in the Grand Jury room that the hearing is held in secret and you are bound to keep all the proceedings secret except your final judgment. You may proceed to the Grand Jury room."

Since Joe would not be called to testify before the Grand Jury, he decided to go back to the office, certain that an indictment would be the outcome.

Joe thought about it for a while and finally said to himself, *Damn it Joe, call the man.* He picked up the phone.

"Hello, Dr. Theroux's office. Kathy speaking."

"Kathy, this is Joe McGrath. I'm calling to make an appointment with Dr. Theroux. I'd like to talk to him about some personal matters."

Kathy sounded surprised. "Doctor's been busy lately. Let me look at his schedule. . . . Oh, I forgot. We just had a cancellation for Thursday at three. Can you come then?"

Joe looked at his calendar. "Yes, that's fine."

"Please come about a half hour early. New patients need to fill out some paperwork before the consultation. The initial consultation is forty dollars and if you decide to continue with weekly sessions, they are twenty five dollars. Payment is required after each session."

"Okay. I'll be there on Thursday about two-thirty."

"I'll tell Dr. Theroux you called. Any questions?"

"Nope. Goodbye."

Later in the afternoon, Joe's phone rang. "Joe McGrath here."

"Joe, it's Dick. The Grand Jury brought in an indictment. Lance Roberts asked for a November third start date. Judge Overton said he was out of town that week and set the start date for the eleventh."

"Did Roberts present any of the Matthew material I gave you?"

"You know I can't answer that, Joe. Grand Jury proceedings are secret." Dick hung up.

And fuck you too, thought Joe. *Roberts wants to extend the start date two or three weeks so Matthew's wounds heal even more.*

CHAPTER 31

MARCUS GILBERT

TUESDAY—OCTOBER 21, 1947

"M ORNIN', SAM. C'MON IN. How's it hangin'?" Marcus Gilbert ruled his empire from a palatial office complex occupying the entire fourth floor, the top floor, of his corner bank building in Scratch Ankle.

Sam had been there a few times, but he was always taken aback by the room's design. "Can't complain, Marcus. How about you?"

"It's jus' hangin'. Older you gets, that's 'bout all it does." Marcus roared at his joke. "We did some remodel since you last come here. Whatcha think?"

Sam knew better than to laugh at the joke as he looked around the huge room. He figured the room at about fifty by eighty feet, and it had been completely remodeled since he last saw it. The first third of the room featured flooring of Italian tiles in a collage of bright colors and patterns randomly covered with oriental rugs of various designs.

Marcus's desk sat at the corner of the room overlooking the intersection below giving him an expansive view of his Scratch Ankle domain. The red and gold on oak desk, an eighteenth-century Louis XV writing table, had gilt-bronze mounts and a dark leather top absolutely clear of any clutter. Two white marble Corinthian columns stood to each side of the desk.

Behind the French desk and chair was a bloodwood rectangular table with four phones, an intercom, a pad of paper, and a set of fine pens and pencils impeccably arranged as if seldom used. To the right of Marcus's desk was a six-foot round table and eight chairs, also made of bloodwood.

White carpet fully covered the remaining two-thirds of the room. This part of the room had a huge dining table that sat fourteen people. There were three large sofas and several chairs, all covered in animal hides: cheetahs, black jaguars, lions, and zebras. A ten-foot bar with a dumbwaiter next to it allowed food, drinks, and tableware to be sent up and down to the kitchen on the third floor. Hung on the wall behind the bar was the head of a Bengal tiger with its mouth wide open, exposing the fangs. On either side of the tiger were hand-painted replicas of two European masterpieces—right of the tiger Goya's *The Nude Maja,* left of the tiger Titian's *Venus of Urbino.*

Floor-to-ceiling bloodwood bookcases of varying depths filled most of the windowless wall space. The cases held vases, ceramics, jewelry, and small statuary from ancient Greek, Roman, European, and Byzantine cultures. The collection was arranged in a haphazard fashion with no eye to period, shape, size, or purpose.

Finally, the room's corners featured four seven-foot white statues: Aphrodite, a Greek discus thrower, Michelangelo's David, and Zeus.

"Looks great. Real eclectic taste," Sam said.

"'Scuse me? Electric taste?"

"No. Eclectic. Ec–lec–tic. Means using things from a variety of tastes and styles. It's a compliment."

"Ec–lec–tic. You fuckin' college boys gets me. Some of you knows all the right words, but you sure as shit don't knows 'bout the real world." Marcus laughed again.

"I reckon you're right about that." Sam stood looking at the tiger and two paintings. "Wow. Who are those two women?"

"Shit, I don't knows. Jus' two naked white ladies. Yolanda said they was famous. That good 'nough for me."

"Who's Yolanda? And where did you get all this stuff?"

"You gotta meet Yolanda Chaisson. She a Creole lady and a looker. She live in New Orleans and come up here to do my office. Any ways, she a great designer and antique lady. She done all this. Most of the stuff come from New Orleans. But she got good contacts with all the Birmingham white antique dealers. And she can sho'nuff drive a bargain. Course, they's take colored money any day of the week, you jus' gotta go in and out the back door," Marcus said.

"I'd like to meet her sometime. But this office sure is interesting. I'm almost speechless, Marcus."

"Well, that sumthin' for you. What you wanna talk 'bout? Lemme guess. 'Bout them two whores what got killed. C'mon, let's sit down in them animal chairs. Hattie Mae picked out the hides. Great, huh?"

"Fantastic. The chairs are great, also. I bet you also heard about the nineteen-year-old kid, Luke Matthew, who's going to trial for the murders," Joe said.

"Course I heard 'bout him. Shit Sam, I know everthin' goin' on 'round here. Alfred Banks is hepin' him."

"Banks is a good guy. The best. Of course, he's the only colored attorney in Birmingham."

"He'd be doin' bettah if he worked closer with me."

"You mean he won't take your money."

Marcus glared at Joe. "I mean sumthin' like that. Hell, all you gotta do is pay them cracker lawyer fellas good money. They's all dance to any tune you play. Who you thinks git Bongo Drum and them others off when they's busted?"

"You do, Marcus. But I'm sure Matthew's not the killer."

"So, what's new? You knows Big Bob and Ramsey wanna put a stop to this right now 'fore it gets outta hand. And I agrees with 'em," Marcus said.

"Sure. But it won't stop the murders."

"How ya knows that?"

"It just doesn't add up, Marcus. The kid's a pussy. The cops beat the shit out of him to get a confession."

"Who ya workin' for on this?"

"I don't ask about your business. Let mine be. I will tell you they're just interested parties," Sam said.

Marcus's gazed hardened. He didn't like Sam's answer, but he let it pass. "So, what ya want from me? I knows it ain't money."

"No, not money. I talked to Bongo Drum and Black Bronco. They wouldn't give me the time of day."

"They's cautious men. I wants 'em to be."

"I know that. But something weird is going on here, Marcus. It's more than a john trying to show who's the boss. This guy, and I think it's a white man, is crazy. He leaves the bodies in arranged positions like religious symbols, sorta like a Christian cross. This kid wouldn't know that stuff. I need your help to find the murderer."

Marcus paused to think about his next move.

"You knows I works with lots of white men. Some of them's good customers. Me and my boys can't start talkin' 'bout 'em."

"I don't expect names. You gotta protect your interests. But right now, your interests are threatened by a madman. Just gimme something to go on. It's a dead end right now," Sam said.

"I ain't sure. I gotta think 'bout it. Call me tomorrow after ten."

"Okay. But remember, if these murders continue, it's gonna hurt your business and the community might explode."

"Sam, don't preach to me like your papa."

"I don't preach, Marcus. I know you don't like it. Just telling you things you need to think about."

"Call me tomorrow."

After Sam left the office, Marcus picked up his phone and called Bongo Drum.

CHAPTER 32

BRENDAN MEETS SAM

WEDNESDAY—OCTOBER 22, 1947

Brendan ARRIVED EARLY AT JOE'S APARTMENT, eager to meet Sam. After he put his uniform in Joe's place, the two men left for Willie's BBQ in the Plymouth.

Sam, waiting for them at the back door, said, "Well, if it ain't the two Birmingham coppers. Right on time."

"Brendan, meet Sam Rucker. Sam, Brendan O'Connor," Joe said.

Brendan, immediately struck by Sam's size and presence, said, "Nice to meet you, Mr. Rucker."

Brendan's reaction elicited a grin from Sam, who knew he wasn't used to addressing colored men as Mister. "Nice to meet you too, Brendan. Call me Sam. Seems Joe's good manners rubbed off on you."

Brendan blushed, realizing he was being both teased and chided. "Yes sir . . . I mean . . ."

"That's all right. Y'all come on in. We're gonna meet in the card room. Want some coffee?"

Joe answered for the two. "Yeah, thanks."

"Y'all sit down. Whatcha want in your coffee?"

Brendan said, "Cream and sugar," and looked at Joe who added, "Black's fine."

"Yes suh, boss mans. I be right back," Sam said as he played the subservient colored man for young Brendan.

"My God, he's something else. He's so big," Brendan said.

"Shit you ain't seen nothing yet. And I don't mean his size."

Brendan took the cup of coffee Sam held out to him. "Thanks, Sam. Smells real good."

As they sipped their brews, Joe finally broke the ice. "Did you see Ritter's column in the Sunday *News*?"

"Yeah," Sam said. "Is Oliver friend or foe? One minute he supports you and me working together, and then he feeds Ritter this line of bullshit."

"Tough question," Joe said. "Dick's like a chameleon. He changes sides often. He's pretty straight with me. A buffer between me and the chief. At the same time, he doesn't . . . no, he *won't*, cross the chief."

"Is he a bigot?" Sam asked.

"Probably as much as any white man. But he's not a redneck bigot. He comes from a wealthy Birmingham family. Those folks usually act liberal, but you really don't know."

Brendan stared in disbelief as he had never heard a white man and colored man discuss bigotry.

"Can you trust him?" Sam asked.

"Not sure. But we gotta assume we can't," Joe said.

"Damn right. He's doing everything to box you in: searches your desks, sets you up with Ritter, says he'll turn on you if things go bad. Brendan, whaddya think about all this?"

Brendan sat up straight. He was surprised to be pulled into this conversation. "Uh . . . I don't know Dick Oliver well, but I think we gotta work around him and keep as much to ourselves as possible."

Sam and Joe nodded.

"We'll have to move carefully. Sam, did you hear about the Grand Jury's decision and trial date?" Joe said.

"Yeah. Alfred Banks called me. No surprises there. At least the trial date's November eleventh."

"You got anything for us? That's it for me," Joe said.

"Somethin' happened at my church Sunday I gotta tell you about."

Sam told them how Reverend Stockton's sermon had triggered his memory of a sermon his father gave when he was a youngster. He explained that the use of the word "harlots" led him to remember the "kiss of salvation" phrase. "I found the pertinent passages in my Bible. Those bruises on the dead girls' lips were the killer's 'kiss of salvation.'

Add this to the body positions, it's like we thought, he's a religious maniac," Sam said.

Brendan looked at Joe and Sam in astonishment. He was having trouble tracking the conversation.

"Got any more surprises?" Joe said.

"Another thing. I met with Marcus Gilbert yesterday. You guys know who he is, right?"

"Sure," Joe said. "Mr. Big in the colored community."

"You don't know how big. He's the colored Stanford Ramsey and Chief Watson rolled into one. If you wanna know what's going on, you talk to Marcus. But he probably won't tell you."

"Get anything outta him?"

"I didn't ask him specific questions. I wanted him to tell guys like Bongo Drum and Black Bronco to loosen up with me. He said he'd think about it. I'll call him later today and see what he says."

Joe looked hard at Sam. "He's putting you off. Can you trust him?"

Sam ignored Joe's comments. "Marcus is the colored side of Dick Oliver and Big Bob. He protects his turf first and foremost. If he can find a way to throw us a scrap, he will. But he don't take no shit."

Brendan, unsure what to think about this back and forth between Sam and Joe, kept his mouth shut.

"So, is that where we are? We got nothing," Joe said.

"No, there is something. I don't know what to make of it. You guys gotta keep your mouths shut, you hear."

"Sure," Joe said. "Right, Brendan?"

"Yeah, sure," Brendan said, thoroughly confused.

"I was working the streets Monday. I talked to a few of the pimps and their gals. Got nowhere. Later, I asked another gal I saw on the street where her pimp was. I hadn't seen him in—"

"What was the pimp's name?" Joe asked.

"Can't tell you. Guy's life might be in danger. Anyway, the gal didn't wanna talk. She finally admitted she no longer worked for him. She said he got in trouble with one of Marcus's lieutenants. Probably over money, usually is."

"What was the gal's name?" Joe said.

"C'mon, Joe, you know I can't tell you that," Sam said angrily. "As I was gonna say, I went to the guy's house. He told me he was short-ing Marcus. Hell, the pimps short what they pay the girls and Marcus all the time. He just got caught. He's lucky they just canned him. He wouldn't say anything about the two murders. Just before I left him, he said, 'Sam, 'member two words . . . mahogany hall.' I asked him what it meant. He repeated, ''Member two words . . . mahogany hall.' That was it," Sam said.

"Any idea what it means?" Joe asked.

"No. Could be the name of a house, a meeting hall, or a dead end."

Brendan spoke up. He finally had something useful to add. "Mahogany hall was also Victorian furniture popular in the latter part of the nineteenth century. My mother had a mahogany hall table in our home that she was very proud of."

Sam smiled at Brendan. "That's interesting. I've never heard about that style of furniture. But you can bet a bundle that the guy who mentioned mahogany hall to me doesn't know shit about it."

"Do you think it's important?" Joe asked.

"Hell, I don't know. It is interesting that he told me about it right after I asked him about the murders."

"What are we gonna do with it?"

"You and Brendan do nothing. Don't mention mahogany hall to anyone. I'll follow-up. Hands off. Okay?"

Joe frowned at Sam, making his irritation clear. "All right, for a while. I thought we were gonna work together on this."

"We are and we will, Joe. But if mahogany hall is important and the wrong people hear us asking around about it, this guy might be dead. These people don't fuck around."

Joe backed off, but he was still not happy about the situation. "We can't seem to get any traction on this case. Nobody's talking except your guy in a two-word code."

"These things move slowly. You gotta go where it takes you. I'll call Marcus today and see if we're gonna get any cooperation from him," Sam said.

Joe looked at Sam with a hard frown on his face. "We're pinched in. Maybe we're fucked. Brendan and I have Oliver and the chief squeezing us on one side. You got Marcus and his pimps holding out too."

"I'll get us a break. You wait and see," Sam said.

During the drive back to the city, Joe said nothing for the longest time. Brendan could tell something was eating at him.

"You okay, Joe?"

"Yeah . . . Fuck. Hell no, I'm not okay. Sam pissed me off. I'm still mad at him. But you know what?" Joe said.

Brendan shook his head.

"Sam's right, and he usually is. But I'm still mad at him."

"Well, he's colored, Joe."

"Yep. I'm white and I'm right. That stupid cliche. Even when you think you're liberal, our damn prejudices bubble up." Joe paused to compose himself. "What do you think, Brendan?"

"My head's spinning. I've never heard a colored man talk to a white man like you two did. But he sure seems to know what he's talking about. We gonna keep working with him?"

Joe laughed. "Of course we are. One, we got no one else to work with. The department's ready to pin it on Matthew and move on. And two, Sam probably will find us a break."

From Willie's, Sam went back to his downtown office. At ten, he called Marcus Gilbert. His receptionist put Sam through to Marcus.

"Hi, Sam. How's it hangin'?"

Sam ignored the question. "Morning, Marcus. You said to call about our talk yesterday."

"Yeah, s'pose I did. . . . Hey, guess who comin' to visit me today?"

"Let's see. Stanford Ramsey."

Marcus roared with laughter. "Right. And Big Bob Watson. We gonna solve them two murders, ya smart ass."

"That's good. Lemme know who dunnit."

"No, goddammit. It's Yolanda Chaisson. That New Orleans lady I tole ya 'bout. Wanna meet her? She be here 'bout eleven."

Sam wanted to get down to business with Marcus, but decided to play along. "Yeah, I'd like to meet her. I got a few things to do. Okay to come after eleven?"

"Sure. We gonna do design work. The wife's comin' later to hep."

"Good. I'll see you soon."

Sam entered Marcus's office at half past eleven. Before Marcus spoke up, Yolanda nearly stopped him in his tracks. She was a knockout. Late thirties, early forties. Lovely figure, dressed in the latest New York fashions, dark hair with a hint of red. But her skin color was her stunning attribute—a light brown that glowed with a tan patina.

Marcus chuckled at Sam's reaction. "Yolanda, this Sam Rucker, the man I tole ya 'bout. Sam, this Yolanda Chaisson from New Orleans."

"Nice to meet you. Is it Miss or Mrs. Chaisson?"

"Miss. Please call me Yolanda. How are you, Mr. Private Eye?"

"So Marcus has been talking. I'm fine, thank you. Enjoying our fair city?"

"Birmingham and Marcus are treating me well. But it's always nice to get back to New Orleans. You been to my city, Mr. Rucker?"

"Sam, please. Yes, a few times."

"Business or pleasure?"

"Mostly business."

"Next time you come, let me show you around. I have a—"

Marcus, tired of the small talk, said, "What's on your mind, Sam?"

"Several things. Are your boys gonna cooperate with me and answer some questions?"

"I tole them to hep ya out. But we gotta protect our interests."

"Your interests are where the answers might be, Marcus."

"Best I can do, Sam."

Not surprised, Sam said, "Well, thanks for that. . . . Oh, one more thing. I don't remember where I heard it 'cause I've talked to so many people over the last few days. Somebody said something about mahogany hall. You ever heard that before?"

Marcus stood with his mouth agape, but Yolanda spoke up before he could regain his composure. She looked at Sam with a wicked grin. "Sam, Mahogany Hall was a famous, high-class brothel in New Orleans years ago. You sure all your trips were for business?" She laughed.

Sam laughed with her. "That must be it. Somebody else did mention New Orleans when Mahogany Hall came up. I didn't connect the two. I'll be damned. And no, I ain't had the pleasure."

Yolanda, enjoying the exchange, said, "Marcus, you know the place. I showed you where it used to be on one of your trips to New Orleans. It was a place run by a colored lady who was from Montgomery, but said she was from Jamaica. And she had all those Creole and light-skinned Negro girls working for her."

Marcus, clearly agitated, muttered, "I don't 'members. 'Scuse me. They's sumthin' I gotta tend to. Take a few minutes." He went into the reception area.

"Marcus seems upset. I'm sure he knows about Mahogany Hall," Yolanda said.

"Maybe there's another one."

"In Birmingham?"

"I don't know," Sam said.

The two stood quietly, staring intently at each other.

Yolanda broke the moment. "Sam, I'm staying at the New Home Hotel if you'd like to meet for a drink later."

"Yes, that would be nice. Six o'clock? Can we keep it quiet?"

"Of course. The only way."

Marcus came back into the room, appearing more relaxed. "Took care of that. Ya got anythin' else, Sam?"

"No. That's it."

Smiling at Yolanda, Marcus said to Sam, "Well, now ya knows 'bout a great whorehouse in New Orleans. Or, I reckon it useta be great."

"In my business, it's always good to learn something new. Even if it's old stuff. Goodbye, Miss Yolanda. Nice to have met you. So long, Marcus. Thanks for your help."

CHAPTER 33

YOLANDA'S SCENT

WEDNESDAY—OCTOBER 22, 1947

Sam got to the New Home Hotel at six fifteen and parked two blocks west of the hotel. Hoping to approach the hotel unseen by any acquaintances or any of Marcus's people, he walked in an alley toward the hotel, ever vigilant for an alcove or doorway to jump into if someone came along. He went to the hotel's back entry and planned to return to his car the same way.

Yolanda was waiting in the hotel lobby. When Sam saw her, he was again stunned by her beauty and felt every sexual nerve ending in his body respond. She was dressed in a loose-fitting, low cut, robin's egg blue silk dress. The dress hung loosely off her shoulders accentuating her skin color and figure.

"Hi, Yolanda. Sorry I'm late. That's a beautiful dress," Sam said as his eyes wandered over her body.

"Thank you, Sam. I just got downstairs."

He enjoyed her playful gaze.

"What a lovely sport jacket you're wearing," she said.

"Thanks. I just bought it a few weeks ago for the cooler weather. Do you mind if we have a drink here? Their restaurant is good if you'd like to have supper with me."

"A drink and supper sounds nice. I also have something I want to tell you. The fewer people that see us together the better."

"Oh. You certainly have my attention in more ways than one," Sam said.

Yolanda smiled warmly and took his arm. "Shall we have a drink?"

They sat at the bar in the back corner of the lobby. As they sipped their drinks, Yolanda asked, "What do you think of Marcus's office?"

Sam knew she was asking about the decor. He repeated what he said to Marcus. "It's an interesting, eclectic design and collection."

Yolanda grimaced and then smiled. "You're quite the politician. I hate it, but I can't afford not to do it. In the last few years, Marcus has paid me more than all my other clients combined."

"Marcus is generous with his money when it serves his purposes."

"Thank God, my New Orleans clients can't see it."

"Marcus told me you did it all. Acted like he knew little about any of the items and didn't care to know," Sam said.

"That's true. He doesn't know anything about the background of most of the items and design. His wife, Hattie Mae, got involved. You know you're in for trouble when the wife wants to do interior design. She chose most of the colors and the hideous sofa and chair coverings. Thank goodness they pay well."

Sam couldn't resist asking, "Who picked the paintings of Goya's *Naked Maja* and Titian's *Venus*?"

"My goodness, a man who knows his art."

"I graduated from the University of Chicago. I also took some classes at the Art Institute."

"Painting classes?"

"Nope. Can't draw. Art history and appreciation classes."

"What'd you study at the university?"

"Criminology."

"Criminology and art. Sam Rucker, you continue to amaze me." She added, "Marcus told me he wanted two paintings of naked white women over the bar. I selected the paintings."

"You're an interesting woman, Yolanda." He felt that the sexual energy flowing between them could have lit the chandelier in the center of the lobby.

After they finished their drinks, he took her by the hand into the hotel's restaurant. The restaurant was small—ten tables arranged close together. There were two other couples already dining when they sat down. Their conversation turned to small talk as they ate. By the time they ordered coffee, all the tables were full, making conversation difficult and discreet exchanges impossible.

Yolanda leaned across the table and whispered in Sam's ear, "We can't talk in here. Too many ears. Do you mind going up to my room?"

Sam tried not to smile, but couldn't suppress it. "No. That's fine."

"Now don't you be a devil," Yolanda said. But her eyes and smile belied her words.

Sam paid the bill and they went upstairs. He had never been in a room in this hotel, but this had to be one of its suites. It had a well-decorated, large outer room that served as a living room and working space. The bedroom had a large bed with an antique armoire, and matching bedside tables and a chest of drawers. Yolanda asked Sam to have a seat on the sofa. She sat beside him.

"You're probably wondering why I'm being so mysterious about what I want to talk about."

"Yes."

"You asked this morning if we could keep our meeting quiet and I said, 'Of course. The only way.'"

"Yeah. I remember."

"Let me explain. I've been doing interior design and decoration work for Marcus for over five years. He's been a good client and friend. I know all about his legit businesses for Negroes. I also know his dark side—the gambling, prostitution, and other activities he controls. I work for guys in New Orleans just like Marcus, white and Negro alike. They're no different. They're tough and ruthless, but pay well if you keep your mouth shut. And I do. I'm not a cop or do-gooder. As long as you treat me and those around me fair, I can usually work with you. I'm not gonna call anybody out or snitch on them, including Marcus," Yolanda said.

"Sounds familiar. I'm in the same boat. I've done some investigations for him, but he paid me. I won't take his bribe money."

"So, you're holier than thou?"

"No. Some would probably say I'm dumber than thou. I just won't take his tainted money. Believe me, I'm not perfect," Sam said.

"Oh, I believe you. Marcus told me about the two recent murders of colored prostitutes. I'm not sure why he told me 'cause it's none of my business. He said someone hired you to look into the murders. He sounded concerned about your involvement in the case."

"Marcus is concerned about things he can't control," Sam said.

"I know he is. But when girls that work for a living with their bodies get a raw deal, especially the ones that work the streets, I get real worked up. I support a group of women in New Orleans who help these girls. Marcus doesn't know about it. When you asked him about Mahogany Hall, he seemed agitated. What did you think?"

Sam thought long and hard before responding. *Christ, she could be a Marcus plant, a Mata Hari to find out what I know. But neither she nor Marcus knew I was going to mention Mahogany Hall before we met this morning. I have to either stop this conversation now or go on at some risk.*

"Yeah, something got under his skin. Maybe Mahogany Hall. Or maybe the way you and I were relating."

Yolanda sensed the tension in Sam's voice. "After you left this morning, Marcus also told me about the nineteen-year-old colored kid that's been charged with the murders. He said you were positive the kid didn't do it. How do you know?"

Sam didn't like this turn in the conversation. He replied simply, "Just a hunch. Some things don't add up."

"In spite of his denial this morning, Marcus knows about New Orleans's Mahogany Hall. I even showed him the building when he was in New Orleans earlier this year. He said, 'Too bad it ain't still open. I mighta checked it out.' He tried to act like he was joking, but I think he was serious. The building's a mess now. I hear tell it's gonna be torn down soon."

"You got any idea why he acted like he did today?" Sam said.

"Now we're getting to what I wanted to tell you. I gotta have your word this won't get back to Marcus. Can I trust you?"

"Yes. I deal on this level everyday in my work." Sam smiled to break the tension that had formed between the two. "Hell, you just asked the question I'm usually asking."

Yolanda seemed to relax a bit. "Good. And you can trust me. On one of my trips up here last May, I was working in Marcus's bedroom. You know where it is?"

Sam was surprised. "No."

"There's a door to it on the back wall to the left of the bar. Marcus uses it when he works late. I think he also uses it for his personal pleasure. You should see how he wanted it decorated. Anyway, no one was in the office suite when I started doing some measurements in the bedroom. The door was partially open. I heard Marcus come into the office. Before I could say hi, he was talking on the phone. I only caught bits of his conversation. He told someone they needed to get Mahogany Hall set up for Halloween Night. I didn't hear much more except just before he hung up and left the office, he told the person not to fuck up 'cause Ramsey wouldn't like it."

"You sure you heard that right?" Sam asked.

"Yeah, I'm sure. When you asked Marcus about Mahogany Hall this morning, it all of a sudden hit me what the connection was all about. I played along with our little word game. But I decided on the spot that I wanted to tell you."

"So there is a Mahogany Hall in Birmingham."

"Apparently."

"And Stanford Ramsey's involved."

"Apparently. If that's the right Ramsey."

Sam chuckled. "Now you're starting to think like a private eye. Miss Yolanda, you been holding out on me?"

Yolanda giggled like a schoolgirl. "No, Mr. Rucker."

"You've certainly opened a new door in this case. We've made no progress on it. Maybe Mahogany Hall has nothing to do with the murders. But we'll see. Don't worry. Marcus won't find out about our conversation. Well, I guess I better say good night."

Yolanda and Sam got up from the sofa. There eyes searched each other eagerly. He could tell that saying good night was not on either of their minds. He stepped closer to her, leaned over, and kissed her. The gentle kiss quickly became a passionate embrace.

Sam placed his hand on her bare shoulders and slowly caressed her bronzed skin. He slipped her dress off her shoulders. It fell effortlessly to her waist. As he had suspected, she wasn't wearing a bra.

Yolanda slipped his sport jacket off, unbuttoned his shirt, and removed it. She gently scratched his nipples.

In a few moments, all their clothes laid strewn about the floor.

"God, you're a beautiful lady," Sam said.

Yolanda surveyed his massive frame in awe. "You are one handsome man." She looked at his legs and hips and exclaimed, "I can't take my eyes off of you."

Sam kissed her again and then let his lips and tongue explore her whole body starting with her breasts. He worked slowly down her torso toward her sweet spot. She stood on her tiptoes and held on to his shoulders while his tongue searched and found the place they both wanted. As his mouth and tongue slowly caressed her, she moaned, thrusting her pelvis forward.

Yolanda pulled Sam's head up. "My turn."

He stood up as she knelt down and took his hard manhood into her mouth. She ran her lips and tongue around and up and down until he thought he would lose control.

Sam pulled her up and lifted her into his arms in one motion. He carried her into the bedroom and held her with one arm while he pulled the bedspread down.

He lay her on the bed, never taking his eyes off her body.

Yolanda moved to the center of the bed. "Lie down here, Sam. It's been a long time for me. I want to be on top. Okay?"

Sam could barely mutter, "Yeah."

He lay down, his erection hard and tall.

As Yolanda straddled his body, she reached for his member with one hand. With her other hand, she turned off the bedside lamp.

CHAPTER 34

JOE'S THERAPY

THURSDAY—OCTOBER 23, 1947

S AM AND YOLANDA WOKE at first light Thursday morning. They quietly and slowly made love, unlike their carnally charged couplings last night.

Yolanda watched as Sam got dressed, knowing she might never see him again. "Will you come to New Orleans and see me, Sam? I don't know if I'll be coming back to Birmingham anytime soon."

Sam looked embarrassed. "I got a lot of work to do on these murders. . . . Yolanda, I'm not married, but I got a serious lady."

She smiled. "I'm not surprised. I don't want to get in the middle. I'd like to see you again. No strings."

Sam sat on the bed and took Yolanda's hand. "I'd like to see you too. But I got a lot to sort out. Janice, that's my lady friend, says men want it all, but when they get it, they don't know what to do with it."

"Your Janice is right. What're you gonna tell her?"

"That's one of the things I gotta sort out. Are you working for Marcus today or headed home?"

"I'm leaving for New Orleans as soon as I get dressed."

"You're not driving? It wouldn't be safe for a good looking women."

"You're sweet, Sam. No, I'm taking the train. It's much safer."

"Good. How do I get in touch with you?"

"Well, now that's promising. You can reach me at my business, Chaisson's Interior Design and Imports. Phone HEmlock 1066. My home's near the shop. Number's HEmlock 1604." She wrote the num-bers down and handed it to Sam.

"Thanks. They're easy to remember. Work is Socrates and the Battle of Hastings. Home is Socrates and Shakespeare's *Othello.*"

"Huh, so you're a historian and Shakespeare buff too?"

"Nope. Just read a lot. I better say goodbye."

Sam leaned over and kissed her. The gentle kiss lingered longer and longer. He stood up, their eyes not wanting to let go.

Sam used the stairs to get to the lobby. The lobby was empty but for one man talking with the check-out clerk. Sam slipped out the rear door unnoticed. He returned to his car as he came, saw no one, and drove home to change clothes. It was too early to call Janice.

While he showered, shaved, and dressed, he thought about what he'd say to Janice. *I'll tell her the truth. I'll just have to fess up and work it out with her. It'll be . . . Oh shit, what if she tells her family or mine. I can't face that. I'll lie. That's easy. Had a late working dinner with Marcus and two of his boys at his bank. That's it . . .* He sat tying his shoes. *Oh, goddammit, I'm gonna tell the truth. Get it over with.*

He put on his coat to leave. The phone rang. He knew it was Janice.

"Hello."

"Sam, are you all right?" Janice said.

"I'm fine, honey. Got home late."

"I was worried. I called a couple of times last night. No answer."

"I called your office yesterday. You were busy, so I left a message."

"I got it. It just said you had to work late."

Before he spoke, Yolanda's naked body flashed through his mind. "Yeah, I had a late working dinner with Marcus and a couple of his guys. I'm trying to get them to cooperate with me on the two murders. They don't move easy. Say they gotta protect their 'interest.' I didn't get home until about one. And damn it, I had too much to eat and drink. I feel like shit this morning."

"You going to the office this morning?" Janice asked.

"I was just leaving when you called. I was gonna call you when I got to the office. You going to work?"

"Yes, I'll leave soon. Want me to come over tonight?"

"You bet. I'll make a nice dinner, and we'll have a quiet evening. I should be home by five."

"I'll see you. Love you," Janice said.

"Love you too, honey."

Sam hung up and looked at himself in the mirror above the table. *You lying son of a bitch.*

JOE'S THURSDAY MORNING WAS SPENT BROODING. The murder investigation was going nowhere. He was unsure which way to turn. He could only hope that Sam's potential lead worked out. In addition, he was having second thoughts about seeing Dr. Theroux, where he'd have to reveal his thoughts to someone he hardly knew. *What the fuck difference would it make. I need the money, not the head-shrink.*

After lunch, he sat at his desk about ready to call Theroux and cancel the appointment when the phone rang.

"Joe McGrath here."

"Hi, Joe. It's Diane Lightfoot."

Joe had meant to call Diane, but the week's events had overwhelmed him. "Hey, Diane. I've been meaning to call you."

"Joe, a woman can only wait so long for a fella to call, so I called you. I'm not bashful."

Joe spirits lifted. "You're certainly not. I'm glad you called. My work hasn't been going well."

"Nothing serious I hope."

"It's this damn murder case. It's not going anywhere."

"Is this the one about the two colored prostitutes?" Diane said.

"Yep. That's the one."

"The newspaper said a colored kid has confessed to the murders."

Joe knew he should keep his mouth shut, but he couldn't contain his frustration with the case. "He didn't do it. But I'm in the minority. The department thinks they have the right guy."

"Well, let me help you at least relax. I've been invited to a dinner party at Stanford Ramsey's Friday night. One of his frequent galas to entertain his minions. How would you like to be my escort? You might even get a chance to meet my ex."

"Can't pass that opportunity up. Yes, I'd love to. But you gotta know, this is way out of my normal social circles."

"You'll charm the socks off this crowd. Their pretensions are overcome by their curiosity in a new face, especially a good looking one."

"If you say so. Can I pick you up?" Joe said.

Diane laughed. "I'm not a pick up, Joe. Of course you can." She told him her address, adding, "Is six okay? Please wear the suit you had on last Friday night. You look great in it."

"Thanks. I'll be there at six."

"See you then," Diane said.

He laughed at himself and thought, *You're so transparent, McGrath. A pretty lady says hi and then calls you. And you brighten up like a sunny day. Okay, Theroux, I'll keep the appointment.*

Joe filled out new patient forms in Theroux's outer office and handed them back to Kathy. She sent him into Theroux's office.

Theroux reviewed Joe's forms. He explained that today's session was a consultation to determine what, if any, future sessions might be appropriate and necessary. He added that everything discussed in these sessions and all his notes were held in complete confidence.

He then asked Joe, "Please explain to me a bit more why you decided to seek psychoanalytic therapy."

Joe sat quietly, trying to decide where to start. "I . . . I'm not sure—"

"I know it's hard to talk about personal feelings and possible problems. Don't worry, I won't be judgmental."

Joe relaxed. "In a word, jealousy. My wife of twelve years and I separated last February. My work may have had something to do with it, but Mary says it was my almost constant jealous outbursts whenever another man showed any interest in her."

"How did she deal with other men's attentions?" Theroux said.

"Well, I think she enjoyed it, but she said it was all flirtatious stuff."

"Did she have any affairs?"

"She says no. I believe her. I recently met an attractive woman and have already felt pangs of jealousy. And we haven't even started dating. I know it's irrational, but I can't seem to control it."

"That's good," said Theroux. "You recognize these feeling are likely irrational. Many people become so consumed by their feelings that they perceive them as normal, but difficult, parts of everyday life. Our challenge is to identify the source or sources of your irrational jealousy. Would you like to relax on the couch beside my chair as we continue talking?"

"If it's okay, I prefer to sit here talking face to face."

"That's fine. I just want you to be comfortable. I'd like you to take your time and explain your family background, your parents, and your earlier years, up to and including your college years."

Joe talked for about ten minutes about his parents and his early years in Montevallo.

He stopped and smiled at Theroux. "I think I will use the couch."

Theroux smiled back at him. "Good idea. Most of my patients find it more comfortable. Joe, were you an only child?"

As Joe lay down on the couch, he said, "Yes."

He continued to talk for some time about his father's murder, the unresolved case, and the impact it had on him. He explained how loving and caring his mother had been in helping him deal with the trauma and move on. As he started to talk about his college years, Theroux interrupted him.

"Joe, you probably don't realize it, but you've been talking for almost forty minutes. We are near the end of this session. I strongly suggest we continue to meet. There are a number of areas and issues we need to explore in more detail. I'm confident that together we can help resolve what you properly call your 'irrational jealousy.' Can we schedule some more appointments?"

Joe wasn't sure why, but he trusted Theroux and felt secure in his care. "Yes, I would like to do that."

Joe left Theroux's office, and as he drove to headquarters, he thought, *Well, I'll be damned. I don't know why, but I think this might be worth the time and money.*

CHAPTER 35

SAM'S DILEMMAS

FRIDAY—OCTOBER 24, 1947

Sam rolled over in his bed and nestled up to Janice. Sam nuzzled his nose in her ear. "I've got to get an early start. I learned something from Marcus last night that may be important in this murder case. I gotta chase it down."

"What'd you learn?" Janice asked.

"If what I heard is true, it could be risky to anyone who knows."

"Including you?"

"Yep. Including me."

"I don't want you to get hurt."

Sam shrugged. "Don't worry. I'll be careful. "

"Honey, you sure are preoccupied. You sure everything is all right?"

"Yeah. But I have to check out this Marcus lead. I gotta get going."

Sam dressed quickly and kissed Janice goodbye.

"Wanna come over to my house tonight?" Janice said.

"Sure. What time?"

"Five or six."

"Okay. I'll call if my work holds me up. See you," Sam said.

Sam sat in his downtown office thinking about his two dilemmas. Both offered problematic alternatives—investigation of the murders was stymied. He was in difficult positions with Yolanda and Janice.

Sam decided to ignore the women problems since he had no clue which way to turn. He phoned Joe's office number. If someone else answered, he would hang up.

"Joe McGrath here."

"It's Sam. Can you talk?"

"Hold on. Gotta close the door."

Joe stuck his head out the door. "Sally, I'm on a private call. No interruptions." Sally nodded.

"I'm back, Sam. If someone comes into my office, I'll hang up and call back later. What's up?"

"Remember that Mahogany Hall thing the pimp told me about?"

"Yeah."

"I went to Marcus's office on Wednesday. His interior decorator was there, a Creole lady from New Orleans named Yolanda Chaisson. I told Marcus that someone on the street had mentioned something called Mahogany Hall. I asked him if he knew anything about it. Before he said anything, Yolanda laughed and said it used to be a high-class whorehouse in New Orleans. She told Marcus that she showed him the building on one of his trips to New Orleans. Marcus was upset and left the room. While he was out, Yolanda asked me to meet her at the New Home Hotel at six for a drink."

"Did you go?"

"You bet. She's a damn good-looking woman, Joe."

"Did you learn anything, lover boy?"

"Very funny, Detective. After we ate in the restaurant, she asked me up to her room to talk where it was quiet." Sam told Joe about the conversation Yolanda overheard.

"Jesus! Do you trust her, Sam?" Joe asked.

"At this point, no reason to distrust her."

"Lots of reasons. What happened?"

"We'll talk more about her later," Sam said.

"If Mahogany Hall is real, it could be big. Interesting that Ramsey's name came up. I met a lady at the White Stag in Five Points last week who comes from Birmingham money. She's invited me to be her escort to a party at Ramsey's house tonight."

"Have fun. I'll talk to a few of Marcus's guys again today. I gotta be careful what I ask them. But I think it'll be a waste of time. I'm pretty sure Marcus told them to keep their mouths shut. I got a couple of other people I'll talk to if I can find them. They might be more coop-erative. We both gotta watch what we say about Mahogany Hall. If it's real, both Marcus and Ramsey probably have a big interest in it," Sam said.

"Right. Let's compare notes this weekend or Monday."

There was a knock. "Somebody's at the door. Gotta go."

SAM WANTED TO ASK THE PIMP who had first mentioned Mahogany Hall more questions. The guy's name was Eddie Johnson. He had worked for Marcus for years and was older than most of the young bucks on the street. He was tagged "Pops" because of his age. Sam parked a block from Johnson's home on the edge of North Birmingham.

Sam knocked on the door.

"Who dat?" came the reply.

"Pops, it's Sam. Can I come in and talk?"

"Hell no. Did you tell someone I tole you 'bout Mahogany Hall?"

"No. Why?"

"Black Bronco come here Wednesday. He ask all kinda questions. He say Marcus unhappy 'bout what he hearing. I think he was gonna work me over. But he didn't. He tole me to keep my mouth shut or else."

"Guys like Marcus and Black Bronco play hardball, Pops. Guys like you and me gotta move carefully. I didn't tell anybody that you told me about Mahogany Hall. But I think I know what goes on there."

Pops opened the door. "Git in here 'fore somebody see you."

Once inside, Sam said, "Pops, you don't owe those motherfuckers a thing. I'm sure they cut you loose over a few bucks. And now these colored girls are getting killed and nobody wants to say anything. Where is Mahogany Hall?"

Pops hesitated, but finally said, "I don't know fo' sure. I think it south of Birmingham."

"You ever been there?"

"Yeah. But we goed in a bus with drapes on the windows, and we all's blindfolded."

"Who was on the bus?" Sam said.

"Some guys like me what works fo' Marcus, and a buncha gals."

"You sure Mahogany Hall's south of town?"

"Ain't fo' sure. I knowed the bus were goin' south when it left town. But after a few turns, I can't tell nothin'."

"Where did you get on the bus in Birmingham?"

"At a downtown warehouse. Morris Avenue and Sixteenth Street. I reckon Marcus own it."

"Who organized the people on the bus?"

"Black Bronco and Bongo Drum. After we's on the bus, they put blindfolds on all us. They say don't you dare take it off 'til we say so. If'n you do, they say they's gonna bash your head in. I don't think they wore no blindfolds on the bus."

"What time of day did you go?"

"Anytime I goed with 'em, it was at night. 'Bout seven or eight."

"How long did the ride take?"

"I ain't sure. Maybe an hour."

"How long did you stay at Mahogany Hall?"

"'Bout two or three hours."

"What's Mahogany Hall look like?"

"Never seen the outside. They's always take us in and out blind-folded. The inside mighty fine."

"What'd the inside look like?"

"Well, I ain't good at saying 'bout that sorta thing. Lotta fine wood and drapes and rugs. I could tell it were two stories."

"What happened in there?"

Pops hesitated before he spoke. "Sam, you ain't gonna tell any-body what I'm telling you, are you? I be a dead man if you do."

"Pops, no one who might hurt you will ever hear anything about this from me. I promise."

"Okay. The place had one real big room and a lotta small rooms. All coloreds goed to a room jus' fo' us. After they's took off our blind-folds, us colored guys put on fancy black robes with hoods and the—"

"You mean no one could see your faces?" Sam asked.

"That's right. The hood jus' had holes you could see outta."

"What happened next?"

"The colored girls goed to some other room and change into sexy clothes what showed off they's stuff. Then all us colored folks stand on one side of the big room. Somebody ring a bell," Pops said.

"Who rang the bell?" Sam asked.

"How the hell I know? The bell jus' ringed."

"Right. Just wondered," Sam said.

"You ain't gonna believe what happened next. Mens, white mens, in red robes and hoods come out into the big room and stood on the other side of us. You could see their white hands and their eyes starin' outta slits in they's hoods."

Sam asked, "How many white men were there?"

"Oh, I reckon 'bout twenty or thirty 'pendin' on the night."

"And then?"

"This here white man in a red robe with a gold stripe on it, he step out. He goed to this box in the middle of the room and pull out what look like a big dice. It musta had a number on it 'cause he'd call out somethin' like 'three.' Then a white man in jus' a red robe step out. I s'pose he were that number. He walk around looking at all the girls 'til he jus' point to one. Sometime he add, 'That one.' "

"Kinda like shopping for a good piece of meat, right Pops?"

"Yep. That's 'bout right. The white man then goed to one of them small rooms. He—"

"Did he go by himself?"

"I's trying to tell you. He goed by hisself," Pops said.

"Thanks. Sorry I interrupted."

"Well, after that white man goed from the big room, a colored guy in a black robe with a red stripe step out. I think it were Bongo Drum. Anyhow, he had a piece of paper and he look at it. Then he point at one of us colored guys and say somethin' like, 'Escort this girl to room 104.' So we take the girl the white man point at to the room."

"Did the escorts go in the room?"

Pops laughed. "Hell no. She not fo' us. She fo' that white man."

"Did you ever see the faces of any of the white men?"

"Nope. We was told to knock on the door and come right back to the big room 'cause we had to escort more girls. If'n the white man opened the door 'fore you left, he always have his robe and hood on. Sometime he jus' open the door so you can't see him. I guess he be behind the door. Any ways, I ain't never seen any of 'em."

"What happened after all the girls were escorted to the rooms?"

Pops sounded frustrated."The white mens and the girls git it on."

Sam laughed. "I know. But what did you guys do while all the fucking was going on?"

"We goed back to our room and jus' wait. Some white guys in green robes brings in food. Hell, I'd goed up there jus' fo' the food."

"You think the guys in green robes worked for the place?"

"Never think of it like that. But sounds right," Pops said.

"So you'd eat and wait for the girls. Then what?"

"Some girls come back pretty fast. Others gone a long time. They's clean up and change clothes and eat somethin'. When everybody ready, they's blindfold us and take us to town on the bus."

"To the warehouse?" Sam said.

"Yep. Right back where we's started."

"Were any of the girls mistreated or hurt seriously?"

"I see a few what been hit a little. But not too bad. One time I not there, I heared a girl was hurt somethin' awful. That's all I knows 'bout it," Pops said.

"How many colored guys usually came to escort the girls?"

"Three, maybe five or six come. We was called 'poontang pilots'. I reckon it depended on how many girls and white gentlemens they was that night."

"Pops, if I didn't know you so well, I'm not sure I'd ever believe this story."

"It ain't no story. It true."

"I believe you. Look, I know you're out of work. Maybe I can find something for you. Want me to check around?"

"I be much obliged. I ain't had no luck. I s'pect Marcus done put out some bad words on me."

"He probably has. I'll let you know if I find anything. I appreciate what you told me. I know it ain't easy. Like I said, nobody you gotta worry about gonna hear about this."

"Okay, Sam. I gotta trust you."

"Don't worry. You can. I gotta go."

"Lemme check the street." Pops went outside and looked up and down the street. He called back to Sam who was standing inside the door. "It's clear, Sam."

CHAPTER 36

RAMSEY'S GALA

FRIDAY—OCTOBER 24, 1947

J OE GOT DRESSED IN HIS FINEST SUIT FOR THIS EVENING with Birmingham's wealthy and social elite. He wondered how he would interact with such people. Then he remembered what his mother had said to him years ago when he insulted their Negro maid. "Joe, you apologize to Martha and always treat Negroes with the same respect and courtesy you do whites." He smiled. *Well, I guess I can treat this crowd the same way I did Martha after Mom set me straight.*

He got to Diane's apartment just after six o'clock. Joe's eyes almost popped out when he saw how stunning she looked. She was wearing a full length dark black gown. It had thin, vertical crimson stripes with a narrow crimson belt. The gown clung to her body, accentuating her lithe figure. The gown was sleeveless, low cut in the back and the front.

"Diane, you look gorgeous."

She wrapped a dark gray cashmere shawl around her shoulders. "You look very handsome tonight, Detective McGrath. And when you meet Mummy tonight, don't you dare tell her that this gown is a loaner from Maxine's."

Diane directed him to Ramsey's estate in Mountain Brook, Birmingham's upscale, residential community. She described some of the people he would meet including her parents and ex-husband.

"This will be as formal and overdone an affair as anything you've ever attended. Stanford claims to be a descendant of a Highland

Scottish chief and fancies himself a modern-day Scottish lord. Now I'm gonna get gossipy. I heard that his early descendants, who came to this country around 1820, were Lowland Scots. He ignores famous Lowland Scot warriors like William Wallace and Robert the Bruce in favor of the warrior myths of the Highlands. His wife's name is Dorothea. You can't miss them. They'll be dressed in their formal Scottish attire."

Joe smiled. "I'll have to work on my Scottish brogue."

"Don't even try, Joe. Your southern accent will betray you. After drinks and hors d'oeuvres, their butler, a stately colored man, will announce dinner. Their party planner arranges the seating. It's unlikely we'll be seated together. When those around you realize who you are, you'll be besieged with interest and questions."

"Kinda like I'm on trial?" Joe asked.

"Yep. Everyone's always on trial at Stanford's galas. He does them twice a year to show off his wealth and power and control. One of the more interesting games he plays is his version of musical chairs. People who have been invited to these galas for years, his inner circle, are assigned the same seats at the two big tables in the dining room. If a person has been excommunicated, their seat is left vacant for two galas to let the other minions know. Fun, huh?"

"I think we can rest assured my seat will be vacant at the next gala."

"No, you'll likely be located in one of the guest seats next to Dorothea as a special guest. Get ready. Like they say in New Orleans, 'Laissez les bons temps rouler.'"

Diane told him to turn onto a winding, slightly uphill road, festooned with torches and Scottish heraldry. At a gate, a guard checked their names against the guest list, welcomed them, and told them to drive to the mansion where a valet would park the car.

Joe smiled at Diane. "So far the service ain't too bad."

"You ain't seen nothing yet, Joe."

They rounded a sharp curve up a final steep hill as the mansion came into full view: a huge, dark gray structure, bathed in fog and floodlights, sat on the hilltop. The mansion, modeled after a Scottish baronial castle, was three stories high with a central tower above the main entrance. A faux portcullis, a steel lattice-like gate that raised and lowered like a guillotine, protected the front entrance. Turrets were on each corner of the castle, and the roof lines featured battlements and steep gables. The castle occupied almost an acre.

As the valet took Joe's car, he was surprised he felt overwhelmed by the mansion and the surroundings. "Where did the fog come from?"

"I understand they have some machines buried around the castle to create fake fog." Diane sensed his discomfort and took him by the hand and led him across a wooden bridge over a dry moat through the portcullis into an inner courtyard.

A white man in a Scottish kilt greeted them on his bagpipe, and a colored man dressed in a tuxedo directed them toward the second portcullis into the main house.

"Do they come and go this way every day?" Joe said.

Diane laughed. "No. There's another private road that goes to the rear of the castle. The family uses that. Don't worry, the back entrance is also pretty spectacular."

As they walked into the entry hall, another colored man in a tuxedo called out, "Miss Diane Lightfoot and Detective Joe McGrath." Just beyond stood Stanford and Dorothea Ramsey, waiting to receive their guests. Stanford wore a formal tartan kilt of the MacLeod clan. Dorothea was dressed in a full length wool dress in the same tartan pattern.

"Diane, welcome. It's been too long. How are you?" Stanford said.

"Hello, Stanford. I'm fine, thank you. You and Dorothea look marvelous. I'd like to introduce my friend, Joe McGrath."

"Detective McGrath, it's a pleasure to finally meet you. I continue to hear good things about your work from Chief Watson and others."

"Thank you, Mr. Ramsey. Mrs. Ramsey, your home is stunning. And I must add, for a simple boy like me, it's overwhelming."

Dorothea smiled at Joe. "Thank you and welcome, Detective McGrath. You look lovely, Diane. Is that dress from Maxine's?"

Diane said, "Yes, it's the latest fashion from New York." And she added even though she knew that Dorothea had her own personal couturier, "You should come in and see some of our new offerings from New York and Paris."

Dorothea sniffed the air in disdain. "Perhaps I will, darlin'."

Stanford broke the icy air. "Detective McGrath, we must talk later this evening."

"At your pleasure, Mr. Ramsey."

Diane discreetly took Joe by the elbow. As she led him toward the huge reception room, he marveled at the mansion's interior.

The granite floors were partially covered by Scottish carpets. The dark wood walls and high ceilings were decorated with paintings of famous Scots and Scottish scenes, and ancient implements of war. Suits of armor stood along the entry hallway. The reception room had a large fireplace burning brightly. Hung above the fireplace stood the MacLeod crest etched with the clan motto, "Hold Fast."

Joe followed Diane around the room as she introduced him to friends and acquaintances. She had to pull him away from each encounter because people couldn't stop asking Joe questions once they learned he was a police detective.

"Oh, there's Daddy and Mummy. Let's get this over with. I hope Mummy's civil," Diane said.

"Hello, Daddy and Mummy. Meet Joe McGrath."

"Hello, Joe, I'm Walter Lightfoot. This is my wife, Cynthia."

They were both polite and cordial until Cynthia said, "Well, Detective McGrath, I'm sure you find police work rather boring and below your station in life."

Before Joe could respond, Diane said to her parents, "We must get a drink. We've been talking nonstop since we arrived. We'll see you again soon." She led Joe to a bar in one corner of the room, and they each got a glass of champagne.

They stood to the side of the room, laughing about the social snobbery that abounded around them when someone tapped Diane on the shoulder.

"Diane darling, how are you?"

"Hello, Warren. I thought you might be here."

"You know I never miss anything that Stanford puts on. And who's your handsome friend?"

"Warren, this is Joe McGrath. Joe, this is Warren Abernathy, my ex-husband."

"Joe McGrath. Why do I know that name?"

"Hi, Warren. I'm a homicide detective with the Birmingham Police Department."

"Of course. I just read about you in the newspaper. Congratulations, Diane, you're going with a real hero," Warren said.

"Diane and I just met, Warren. We're just friends."

"As you wish, Detective. With your investigative skills, I'm sure that's accurate."

Diane interrupted, "Oh, there's someone over there I want you to meet. Excuse us, Warren."

As they turned away, Joe said, "Does he always talk with a partial British accent?"

Diane whispered in Joe's ear, "Yes. He's insufferable. Don't believe a thing he says. He's a pathological liar."

"Is this going to go on all night?" Joe asked.

"With this group, it's the national pastime: double entendres, snide comments, haughty looks. Welcome to my world."

A gong sounded and a colored man entered the room, He intoned in a deep, bass voice, "Ladies and gentlemen, dinner is served."

Joe estimated there were well over one hundred guests at the party, and he felt they were all watching his every move with Diane.

Dorothea Ramsey walked up and took Joe by the arm. "Detective McGrath, you'll be seated next to me for dinner. Let me show you to our chairs." She smiled at Diane. "Don't worry, dear. I won't hurt him."

The dining room was across the entry hall and was a mirror image of the reception room except that it contained two long dining tables, each of which accommodated sixty people.

Dorothea led Joe to the center chairs at the first table. "Detective McGrath, we'll sit here. Please take the chair to my left."

Dorothea remained standing as did everyone else in the room. A colored waiter stepped forward to assist her. She turned to the waiter. "Just a moment."

Looking around at those standing nearby on both sides of the table, she said, "Ladies and gentlemen, I'd like to introduce my table guest, Homicide Detective Joe McGrath with the Birmingham Police Department. He's Diane Lightfoot's escort tonight. I'm sure you join me in welcoming him with open arms."

Joe tilted his head in Dorothea's direction to recognize the kind introduction. She then introduced Joe to the individuals nearby, starting with the woman to his left. "Detective McGrath, let me introduce Penelope Griffin."

Joe nodded. "Good evening, Mrs. Griffin."

"And good evening to you, Detective McGrath. How exciting to have a homicide detective sitting next to me. I can't wait to hear about some of your murder cases."

"I'm afraid you may find the stories inappropriate for dinner conversation, Mrs. Griffin."

"We'll see."

As Dorothea continued with introductions, Joe noted that the chair opposite Mrs. Griffin was empty. *Well, it looks as if someone has been exiled to limbo.*

When Dorothea completed the introductions, she nodded to the waiter, and he helped her with her chair. After she sat down, all the others in the room sat.

The multi-course dinner proceeded as colored maids and waiters appeared. There were generous portions of everything including roast beef, salmon, scalloped potatoes, carrots and string beans, and the traditional haggis. The maids held the food trays while the waiters served each person. Food and wine flowed freely as did the table conversations. As Diane had predicted, the conversations centered on Joe. When asked to describe some of the murder cases he had worked on, he chose ones he hoped the audience would find less offensive. When asked about the most recent murders, he simply replied that Luke Matthew's trial would start in a few weeks.

At one point, Dorothea pressed him on Luke's arrest. "Detective, do you think the colored boy is the murderer?"

Joe was aware of the relationship between Stanford Ramsey and Chief Watson. He also suspected that he wasn't sitting next to Dorothea by accident. He thought she might be questioning him on Stanford's behalf. "District Attorney Roberts presented a compelling case to the Grand Jury, and they returned an indictment the same day. The trial and the jury will determine the final judgment."

"Rather an oblique answer to my question," Dorothea said.

"In my profession, Mrs. Ramsey, one learns to speak carefully. Legal provides the answers. I'm just a cop doing my job."

After dessert and coffee had been served, the piper came into the dining room and played, "The Skye Boat Song."

Stanford stood up when the piper finished. He said, "Ladies and gentlemen, I trust you enjoyed your dinner." After a rousing round of applause, Stanford continued, "Ladies, please follow Dorothea to her salon for after dinner drinks and conversation. Gentlemen, after the ladies have exited the dining room, please follow me to my study for brandy and cigars."

Dorothea rose slowly from her chair, thanked Joe for being a gracious guest, and turned to lead the women to her salon. Since Stanford was at the far table, Joe had to wait before he could follow Stanford's entourage to his study.

Penelope Griffin also waited while the other women formed behind Dorothea. "Detective McGrath, may I call you Joe?" she asked.

"Of course, Mrs. Griffin."

"Penelope, please, Joe. I certainly enjoyed your company."

"Thank you, Penelope. I enjoyed yours also. Tell me, why was the chair opposite you empty?"

Penelope sighed as if in mortal distress and spoke quietly. "Oh my, one of the cruel practices of Stanford's galas. If one of his business or social associates crosses him, the man and his wife are no longer invited to the galas, and their chairs remain empty for at least two galas until everyone is fully aware of their loss of status."

"Who occupied that chair?" Joe asked.

"Franklin Pierce. I really grieve for his wife, Caroline. These events were so important to her. I know she's devastated."

"It does seen rather draconian."

"Stanford can be very cruel, Joe. And in more ways than one."

"How so?"

Penelope looked around and lowered her voice. "I've said too much. I must catch up with the ladies."

She turned and joined the women. When the woman had left the dining room, Stanford led the men to his study.

CHAPTER 37

STANFORD'S OFFICE

FRIDAY—OCTOBER 24, 1947

J OE WAS STANDING TO THE SIDE IN THE STUDY, observing the other men. *Wonder if I'm looking at the murderer?*

A waiter offered him a brandy and cigar. He took the brandy, but declined the cigar when he saw Dick Oliver walking toward him. He was surprised to see Dick, but then he remembered that Dick was from a wealthy Birmingham family and this was his natural milieu.

"Well, Joe, welcome to Birmingham high society. What do you think of Stanford's little party?"

"Dick, I didn't see you earlier. This is splendid and way out of my social realm. I've never seen a mansion anything like this."

"Stanford likes to make a statement in everything he does. So it was Diane Lightfoot you were seeing last Friday night. Congratulations. She's a lovely lady, but considered something of a renegade."

"I find her interesting, Dick. We just met a little over a week ago."

"I'll bet you're getting bombarded with questions about your police work. People look down on us for what we do, but they love to hear all the gory details."

"Yes, at times I feel as if I'm on the witness stand."

"You are. The politics and backbiting in our office pales compared to this group. Everyone is trying to achieve a business or social advantage. They would love to get a good tidbit from you. It might serve one of them well."

Joe knew where Dick was going with his last comment. "Everyone wanted to talk about the two murdered prostitutes and Luke Matthew's arrest. I just repeated what was in the newspapers," Joe said.

"Good. Enjoy the rest of the evening, Joe. See you Monday."

Joe now realized that Dick was one of Stanford's sources. In fact, he thought that Dick might be his prime source, not Chief Watson.

Joe needed to go to the restroom. He asked one of the waiters where it was, and he directed him down the entry hall to a door marked Gentlemen's Lounge. Like everything in this mansion, it was huge. There was an outer sitting room with a colored attendant to assist any needs. Through another door was the restroom with twelve urinals separated by a wall from a row of six stalls. The restroom was empty when he entered. He needed to use a stall, and soon after he sat down, he heard someone else enter.

Two men stood at adjacent urinals, and Joe could hear them talking.

"You goin' to Mahogany Hall next Friday night?"

"You betcha. Wouldn't miss it. A good fuck and good food. Maybe some poker. What else does a guy need?"

The other man laughed. "I sure hope they bring up some of those gals from New Orleans again. Those babes are hot."

"Damn right. Wanna ride with me?"

"Sure. What time?"

Joe heard sounds of running water as the men washed up. "I'll pick you up about eight. Whatcha gonna tell your wife this time?"

"I'll tell her there's a big poker party at one of Stanford's—"

The door shut behind the men as they left. Joe waited in the stall for about five minutes before he left the restroom.

After Joe got back to the study, he took another brandy from a waiter's tray and stood surveying the scene when Stanford Ramsey came up to him. "Ah, there you are, Joe. I've been looking for you."

"Mr. Ramsey, I was in the restroom. Sir, the dinner was superb."

"Thank you. But in truth, all thanks go to Dorothea, the chef, and our fine staff. And Joe, please call me Stanford. Did you have a pleasant time with Dorothea at her table?"

"Very much so, Stanford. She's a delightful lady."

"I want to talk to you in my private office down the hall."

Joe followed Stanford to his office.

"Would you like a drink, Joe?"

"No thank you. I just finished a brandy."

"Please have a seat by the coffee table."

Stanford sat down and looked at Joe seriously. "I trust the conversations were interesting at your table."

"Yes, although I was surprised how much people wanted to talk about my police work and murder cases," Joe said.

"I'm not. These people try to act like police work is below their station in life, but their prurient curiosities always overcome them when they meet someone like you."

"I hope they don't think I'm an oddball."

Stanford laughed. "No, they don't. They just know you deal with things that are macabre and sexual." Then he abruptly considered Joe with a stern expression. "Like the recent murders of the two colored prostitutes, and the arrest of Luke Matthew. Did people ask you about that?"

Joe, now knowing that both Chief Watson and Dick Oliver were Stanford sources, realized he had to be straightforward with him. "Yes, many did including Mrs. Ramsey. I told them that the DA had presented a compelling case to the Grand Jury, which issued an indictment. I also said that Matthew's trial starts in a few weeks, and the jury will determine his guilt or innocence."

"Good. That was fine. But I understand you don't think Matthew is the murderer."

"That's correct."

"Why?"

"Both Chief Watson and Dick Oliver made it clear that Matthew was going to trial. They said they had a signed confession, and the DA was satisfied with it. I was told not to talk to anyone about the case including the DA and the press. And I haven't."

"I don't care what Watson and Oliver told you. I want to hear what you think," Stanford said.

Joe paused.

Stanford relaxed and smiled. "Joe, I admire your loyalty to your superiors. Don't worry, there will be no repercussions from our talk."

Joe doubted he could trust Stanford, but he knew it was best to tell him what he thought. He explained the interview with Matthew, the follow-up work that corroborated key elements of his story, and the tests of the semen samples.

"What about the confession? That seems pretty damning and incriminating."

"Stanford, it was beaten out of him. Brutally beaten."

Stanford rubbed his chin in thought. "Joe, this is a difficult situation. I'm sure you know that. We're always working through the police department and city hall to maintain the status quo in the colored community. In fact, I also talked to Marcus Gilbert today about the upcoming trial. You know him, don't you?"

"I know who he is. I've never met him."

"He agrees with me that the sooner we get this over with the better for both the city and colored community. Like me, he wants the races to live in harmony. I'm sure you understand."

"Yes, I understand the need for harmony. But at what price? An innocent colored boy will probably die in the electric chair."

"Joe, you know you could be wrong about Matthew. He did confess and he may be guilty."

"I know. I might be wrong." Having gone this far with Stanford, Joe decided to tell him everything. "There's some other things you should know. I think it's likely that another murder will take place on November fourteenth with the same MO."

"Why?" Stanford's tone was harsh.

"The first two murders took place on new moon dates. November fourteenth is the next new moon. Both bodies were arranged in shapes approximating Christian icons."

Stanford was taken aback, and there was an edge to his voice. "Why wasn't I told this earlier?"

Joe sighed, fully realizing that his police career may be coming to an end. "I was told to keep my mouth shut. I have no idea what the chief or Oliver chose to tell you."

Stanford stood up and stalked about the study talking to himself. "This could go one of three ways. The jury could find Matthew innocent. That is so unlikely we can discard it. The jury finds Matthew guilty and no additional murders take place. Tells me we've got the right guy. Or the next murder happens as you suggest." He finally turned to Joe and asked, "You agree, Joe?"

"Yes, unless the murderer decides to take a month or two off and then strikes again."

"A risk I'm willing to take. Here's what we're going to do. You continue, as you put it, to keep your mouth shut. I don't want to hear anything about you coming from other sources on this case. I'll talk to Watson and Oliver and make sure they don't withhold information from me. I don't like to be surprised. Makes me angry. And don't worry, I won't tell Watson or Oliver about our talk. Let me know if they start giving you a hard time in any regard. Can you go forward this way?"

The only risk you're taking is with Matthew's life. "Okay."

"One other thing, Joe. I hear you're still working with Sam Rucker."

So, Oliver told Stanford about Sam. "Yes, we're working on the case, very low key. Sam's a good man."

"I know. I met him once. Well-educated, well-spoken, but don't forget, Joe, he's colored. He cares only about his own people. He'll use you if need be."

"Do you object if I keep working with him? We haven't made any significant progress on the case, except for what I've told you tonight."

"No, but keep it low key." Stanford got his business card, and handed it to Joe. "Call if anything significant turns up. That's my direct number. We need to get back to the study. We'll have to join the ladies soon. You go first. I'll come shortly. I have a couple of things I need to do in here."

As Joe walked back to the study, he came to another realization as this night of surprises continued to unfold. *Stanford has reeled me in as another of his confidants and sources. I'm sure he sees it as a means of gathering information and maintaining control. Move cautiously, Joe. There are unknown pitfalls everywhere.*

Joe joined the other men in the study. Soon after Stanford returned, Warren Abernathy approached, "Well, Joe, I see you and Stanford have returned from your private meeting."

Joe smiled at Warren and then laughed. "Seems a guy can't even go to the restroom without someone watching him."

Warren stood eye-to-eye with Joe. He was a good looking guy, well-dressed. Fiftyish. Brown, graying hair.

"It's Stanford everybody is watching. You just happened to be his guy in tow for whatever reason. I remember what I read about you in the paper. You nailed the colored kid that killed the two whores. Good work. You nabbed two people lately—a murderer and my ex-wife," Warren said as he laughed at his tasteless joke.

Joe looked hard at Warren, but ignored the joke. "Diane is a delightful and gracious lady. I enjoy her company."

"I'm sure you do. I hope you two are happy. And, gumshoe, con-gratulations on the arrest. I'm glad you got that creep off the streets. See you around," Warren said.

Joe watched him stagger over to the bar. Warren had obviously been drinking too much, so Joe decided that most of what Warren said was liquor induced. He wondered what would transpire next when, as if on cue, Stanford announced it was time for the men to join the women in the reception room.

As Joe and all the men moved toward the reception room, the women were also moving up the entry hall, and the two groups merged. Diane caught up to him and took his arm.

CHAPTER 38

DIANE'S APARTMENT

FRIDAY—OCTOBER 24, 1947

"W̲ELL, MY DETECTIVE, HOW ARE YOU DOING?" Diane said.

Joe leaned over near her ear and whispered softly. "What an evening." He gave her hand a light squeeze. "I don't know where to start, so I do what I always do when overwhelmed and can't find words; I reach for Shakespeare. How about, 'Lord, what fools these mortals be!' Or, 'All the world's a stage, And all the men and women merely players.' Or, 'For nothing can seem foul to those that win.' Stop me, Diane, I'm running off at the mouth."

Diane looked at Joe in amazement. "My God, how do you pull all those up at a moment's notice."

"I'll tell you when it's less crowded."

In the reception room, a small orchestra was playing popular dance tunes. Diane pulled Joe over to a quieter corner.

"Now tell me about the Shakespearean quotes," Diane said.

"Okay, you asked. 'What fools' is from *A Midsummer Night's Dream*. Puck is referring to the young lovers confused by the night's events and trickery, so it's not directly applicable to tonight, but the words are perfect for this crowd. Actually, the phrase was first written by Seneca the Younger, a Roman philosopher, in his *Moral Letters to Lucilius* in the first century A.D. 'All the world's a stage' is from *As You Like It* when Jacques describes the seven ages of man. And 'For nothing can seem foul' is King Henry speaking in *Henry IV, Part One*.

Oh, I just thought of another good one: 'Here's a night pities neither wise men nor fools.' That's the Fool in *King Lear*."

"How the hell do you know all this on demand, Joe?"

He laughed. "I'm an idiot savant."

"Aw, c'mon."

"Okay, straight scoop. My mother teaches English lit at Alabama College in Montevallo. I took some of her courses on Shakespeare's plays when I was in high school. I majored in English lit at Alabama with an emphasis on Shakespeare, and I taught English lit for a few years in a Tuscaloosa high school. After a while, it sticks."

"I'll say, but how did you become a cop?"

"Simple. I took criminology as a minor at Alabama and completed the degree while teaching high school English in Tuscaloosa."

"My God, a 'man of crime' and a 'man of letters,'" she said in a slightly elevated voice. "What's next?"

Joe noticed that people standing nearby turned their heads and stared at them. The orchestra started playing a slow dance tune. "May I have this dance, Miss Lightfoot?"

"Why, Mr. McGrath, I thought you'd never ask."

They danced rigidly at first, getting used to being dance partners and being so close together. Slowly they melded together, and Joe was intoxicated by the smell and feel of this beautiful woman.

Near the end of the dance, Diane whispered, "I've had enough of this party. How about you?"

"More than enough."

"Let's go to my place and unwind. I'll fix some nice tea."

She looked around for Stanford and Dorothea, and saw them across the dance floor. She took Joe's hand, and they went to their hosts. "Dorothea and Stanford, Joe and I are going to take our leave. It was a wonderful evening as always. There's no doubt that you two are Birmingham's premier host and hostess. Thank you very much."

Dorothea gleamed with pride. "It was our pleasure. And Joe, you were a delightful table partner. Everyone loved your stories about your police work."

Stanford added, "Joe, don't forget to get in touch if anything important comes up."

"I will, Stanford. Thank you."

As they left the mansion, Diane asked, "What was that all about?"

"Tell you later."

Joe's car was waiting. "Well, they certainly time everything."

"The whole night's orchestrated, Joe."

Joe drove away from the mansion and looked briefly at Diane before explaining, "While all the men were in the study, Stanford approached me and said he wanted to talk to me in his office. He asked me questions about the conversations at Dorothea's table and the murders of the colored prostitutes. Everybody asked about the murders. He already knows that I think Luke Matthew, the kid going on trial for the murders, is not the killer. I'm sure either Chief Watson or Dick Oliver told him. I told Stanford that when people asked me about the murders, including Dorothea, I told them the jury would decide Matthew's guilt or innocence. He seemed satisfied and asked me to call him—no, he really instructed me to call him—if anything significant happened in the case."

Joe didn't tell Diane about Sam Rucker or what he heard about Mahogany Hall in the Gentlemen's Lounge.

"I think both Stanford and Dorothea enjoyed your company, Joe. She told me that you were a delightful addition to her table."

"I'm sure I was seated next to her so she could ask me about Matthew and listen to my conversations with others. I tried to be discrete."

"'The better part of Valor is Discretion.' Falstaff in *Henry IV, Part One*," Diane said.

Joe roared with laughter. "Touché and very apropos."

Diane, pleased with Joe's reaction, said, "Did you enjoy the party?"

"I enjoyed being with you. I felt I was on display, an object of curiosity. I even had another encounter with Warren. He seemed drunk and said several unnecessary things. I just shrugged it off."

Diane rolled her eyes. "Wise. Warren has a drinkin' problem. Always has. You can't trust him." She looked away.

Joe reached over and squeezed her hand. "It's okay. I've known a number of Warrens in my life."

They didn't speak for the remainder of the ride.

When Joe parked at the apartment, Diane turned to him. "Please come in. I'll fix a pot of tea."

Entering the apartment, she threw her wrap on the entry chair. "Take off your coat and tie and get comfortable. I'll make the tea."

Joe hung up his coat and tie and looked around the living room. It was tastefully decorated. Unsure of the style, he thought it might be French Provincial. All the colors matched perfectly, which didn't surprise him since he had seen how well Diane dressed.

Diane came in with the tea. "Aha, inspecting my humble environs."

"Not the words I would use."

"C'mon, sit down and have some tea."

Joe joined her on the sofa and reached for a cigarette.

"Joe, I wish you wouldn't smoke in my apartment. The smell hangs on everything."

"Okay." Joe was embarrassed. "I need a push to stop again. Waste of time and money."

"Thanks. Now Detective McGrath, I know you're well-educated. Tell me more about yourself."

"My childhood in Montevallo was fine until my father was murdered when I was thirteen. Dad was the only lawyer in town who handled cases for coloreds and whites. Many thought one of his clients did it, but the murderer was never found. Someday I'm going back and find the killer." Joe looked at Diane, fighting back his tears.

She took his hand. "I'm sorry, Joe."

Joe cleared his throat. "Thank you. . . . One more thing. I'm married. My wife, Mary, and I separated last February. I just started smoking again after she left me."

She didn't look surprised. "So I'm seein' a married man?"

"Technically, yes." Joe paused, finding it difficult to continue. "It's been a hard time for me. You're the first woman I've gone out with since we separated. I also have a ten-year-old daughter. Soon after we separated, they moved to Huntsville."

"What's your daughter's name?"

"Jane. I miss her more than I can tell you. With my work and the distance, I don't see her often." He stopped talking and looked away. He felt empty, thinking any chance of a friendship or relationship with Diane was now out of the question.

"I know how you feel, Joe. Although we've both had rocky marriages for different reasons, the hurt's the same. We didn't have a child, thank goodness. It would have made things more difficult." Diane sat up straight and looked forlorn. "I married Warren soon after I graduated from college. He was thirty-seven. I was smitten with this older, suave gentleman. My parents loved him, especially Mummy. He was Birmingham old money, or as old as any money gets in Birmingham. When I agreed to marry him, they thought it was a marriage made in heaven. It proved to be hell. It was fine for six months, then his drinkin' got worse. He started stayin' out all night. He never told me where he had been and wouldn't talk about it. He didn't hurt me physically, but it was emotional hell. When we did talk, it was a constant barrage of insults. I left him a year later. I don't regret it, but it still hurts. I've had a few flings but nothin' serious. You're the first man I've met who's even interested me."

"There's something else I need to tell you, Diane. This is hard for me. . . . I'm seeing a psychiatrist. Not because of work or anything like that. One reason Mary left me is that I have a problem with jealousy." He paused, unable to go on.

Diane took his hand. "That's okay, Joe. You don't have to talk about it."

He held her hand tightly. "I want to. That's why I'm seeing the psychiatrist. At times, jealousy consumes me. I hate what it does to me."

"Joe, that's the most honest and open thing a man ever told me about himself. I appreciate your telling me. Have you had those feelings about me since we met?"

Joe smiled weakly. "Not tonight. But maybe because we weren't together that much at the gala. I don't know; it's a strange thing. My doctor says my openness and willingness to deal with the problem is a good sign. I see him again next Thursday. We'll see."

Diane looked at Joe in a stern manner. "Well, Detective McGrath, I concur with my colleague's diagnosis. Take two aspirin. Eat a lot of chicken soup. I'm sure it'll pass." She relaxed and smiled. "And Joe, I like and trust you."

She moved closer to Joe and put her head on his shoulder. He put his arm around her. She turned to him and they kissed. In no time, the kisses became more intense. They lay back on the sofa. Her dress slid up her legs, and Joe started caressing her thighs.

Diane sat up abruptly, straightening her dress. "Oh, Joe, I want you to stay the night so badly. I just think it's too early. I know it is for me."

Joe remained on the sofa. "You're right. But I sure wish you weren't." He sat up and held both of her hands. "How about dinner tomorrow or Sunday night, or, hey, both nights?"

"Yes, I'd love to Sunday night. Tomorrow night, I'm committed to have dinner with Daddy and Mummy. My older brother will be there also. I'd invite you to come if I didn't think Mummy will be hurling lightning bolts at me about inviting a cop to Stanford's gala. If she only knew how badly Stanford wanted to talk to you alone." She feigned seriousness. "You won't be jealous, will you?"

Joe put his arms across his chest, acting outraged. "Of course, I will. But only of your parents for stealing you away from me. God, I love jousting with you. I never met a woman like you. You're a paradox, Diane Lightfoot. You reject your wealth and high society on the one hand, and on the other, you seem to embrace it."

"Guilty as charged, counselor. But who isn't? You can't run away from some things. I'm just a rich, spoiled girl at heart."

Joe wanted to carry her into the bedroom, but instead he stood up. "Okay rich girl, jealous guy is going home. Is six o'clock okay Sunday night?" She nodded. He gave her a gentle kiss and said good night.

As Joe entered his apartment, he pulled the pack of Camels out of his shirt pocket and threw them in the garbage can.

He sat down in his big chair, lost in thought. *What an evening and what a woman. McGrath, are you up to handling everything that happened tonight? Diane, Stanford, Warren, Mahogany Hall, Birmingham's high society, and quitting smoking. Gotta call Sam tomorrow morning.*

Sam was becoming Joe's go-to guy.

CHAPTER 39

SAM'S LAMENT

SATURDAY—OCTOBER 25, 1947

JOE ATE A QUICK BOWL OF CEREAL, drank a cup of coffee, then jumped into his Plymouth and headed for the office. He wanted to see if his latest expense report had been paid, as he needed to pay Sam. But mostly he wanted to talk to Sam. He had tossed and turned most of the night, alternating between pleasant thoughts about Diane, and concerns about Ramsey and Mahogany Hall.

The expense check was on his desk. He wrote a personal check to Sam for the same amount. At nine, he closed his office door and dialed Sam's home phone.

"Hello."

"Sam, it's Joe. Can you talk?"

"Yeah. What's up?"

Joe noted a lethargic tone in Sam's voice. "Incredible night at Stanford Ramsey's party. Can I come over? I heard a guy mention Mahogany Hall. I think we're onto somethin'."

"Sure, c'mon over. Park and enter the house like last time. I'll move my car. Don't worry, we'll be alone. Janice won't be comin' over." He paused again and then spoke in a more upbeat voice. "Hey, are you dressed like a detective?"

"No dammit, you've got me trained. Is anything wrong?" Joe said.

"I'll tell you about it later. You comin' now?"

"Yeah. I'll be there in a few minutes."

Sam was waiting and opened the back door for Joe. "So how was your evening with Birmingham's high society, Mr. Detective?"

"You won't believe it, Sam. Ramsey's house is a huge Scottish castle. Stone, turrets, fake fog, a moat, kilts, bagpipes, the whole bit."

"Yeah, I heard about it from a white Birmingham businessman who had me do a job for him in the colored community. Want some coffee before we get started? I got a pot on."

"Sure. Who was the white client?" Joe said.

"For your ears only. Franklin Pierce. He had a beef with a colored businessman. He wanted it taken care of quietly, and I got it done. I'll get the coffee. Have a seat in the dining room."

Franklin Pierce again. Another connection. He pulled out his notepad and wrote, "Talk to Pierce on the q.t."

Sam served the coffee and took a seat.

"Thanks. I just got paid for my expense report. Here's my check for your most recent invoice," Joe said.

"Good. I need this. So what'd you hear about Mahogany Hall?"

"I overheard two guys talking in the men's room. One guy said, 'You goin' to Mahogany Hall next Friday night?' His buddy replied, 'Wouldn't miss it. Good fuck, good food, good poker.'"

Sam's face lit up. He whistled in delight. "Well, we just might have to lift a glass to overheard conversations when this thing's all over. I got somethin' that ties this together even more." His facial expression went flat. "You sure nobody else was in there with you?"

Joe explained the layout of the restroom and how he waited after the two men left. "I never saw their faces."

Sam relaxed. "Good. I talked again to the guy who first mentioned Mahogany Hall to me. He's been there. When an evening's on, Black Bronco and Bongo Drum take a busload of blindfolded colored prostitutes and guys to the place. My guy thinks the place is about an hour south of downtown. The bus leaves from a warehouse owned by Gilbert on Morris Avenue, right where Morris and Sixteenth Street North form a tee intersection. I drove by there yesterday, and there was the warehouse. We can stake it out next Friday night and follow the bus. I found a good place to park for the stakeout. You game?"

Joe wasn't sure it was a good idea, but he couldn't back down from Sam's challenge. "Absolutely. But we gotta be careful. If we're seen, we're done working together. Sometimes you gotta wonder: Are we the suspects or is the killer?" Joe told Sam about his conversation with Ramsey in his private office. "He agreed to let me continue working with you low key. But he wants me to call him with any developments. Now I'm just another one of his sources like Oliver and Watson. I'm also sure it's a way to control me."

"You wanna back out?" Sam said.

Joe leaned back in his chair, hands interlocked behind his head. He gazed at the ceiling. In a low voice, he said, "This is getting fuckin' complicated." He paused, lowered his head, looked at Sam, and with his voice rising, said, "No, goddammit. I'm in. This is too good a lead. We gotta follow it up."

"Maybe Mahogany Hall has nothing to do with the killings."

"You don't really believe that, do you?"

Sam smiled. "No."

"I don't either," said Joe. "There's something else I gotta tell you. One of the guys in the restroom said, 'I hope they have some of those gals from New Orleans again. They're—' "

Sam leapt up. "What?"

"Apparently, someone brings New Orleans prostitutes to Mahogany Hall for their fun and games."

Sam slumped back down in his chair so far that he looked smaller. "Son of a bitch, I shoulda known better."

Joe was confused, and then he got it. "Is it that Yolanda lady?"

"Yeah."

"What's the problem?"

Sam unloaded the whole story. Once he got going, it seemed he wanted to get it off his chest. Most importantly, he told Joe about their meeting at the hotel and everything that happened.

"Joe, after she told me about what she heard about Mahogany Hall, we couldn't wait to get at each other. We fucked all night. I gotta tell you, it was great."

"Coulda been just a one-night stand, Sam. So you think she's the New Orleans supply source for the girls, right?"

"Christ, it makes sense. Marcus, Yolanda, Mahogany Hall, New Orleans prostitutes. Who else could it be?"

"Slow down, Sam. You're not focusing. It could be a lot of other people. Think about it. Have you heard anything from Marcus?"

"No," Sam said, but he looked confused.

In the span of a few minutes, Joe realized their roles had reversed. For the first time since they met, Sam had gone from his usual confident, in-control self to a brooding, unsure wreck.

"Sam, let's go over events carefully. You told me a few days ago that you met Yolanda at Marcus's office, the same day you asked him about Mahogany Hall. She piped up and said there was once a Mahogany Hall brothel in New Orleans. Marcus denied knowing about it. And then, while he was out of the room, she invited you to her hotel for a drink. Have I got that right?"

Sam sat straight in his chair, looking less distraught. "That's right."

"At the hotel, Yolanda told you what she overheard during Marcus's telephone conversation. And you two had sex." Joe paused and put on his best deadpan expression. "Sounds like it was pretty hot stuff. Right so far?"

Sam couldn't help laughing. "That's right on all counts, Detective."

"Okay, here's my take. When you went to Marcus's office, he had no idea you would ask about Mahogany Hall. How could he? Yolanda asked you to come to her hotel while Marcus was out of the room. When and why would Marcus have told her to invite you to the hotel? To tell you about the phone conversation and Mahogany Hall? It doesn't make sense. It sounds like Mahogany Hall is a cash cow for him. Hell, maybe he even owns it."

Sam thought about Joe's analyses for a few moments. "Yeah, could be. But maybe he sent her to fuck me and confuse me."

"If he did, she succeeded. But I don't buy it. You sure are whacked out by the thought of her supplying the New Orleans girls."

Sam turned grim again. "I'm emotionally involved. I like her. Christ, I may be in love with her."

"The perfect private eye has a weakness, women problems. Welcome to the club, Sam. It's not very exclusive. What about Janice?"

"I wanted to tell Janice. I couldn't get it out, so I lied. It's a mess, but I gotta go to New Orleans and get straight with Yolanda on this. I'll go nuts if I don't sort this out," Sam said.

"What if I'm wrong? She'll be on the phone to Marcus in a flash."

"Shit, if you're wrong, we're already cooked. I'll leave early in the morning. I can be there by around six."

"Okay, but I wanna do one thing. A guy I studied criminology with is a good friend. He's a New Orleans PD lieutenant. I'll call him and see if I can get a fix on her. Okay with you?" Joe said.

"Yeah. Don't use my name."

Joe didn't respond to Sam's comment. "What's her last name?"

"Chaisson."

"How do you spell it?" Joe asked.

"c - h - a - i - s - s - o - n."

"I gotta get back to my office. My friend's phone numbers are there. I'll call you whether I get him or not. You gonna be here?"

"Here or at my office."

"Hey, you seemed pretty glum when I got here. Even before I told you about the New Orleans girls. Something else wrong?" Joe said.

Sam looked distraught. "Janice knows something's not right. Women have a good sense for these kinda things. I'll have to deal with it soon. I been with her for years. I love her. How'd this happen?"

"It's tough. Sorry."

"Yeah, tough." Sam tried to smile. "Well, how's your love life?"

"Actually, it's looking up. My wife wants a divorce. She also wants to try and get an annulment from the church. We'll see how that goes." With a big grin on his face, Joe added, "I think I've got a new lady friend, Diane Lightfoot. She asked me to go to Ramsey's party. She's from a wealthy Birmingham family. They're Coca-Cola rich. We'll see. But there's definitely something going on between us."

Sam laughed sarcastically. "I can't match Coca-Cola. But I'll be glad when we're both on the same life path in the love department."

JOE GAVE THE LONG DISTANCE OPERATOR his friend's office phone number.

"New Orleans Police Department. Lieutenant Terry Crowe."

Joe faked a female voice with a heavy southern accent. "Oh, Mistah Po-liceman, you jus' gotta hep po' ol' me. Sum smooth fella tried to despoil my vir-gin-i-ty."

Terry knew immediately it was Joe. "You po' darlin'. I knows jus' who done it. It's a dastardly fella named Joe McGrath who preys on innocent, unsuspecting southern belles."

After they both stopped laughing, Terry said, "Goddamn, how are you, Joe?"

They caught up on their lives for a few minutes, and then Joe got to the point. "Terry, business. I need your help. Ever heard of a Yolanda Chaisson?"

"You bet I have. I know her. Yolanda runs one of the city's best interior design businesses. She's a solid citizen."

"She's not involved in prostitution?" Joe asked.

Terry sounded surprised. "Joe, the Chaissons are one of the more prominent Creole families in New Orleans. If she's involved in prostitution, it's the best kept secret in town. Hang on. A guy that works vice is here. Lemme ask him. Be right back."

Terry came back on the line. "Joe, I'll quote what he said after he stopped laughing. 'You gotta be fuckin' kidding me. If that lady is involved in prostitution, I'm a madam in a local whorehouse.' Forget it, Joe, you're barking up the wrong tree."

"Thanks, Terry. I didn't think there was anything to it. I can get back to serious business. One other thing. Please don't tell anyone about our conversation. It'd be real embarrassing if Yolanda should hear about it."

"Okay. And Joe, someday soon you gotta tell me why you called about Yolanda."

"I will. We'll talk soon."

JOE SAT BROODING ABOUT HIS CONVERSATION WITH TERRY. He had tried to be circumspect with his questions about Yolanda. What he hadn't expected was that Terry would know Yolanda so well. Clearly, Terry knew there were other motives for his call. *It seems obvious that Yolanda was not playing games with Sam. So who is Marcus's source for the New Orleans girls?*

He called Sam's home phone.

"Hello," Sam said.

"Just got off the phone with my New Orleans PD buddy. He knows Yolanda and says the Chaissons are a prominent New Orleans Creole family."

"So she's not the one providing Marcus the New Orleans girls?" Sam said, sounding relieved.

"Nope. My buddy also asked a guy in vice if she was involved in prostitution. He said absolutely not. Of course, the real question is, who is Marcus's contact in New Orleans?"

"Yeah. Thanks, Joe. I feel better but still gotta go see her."

"I figured you would. When will you be back?"

"Tuesday or Wednesday. I won't miss our stakeout Friday night."

"Good. Let's talk about how we're gonna approach it," Joe said.

"I've been thinking about it. I'll drive my car. I'll dress in a black coat and tie and hat like a chauffeur. You sit in the back like a wealthy white man. Nobody will pay much attention to us," Sam said.

"A stakeout in style. It'll work. What time and where do we meet?"

"Lets' meet on Park Place by the downtown library a little before six. It's usually quiet there by then. I'll park, and you walk along the sidewalk and find me. If it's clear, get in the back seat. If it's not, keep walking and double back and get in when it is clear. Bring something to eat and drink. "

"Okay, but let's talk after you get back. How do I get in touch with you while you're in New Orleans?" Joe said.

Sam read him Yolanda's phone numbers. "Call me. If I'm not there, leave a message. I'll call you back."

"Okay. Have a safe trip. I hope things work out."

"Thanks. Joe, I appreciate your understanding and help with Yolanda. I must sound crazy about the whole thing."

Joe chuckled. "Women troubles are one of our common denominators, Sam. Smooth sailing."

Sam got the long distance operator on the phone.

"Miss Yolanda Chaisson's residence. Frederick speaking."

"I'd like to speak to Miss Chaisson. This is Sam Rucker."

"Just a moment, sir."

"Sam, I'm so glad to hear from you. How are you?"

"Hi, Yolanda. I'm fine. I wanna come down to see you for a few days. Will that work?"

"Of course it will. I can't wait to see you."

"I'm gonna leave early in the morning. I should be there by five or six. Is that okay?" Sam said.

"I've been missing you." She giggled. "Get on down here."

"I've missed you too. You're always on my mind."

"Well, the sooner you get here, the sooner we'll solve that problem."

"Who answered the phone?" Sam said.

"Ain't you nosy. That was Frederick Russell. He's my butler. A wonderful man. You'll like him."

"If you like him, I know I will. I'll see you tomorrow."

"Can't wait, Sam."

CHAPTER 40

SAM ON THE ROAD

SUNDAY—OCTOBER 26, 1947

S AM LEFT BIRMINGHAM at seven o'clock Sunday morning for the 370-mile drive. It was a straight shot on U.S. 11 on a long southwest diagonal through west central Alabama's Black Belt region, into Mississippi's piney woods and down to the Pearl River swamps, across the five-mile-long Lake Pontchartrain Bridge, and into New Orleans.

When he got to Laurel, Mississippi, he needed gas. As he drove through town, he saw a Gulf gas station with a canopy. Since it was raining hard, he slowed down to take a look.

Sam saw a colored man just pulling away from a pump to leave the station. There were no other cars being serviced. He pulled up to a pump under the canopy.

A skinny white kid in a Gulf uniform ran out from the office gesturing wildly at Sam. "Hey, boy. You move yer ass to the pump out yonder," he said, pointing to a pump clear of the canopy. "This here pump for white folks."

Sam nodded, held up his hand in recognition, and drove his car to the pump. He got back under the canopy to get out of the rain.

When the kid saw him, he jumped. "Whoa. You sum big darkie. You ain't gonna be no trouble now?"

Sam played to the kid's fears and prejudices. "Oh, no suh. I jus' needs some gas, and I be on my way. Yes suh, no trouble."

The kid relaxed. "Okay, how much gas you want?"

"Fill 'er up, please."

"You gotta pay me first. That's the rules."

"I ain't never heard that rule," Sam said.

The kid bristled. "That's our rules. You give me five bucks. If'n it don't cost that much, you get the change."

"What if it cost more'n five dollars?"

"I stop pumping at five. You gotta give me another five."

Sam didn't like it, but he handed the kid five dollars. The kid started pumping gas. At five, he stopped pumping. Sam knew his tank was almost full. He was tempted to leave, but he handed the kid another five. Right after the kid started pumping again, another car drove into the station and parked by a pump under the canopy.

Two bulky white men in coveralls got out, looked at the kid pumping gas for Sam, and yelled, "Hey kid, git over here and pump us some gas. That big darkie can wait."

The kid moved immediately to the white men's pump. Sam got anxious; he smelled trouble coming. The two men walked over near Sam. "You from around here, darkie?"

"No suh. I's from Birmingham. I's on my way to New Orleans."

"Well, big city darkie, get your ass out of Laurel right now. We don't like no strangers, 'specilly ones like you."

Sam wanted to kick the shit out of the two men, but he said politely, "Yes suh, I be on my way right away. Uh, that station man owe me a few dollars in change."

"You ain't gonna tip that boy? What's the matter with you? Are we gonna have to teach you some manners?" Turning to his friend he said, "Bubba, go git that crow bar in my car."

Sam knew when to get moving. "Yes suh, you right. He can sure keep the change. I be on my way."

Sam quickly took the gas nozzle out of his tank and put it back on the pump. He jumped in his car and drove away as Bubba approached with the crow bar.

THE REMAINDER OF THE TRIP was uneventful. He arrived at Yolanda's home just before six. When he got out of his car, he stared at a house unlike anything he had ever seen.

Yolanda's home was a stunningly renovated New Orleans Creole townhouse, so bright and clean, one would be hard-pressed to guess its age. It had a brick exterior that had been painted with an off-white base and a random scattering of light red, which gave the appearance of age and elegance. The house had three stories with a steeply pitched roof featuring two dormer windows. The front of the house had a large double door extending from the street level to near the second floor. Two elegant, multi-paned windows sat on either side of the door and were rounded at the top. The second and third floors had high, narrow rectangular windows framed by shutters painted a dark green as was the other trim on the house. Both upper floors featured balconies facing the street decorated in lacy, wrought iron.

Sam knocked on the front door.

"I'll get it, Frederick," Yolanda called. She opened the door, saw it was Sam, and put her arms around him. "I'm so glad you're here. I thought it might be months before I saw you again."

He pushed her back enough to kiss her. Just the feel and taste made his heart race. "Hi, Yolanda. I'm sorry I'm late. Heavy rain in Mississippi slowed me down. God, this house is beautiful."

She took him by the hand and led him into her home. "First things first. I want you to meet two important people in my life." She called out, "Frederick. Pearl. Come meet Sam Rucker."

The two came into the hallway. Frederick was a short, stout man, maybe fifty years old with graying hair. He was dressed in a dark suit with a gray tie. He stood erect, his head held high, his shoulders back, projecting a regal bearing.

Pearl was even shorter than Frederick. Her hair was stark white. She had a round face to match her round body, and she smiled constantly. When she laughed, which was often, a wave of motion flowed up and down her round body in a joyful exclamation of life. She was dressed in a long, black dress and wore a white apron splattered with food stains and hand wipes. Sam thought they must not be Creole since their skin color was dark black.

"Pearl, this is Mr. Sam Rucker from Birmingham. Pearl is our cook, and lemme tell you, she's the best cook in New Orleans."

Pearl's face lit up. "Oh, Miss Yolanda, you knows that not true." Pearl turned to Sam. "Nice to meet you, Mr. Rucker. Welcome to New Orleans."

"Thank you, Pearl. Please call me Sam."

"And Sam. This is Frederick, my major domo. If you need anything or want to know anything about New Orleans, Frederick is your man," Yolanda said.

Sam offered his hand. "Hello, Frederick. It's a pleasure to meet you." The two men shook hands.

"Thank you, sir. If you don't mind, we'll call you Mister Sam. It's the New Orleans way."

"That's fine with me, Frederick."

Frederick looked at Sam with a quizzical eye. "Mister Sam, did you know a Reverend Angus Rucker in Birmingham?"

At first taken aback, Sam grinned. "Yes, I knew him well. He's my father. He died in 1934."

"My goodness, how about that. Your daddy came to New Orleans, oh, maybe twenty-five years ago, and preached at the St. James AME Church. I never heard such a sermon. I talked to him after the service. Your daddy was filled with the holy spirit," Frederick said.

"Yes, he was. Thank you for saying that."

Yolanda was beaming. "Sam, Pearl told me she's gonna cook a special New Orleans dinner in your honor. Let's go sit in the living room while they finish the preparation. And Frederick, please bring us a couple of Vieux Carre cocktails. Sam has to try a New Orleans drink."

Frederick brought the drinks to the living room and explained with precision, "Mister Sam, many famous drinks come from New Orleans bars and speakeasies, like the Sazerac, the Ramos Fizz, and the Absinthe Frappe. The Vieux Carre was created by a bartender in the Carousel Bar at the Hotel Monteleone in the thirties."

Sam tasted the drink. "Thanks, Frederick. It's delicious."

Frederick bowed and went back to the kitchen.

Yolanda moved next to Sam on the sofa and took his hand. "I hope you're not too tired after the long drive." Her voice sounded like a plea as she was more than ready for another night in Sam's arms.

He moved closer to her, anticipation written all over his face. "I'm a little weary. But as soon as I saw you, I felt invigorated."

With youthful abandon, Yolanda said, "I feel invigorated too. Sip your drink. I need to see how Pearl is doing."

During the drive, he had thought long and hard about how to approach Yolanda. He didn't want to insult or alienate her, but he had to find out if she was doing work for Marcus other than interior design. *Joe's right*, he thought. *If all she knows about Mahogany Hall is what she heard on that phone conversation, she can't be the one supplying Marcus with New Orleans women. I'll go slow and easy on her tonight.* His loins stirred at the thought. *Hell, Rucker. Admit it. The only thing you want to do tonight is go slow and easy with her in bed.*

His thoughts were broken when Yolanda came back into the room. "Sam, dinner is served."

As she led him into the dining room, he realized how elegantly decorated the house was. It was a tasteful mix of antique and modern furniture, fine art, and gorgeous light fixtures, all of which fit the Creole townhouse perfectly. It was clear why she was upset with the design choices she had to make to satisfy the Gilberts.

Frederick served the first course, a selection of fresh Gulf oysters on the half-shell.

Yolanda leaned over and whispered, "These'll make you stronger and bigger."

Sam's grinned devilishly. "If I get any stronger than I am right now, you better watch out, Yolanda." Out of the corner of his eye, he saw Frederick smiling as he left the dining room.

The rest of the meal included small servings of a number of New Orleans dishes including gumbo, jambalaya, crayfish étouffée, shrimp Creole, and for dessert, Creole bread pudding and coffee.

After dinner, they went back to the living room. Frederick came in and asked, "Would you like an after-dinner drink?"

Yolanda looked at Sam, and he shook his head. She said, "No thank you, Frederick. Please take Sam's bag up to the guest room. I suspect he's tired after his trip. And then you and Pearl go to bed. It's been a long day."

"Yes, ma'am. Good night."

Yolanda's eyes lifted playfully. "I don't know why I play that game. They both know we'll sleep together tonight. Shall we go upstairs?"

Sam looked like a mischievous rogue. "Yep. I think I'm ready for a good night's sleep."

Yolanda blushed. "I hope it's not too good."

He took her hand as they climbed the stairs. "We'll just have to see about that, won't we?"

As soon as Yolanda closed the bedroom door, the sexual gymnastics started and continued on and off throughout the night.

CHAPTER 41

FRANKLIN PIERCE

SUNDAY—OCTOBER 26, 1947

Sunday mornings were a bitch for Joe. In spite of his avowed agnosticism, he always had to struggle with his latent Catholicism. He seldom felt an urge to attend Mass or any other church services, yet lingering in the back of his mind was his youthful enthusiasm for Catholic rituals until after his father was murdered. The finality of his father's death, and the church's inability to provide him solace, started his inexorable drift from organized religion.

He wanted to get out of his apartment, so he drove downtown to the cops' diner. It was always open for breakfast. On his way, he stopped and purchased a *Birmingham News* Sunday paper.

It was Helen's day off, so no sexy repartee. He ordered two eggs over easy, bacon, grits, and white toast. When the food was served, he cut up the eggs and bacon, and mixed them with the grits. He ate with gusto, using his toast to sop up remaining egg and grits. Everything was washed down with generous gulps of orange juice and coffee.

While he ate, he read the newspaper, starting with the sports section. He was pleased to see that Alabama had beaten Georgia 17–7 on Georgia's home turf. Next he went to the society pages, where the Ramseys' party was described in glowing terms.

Returning to his usual Sunday reading habits, he went to the weekly report of police actions and arrests. He read though the list and saw nothing of particular interest to him. But it did remind him that he first learned of Franklin Pierce in an earlier Sunday paper. Joe pulled out his notepad and read what he already knew it said: "Talk to Pierce on the q.t."

Joe jammed the notepad back in his shirt pocket. *Dammit. I'm gonna call Pierce today. We gotta find some movement somewhere on these murders.* He paid the bill and drove to his office.

Joe found Brendan's file on Pierce's arrest in October. It included his home address and phone number.

What the hell. Maybe Pierce doesn't go to church. He picked up the phone and placed the call.

"Pierce residence."

"Good morning. I'd like to speak to Mr. Pierce."

"Who should I say is calling?" the voice asked in a haughty tone.

"Detective Joe McGrath with the Birmingham Police Department."

"This is Franklin Pierce, Detective McGrath. Good heavens, why are you calling me on a Sunday morning? Or more precisely, why are you calling me at all?"

"Good morning, Mr. Pierce. I apologize for calling at this time. I would like to meet with you today to ask you a few questions."

In a voice that was clearly annoyed, Pierce said, "And what would those questions be about, Detective?"

"Your name, along with Stanford Ramsey's, was mentioned in a recent investigation I've been conducting."

"Does this have anything to do with my ridiculous arrest by two of your overeager boys in October? I trust you know that it was a big mistake. The judge dismissed the charges immediately."

"No, sir. It is not about that incident. I know all the details, and you're right. Our boys were overeager and acted improperly." Trying to gain some trust with Pierce, Joe added, "I'm truly sorry you had to put up with the indignation of arrest."

"Well, thank you for that, Detective. What exactly do you want to talk to me about?"

Joe knew this was the dicey part. "As I said, your name was mentioned in a recent investigation. I'd like to ask you about that."

"Detective, are you implying that I may have committed a crime? Am I a suspect?"

"Absolutely not. I just want to discuss a few things with you."

"Completely out of the question, Detective. I see no reasons to meet with you."

Joe realized he had to take a different and more risky approach. "Mr. Pierce, I attended Stanford Ramsey's gala last night in his castle. I understand you have attended the galas on numerous occasions. I went as the escort of a regularly invited guest." He mentioned the empty chair and its meaning. "I asked the woman seated next to me whose chair it was. She said it was yours. Quite frankly, she was more concerned about your wife's reaction to this than yours. I'd like to understand the events that led to this."

Pierce paused a moment. "So do you want to talk to me as a detective or on behalf of the *Birmingham News* society pages?"

"The society pages are definitely out of my bailiwick. I want to talk to you in confidence about Ramsey. I know he controls the police department through Chief Watson and most other things in the city with an iron fist. It's the other things I'm interested in."

There was a sharp, angry edge to Pierce's voice. "Add brutal, malicious, and cruel to your list. Be at my home at one. I can talk for no more than an hour. Do you have my address?"

"Yes, sir." Joe read Pierce's Mountain Brook address to him.

"That's correct. If you ask me anything threatening or suggestive of criminal intent, I will terminate the talk and call my lawyer immediately. Understand?"

"Completely. I'll be there at one." Joe hung up. *He's angry at Ramsey. Hopefully, he'll be cooperative if he thinks he can strike back at Ramsey.*

JOE WENDED HIS WAY ALONG THE STREETS in Mountain Brook to Pierce's home. He always marveled at the houses. Set back from the street on one-acre lots were lovely houses, although none rivaled Ramsey's castle in size or pretentiousness. The architectural styles included English Tudor, French Provincial, American Colonial, and Southern Plantation.

He turned into Pierce's ungated driveway. It was a short drive up a slight rise. The lawns and gardens were immaculate, the house, an English Tudor, modest in size compared to others in the neighborhood.

Joe rang the doorbell.

A colored man in a black suit and tie answered the door. "May I help you?"

Joe recognized his voice as the man who answered his call. "I'm Detective Joe McGrath. I have a one o'clock appointment with Mr. Pierce."

"Ah, that's correct, Detective McGrath. Please follow me."

Joe followed the butler down a hall. *Well, snobbery is not limited to only Mountain Brook's whites.* Just past the dining room, the butler knocked on a door.

"Yes?"

"Detective McGrath is here to see you, Mr. Pierce."

The door opened. "Thank you, Paul. Come in, Detective McGrath."

Joe was welcomed by a man in his fifties, maybe six feet tall with rusty, graying hair. He had a lean physique. His complexion was shallow, a pale pallor, scattered with freckles. He appeared to have had few encounters with the sun. His narrow face seemed frozen in an eternal sneer, accentuated by thin, taut lips. His dress was casual: light tan gabardine slacks, a dark blue silk shirt, and penny loafers.

"So, we have before us the famous Detective McGrath," said Pierce.

Christ, this guy thinks he's something, using the royal We. Joe said evenly, "No, not famous at all. Just a hard-working cop."

"Jack Ritter disagrees with you. He calls you Birmingham's best detective. His column said that you were responsible for the arrest of the colored kid that killed the two prostitutes."

"Yes, sir. His trial starts in about two weeks."

"Good. I'm glad that is almost behind us. Well, Detective, it seems you have entered the upper echelons of Birmingham's society."

Joe laughed softly, having decided not to play the tough detective with Pierce, at least not initially, in hopes of gaining his confidence. "Not quite. I was completely out of my social circles last night. A young lady I met recently asked me to go to the Ramseys' gala as her escort."

"And who might that lady be?"

At this point in most interviews, Joe would have said, *I'll ask the questions, Mr. Pierce.* "Diane Lightfoot."

"I know Diane and her parents well. You keep seeing Diane and you'll become part of high society, like it or not. Although, Diane can be something of a troublemaker. Is she using you to make trouble?"

Joe was startled by the question. "We're just friends."

Sarcasm dripping from his thin lips, Pierce said, "That's nice." He added in a more civil tone, "How did the Ramseys treat you?"

"They were gracious hosts and treated me well. Why was your chair empty, Mr. Pierce?"

"Ay, there's the rub. Why indeed?"

Since Pierce used a famous Shakespearean quote, Joe seized the moment to bond with the man. "*Hamlet*, Act Three, Scene One. Maybe Touchstone, the jester in *As You Like It,* provides some insight into your misfortune. In Act Five, Scene Four, he says, 'an ill-favored thing, sir.'"

"A Shakespearean scholar, Detective? I certainly fancy myself one."

"I'm hardly a scholar. I have an English lit degree. So what do you think the 'ill-favored thing' was, Mr. Pierce?"

Pierce lips pulled even tighter. His voice rose in anger. "An 'ill-favored thing,' indeed. I'm speculating, you understand. I haven't talked to Stanford in almost two months. I suspect it was that god-damn arrest your enlightened cops put me through. Stanford likes to act as if he's free of sin, but woe be to he that wanders, even if it's not true." He slammed his fist on a table. "My poor wife is distraught. She loves our circle of friends, and now she feels like an outcast." His head drooped and his voice faded to a whisper. "Christ, that son of a bitch."

Joe sensed this was the time to push. "Have your ever heard of a place called Mahogany Hall?"

Pierce's head popped up, as if momentarily startled. "No. I've never heard of such a place. Why?"

"Someone mentioned it in passing during my murder investigation. I couldn't get a handle on it anywhere else. You'd be amazed at the things people tell cops to throw us off the trail," Joe said.

"I wouldn't know about that. Anything else?"

"No. Thanks for your cooperation, and rest assured, this conversation is confidential."

"Good," Pierce said.

Joe got up and walked toward the door.

"Detective McGrath," Pierce called out. "I assume you know that Stanford had a colored mistress."

Joe didn't try to suppress his surprise. "No. When was that?"

"She was a young, beautiful girl he met about ten years ago. He bought her a nice house in Ensley. It was the worst kept secret in town, but people kept their mouths shut. Five or six years ago, a business associate of his threatened to go public with the news. Blackmail I guess. Stanford sent the woman to New Orleans and set her up in business. One friend told me it was a brothel."

"Do you know the woman's name, Mr. Pierce?"

"Loretta Langtree." Pierce spelled Langtree and laughed. He was having fun with this. "I'm sure it wasn't her real name. I think Stanford gave it to her. A play off Lily Langtry, the English actress who had affairs with a number of English royals including the Prince of Wales."

"I know Lily Langtry's story. I'll say goodbye," Joe said.

"One other thing, Detective McGrath. Perhaps someday you can join me and a few friends for a round of what we call, 'Identify That Quote.' Each participant picks out five Shakespearean quotes and reads them aloud. You identify the quote on a piece of paper in five attributes: the play, the speaker, the act, the scene, and the line number. You score a point for each correct attribute, but a five is unusual. Highest total score wins."

"Sounds like fun, Mr. Pierce. Thanks for your help."

As if on cue, the butler appeared and showed Joe to the front door.

He drove back to Birmingham, his thoughts on the conversation. *He's lying about Mahogany Hall. Ramsey or whoever controls the place must have a tight grip on people like Pierce. Gotta call Sam in New Orleans tomorrow and tell him about Loretta Langtree. She might be the source of the girls.*

CHAPTER 42

PAOLO'S RISTORANTE

SUNDAY—OCTOBER 26, 1947

Paolo came to the table and placed the vase of roses in front of Diane. "Signorina Lightfoot, compliments of Signore McGrath."

Joe had brought her to Paolo's Ristorante, a small Italian restaurant in Homewood, a white, middle-class suburb of Birmingham nestled next to Mountain Brook. The owner, Paolo Pizzini, was a good friend, and Joe had prearranged for him to bring the bouquet to Diane. He felt like a teenager as he watched her bury her nose in the roses.

She giggled. "You silly boy. They smell wonderful. Thank you."

He took her hand. "I couldn't wait to see you again."

She squeezed his hand. "Me too. You look so handsome tonight."

Paolo returned with a plate of antipasti. "Detective, you know it's Sunday and we can't sell liquor." He winked at Joe. "But I have a special bottle of my best Chianti that I share with my friends. I'd like to offer you both a glass."

Joe smiled knowingly. "Paolo, that's kind of you. I accept as your dear friend."

Paolo returned with the bottle of Chianti and poured two glasses. "Let me make several main course suggestions. Tonight, I highly recommend our veal piccata, ossobuco, or risotto alla milanese."

Joe nodded to Diane. "I'd love the veal piccata," she said.

"I'll have the risotto, Paolo. And two salads please."

Paolo beamed at them. "Of course, insalate, veal piccata, and risotto for the two young lovers."

"He's delightful, Joe. How did you find this place?"

He turned on a stern face. "Cops' ABCs: arrest, bribery, coercion."

She poked him softly in the ribs. "Get serious. Tell me more about Mary and Jane. Where do you think it's going?"

Joe sat up straight and stared right through Diane. "Mary wants a divorce. At first, I hoped we could get back together, but now I know it's the right thing to do. She also wants an annulment so she could remarry in the church."

"Are you going to do it?"

Joe looked confused. "Do what?"

"Get a divorce and an annulment?"

"Oh. Yes. I'm going to start the divorce proceedings. Mary will take care of the annulment." Joe was surprised at his response since he hadn't made any moves toward getting a divorce.

"It sounds like the best solution," Diane said.

"Yeah. I just made up my mind as I was answering your question. You know why, don't you?"

"I think so, but tell me," she said.

"I'm crazy about you, Diane."

"If we weren't in a restaurant, I'd jump into your lap."

Joe leered with his arms spread open. "Be my guest."

"You big lug. I think I'm falling in love with you too." She laughed and lowered her voice. "No, I have fallen in love with you."

Paolo appeared with the salads. "Shall I come back?"

They both laughed. "No. We're hungry," Diane said.

Paolo smiled coyly at them and served the salads. "I can see that."

Joe looked around the small restaurant as they ate. Sunday nights were slow, and there was only one other couple seated across the room.

"At the Ramseys' party, Penelope Griffin told me that the empty chair at our table used to be occupied by Franking Pierce."

"That's right. At my table, his wife Caroline's chair was also empty."

"Ramsey plays hardball, doesn't he?"

"All the time."

They picked at the antipasti and salads, more interested in each other than the starters. Joe motioned to Paolo.

"I think we're ready for the main courses, Paolo."

"It'll be right out. Allow me to pour you more Chianti."

As they were eating their entrees, Joe said, "Did you know that Stanford had a colored mistress?"

She nodded. "There were rumors, but nobody talked about it. They didn't want to rile him. But hell, Joe, most of these guys were screwing anything they could, black or white. I'm sure Warren was."

"Stanford gets his cake and eats it too, huh?"

"He usually does. I heard he sent his mistress to New Orleans. And people say he prefers colored women for sex."

"Stanford's an interesting character," Joe said.

"Why are you so interested in him? Does it have anything to do with the recent murders."

"Probably not. I just keep my eyes and ears open to all possibilities."

"Can I help?"

Joe groaned inwardly, but said in jest, "Oh, my goodness. Besides a beautiful woman, I also have an aspiring detective on my hands."

"Be serious, Joe. I do want to help."

"Sorry. I know you do. Like me, just keep your eyes and ears open If you hear anything interesting, let me know. Okay?"

"Of course. I'll be a good girl, Detective McGrath."

Joe grinned. "Oh, please don't be too good."

She put on her best mischievous face. "Aye, aye, sir." She added, "I know. We can work together like Dick Powell and Myrna Loy."

Joe played along. "Right. I'm the hard-drinking, witty private eye. You're my wealthy socialite wife. Perfect. When do we start?"

"Tonight," Diane said.

"What do you have in mind, Mrs. Charles?"

"We'll talk about that later, Mr. Charles. Shall we finish our meal?"

"Excellent idea, darling. I'm sure Asta's awaiting us at home."

WHEN THEY ARRIVED BACK AT DIANE'S APARTMENT, Joe walked her to the door, kissed her, and said good night.

"Not so fast. Remember, we have to talk."

Joe helped her off with her coat and removed his sport coat. As they looked at each other, knowing what they wanted, Joe said, "Diane, I think we've known each other long enough, don't you?"

Diane couldn't contain her eagerness and blurted out, "Oh, yes."

She took him by the hand and led him into her bedroom. They struggled so fast to get their clothes off, they almost fell on each other.

Joe gasped. "Let's slow down. Here, let me," he said. He slowly unbuttoned, unhooked, and dropped each piece of her clothing to the floor. He looked at her naked body. "Oh, my God. You're exquisite. Now it's your turn."

Joe stood still as she reciprocated and undressed him. She stepped back. "You look like an Adonis."

Joe put his arms around her and pulled her close to his body. They kissed with abandon, their tongues intertwined, seeking the secret passages to ecstasy. He lifted her over his rock hard erection. They undulated to the rhythm of their thrusting tongues.

They separated, looked at the bed, and together threw the covers back. Both were so ready that Joe immediately entered her as soon as she opened her legs. He thrust with an urgency of a man possessed, afraid the moment might pass. Joe moved his lips between her nipples and mouth.

Joe lifted himself up so he could gaze at Diane's face as he kept thrusting. Her mouth was wide open and her eyes rolled back in pure pleasure. She was moaning softly when Joe arched his back and uttered an indistinguishable scream of primal release and emotional catharsis that he didn't know he was capable of.

He wrapped her in his arms, and rolled to the side, still coupled.

They muttered post-coital gibberish to each other for a few moments, and then Joe said, "I love you, Diane. Please, don't ever leave me."

She nibbled his ear and whispered, "Don't worry. I'm not letting you out of my sight."

Joe wrapped his arms around her, acutely aware of every breath she took, feeling a contentment he hadn't felt in months. Soon, they were sound asleep, wrapped together like one cocoon.

CHAPTER 43

NEW ORLEANS

MONDAY—OCTOBER 27, 1947

S AM WOKE AT EIGHT O'CLOCK. Yolanda was still asleep. He scooted over and wrapped her in his arms.

She nestled right up to him. "My, my. Who's this big man in bed with me this morning. Sir, did you take advantage of me last night?"

Sam nibbled her earlobe. "Yes, ma'am, I sure did. And it was mighty fine. Yolanda, I haven't had you off my mind since you left Birmingham. You've turned me upside down."

"I'm glad, 'cause I haven't stopped thinking about you. I've been a real good girl of late until you came along. Although at first, I thought it was just gonna be about having good sex."

"You been married or had any serious fellas?" Sam said.

"Haven't been married. Too busy for that. My last serious relationship ended two years ago. He ended it." She turned away, too embarrassed to look him in the eye.

"He must be an idiot," Sam said.

"No, I was the idiot." She turned back, still looking chagrined. "I knew better, but I got into a relationship with a white man. Nice guy, I thought. It took me a while to realize all he wanted was a Creole mistress. When I told him I was not happy with the arrangement, he walked away. Hardly said a word. Just as well. . . . How's your Janice?"

"She's fine." Sam shook his head nervously. "I'm not. It's a problem. She suspects something. I don't know what I'm gonna do about it."

Yolanda sat up straight in bed and stared hard at him. "Sam, I'm a patient woman, but I'm not gonna get strung along again. You gotta talk to Janice and decide what you want, her or me."

"I will when I get back to Birmingham." Sam took her two hands. "I don't want it to go on like this either."

"Good." Yolanda jumped out of bed and threw her arms up in glee. "Well, let's don't worry about all that right now. I wanna enjoy our time together. I need to go to my shop this morning and make sure a new employee is comfortable with our routines. I'm going to take a bath and get dressed. You can use the bathroom in the guest room." She pointed at a door on the opposite wall. "That door next to the chiffarobe opens to the guest room."

Joe got out of bed and laughed. "So the charade goes on?"

"Why not? It's fun. I know Pearl and Frederick get a kick out of it. I gotta hurry. If I'm gone when you get downstairs, ask Pearl to fix you some breakfast. Please come to my shop later this morning. I'd love to show it to you. Then we can have lunch somewhere nearby."

"Okay. I'd like that. How do I get to the shop?"

"Frederick will give you directions and an umbrella. It's only four blocks, but it's been raining some the last few days"

Sam picked up his clothes, opened the door to the guest room, and smiled. "Thanks for the evening. It was memorable."

She had left when Sam came downstairs and ate a light breakfast. He sat in the living room sipping coffee, reading the *Times-Picayune* newspaper when the phone rang.

Frederick answered the call in the hallway, and Sam heard him say, "Yes, he's here. I'll get him." He stuck his head inside the living room door. "Mister Sam, you have a long distance call from Birmingham."

Sam was surprised. "Oh, okay. Where do I take it?"

"Miss Yolanda's office is fine. It's private," Frederick said.

Frederick showed Sam into Yolanda's office. "I'll hang up the hall phone when you get on."

Sam picked up the receiver. "Hello, this is Sam Rucker." He heard a click as Frederick hung up the other phone.

The operator said, "I have a call for you from Joe McGrath in Birmingham. Go ahead, Mr. McGrath."

"Hey, Sam. Glad I got you. I learned something yesterday that you need to know. I'm gonna be short on detail because we're on a long distance line. I worry someone might be listening in. See if you can nose around and find out anything about a lady named Loretta Langtree. She may be providing the New Orleans product we heard about. Savvy?" Joe said.

"Yep. I get it. Spell that woman's name. I wanna be sure I have it right." Sam wrote the name as Joe spelled it.

"When are you coming back, Sam?"

"I was planning Wednesday, but now it may be Thursday. Don't worry. I'll be back for our Friday night party. Anything else?"

"Nope. Lemme know if you learn anything."

"Will do. See you Friday."

Sam leaned back in Yolanda's office chair thinking, *This changes everything. But I'll have to see how Yolanda reacts to Joe's news.* He got his coat and hat, and asked Frederick for an umbrella and directions to Yolanda's shop.

He enjoyed the walk through the heart of the French Quarter. The old homes, shops, bars, and restaurants were a distinct cry from Birmingham's architecture and ambience.

At the shop, Yolanda introduced him to her assistants, two attractive, younger Creole ladies, and then gave him a tour of the place. The antiques and other imports were displayed on the first floor. Most of the upstairs space was devoted to Yolanda's interior design work.

About an hour later, Yolanda said, "Let's go have some lunch. There's a nice cafe around the corner run by a sweet little Creole lady."

They both ordered a bowl of gumbo and iced tea. After they ate a few bites, Sam said, "I got an interesting call from Birmingham."

Yolanda raised her eyebrows. "Oh. Did Janice call?"

Sam couldn't help but smile. "No. But that would have been interesting. She doesn't know I'm in New Orleans. It was a guy I'm working with on the murders. He learned something Sunday that may have a bearing on the case."

"What?"

Sam knew this was the moment of truth about the case with Yolanda. First, he told her more about the murders: the strangulations, the bruised lips, the religious significance of the body positions, and the moon theory. Sam added that they had an additional confirmation on the existence of Mahogany Hall.

She listened quietly, her face a mask of stoicism.

"Stanford Ramsey had a mistress in Birmingham named Loretta Langtree. He had to send her to New Orleans over a blackmail issue," Sam said.

At the mention of Langtree, Yolanda looked surprised. "I know Loretta. Not well. But she's been in my shop a few times."

"Is she a madam? Does she run a brothel?"

"Yes and yes. It's a well-known, high-class brothel in the city. It's called Maison de Créole. She must pay off the cops 'cause they've been hard on prostitution lately. I told you about the group I work with helping prostitutes who get in a bad place on the streets or with their pimps. We've never had a girl come to us that worked for Loretta."

"Do you think she's sending girls to Birmingham for Marcus to use at Mahogany Hall?"

"Loretta's tied to Ramsey. Marcus is tied to Ramsey. Yeah, could be," Yolanda said.

"Do you know those two men control Birmingham? Ramsey the whites. Marcus the coloreds."

"Yes. That became obvious soon after I started working for Marcus," Yolanda said.

Sam had been tense, his lips taut since he brought up the subject of Langtree. He relaxed. "You sure you don't also run a private investigation business on the side?"

"Oh, yes. But it's a big secret. I'm the best PI in New Orleans."

"Miss PI, I need to see if I can verify that Langtree is working in cahoots with Marcus. Any ideas?"

"Well, you could go to her place tonight, play customer and see what you can learn." Yolanda frowned. "I don't really like that idea. Let's think of something else."

"I don't like that idea either. But for a different reason."

She slapped his arm. "You bad boy."

"Seriously, she might recognize me. I don't remember meeting her, but coulda happened. And if she smells anything fishy in what I say or do, she'll be on the phone to Marcus or Ramsey before I can get outta the place. Any other ideas?" Sam said.

They sat thinking for a few moments, then Yolanda said, "If you ever tell Pearl or anyone about this idea, I'll never speak to you again."

"Yolanda, you gotta know that in my business the first thing you learn is to keep your mouth shut. Everything's confidential. Now, I gotta ask you to do the same with this whole mess in Birmingham."

"Sam, I'm a big girl. I know when to keep quiet. Confidentially is important in my business too."

"Good. If anything I've told you got back to Ramsey or Marcus, I'd be cooked. Maybe literally." He took her hand. "I trust you. We can work together. So what's the new idea?"

"Frederick visits the brothels every now and then. Maybe he even goes to Langtree's. Anyway, we could ask him to go there tonight and see what he can learn. He's a smart guy. I know he'd be sympathetic to what you're trying to do. I'd trust him with my life."

"Maybe Langtree or some of her girls know he works for you. If things got out of hand, that could lead back to us."

She flipped her hand, dismissing his concern. "Won't happen. When I hired him twelve years ago, I told him that his personal life was his own, but not to tell anyone he worked for me. When I learned about his nighttime habit, I made it real clear to him not to mention me. I'm sure he hasn't."

"Hmmm. Might work. We'd have to tell him why we want him to do this. I understand you trust him. That's good, but the fewer people that know the better. Let's talk to Frederick. Can he do it tonight?"

"I have to go back to the shop for a couple of hours. I'll call him when we get there," Yolanda said.

Sam paid the bill. When they got back to the shop, Yolanda called Frederick and talked to him alone for a few minutes.

After the conversation, she said to Sam, "He's available tonight. I didn't tell him much. I told him I'd be home about four, and we'd talk some more. I need to do some work now. It's a nice day. No rain yet. You could walk around the Quarter or go back to my house."

"Yeah. I'll walk around a bit. I'll see you at four." He gave her a soft kiss and left.

CHAPTER 44

FREDERICK'S PLEASURE

MONDAY—OCTOBER 27, 1947

Yolanda joined Sam in the living room and asked Frederick to bring all three of them some hot tea.

"Thank you, Frederick. Please close the door and sit down. I don't want to bother Pearl with this."

Frederick did as instructed and sat down, his posture ramrod straight.

"Frederick, Sam is a private investigator. In the last two months, there were two murders of colored prostitutes in Birmingham. He thinks there'll be more if he can't find the killer soon. He needs your help to investigate something in New Orleans that may be connected to the murders. Sam will explain."

Sam described all the gory details of the murders. When he got to the possible New Orleans connection, he didn't hesitate and asked, "Frederick, do you know a Loretta Langtree?"

Frederick had not moved a muscle or as much as blinked an eye. "Yes, Mister Sam, I know Miss Loretta. She operates a brothel called the Maison de Créole. I take my pleasure there occasionally."

"I think she's supplying young ladies to a Birmingham gentleman who operates an exclusive brothel called Mahogany Hall. I don't know that she's doing it. I need to verify it. If she is, it may be related to the murders," Sam said.

"Do you think Miss Loretta is involved in the murders?"

"No. I'm sure it's just a business deal with her Birmingham friends. Did you know she came from Birmingham to New Orleans about five years ago?"

"Yes." Frederick's somber facade finally cracked. He looked around nervously, trying to settle back down. "Mister Sam, I've never been married or had a serious lady friend. But I have the same needs as all men. The young ladies at Miss Loretta's treat me just fine. I don't mistreat them. It makes me angry to hear about those murders. I work with Miss Yolanda to help young ladies in trouble."

Sam responded in a soft, comforting tone. "Frederick, I don't fault you for your desires. When I was a college student in Chicago, I went to a nice Miss Loretta-type place a few times." He could see out of the corner of his eye that Yolanda had a wry smirk and was shaking her head as if to say, *Men! They're all alike.* "I know you help Miss Yolanda in every way. But young ladies are being killed. I need your help. I gotta find the killer soon."

"What do you want me to do?" Frederick said.

"Go to Miss Loretta's place tonight and see if you can find out if she's sending women to Birmingham. You'll have to be discreet and indirect. You can't just ask, 'Does Miss Loretta ever send girls to Birmingham to work?' I'm sure it'd get back to her Birmingham friends and cause us a lot of trouble. I'll give you some money to help pay for the evening."

Frederick thought about how to get the information Sam wanted and decided there was only one way to proceed. "I'll do it. I don't need your money. I usually see the same woman there. I'll call and make a reservation to see her later tonight. I don't promise I can find anything out. I'll try my best."

"Thanks. I know you will."

Sam looked at Yolanda, hoping she would speak.

She took the cue. "Frederick, I don't want you to take any risk."

"Yes, ma'am. Don't worry. I won't get in trouble."

"Are you gonna wear that black suit tonight?" Sam said.

Frederick finally broke into a big grin. "No, Mister Sam. I'll wear something appropriate for the occasion. I'll probably go over there about nine for an hour or so."

"Thank you, Frederick. But you know, you don't have to do this," Yolanda said.

Frederick smiled, "I want to, Miss Yolanda. I get to have some pleasure and play detective."

Yolanda had planned to take Sam to a fine restaurant tonight, but in light of the day's events, she asked Pearl to fix them a light supper of salad and soup. She and Sam were sitting in the living room sipping coffee when Frederick walked past the living room to leave.

Yolanda called out to him, "Frederick, just a minute." She went into the hallway, and Sam could see her hand something to him. He was sure it was money.

For the first time since they met, they were less focused on each other and more focused on Frederick's visit to Maison de Créole.

FREDERICK RANG THE DOORBELL of Maison de Créole. Jerome, a stately colored man opened the door. "Ah, good evening, Mr. Russell. Come right in."

Frederick nodded at Jerome and entered the parlor. The room was a mix of dark red and purple. There were several sofas and a number of chairs in Victorian and French Provincial styles. Plush oriental carpets covered the entire floor. A well-stocked bar was in the corner.

Miss Loretta sat in a chair in the far corner of the room. She was surrounded by several of her young ladies, all dressed provocatively to entice the most timid of visitors.

When Frederick came into the parlor, Loretta looked delighted, he was one of her favorites. "Frederick, darling, so good to see you. It's been too long."

He took her hand and kissed it. "Yes, too long, Miss Loretta. You look beautiful as usual."

She was forty years old and many said she looked exactly like Lena Horne. "You're so sweet. Belle was excited to hear you were coming to see her. She misses you." Loretta looked over at the young lady near her. "Please go tell Belle that Frederick is here."

Belle came into the room, a thirty-something, attractive woman with darker skin than most of the ladies in the house. She ran up to him, hugged him, and squealed, "Oh, Freddie. I've missed you so." Then she pouted and said, "Why haven't you come to see me? I've been so lonely."

Frederick hated that nickname, but tolerated it from Belle because she was so special. "I've missed you too, Belle. Too much going' on. You look delightful."

"You want a drink?"

He looked longingly at her. "No thank you."

She took him by the hand. "C'mon. I've got a special room for us."

She led him to a large bedroom decorated much like the parlor aside from ample mirrors on all of the walls and the ceiling. They sat on the sofa talking for a short time. She led him into his routine that she now knew as well as he. His tastes were simple: a bit of adolescent-style petting and then he would let Belle take over. After they had petted for a while, he lay on his back on the bed and she mounted him. She purposely went slow, but Frederick came soon, as it had been a while since he had visited Belle or any other lady.

They washed up and sat on the sofa. Frederick thanked her profusely for her favors. Then, as always, they sat quietly and had an open and candid conversations.

Frederick started and said, "How have you been?"

Her usual radiant smile faded to despair. "I'm so tired. We've been busy lately and it's usually slow this time of year."

"Why don't you take some time off? Go on a trip. Visit your family."

"I had something planned starting Friday, but last week that damn Miss Loretta said I had to go on a business trip."

"Well, maybe you can relax on the trip and do some sightseeing."

She was clearly upset. "You don't understand. It's our usual business." She was real angry. "I'm just gonna be fuckin' some more white men in Birmingham. We're leaving on the Southern Railway Thursday morning."

Frederick tried to look calm, although he realized what Belle had just told him might put her life at risk. To hide his anxiety, he put his arm around her. She put her head on his shoulder. He could feel her anger subsiding. "Did you tell Miss Loretta you already had plans?"

"Yes, but she said I had to go 'cause the men in Birmingham asked for me. I've been there two times before. I guess I did a good job."

"Is Miss Loretta going with you?"

"No, she never goes. She has Jerome look after us. He's nice, but when we get to Birmingham, the other guys take over."

"I hope you get treated well in Birmingham."

"I wish. Freddie, they push us around. They blindfold us, drive us in a bus to some big house. White men in robes and masks choose a lady. Then they go at us all night long. If you get picked by the wrong guy, you can be treated real bad. It's an awful trip." Belle began to cry.

"That's okay, honey. You know I'm always here for you."

"I know. Freddie, don't tell Miss Loretta I told you about this. She'd be real mad. I don't know what she'd do to me."

"Don't worry, I won't say a thing to her. Here, take this. I know you can use it." He handed her a hundred dollars.

She kissed him with a renewed passion. "I don't know what I'd do without you."

They talked a while longer, then Frederick said good night to Belle and Miss Loretta.

SAM AND YOLANDA WERE PLAYING GIN RUMMY to pass the time when Frederick returned just before eleven.

Yolanda heard the front door open. "Frederick, we're in the living room. We can't wait to hear about your evening."

He entered the living room and waited.

Somewhat exasperated, Yolanda said, "Oh, sit down, Frederick. You don't have to wait to be asked."

"It's just my way, Miss Yolanda." He sat and said no more.

Yolanda blurted out, "Well, what happened?"

"Miss Loretta is the one sending ladies to Birmingham."

"Is that all?" Yolanda asked.

Frederick had a mischievous glint in his eyes. "You want to hear it all, Miss Yolanda?"

She blushed. "No, I didn't mean that. How did you find out?"

Frederick answered in a matter-of-fact voice. "After I had my pleasure, I sat and talked with my lady. We talk about whatever's on her mind. I asked her how she'd been doing. She said she'd been too busy and was real tired. I told her to take some time off and relax. She got real agitated and said something like, 'That damn Miss Loretta. She gonna send some of us to Birmingham.' "

Sam spoke up. "Did she say anything about what she and the other ladies did in Birmingham?"

"She said they were all blindfolded and rode on a bus to some big house. Then white men in robes and hoods would pick a girl and have at 'em all night long." He stared at Sam, his lips pursed in a grim expression. "Mister Sam, is my lady in danger? Do you think the killer is one of the white men in that Birmingham house?"

Sam thought carefully about his answer. "I don't know any of the men who will be in that house, and I don't know who the killer is. Your lady's not in danger. The two women killed were street prostitutes. Are you all right?"

Frederick sat back and took a deep breath. "Yes. But playing detective's not easy."

"Sometimes I wish I wasn't one. It's a tough business. When are the ladies leaving? Is Loretta going with them?" Sam said.

"Thursday morning on the Southern Railway. Miss Loretta's not going. Her man Jerome chaperones the ladies."

Sam couldn't help grinning. "Well, that's a polite name for the guy. Thanks a lot, Frederick. This is helpful information."

Frederick said simply, "Yes sir."

Yolanda added, "Frederick. I hope it wasn't too difficult."

"No, ma'am. I didn't have to ask any hard questions. My lady was upset and ready to talk. You have to promise me something, Mr. Sam. If anything gets out about what I just told you, my lady would be in big trouble. So would Miss Loretta and all the other ladies." Frederick shifted around nervously. "You're not gonna tell anyone or go after Miss Loretta and Maison de Créole, are you? I care about my lady a lot. I don't want to see her get hurt."

"I won't say anything about this to anyone except the guy who's working with me on the case. We're not interested in Loretta or Maison de Créole. We want to find the killer. What you've told us tonight just gives me another lead to work," Sam said.

Frederick nodded and got up slowly. "Thank you. I'm going to bed. Good night."

"Let's go to bed too, Sam. It has been a long day," Yolanda said.

They undressed quietly and separately, unlike last night's frenzied activities. They lay down in bed, deep in their separate thoughts.

"Where are you going with this, Sam?"

He stared at the ceiling. "I'm not sure, but now we know Loretta sends her ladies to Marcus. They're going to be used this Friday night.

We're gonna follow the bus to Mahogany Hall. We wanna get a good look at it."

"My God, Sam, this thing is really complicated and unsafe."

"And illegal. What Loretta's doing is a felony under a federal law called the Mann Act. And I mean beyond the issue of prostitution in New Orleans or Birmingham. It's a felony to transport a woman over state lines for the purpose of prostitution. Big fine, big prison sentence. Loretta probably thinks she can avoid a problem by not accompanying the ladies. But I think a good prosecutor could easily show that Jerome is working under her direction," Sam said.

"Are you gonna try to get her arrested?"

Sam turned his head, a startled look on his face. "Of course not. I didn't lie to Frederick. I want the killer, not Loretta."

"I'm just being protective of Frederick and Loretta."

"Yeah, I know. The whole situation is touchy," Sam said.

Yolanda looked slighted. "You mean us too, don't you?"

Sam pulled her close. "No, not you. I've fallen in love with you. You've helped me in ways I could never have imagined. But yes, it will be touchy with Janice."

She held on to him tightly as if afraid to let go.

Sam said, almost in a whisper, "I think I better drive back to Birmingham tomorrow. So much to do. The case, Mahogany Hall, Friday night, Janice—" His voice trailed off.

"I understand. Damn it, I'm in love with you too, Sam. When will you come back to New Orleans?"

"As soon as possible, but I can't promise with all that's going on. You got any trips planned to Birmingham?"

"No plans." She pulled back from him and smiled. "Maybe I'll dream something up."

"Come here, you." He pulled her close again and started caressing her. "I'll give you something to dream about."

They made slow, tender love for a while and then quickly fell asleep.

CHAPTER 45

BACK TO BIRMINGHAM

TUESDAY—OCTOBER 28, 1947

S AM WOKE EARLY TUESDAY MORNING, well before sunrise. He got
out of bed, trying not to wake Yolanda. He gathered his clothes,
and as he opened the door to the guest room, Yolanda stirred.

"Sam, you're not gonna leave without saying goodbye, are you?"

"Of course not. It's just five-thirty. I didn't want to bother you."

She sat up, kissed his cheek. "You get dressed. I'll go make some
breakfast and coffee."

"Thanks. I'll be down in a few minutes. Can I use your phone to
make a long distance call? I want to tell my guy in Birmingham about
Loretta. I'll pay you for it."

"Don't be silly. You can use the phone in my office. Who is this guy
in Birmingham you keep talking about?" Yolanda said.

"I don't want to sound evasive, but it's best you not know. The situation is pretty sensitive."

She nodded. "Okay. Get going."

Sam showered and shaved and was downstairs in fifteen minutes.

Yolanda was in her bathrobe and had eggs, bacon, and toast ready.
As they ate breakfast at the kitchen table, Pearl came in.

"I thought I heard somebody in my kitchen. Miss Yolanda, you
shoulda called me," Pearl said.

"It was so early. You know I cook a good breakfast. Sam has to get
an early start. He's driving back to Birmingham today."

"Mister Sam, why you leavin' us so soon? We just gettin' to know you. Don't you like my cookin'?" Pearl said.

Sam got up, put his arms around Pearl's plump body, and hugged her. "Pearl, I love your cookin'. I'll never forget the meal you cooked for us Sunday night."

"Oh shucks," she said, laughing in delight.

"Yolanda, I'm gonna go make my phone call. Is that all right?"

"Of course, Sam. I'll sit here and have coffee with Pearl."

Joe's sleepy voice answered the phone, "Joe McGrath here."

"This is the long distance operator. I have a call from New Orleans. Just a moment."

"Hey, Joe. Sounds like I woke you up."

"Yeah. What's up?"

"I wanna keep this short. I'm on my host's nickel. I'm leaving soon for Birmingham. I should be back late this afternoon. I'll call when I get there. But I want you to know that we confirmed last night that the person we suspected is supplying the goods. In fact, the goods will leave New Orleans on Thursday morning on the Southern Railway."

"Not surprised. Thanks for the update."

"Right. Goodbye."

Sam hung up and went back to the kitchen.

Frederick saw Sam first. "Good morning, Mister Sam. I hear you're leaving us."

"Good morning, Frederick. I'm afraid so, gotta get back to Birmingham. Lots to do."

"I hope we'll see you soon."

Sam glanced at Yolanda as he said, "Frederick, don't worry, you'll be seeing me soon. Excuse me, I gotta get my things upstairs."

Yolanda followed him upstairs. As he packed his small bag, she said, "Did you mean what you said to Frederick?"

"Yes. I wish I could say it'd be next week, but I just don't know. I don't know how, but we'll work things out."

"Can I have your home phone number?"

"Not yet. You have my office number. Use that. Until I get things sorted out with Janice, it's best you not call me at home." Sam knew she wouldn't like his answer.

And she proved him right. "I'm number two, huh?"

He took her face in his hands. "No. I love you." He kissed her, at first lightly and then more intensely. He stepped back. "I'll talk to Janice. I better get going."

After he was gone, Pearl said, "He one mighty fine man."

Yolanda smiled tenderly at Pearl.

Sam headed out of town on Highway 11. *God, what an amazing two days. Yolanda stole my heart. And Loretta Langtree sends her ladies to Birmingham for the fuck party.*

THE WEATHER WAS MUCH BETTER than it had been on his trip down to New Orleans. The drive back took almost two hours less, and he had no problems along the way. As before, he carefully observed all highway and local speed limits, and he purposely did not stop and pay his respects in Laurel, Mississippi.

Sam got home before four. He immediately called Joe at his office.

"Joe McGrath here."

"I'm back. Can you talk?"

"Yeah, let me close the door."

After Joe sat back down, he said, "The trip okay? Any problems?"

"Went all right except for some rednecks in Laurel. Usual shit a colored man has to put up with."

Joe shook his head. "How did you find out Langtree was the one?"

Sam told Joe about Frederick and how he had so adroitly gotten the information about Langtree without asking a revealing question. He added, "When this thing's all over, we gotta do something for him."

"Yes, and for Yolanda too. Good work. So I know you're happy Yolanda's not the source," Joe said.

"You bet. Joe, I'm crazy in love with the lady. I don't want to, but I gotta talk to Janice. Got any suggestions?"

Joe laughed so hard, he couldn't speak. Finally, he said, "Christ, you gotta be kidding. I'm the last guy you want advice from. You know how screwed up my marriage is."

Sam chuckled. "Yeah. We better stick to solving these murders. Women problem solvers we're not."

"Crime work it is, sleuth."

"Yep, our only skill. You gonna meet me at six Friday night at the library, right?" Sam said.

"I'll be there looking for my chauffeur," Joe said.

"Dress nice so you look like a right proper white man that deserves to be chauffeured around."

"Yes suh, boss."

"See you then, smart-aleck cracker."

Sam sat brooding over his next call. He couldn't come up with anything brilliant, so he just picked up the phone and called.

"Hello," Janice said.

"Hi, honey. I just got back from New Orleans. I was chasing a lead on those murders."

"Sam, you sure that's all you were chasing? I'm coming over right now. We have to talk."

"Good. I wanna see you. What's the problem?" Sam knew immediately he had said the wrong thing.

In a harsh, abrupt voice, she said, "I think you know. I'll be there in a few minutes."

He asked lamely, "You want me to fix something to eat?"

Even more stridently, she said, "No."

Ten minutes later, Janice walked in the house and sat on the sofa. She said nothing.

Sam fidgeted like a schoolboy. "You want a drink?"

"No. Sam, what's going on?"

"I had to go to New Orleans on business related to the murder cases Joe and I are working on."

Janice rolled her eyes in exasperation. "You know that's not what I'm talking about."

Sam slumped down in a chair opposite the sofa. "I've met someone." He couldn't bear to look at her, his head almost on his chest.

"Is that the lady you were with at the New Home Hotel?"

Surprised, Sam's head popped back up. "Who told you that?"

"You fool, you didn't even notice her. Thelma from our church. You know her, right?"

He nodded.

"She was there last Wednesday night with her husband to have dinner. She saw you walk out of the restaurant with a beautiful lady on your arm and go to the elevator. She was almost right in front of you, but you didn't notice her because your eyes were all over the lady."

Joe stammered, "Honey, I don't—"

"Sam, don't call me honey. Who was that lady?"

He was distraught. It wasn't shame. He felt like a cornered animal with no way to turn. He blurted out, "Her name's Yolanda Chaisson. She's an interior designer from New Orleans and does work for Marcus Gilbert. I met her in his office. I don't know how these things happen. They just do, I guess."

The toughness Janice had displayed since she arrived started to crumble. Her voice cracked. "Did you sleep with her?"

Sam looked down again. "Yes. . . . I really did have business in New Orleans, but I stayed with her. I'm sorry, Janice. I love you. I know that sounds crazy, but I still do. Damn, I'm confused but things have changed."

Tears welled up in her eyes. "How can you say you still love me? What did I do to deserve this?"

"Nothing. That's just it. You did nothing. That's what so crazy."

Crying hard now, Janice spoke in a sobbing whisper. "So after all these years of promises and let's wait a while, it's just all over."

Sam said nothing.

As Janice headed for the door, she said, "I'll come over in the morning to get my things. Will you be here?" She added in a brittle tone, "You better tell your mother. I'm not gonna lie if she asks me."

Sam didn't move. He sat staring at the floor.

CHAPTER 46

JOE'S REVELATION

THURSDAY—OCTOBER 30, 1947

Today Joe wanted to talk to Brendan about other cases they were investigating before his appointment with Dr. Theroux at two. They were reviewing witness notes when Dick Oliver came in.

"Mornin', gents. Joe, the chief wants us right now," Oliver said.

"Are we in hot water?" Joe said.

"Don't know. Guess we'll find out."

The chief glowered at Joe. "Well, so you done moved up the social ladder. How you doin', Mr. High Society?"

Joe glanced at Dick who looked straight ahead. "I haven't moved anywhere, Chief."

"That ain't what I been hearin'. Now you're rubbin' elbows with Stanford Ramsey and the other bigwigs."

Joe felt his shirt collar tighten as his anger bubbled up. "I was invited to Ramsey's party by a lady friend. I was there as her guest. I doubt I'll ever be invited again. I felt like a fish out of water." He couldn't resist dragging Dick into this discussion. "Dick was there too. He saw how uncomfortable I was."

Dick didn't move. He said nothing.

The chief continued, "Dick ain't got nuthin' to do with this. Why'd you disobey my orders?"

Joe's face was burning. "What're you talking about?"

Watson shouted, "You talked to Stanford Ramsey, didn't you?"

"Of course. You shoulda been there, Chief."

Watson exploded. "Goddammit it, I wasn't invited." In a quieter voice, Watson asked, "Did he ask you 'bout the murder of them two whores?"

"Yes," Joe said.

"What didya tell him?"

"I answered his questions. I didn't tell him anything you don't already know."

Watson's voice rose again. "Oh fuck, stop it. What didya tell him?"

Joe suddenly felt completely at ease, and said in a matter-of-fact voice, "You better ask Mr. Ramsey that question, Chief."

"You're skating on thin ice, McGrath."

"I've never ice skated, Chief."

"Get outta here! Stay put, Dick."

AFTER JOE LEFT THE OFFICE, Watson turned on Dick. "I thought you could control him."

"I didn't invite him to Ramsey's," Dick said.

Watson's eyes narrowed and he stared intently at Dick. "Christ, I know you're Stanford's boy. Hell, the only reason you're here is 'cause he wants you on the force. You his watchdog?"

Dick looked hard back at Watson. "Be that as it may, I wouldn't do anything rash about McGrath. Ramsey took him to his office during the party. I don't know what they talked about, but Ramsey didn't looked displeased afterwards." He added with a sneer, "The watchdog had his eyes open."

Watson's face turned grim. "Ramsey called me t'other day and reamed my asshole out. He knowed things 'bout Matthew I didn't tell him. Unless you told him, it musta been McGrath."

"Whoever told him, Chief, move carefully. If Ramsey's taken a liking to McGrath, you don't want to get in the middle."

Watson took a deep breath. "Is McGrath still working with that darkie Rucker?"

"Yeah, but only on the side. I don't think they've had much luck on the case."

The chief waved at Dick to leave. "Okay, I'll take care of this."

As soon as Dick closed the door, Watson dialed the phone.

When someone answered, Watson said, "Meet me at Dolly's at seven. I got sumthin' I want you to do." He hung up.

Dolly's was a bar frequented by the Klan.

JOE HAD BEEN SITTING IN DR. THEROUX's waiting room for ten minutes, when he came out of his office and invited Joe in.

After exchanging pleasantries, Theroux asked Joe if he preferred to sit in a chair or lie on the sofa. Joe chose the sofa. Theroux led Joe through a brief review of his notes from their first meeting.

When Theroux was finished with the review, he said, "Joe, I'd like to go back to the period in your life right after your father was brutally murdered."

Joe's body tensed up at the mention of his father's murder.

"Tell me more about that period: your feelings, your thoughts, your interaction with your mother and uncle, and anything else that comes to mind," Theroux said.

Joe talked for fifteen minutes about his initial denial, then anger, and the tough time in school with his studies. He told Theroux that his mother and uncle, who had become something of a father figure for him, helped him through the first couple of difficult years. He said that his mother had used Shakespeare as a therapy tool, which led to his continued studies and love of the Bard's canon. He added that his uncle had helped by letting him become involved in the investigation, which led to his interest in police work.

When Joe stopped talking, Theroux asked, "How do you feel about your father's murder today? Does it haunt you?"

"Maybe. . . . Yes, it does. I know the murder trail is old. But someday soon, I'm going back to Montevallo to find his murderers."

Theroux wrote some notes. "I wish you well with your efforts. I hope you have some success so you can exorcise those demons from your mind. Joe, how was your relationship with your mother up to the time you left home for college?"

Joe didn't say anything for several minutes. "I never told anyone this. It embarrasses me."

"Joe, it's all right. There are no secrets or anything too embarrassing to discuss here. It's all confidential."

Joe fidgeted about and then seemed to relax. "A few months after Dad was killed, I turned fourteen. I couldn't go to sleep. I was crying pretty hard. Mom heard me. She came into my bedroom and sat on the bed. She rubbed my head and said everything was going to be okay, that I'd be fine. I continued crying. I was laying with my back to her when she pulled the sheet aside and lay down. She wrapped her arm around me and cuddled up to me and continued to rub my head. She had, and still does, a good figure. She was in her sleeping gown. I felt her whole body against mine, her breasts against my back. I stopped crying, focusing on the feel of her body."

Joe paused and took a deep breath. "I . . . I got an erection. She held me tight, stroking my hair. I had an orgasm. I felt the spurts filling my pajama bottoms. My whole body shuddered with each spurt. Mom knew immediately what had happened. I'll never forget what she said. 'Joe, that's all right. Boys do that all the time. Now go to sleep.' She sat back up and rubbed my head some more. I got drowsy and fell asleep."

Theroux made more notes. "Did you and your mother ever talk about that night? Did it happen again?"

Joe was abrupt. "No to both questions. I was too embarrassed. Maybe Mom was too."

"After that night, what did you think about it?"

"Not much. Life went on. . . . No, that's not true. I couldn't get it out of my mind. Many nights I lay in bed making noise in hopes that Mom would come in again. She never did. Well, not quite true. She did come in a couple of times and ask if I was all right. She'd just stand by the bed. She never even sat down."

"Did your mother start seeing other men?"

"Do you mean dating them and stuff?" Joe asked.

"Yes."

"A year or two after Dad was killed, she started seeing one of the philosophy professors at the college. They'd go to plays and concerts. Sometimes they'd take me. They also went out to dinner a lot."

"Were they serious?"

"I'm not sure. They didn't get married. Mom saw a few other men. But she never married."

"Do you know if she ever slept with one of the men?"

"How would I know that? I didn't sneak around the house at night." Joe sighed, "I guess she could have. I don't know."

"How did you feel toward the men in her life?"

Joe hesitated and then said in an angry voice, "I hated them. I . . . I . . ." He started weeping like the boy twenty-four years ago. "I was jealous of the men. I was also mad at Mom. I thought I was losing her I thought I would lose her and be alone. I—"

Joe cried softly.

Theroux let Joe weep until he calmed down. Then he said, "Joe, do you realize what you just said. While there may have been other events earlier and later in your life that added to what you call your 'irrational jealousy,' I suspect the root of your jealousy grew out of that night with your mother and your subsequent reactions to the men she dated. Can you see that?"

Joe swung his legs off the sofa, sat up, and faced Theroux. "Yeah, I guess. So I wanted my mother."

"Most boys want their mothers, Joe, including me. It's not unusual to want your mother, both as a nurturing mother and as a sexual object. What you feared most and continue to fear is being left alone, abandoned. It started with your father's murder and continued to your mother and now to your wife."

Joe was perplexed. This was difficult stuff to comprehend and accept. "I'll have to think a lot about this. I'm a little insecure. I also feel stupid. Why couldn't I see these things?"

"Because you're living them, Joe. When we're not involved in a situation, we see things more clearly. But put us in the middle of a personal crisis, and our ability to see clearly gets clouded by emotion and insecurity. Sorry, our time's almost up. Think about today's discussion. It's been useful. We can talk some more next week."

Joe stood up and stretched. "Yes, I will. Thank you."

He drove back to headquarters, his mind roiling with thoughts about the past hour. *It can't be that simple. Shit, maybe it is. Theroux is right. That night with Mom, her boyfriends. I was as jealous as hell of them. And I missed what happened that night. I wanted more. Christ, you're fucked up, McGrath.*

CHAPTER 47

MAHOGANY HALL

FRIDAY—OCTOBER 31, 1947

S AM PICKED UP JOE AT THE LIBRARY FRIDAY NIGHT. At six twenty, Sam parked in the alleyway across from Gilbert's warehouse. The parking spot provided unobstructed sight lines to the one door large enough for a bus to use. It was a clear night with ample moonlight, as it was two days past the full moon. The parking spot was in the dark shadows of the two buildings, and no direct streetlights or moonbeams shined on them.

Sam sat in the front driver's seat, dressed as a chauffeur in a black suit and tie, complete with a chauffeur's black hat. Joe wore his oldest, somewhat worn, black suit and gray hat, but looked presentable enough from a distance. He sat in the rear on the passenger's side.

Both Sam and Joe had tailed vehicles many times. They knew that tailing a vehicle in a criminal investigation was more an art than a science with many variables: time of day, weather, road traffic, ambient light, speed, and traffic lights

As they sat hunched down in the car, their eyes fixed on the warehouse, they discussed how to follow the bus and what to do when the bus neared its destination. Since a large bus could be tailed easier than a smaller automobile, they decided city traffic lights would be less of a problem, although they agreed it best not to get separated by a light if possible. On the more open roads, Sam would stay close enough to maintain eye contact with the bus's taillights. They agreed to play it by ear once the bus turned off the main highway.

As they observed the warehouse, Sam spoke in a quiet voice. "I gotta get somethin' off my chest. After I got back from New Orleans, Janice came over to my house. She knew something was going on."

"Yeah. How'd it go?" Joe said.

"Not well. A friend of Janice's saw Yolanda and me at the New Home Hotel. I told Janice about Yolanda and my feelings for her. Janice started crying and couldn't understand how this could happen after we'd been together so long. I don't understand either, but am incapable of doing anything else. She's hurt. I'm hurt too. I know I'm in the wrong here. But goddamn, Joe, what else could I do?"

Joe listened carefully, kept his eyes on the warehouse, and said nothing.

When it was obvious Joe was not going to answer, Sam said, "I had to call my mother and sisters. That was almost the hardest part. They all know Janice well and think she's perfect for me, especially Mom. She was real upset. She got so mad, she said, 'Your Daddy was right when he told you years ago you weren't welcome at home.' She hung up. She did call back later to say she didn't mean it. But she added that I need to think long and hard about my life. Dammit it, Joe. Why is family and love so much more difficult than working a case?"

"Don't know. But it is. You gotta get—"

A car stopped by a door entrance to the warehouse. Black Bronco got out with five young colored ladies. Two men who appeared to be guards came out of the warehouse. The guards directed them into the warehouse. A few minutes later another car pulled up. The guards assisted Bongo Drum and five more women. Two more carloads came, five women in one and three in the other. Unless some women came before Sam and Joe started their stakeout, it appeared eighteen women would be on the bus. It was almost seven o'clock.

Sam said, "That's probably the New Orleans women. Frederick said that Loretta usually sent about twenty."

Ten minutes later, four more cars arrived: three with fifteen more women and one with six colored men.

"I recognize some of those ladies and a few of the guys. All Birmingham folks. The ladies work the streets. The guys are pimps. Most of 'em work for Black Bronco and Bongo Drum. That makes thirty-three women. The guys are probably poontang pilots. At Mahogany Hall, they escort a woman to the room of the white guy who picked them," Sam said.

"Goddamn. This is coming together just like you heard from your Birmingham informant and in New Orleans."

"Yep," Sam said. He added in a harsh tone, "He's not an informant, Joe. He's a guy caught in the middle."

Just before eight, the warehouse's big, roll-up door opened. The two guards came out and looked up and down the street. When they were sure it was clear, they signaled the bus to pull out. The bus turned right and headed east on Morris Avenue. The only windows not tinted black or covered with dark drapes were the driver's windshield and the small windows to the driver's left and right. There was no rear window.

"It's gonna be easier to tail," Sam said.

When the two guards went back into the warehouse, Sam waited until he was sure it was all clear. Then he started the car, pulled out slowly, and didn't turn on the car's headlights until he had turned left onto Morris Avenue and driven half a block. Stop signs at Seventeenth and Eighteenth were easy to handle. As the bus pulled away from a stop sign, Sam would speed up, stop, and proceed more slowly to maintain space. A traffic light at Nineteenth stayed green for both vehicles. At Twentieth Street North, the bus turned right heading south. Sam sped up as the bus turned and made the same green light. There was moderate traffic on Twentieth, which made it easier for Sam to follow the bus more closely. He stayed in the lane behind the bus to limit the driver's or anyone else's ability to see the car.

They passed the university hospital and Five Points, and drove over Red Mountain near Vulcan, a 56-foot cast iron statue of the Roman god of the forge and fire that stands on a 126-foot pedestal overlooking Birmingham and the Jones Valley as a tribute to the city's founding industries. They followed the bus into Homewood, where it turned left and made its way to Highway 280 south.

They left Homewood, the traffic lessened noticeably, and the area became less populated. The bus proceeded over Shades Mountain, past the Birmingham Water Works reservoir and between Mountain Brook and Vestavia Hills, a newly developing community of upscale homes.

Sam pointed to a sign advertising the new community. "Well, I reckon Mr. Boss that thar ain't no Vestal Virgins on that thar bus."

Joe snickered. "No, I reckon you 'bout right. I gotta tell you Sam, you one helluva chauffeur and even bettah tail man."

"Yes suh, Boss. I's does my best."

The men stopped joking around and focused on the rear of the bus. The highway was now in the countryside, and Sam stayed farther back. The bus was going forty-five miles per hour, so occasionally a car would pass them, but they had no trouble maintaining reasonable contact with the bus. Thirty minutes later on a straight section of highway, the brake lights engaged as the bus slowed.

Sam slowed down. "Joe, I think the bus is getting ready to turn. If it turns, I'll drive by at normal speed. You look down the road where it turns and check it out. I'll make a U-turn down the highway, and we'll decide what to do."

"Right," Joe said.

The bus did turn right, heading west. Sam drove by, and Joe got a quick glimpse of several "No Trespassing" signs spotted around the gravel-covered dirt road. He also saw that two armed guards had stopped the bus, its tail and brake lights glowing in the dust kicked up on the gravel road.

"There's two armed guards. Don't make a U-turn," Joe said.

Sam continued south for several hundred yards as the highway curved to the right. When Sam was sure they couldn't be seen from the gravel road, he slowed down and saw another dirt road to the left. Since no cars were coming in either direction, he quickly turned onto the dirt road heading east and drove slowly until he was well off the highway, pulled to the side, and turned the car off.

Sam looked at Joe in the backseat, the moonbeams providing a hint of light through the trees. "We have two choices. I think we know where Mahogany Hall is. We can either come back later in the daylight or try to walk in now. What do you think?"

"The first choice is safer. The second's tougher. We don't know how far it is. Cars will continue to come and go. They probably have more armed guards." Joe smiled in the dim light. "What the hell, we've come this far. Let's do it."

Sam said, "I'm game. The gravel road works in our favor. We can hear a vehicle before it gets too close. We'll have to scramble into the trees and brush and lie down."

"Yep. We better cross the highway at this dirt road and work our way through the trees and try to come out on the gravel road a few hundred yards from the highway. We can't enter on the gravel road at the highway. The guards or a car entering the road will see us."

"Yep. Ready to go?" Sam said.

"Think the car's okay here?"

"Let's take a look around."

They walked to the east on the dirt road a short distance and saw an even smaller dirt road to the left. The roadway was covered with grass, and tree branches obscured it, indicating it was seldom used.

"Ill get the car and park in here," Sam said.

Sam drove the car well into the small side road, concealing it from the dirt road and the highway. They left their hats in the car, knowing they would likely lose them as they struggled through the trees and brush. Back at the highway, they waited until no sounds or lights were obvious, and ran to the other side into the woods. The pines and oaks were thick and, coupled with the brush, made for tough going. They took turns leading, as the lead man had to feel ahead to find a way since the moonlight didn't penetrate the woodland canopy very well. Sam counted his paces as best he could to get a rough measure of their distance.

After about twenty minutes, Sam touched Joe's shoulder and whispered, "I think it's okay to turn north and look for the gravel road."

In another ten minutes, the trees opened up and they were on the gravel road. As they started to turn left, Sam said, "Let's look for a landmark so we know where to get off the gravel road when we leave." In the dim moonlight, they could see a broad clearing in the trees on the opposite side of the road.

Joe said, "I think that clearing will work."

Sam nodded.

They turned to the left and walked westbound as close to the trees as possible, ever alert for lights and sounds.

Over the next twenty minutes, they scrambled into the trees twice and lay down as cars continued to drive toward Mahogany Hall. They couldn't see the cars' occupants since they kept their heads facing down on the ground.

After continuing on the gravel road for another fifteen minutes, the road curved gently to the right. They saw some lights through the trees in the direction the road curved. Joe motioned to the left, and they went into the trees. They moved forward and laterally to the right slowly, taking care to make as little noise as possible.

As they tracked toward the lights, it soon became apparent that a number of lights were shining in different directions including toward the woods. The trees were still thick when they got their first glimpse of the hall. They stopped and surveyed what lay ahead. The hall was two hundred yards away, and the trees thinned noticeably in a hundred yards. Just beyond the thinned trees was a chain link fence topped with barbed wire. Wanting to maintain good cover, they decided to proceed to a point just before the trees started to thin. Moving as slowly and quietly as possible, Sam inadvertently stepped on a large, dry branch that broke with a loud crack. Both men immediately dropped flat on the ground.

A voice called out, "Did you hear that? Sumthin's out yonder in the woods."

"Yeah, I heared it. Sounds like it come from out front. Lemme look around."

Sam and Joe had their faces buried in the damp soil. They could taste the dirt in their mouths, and their nostrils were filled with the pungent odors of the earth. They remained motionless, listening to the footsteps walking around the gravel area just beyond the fence. Occasionally, they would sense a beam of light sweeping through the woods, but they were well concealed in the trees and brush.

In a couple of minutes, one of the men announced, "I reckon it was an animal. Maybe a coon."

"Reckon you're right. Want me to get the dogs?"

"Nah. Didn't see nuthin'."

"Just keep your eyes and ears open, you hear?"

"Will do." They could hear the man's footsteps receding as he went back to the hall.

They sat up behind two large trees, cleared the dirt off their faces, and peered out carefully at the hall. They knew they couldn't risk getting any closer. Their views were square on to the hall's front. It was red brick, three stories, a hundred to a hundred-fifty feet wide, and rather plain in appearance except for one feature. An ornate porte-cochere covered the hall's entrance and had two facing bronze statues on top: the goddess Venus and the god Bacchus. The front and side areas were also graveled, and there were a number of cars and the bus parked on the sides.

Five men were standing around the hall's entry area: four armed guards and one car valet. The cars they could see were late model Cadillacs, Oldsmobiles, Lincolns, and Buicks, a veritable car lot of pricey vehicles. Joe tried to count them, but they were parked side by side in a column to his eye, and he couldn't see them all. He guessed there must be at least twenty to thirty.

It was quiet except for the chatter among the men in front when they heard a vehicle approaching on the gravel road. When Joe first saw the fence, he figured there must also be a gated entry where people were identified for a second time. He listened carefully as the car approached, and it did stop. In less than a minute, he heard it proceed again on the gravel. As the car pulled under the porte-cochere, Joe realized it was a 1947 light blue Cadillac like the one Dick Oliver drove. Three well-dressed men got out of the car and entered the hall. Joe recognized Dick but didn't have a clue as to the identity of the other two. The valet parked the Cadillac.

Joe and Sam sat for another hour. No cars arrived and no one came out of the hall. They heard some music. It sounded like jazz.

It was almost midnight. Joe leaned over to Sam and whispered, "I think we should go before they start to leave."

"Are you sure? Don't you want to see who comes out later?" Sam whispered.

"Yeah. But it's too risky. I got a hunch the killer's here tonight. But even if we saw him, we wouldn't know he's the guy. We have no leads, no evidence, and it's hard to see faces clearly from this distance. Well, I do have one possible suspect now. I'll tell you about it after we get back to the car."

The men slowly got up and carefully worked their way through the trees and brush in the direction they had come from. When they got to the gravel road, they followed along its side until they were sure they were adjacent to the clearing in the trees on the left. They ducked into the trees on the right and went south and east until they came to the highway. They realized they were about two hundred yards south of the dirt road where the car was parked. They crossed the highway and ducked into the trees and worked their way north to the dirt road and easily returned to the car.

They were well on their way back to Birmingham when Sam finally broke their silence. "Okay, Mr. Detective, who's the suspect?"

"Dick Oliver, my boss. That was his car that came in late, the light blue Cadillac. I shouldn't call him a suspect. We have nothing on him. Not surprising he's here. He's tight with Ramsey's social circle."

"How you gonna approach him?" Sam said.

"Don't know. Can't ask him about it. That would blow our cover. I guess I'll play around the edges with him and see if he says anything interesting."

Sam dropped Joe off at the library. It was after one. As Joe got out of the car, Sam said, "When do you wanna go back and try to check the place out? Say, that suit looks like shit."

"It's headed for the garbage can. I'll bet yours is too. Let's talk about Mahogany Hall on Monday," Joe said.

Sam nodded and drove off.

CHAPTER 48

THE KLAN'S CALLING CARD

MONDAY—NOVEMBER 3, 1947

I T was a nice, crisp fall day, and Diane and Joe had decided to spend most of Sunday with each other. They started the day with a leisurely picnic lunch in the park adjacent to Vulcan's statue atop Red Mountain. After eating, they lay on their blanket enjoying the afternoon sun.

"I've started the divorce," Joe said. "My attorney says the Alabama process can be lengthy. But he knows the judge who handles many of the divorce cases, and he thinks it might be done within a year."

Diane perked up. "Yep, it can. With my family and Warren's connections, our divorce was final in less than a year."

"Good news. I told him to get started. We'll see how it goes."

Joe decided it was best not to tell Diane about Mahogany Hall and Friday night. Late in the afternoon, they went back to Diane's apartment for a light supper.

MONDAY MORNING, AFTER JOE GOT TO HEADQUARTERS, he went directly to Dick Oliver's office.

"Hey, Dick. Can I come in?"

"Sure, Joe. I was gonna call you. We need to talk."

"Okay. Did you have a nice weekend?" Joe said.

"Yeah. How about you?"

"Nice picnic with Diane yesterday. But everything pales after Ramsey's party."

Dick looked smug. "Stanford knows how to put on a party. You should see some of the things he does."

"Like what?"

"Like none of your business, Joe. Ask Stanford. You two seemed to be buddy-buddy at his party."

"Are you ticked off at me too, like the chief?"

"Just stay outta my social circles, Joe."

"Hey, . . . hey, peace, Dick. I know when I'm outta my league."

"Maybe. You keep seeing Diane, that'll change."

Joe looked hard at Dick and said nothing.

Dick continued. "I'm not gonna fund your little escapades with Rucker any longer. I see no reason to. I just approved a check for your last expense report. That's the last one."

"That's too bad. We are making some progress," Joe said.

"Yeah, what?"

"Can't tell you. Might be a bad lead."

Dick turned bright red. "Goddamn. Whaddya mean you can't tell me? You work for me, McGrath."

Joe said evenly, "If we're wrong, some innocent people might get hurt. Some in high places."

Dick laughed sarcastically. "Well, that's it, Joe. You want money to find leads with your colored buddy, but you won't tell me. No more. You and Rucker stop working together."

Joe decided to end the conversation. "Okay. I doubt he'll continue if we won't pay him." Joe got up to leave.

"Good riddance," Dick shouted.

Back in his office, Joe asked Brendan to leave so he could make a couple of phone calls.

Joe closed his office door and phoned Ramsey's number.

"Hello, Stanford Ramsey's office."

"Good morning. This is Detective Joe McGrath with the Birmingham Police Department. I'd like to speak to Mr. Ramsey."

"Just a moment, Detective McGrath."

Almost immediately, Ramsey said, " Hello, Joe. Glad to hear from you. Got anything interesting for me?"

"No sir. I wish there was. Sam Rucker was out of town a few days last week. I got caught up on some other cases. I don't think Chief Watson or Dick Oliver are too happy about my being at your party."

Ramsey laughed. "Don't worry about those two. They might bark, but they won't bite. Let me know if they do."

"I can handle it, Stanford. Just wanted you to know how it is."

"I know how it is, Joe. Got anything else?"

Joe wanted to drop a hint about Mahogany Hall but said simply, "No sir."

"Call me when you have something." Ramsey hung up.

Damn it, Joe thought, *how am I gonna open the door to Mahogany Hall without blowing the lid off our cover and investigation?* He dialed the phone again.

"Sam Rucker."

"Can you talk?"

"Yeah."

"I talked to Dick Oliver and Stanford Ramsey this morning. No mention of Mahogany Hall," Joe said.

"What'd you expect?"

"I hoped Dick might slip and say something. He's pissed at me, just like the chief."

"They're Ramsey's boys, Joe. No surprise there either."

"Yeah. But get this. Dick signed my last expense report, so I'll have a check for you shortly. That's the good news. The bad—that's the last one. He's gonna stop paying you. And he told me to stop working with you."

Sam sounded nonplussed. "I'll go on without the money. I got a few jobs recently. Bread and butter stuff, but it helps. What do you want to do?"

"If you're game, I'll continue. We'll have to move around like two spooks in the night."

Sam laughed heartily. "I can do that easy enough. But you'll have to cover yourself with black shoe polish."

"Shit. I didn't mean that. I meant like ghosts," Joe said.

"I know. Now I gotta wear a white sheet. Big problem."

"Fuck. Forget it." Joe said.

"Loosen up, Joe. I'm pulling your leg. Ain't the end of the world. Spooks we'll be."

Joe relaxed and realized he was still angry at Dick. "Yep. The Spooks Boys on the case."

"Right. Speaking of the case, what's next? You wanna go out to Mahogany Hall and try to look around?" Sam said.

"It's not a good idea. It's fenced and has guards with dogs. I doubt we could get in. I suppose we could drive up close and walk around the perimeter. Let's wait 'til later this week. They could still be busy with cleanup and stuff after a big night."

"Makes sense. So what can we do now?"

"Gotta find a way to crack the Mahogany Hall puzzle. I'm betting the killer was in the building Friday night," Joe said.

"Any idea who it is?"

"Hell no. Could be anyone. Ramsey or Dick or pick a name. I gotta find the right way to approach them about it."

"Maybe Mahogany Hall is a red herring," Sam said.

"Could be. Got a better idea?"

"No. I could approach Marcus. But I know he wouldn't give me the time of day on Mahogany Hall."

"Bad idea, Sam. He'd figure we know something and raise hell."

"Ideas will come. They always do."

"Before the next killing? The next dark moon is in nine days," Joe said.

"Don't know. How's Matthew doing? His trial starts next week."

"Haven't talked to him lately. I'll have Brendan go see him. I'll call you tomorrow," Joe said.

IT WAS ALMOST MIDNIGHT. Sam was asleep in his bedroom, located on the back corner of his home. He awoke with a start when a car door slammed. He sat up and heard a car pulling away from the front, its engine roaring and tires peeling rubber on the pavement.

He got out of bed and put on his bathrobe to go see what happened when there was a big explosion.

As he heard glass and wood shattering, the concussion from the blast rocked him back on his heels. He quickly put on his shoes and hurried to the front of the house, turning on lights as he went, surprised the electricity was still working. The windows in the living room and study were all blown inward, broken glass everywhere. The front door was loose, but he was able to open it. There was damage to the porch and the facia board and other trim. Sam noticed lights turning on all over the neighborhood. A few people had already gathered in the street. He looked around the yard and saw a large crater in the middle of the lawn about fifteen feet from the porch.

Sam immediately knew what had happened. Whoever threw the bomb, and Sam suspected it was a Klansman, had made a poor toss. In the bomb thrower's haste to toss and safely get back in the car, the location of the crater clearly demonstrated that he was not a pitcher for the Birmingham Barons.

A neighbor from a few doors down the street came up to Sam and said he had called the police. Sam thanked him, knowing full well the police would do nothing. Earlier in the year, another bomb had been planted under a wood frame house near Rickwood Field. It had been purchased by a colored man using his life savings in what many considered a white neighborhood. The house had been destroyed, the man had no insurance, and no arrest had been or would be made. Fortunately, the man and his family had not yet occupied the house. Sam and the rest of Birmingham didn't know it, but the Klan's bombing spree that would plague Birmingham for the next eighteen years had just begun.

A squad car pulled up to the house fifteen minutes later. A night duty sergeant and a patrolman got out of the car.

The sergeant yelled, "Whose house is this?"

"It's mine, sir. My name's Sam Rucker."

"You see anything, boy?"

"No, sir. I was in bed when the bomb exploded."

The sergeant turned to the crowd. "Did any y'all see anything?"

It was silent.

"Well, it's gonna be tough with no eye witnesses."

Sam spoke up. "Maybe you oughta check the yard and house for bomb fragments, sir."

"You trying to tell me how to do my job, boy?" the sergeant growled.

"No, sir. Just a suggestion."

The sergeant glared at Sam, but then proceeded to look around the bomb crater, the lawn, and the porch using a powerful flashlight.

Sam watched as he pick up a few things that might be dynamite fragments and put them in his pocket. Sam knew he'd anger the man more if he suggested to the sergeant that the items be carefully bagged so they could be checked for fingerprints and other clues.

The sergeant walked back to the street and yelled, "Now y'all go home. Nothing else for you to do here. I'll take care of it."

As the crowd drifted away, the sergeant said to Sam, "Lemme get some information on you, boy." He asked Sam for his name, address, phone number, and occupation.

When Sam said he was a private investigator, the sergeant's head popped up from his notepad. "So you that uppity, colored private eye. I reckon you oughta be able to solve this here case."

Sam played the obedient Negro. "Oh, no sir. I ain't never dealt with nothing like this. Y'all gotta find out who done it."

The sergeant was pleased. Sam looked stoic, but was smiling inside. He knew many crackers like this man. They liked to think they had tamed this huge, colored wild beast.

"We'll try, but don't expect much. Not much to go on," the sergeant said. He turned to the patrolman. "Let's get outta here."

Sam went back into the house, got a broom and dust pan and large container. He swept up the glass fragments and wood chips as best he could, and then sat in the living room.

Well, I guess the Klan has finally come calling. I reckon I'm long overdue this visit.

AT THE TIME SAM'S HOUSE WAS BOMBED, Joe was in his apartment. He had been sitting in his comfortable chair trying to read Proust. He put the book aside for the umpteenth time and went back to mulling over the Mahogany Hall situation. He was frustrated when an idea hit him. *Of course. Franklin Pierce. Why have I been blocking him out? I know how to get him to talk now.*

Joe was so pleased with himself, he got up and paced around the room, anxious for tomorrow to begin.

CHAPTER 49

PIERCE TALKS

TUESDAY—NOVEMBER 4, 1947

J OE'S PHONE RANG AT FIVE FORTY-FIVE. He nearly knocked the receiver over. Only partially awake, he mumbled, "Hello."

"Joe, sorry to call so early. I almost called last night."

"Yeah," his voice dripping with sleep, "What's up, Sam?"

"My house was bombed last night."

Joe sat up straight. "Jesus! What happened? Know who did it?"

"Not for sure. But I bet it was the Klan." Sam proceeded to tell Joe the whole story including the visit by the cops.

"Who was the sergeant?"

"His name is Calhoun, a real cracker," Sam said.

"I know him. You're right. He's one of the chief's favorites."

"The Klan doesn't usually do this alone. Somebody put 'em up to it. And you know who," Sam said.

"Sure. The chief. He's so goddamn mad at me, I'll bet he set it up with his buddies in the Eastview klavern."

"Yeah. And probably the bombing out by Rickwood."

"You need some help?" Joe said.

"A friend's gonna do the repairs. Appreciate your offer. But stay away. You come over here and all kinda folks gonna be talking."

"I know. You gotta keep a low profile. I don't want you to get hurt."

"Me either. But I wanna continue working with you when and where I can," Sam said.

"Right. Lemme tell you an idea I had last night," Joe said.

"I hope it was a good wet dream."

"Very funny for a man whose house was almost blown out from under him. I'm gonna talk to Franklin Pierce again. He's so pissed at Ramsey, I'm sure I can get him to open up. Don't know where it'll lead, but we gotta get some movement on this thing."

"If he cracks, let me know. Maybe that's the time for me to hit Marcus again."

"Could be, but I doubt it. I figure if Pierce opens up, Marcus will keep his mouth shut. Pierce wants to see Ramsey hammered on this. Marcus doesn't. It's a meal ticket for him. I'll be in touch. And call me if there's any more trouble," Joe said.

JOE SPOKE BRIEFLY WITH SALLY when he got to headquarters. He had decided not to talk to Oliver or Watson. He'd wait and see if they said anything about last night. Brendan showed up a few minutes later.

"Good morning, young fella. I got something I want you to do. Go over to the jail and talk to Luke Matthew. See how he looks, and if he's being mistreated. Find out if Banks has been spending time with him. I think he's more comfortable with you than with me."

Brendan was eager to be back on the case. "Will do, boss. When do you want me to go?"

"Sooner the better. But before you go, dig out of your files the business address and phone number for Franklin Pierce. I need to talk to him," Joe said.

"I thought the chief told you to stay away from him."

"He did." Joe winked. "I forgot. Lips sealed."

"Got it." Brendan pulled out his file on Pierce and gave Joe the information. "I'll head over to the jail. See you later."

Joe was sitting at his desk when Dick Oliver came in.

"Hi, Joe. Hear about last night?"

"No. What about last night?"

"Somebody threw a bomb at Sam Rucker's house. Did some damage, but nobody hurt. Calhoun took the call and wrote it up. Looks like it was a few sticks of dynamite."

Joe feigned surprise and then disgust. "That makes two this year. Any suspects?"

"No. Rucker says he was in bed when it happened. None of his neighbors saw anything."

"Or just aren't talking. Who do you think did it?"

Dick sat down, shaking his head. "How would I know?"

"Oh, c'mon, Dick. You know as well as I do who did it."

"Tread lightly, Joe. Listen." He spoke slowly, enunciating every word. "We do not have any witnesses or suspects."

Joe couldn't contain his contempt. "Right."

Dick abruptly walked out of Joe's office.

Joe put his feet on his desk and leaned back. *This is getting tougher and tougher. Dick's not gonna cover for me. Gotta get a break. A real break.* He called Franklin Pierce.

"Detective McGrath, to what do I owe this pleasure?"

"Stanford Ramsey and Mahogany Hall. I need to talk to you."

"I told you, I never heard of such a place." Pierce said.

"Well, I know of the place. I'd like to have thirty minutes. This is a request, not a demand. I think you will be pleased the way things are headed."

"What things?" Pierce asked.

"That's what we'll talk about."

Joe could hear Pierce breathing as he paused to decide what to do. "Get over here at ten-thirty. No shenanigans or you're out the door."

"I'll be there."

"Have a seat, Detective McGrath," Pierce said.

He took a chair in front of Pierce's desk. "Joe will do just fine."

"In the interest of fair play and social equality, call me Franklin. Why do you want to talk about this place you call Mahogany Hall? I know nothing about it."

"I do, Franklin. I've seen it. There was a party, actually more an orgy, there last Friday night. I know it was hosted by Stanford Ramsey. I know colored girls are bused there to have sex with the guests, white men. I know the men are hooded and select a girl from a line-up. I know the guests are many of Birmingham's business and social elite."

As Joe reeled off the facts he knew, he watched Pierce's face change. His usual taut lips and sneer softened to a look of confusion, and his eyes darted about seeking a refuge.

Pierce regained his composure. "If you know all that and take it to be true, what could I possibly tell you?"

"I think you participated in the orgies at Mahogany Hall until you fell out of favor with Ramsey," Joe said.

"Even if that's true, why should I talk to you. I can't trust you."

"That's correct. You can't. But you have to take a risk, just as I am by talking to you. As soon as I leave, you might call Ramsey or one of his associates and tell them what I know."

"And if I do, Stanford will cut you off at the knees immediately."

Joe tried to look concerned. "I know. In my case, it would probably be literal, unlike the figurative humiliation you and your wife are suffering."

"Where did you get all this information, Joe?"

"Franklin, I'm not gonna tell you my sources today or ever."

"If that's the case, what's the use in my talking to you?"

"I use whatever I learn discreetly. I'll find a way to use anything interesting you might tell me without revealing your name. That's my business."

"I know this is all about the murder of those two whores. I also know you're looking for the murderer. Do you consider me a suspect?"

"No. And the answer's easy. You won't like the first part. You and I know you were hustling that colored girl in September. You were on the prowl looking for some action. You almost asked for that bust. The murderer doesn't operate that way. He's a late-at-night guy in alleys or parks. Second, your little encounter occurred only four days before the first prostitute was killed. I'm sure the murderer would not have been stupid enough to act right after a bust for suspected solicitation. And you're not stupid. Finally, I think the murderer was in Mahogany Hall last Friday night. You weren't there because you're on Ramsey's blacklist."

"How do you know I've been to Mahogany Hall?"

"Oh, c'mon, Franklin. You know you've been there. You obviously like colored women, and Stanford's place is an ideal setup for a night of fun and games."

"What do you plan to do about Mahogany Hall?" Pierce asked.

"I want the killer of the two colored prostitutes. I don't want to see Luke Matthew electrocuted, and that's what'll happen to him. His trial starts next week. I don't know how it will play out, but I also want to see Stanford Ramsey in a vise over Mahogany Hall. I'd like to see it closed down or at least stop exploiting women so brazenly."

"Aha, you're a do-gooder," Pierce said.

"Not exactly. Prostitution on the local level is okay if the players aren't too exploited. But you gotta agree, Mahogany Hall is excessive."

Pierce looked as if he were brooding. "So you want me to help you write the script so that 'the play's the thing wherein I'll catch the conscience of the King.' I mean Ramsey."

Joe had been waiting for an opening like this to bring Pierce back to the end of their conversation over a week ago. "Play, *Hamlet*. Speaker, Hamlet. Act Two, Scene Two. Lines 606-607, although line numbers vary somewhat depending on the anthology you use."

Pierce's face turned to a rare, almost imperceptible, smile, his taut lips slightly open and curled upwards. He pulled a book out of a bookcase and found what he was looking for. "Five points. I was checking the line numbers. Here's what I'll do. You ask me questions. I'll answer if I want to. If I find a question objectionable, I won't answer. And don't push me."

"Okay. Do you know of Mahogany Hall?" Joe asked.

"Yes."

"Does Stanford Ramsey own it?"

"Yes."

"Does he host the events there?"

"Yes."

"How long has Mahogany Hall existed?"

"The first time I was there was about five years ago. I think Stanford built it right after his mistress, Loretta Langtree, was moved to New Orleans," Pierce said.

"How many times have you been there for the fun and games?" Joe said.

"Maybe ten or twelve," Pierce said.

"What's an evening there like?"

"You summed it up well. Someone supplies a busload of colored girls. The men are in robes and choose a girl. They go to a room to enjoy themselves. Several hours later, the girls leave and most of the men stay. They have a late meal, play cards and pool, and drink a lot."

"Have any of the girls been mistreated or hurt?"

"Not often. A few times a guy has roughed a girl up."

"Seriously?" Joe said.

"Only once that I'm aware of. She had to be rushed to a doctor. I was told that she recovered."

"What happened?"

"I'm not getting into the details," Pierce said.

"Franklin, I can't prove it yet, but I'm sure the man who killed the two prostitutes was in Mahogany Hall last Friday night."

"Well, that's interesting, Joe. But until you can identify a suspect and prove it, you're just speculating."

"Who do you think is capable of such acts?"

"I have no idea. And even if I did, I wouldn't give you names. You must have some names in mind."

"Hell, it could be Ramsey. Dick Oliver was there Friday night. It could be him. I met lots of men at Ramsey's gala. I imagine many of them attend the Mahogany Hall orgies. It could be one of them."

"Sounds like you have your work cut out for you, Joe."

"I do. That's why I need your help. I'm running out of time. I also think it's highly likely there will be another killing. I need some leads, Franklin. Lives are at stake."

"And maybe reputations."

"Possibly." Joe looked hard and long at Franklin. "Who do you think could have done this? Someone must stand out from that Mahogany Hall crowd," Joe said.

"I'll give you two names. Elliott Spencer. Weldon Knight."

"That's it?" Joe asked.

"Yes. . . . No, I've changed my mind. I'll tell you something about the girl that was seriously hurt." Pierce's lean body coiled inward and his mouth thrust forward as if he were about to strike like a viper. "I won't describe the bloody details. I will tell you this since Stanford's beneficent largess is responsible for it." Pierce spit his words out like venom. "After the guests finish with the girls, the guards are allowed, one at a time, to choose a girl and enjoy themselves. It's one of the niceties Stanford offers those guys for their work and silence. Anyway, one guard beat a girl senseless. Another guest happened to be walking past the room the guard and girl were in. He told me he heard the guard exclaim, 'Oh, sweet Jesus, let it come.' I later heard from a friend who was there that the guard was a religious zealot with a fundamentalist Pentecostal church."

Pierce smacked his lips, obviously pleased with all the implications in what he had just told Joe.

Joe grimaced at the awful recitation. "What's the guard's name?"

"How the hell would I know? I don't associate with Stanford's help. I heard others call the staff Billy, Joey, Bobby Joe, Sammy, even Bubba, all those common Southern first names."

What an asshole, Joe thought. "When did this happen?"

"I don't remember exactly. Must have been last summer before my banishment. No more questions."

"Franklin, I'll use the information discreetly."

"Good." And then as if they had been talking about the weather or his next bridge game, Pierce said, "Next Monday night at seven I'm hosting the Shakespearean group at my house. Why don't you join us. I think you'd be an interesting addition."

Joe was surprised at the segue, but realized he shouldn't say no to Pierce at this time. "It sounds interesting. You could keep an eye on me. And I'm sure your well-to-do friends would be intrigued by the cop who knows Shakespeare."

Pierce put his fingertips together and held his hands in front of his mouth, his middle fingers touching the tip of his nose. "Precisely. And your lady friend Diane's ex-husband is one of our group of six. He's good at the game. Frequently wins."

"Is he a Mahogany Hall attendee?"

"I said, no more questions."

Joe nodded. "I met Warren at Ramsey's gala. The game should be fun. I look forward to it."

Joe pondered the interview on the way back to his office. *Well, that went okay. Got more than I thought I would. It's never simple. The guard's a suspect. How do we identify him?*

BRENDAN HAD RETURNED FROM THE JAIL when Joe got back to headquarters. "How did it go with Matthew?"

"Joe, it's amazing. Most of his injuries are gone. The few remaining are hardly noticeable."

"Yeah. Young guys heal fast. How's his frame of mind?"

"He's real worried. He still doesn't understand why no one believes him," Brendan said.

"You and I do," Joe said.

"I told him that. It doesn't help much. Banks has spent time with him. He doesn't know what Banks intends to do in the courtroom. He's just a scared kid, Joe."

"Yep. I want you to attend the entire trial unless something real important comes up. Give me a report every day. Now, here's something else I want you to do. Two names. Elliott Spencer. Weldon Knight. Research our files for any priors and other info on them. Do a newspaper search. I wanna know everything about them: backgrounds, social status, education, work, addresses, phone numbers, family, wife, kids. You name it. You find it. Get on it right away. It's important," Joe said.

"Is this connected to the two murders?"

"Yes, but only you and I know that."

"Gotcha." Brendan rushed out of the office.

CHAPTER 50

THE SUSPECTS

WEDNESDAY—NOVEMBER 5, 1947

BRENDAN WAS AT HIS DESK when Joe arrived Wednesday morning. He couldn't wait to tell Joe what he had found. "Morning, Joe. I got some info on Spencer and Knight."

"Good. Give me a quick summary on their backgrounds. Then we'll get into the weeds."

"Okay. Both are well-educated, successful, run in the highest social circles, members of all the important clubs, married with kids. Spencer's fifty-six, a banker, lives in Mountain Brook. Knight's fifty-four, a lawyer, and lives in Birmingham just off Highland Avenue South."

"Sounds like both are stalwarts in our community, and I'm sure they're paragons of virtue. Whatcha got on Spencer?" Joe said.

"No recorded priors and nothing in records, not even an arrest. But here's the hooker. The *News* reported in its Sunday rundown on arrests that Spencer was booked on May 8, 1944, for solicitation. A few days later the paper reported he was represented by Robert Beauchamp and that his case was dismissed."

"Knight?" Joe said.

"Like Spencer, Knight has no recorded priors and nothing in records, not even an arrest. But the *News* reported that he was arrested on March 16, 1942, for immoral conduct, and assault and battery in a sleazy colored hotel. Then nothing. Not even a mention of a dismissal. Maybe Beauchamp got him off too. That's why no priors are on record," Brendan said.

"Could be. But priors are not that easy to get off the record."

"Does Beauchamp have the connections to make that sorta thing happen?"

"Yep. He sure does. Anything on Knight's arrest and the prostitute?"

"All I got is the initial *News* report of his arrest. Nothing on a prostitute being arrested. Nothing else on Knight."

"Ain't it wonderful. Everybody fucks around. Nobody gets prosecuted but Luke Matthew," Joe said, staring at the ceiling.

Brendan sat quietly. He never knew what to say when Joe took off like this.

Joe growled at Brendan, "Did you visit the courthouse yesterday?"

Brendan looked chagrined. "No, sorry. It was closed when I finished the newspaper search."

Joe relaxed. "That's okay. Then get over there now. See if there's anything in the court transcripts. I'll bet those were purged too. If you're asked, just say you gotta do some research. Also, check a lunar calendar for '42 and '44. See if either arrest date was a dark moon."

"I'll get on it right now."

Joe dialed Sam's home phone.

"Hello."

"It's Joe. How's the house?"

"A guy's doing repairs now. Mostly wood and glass. It'll be fine. I know you didn't call to talk about the repairs."

"Nope. I gotta pick your brain. Do the names Weldon Knight and Elliott Spencer mean anything to you?" Joe said.

"Nothing on Spencer. Knight rings a bell. I don't know why."

Joe explained to Sam what Brendan had learned about the two men, adding, "We know Beauchamp got Spencer's case dismissed. I suspect he also got Knight off. Brendan's over at the courthouse right now looking for transcripts."

"My. My. What a big fucking surprise. Now I remember the Knight incident. I wasn't involved in the case, but I know the owner of the hotel. Later on, the owner told me what happened. You called the place a sleazy colored hotel. That's right on. All the rooms are ground level to make for easy ins and outs. The night clerk was one tough cookie and always packed a Colt 45 'cause of all the trouble at night. The clerk heard a woman screaming. He followed the screams to the room. Knocked on the door. No response. The woman yelled, 'Help me.' He pulled the gun and kicked in the door. A white man was trying to climb out the back window. The clerk forced him into a chair, tied him up with a sheet, and called the police. The woman was bloody with bruises and lacerations all over her body. The cops came, called an ambulance for the woman, and took the white man away. That's the last the owner heard anything. He didn't even know the guy's name. The colored gal probably registered for the room," Sam said.

"And Knight apparently gets off even though he was caught at the scene and there was a witness."

"C'mon, Joe. This is Birmingham. A wealthy white man doesn't go down. Goddamn, I shoulda remembered this when you first contacted me. I never knew Knight's name, but he's gotta be a prime suspect for these recent murders."

"I also asked Brendan to check if either date was a dark moon."

"Yeah. Good idea," Sam said.

"Think the owner has the register with the woman's name?"

"I'll ask him. But I doubt he keeps registers that old."

Joe sighed. "Yeah. At least I got another lead." He told Sam about the guard at Mahogany Hall who brutally beat one of the girls.

"Hmmm. All kinda suspects. Rich white men. Working stiff white man. Where did you get the information on the guard?"

"A confidential source. Best you not know," Joe said.

"Understand. What do you want me to do?"

"Fix your house. I'll let you know what Brendan finds at the courthouse. I'm gonna put a tail on Knight next week, especially the twelfth. I know Oliver and Watson won't do shit about increasin' patrols in the Ankle next week. Can you talk to the pimps and their ladies and see if they'll stay off the streets on the eleventh and twelfth?"

Sam said, "Sure. But it's unlikely I'll get much cooperation."

"We gotta try. Say, you told me a while back that your minister asked the congregation to come forward if they knew anything about the murders. Did anybody talk?"

"Nope. Not surprised either," Sam said.

"Right. I'll call after Brendan gets back from the courthouse."

Brendan returned from the courthouse just before noon.

"Just as you suspected, Boss. Didn't find much. There is a record of the Spencer case dismissal. No details though. There's absolutely nothing on Weldon Knight. It's like it didn't happen."

"Power has its privileges. Was either date on a dark moon?"

"Spencer, no. May 8, 1944 was a full moon. Now it gets interesting. March 16, 1942, Knight's arrest, was a dark moon."

"Could be a coincidence. Especially since Knight's arrest and the recent murders are five years apart. But we gotta take it seriously. Forget what I said yesterday about attending Matthew's trial. I want you to do a stakeout at Weldon Knight's house next Tuesday and Wednesday nights. Wednesday's a dark moon. I want you at his house from dark to daylight. Get an unmarked car with a radio from the carpool. Tell 'em you're on an assignment for me. If Knight leaves the house, discreetly follow him. Call the desk officer when you have a sense of where he's going, and tell him to call me immediately."

"Shouldn't I check his house out before next week?"

"Good idea. Change into your civvies and use your car. Get comfortable with the location. Look for a place to park where it's unlikely you'll be observed. But you want to have good sight lines to the front door and wherever he parks his cars. Have lunch and then get on it."

Joe called Sam again.

"Sam, there are no transcripts or records of any sort in the courthouse files on Knight. Someone made sure no records were created or they've been destroyed. But, get this, the night he was arrested in 1942 there was a dark moon. Could be a coincidence, but we gotta watch him. I just sent Brendan to check out Knight's house. He's gonna do a stakeout next Tuesday and Wednesday."

"Good. You gotta cover him. I called the owner of the hotel where Knight got arrested. He laughed when I asked him about the register and the girl's name. No register. No name. I'll make some more calls and see if I can find anybody that remembers that night."

"Okay. I'll guess we'll just keep plugging along until the trial and the twelfth unless the murderer falls in our laps."

"Very funny, Mr. Detective. Look, I'm gonna be busy with house repairs over the next few days. I will make some calls. I'll let you know if I find anything."

"Likewise."

CHAPTER 51

THE SHAKESPEAREAN GAME

MONDAY—NOVEMBER 10, 1947

"THE MOON'S AN ARRANT THIEF, And her pale fire she snatches from the sun," Joe read. For his opener in the Shakespearean game, he had chosen a selection from *Timon of Athens*, one of Shakespeare's least known and more difficult plays.

JOE ARRIVED AT FRANKLIN PIERCE'S HOUSE precisely at seven. He said hello to Warren and Franklin, but the other four men were strangers.

Franklin took Joe by the arm and announced to the room, "Gentlemen, let me introduce our guest, Homicide Detective Joe McGrath with the Birmingham Police Department."

As Franklin made the individual introductions, Joe enjoyed the humor Franklin exhibited, showing a side of his personality Joe had not experienced in their previous meetings.

"Joe, meet Sheldon Collier, a history professor at Birmingham-Southern College. If we played a game about history, he would win hands down. He even knows who won the War Between the States.

"This is Randolph Neville, our city's most noted surgeon. He's noted for his steady hand, but I hope you never need his services.

"Joe, this is our money man. Meet Wilbur Clampton, the president of First National Bank. Just be sure you pay all your loans on time.

"And last but not least, meet Algernon Fisk, a classic literature scholar. He is the game's most frequent winner, so he's likely your main competitor. But beware the Algernon, he does not like to lose."

Algernon said with an air of decided superiority, "So Detective McGrath, you're the policeman who is the Shakespearean expert. I find that hard to fathom. But we'll see about that tonight." Joe smiled politely, realizing Algernon was more the snob than Pierce.

The other men greeted Joe cordially and told him that Franklin spoke highly of his Shakespearean knowledge. He remembered having seen Collier and Clampton at Stanford Ramsey's gala.

Franklin had told him that the dress was casual, so he wore off-the-rack Pizitz slacks, a cotton shirt that needed ironing, and a cotton sweater. All the other men wore tailored wool or gabardine slacks, fine cotton shirts, and expensive sport jackets. He was particularly impressed with the jackets Franklin and Warren wore. Franklin had on a light wool, herringbone jacket that appeared to be tailor-made. Warren's light brown jacket was even more elegant. It fit him impeccably, and he wore a dark brown, silk handkerchief for accent.

JOE READ THE *TIMON OF ATHENS* QUOTE THE SECOND TIME as the rules of the game required. Four of the players looked perplexed. Warren had a big smile on his face. Algernon smirked.

After two minutes, he collected the answer cards from the six men and tabulated the results on a score sheet for each player. When all five of his quotes were tabulated, he handed them to Franklin who held them until the end of the game.

As the game proceeded, the men were served snacks and cocktails by Franklin's butler, Paul. Joe observed that Warren frequently called on Paul to refresh his cocktail. Joe enjoyed the conversation at the table, generally related to Shakespeare and the quotes. But he mostly studied the men as the evening progressed. He listened for any comments that might allude to Mahogany Hall but none were forthcoming. He wasn't surprised as any mention of Mahogany Hall or Ramsey's gala would have insulted and embarrassed Franklin.

After the last player completed his round, the evening's host was responsible for tabulating the results. However, when Franklin was host, he always had Paul do the final tabulation since he was more accurate and faster with numbers. It took Paul five minutes to tabulate the results, and he then handed the summary sheet to Franklin.

Franklin looked at the results and smiled. "Well, gentlemen, we have a new winner in our midst. Joe McGrath won hands down. And I think we must crown him our new overall champion. Paul also did a quick calculation using averages to correct the scores to our usual six players, and Joe not only won, he set a new scoring record, 132 points. Well done, Joe. Algernon was second, and Warren was third."

All the men, save Algernon, applauded and complimented Joe with words of praise.

Sheldon, whom Joe found the least pretentious in the group, grinned. "Joe, are there any more Shakespearean nuggets in our police department?"

"No, Sheldon. Not to my knowledge. Well, maybe Dick Oliver, my boss, but we've never talked about Shakespeare."

Wilbur jumped right in. "We all know Dick Oliver well. You can rest assured he's no Shakespearean buff."

With a straight face, Randolph said, "Then I'll bet Chief Watson must be." Joe joined all the men except Algernon in a good laugh.

Algernon could no longer contain himself. "Franklin, I insist we check the final figures." His face contorted as if he had swallowed poison. "I can't image a darkie can do arithmetic that quickly and that accurately. There must be a mistake."

As Algernon spoke, Joe observed Paul. He did not move a muscle or alter his stoic facial expression.

Franklin replied curtly. "That won't be necessary, Algernon. Paul takes care of our household accounts. I trust him implicitly."

Algernon stood, glowered at Joe and then Franklin. "Well! I'll take my leave." He walked out in a huff.

Joe sat quietly, unsure of what to say, as did the other men. Sheldon finally broke the deadly silence. "Forgive Algernon, Joe. You forgive him too, Paul. Algernon goes off like that occasionally. He's really a good man, but he can't abide losing."

Franklin said, "Gentlemen, it's been a stimulating evening. One more round of applause for Joe McGrath. I trust you agree with me that we should invite him to our next game." He added, trying to be serious, "We must dethrone him."

The men applauded and nodded to Joe with respect. He nodded back.

"After Algernon's graceful departure," Franklin said, "I think it's time to call it a night. Thanks for coming. Paul will show you out."

As Joe got up to leave, Warren said to him, "The *Timon of Athens* quote was a real curve ball. I knew the speaker and play, but I was unsure about the act, scene, and line numbers."

"You got three points including Act Four. You were incorrect on the other two. The correct answers were Scene Three and lines 439-440. Algernon was the only other player to get points. He got the speaker and play, but missed the other attributes," Joe said.

"I can thank Hugh Stroud," Warren said, continuing to sprinkle his speech with a British accent. "He was a great Shakespearean scholar who still teaches at Alabama. Of course, he taught all the famous plays, but he loved to cover the lesser known and problem plays. He thought they were underrated."

"You're right, Warren. I studied under Stroud too. We would read plays like *Timon* and *King John* at his home in the evening. It was invigorating. Did you take part in readings like that?"

Warren's expression immediately told Joe he shouldn't have asked the question.

"No. I was never invited."

Joe changed the subject. "Warren, I meant to tell you that I've been admiring your jacket all evening. Where did you get it?"

As a chameleon changes colors, Warren's face went from muted anger to delight. "Why, thank you. I bought this, and one just like it in dark blue, when I was in London earlier this year. Oh, I must tell you, London is still a mess from the war. But Savile Row is slowly coming back to life. A tailor hand made these for me in one week so I could bring them back on the Queen Elizabeth. They're worth every penny. Have you been to London, Joe?"

Even if he had been, Joe would have said no. "I'm afraid not. I can't afford the time or money."

"Pity. Well, maybe your new lady friend will take you. I must be going. Good game, Joe. Well played."

CHAPTER 52

LUKE MATTHEW'S TRIAL

TUESDAY—NOVEMBER 11, 1947

J UDGE OVERTON HAD POSTPONED THE START of Luke Matthew's trial until one o'clock. He had to clear up backlogged paperwork that accumulated during his weeklong vacation.

Luke was brought into the courtroom, shackled at the hands and ankles. The police removed the shackles, and Luke sat down beside his attorney, Alfred Banks. District Attorney Lance Roberts and two of his assistants were at the prosecution's table. The courtroom was empty but for a few courtroom regulars, Luke's parents, and three newsmen including Jack Ritter. Dick Oliver was there to observe.

After Judge Overton took his seat on the bench, Roberts said, "The prosecution is ready to proceed, Your Honor."

"Is the defense ready to proceed, Alfred?" Overton said.

"Yes, Your Honor. The defense is ready, but we have one request."

"What is that?"

"The defense requested via subpoena that the prosecution provide a copy of the transcript of the first police interrogation of the defendant on the afternoon of October 15, 1947. The defense has yet to receive the transcript. Homicide Detective Joe McGrath and Officer Brendan O'Connor conducted the interrogation. I respectfully request that their names be added to the defense witness list."

Roberts jumped out of his chair. "Objection, Your Honor."

"On what grounds, Mr. Roberts?"

"The prosecution tried to comply with the request. Apparently, there's no written record of the first interrogation. The prosecution will call Officers Tommy Langford and Bertie Jackson. The defendant signed a confession in the presence of both officers. The confession will be Exhibit A in our case."

"Mr. Roberts, there aren't even handwritten notes available from the first interrogation?"

"No, Your Honor. Apparently, none were kept."

"Objection overruled. Clerk, add the two names to the defense witness list and issue the necessary subpoenas."

Roberts sneered at Banks and sat down.

Banks leaned over to Luke and whispered, "Well, we won that one."

Overton said, "Mr. Roberts, Alfred, anything else before we proceed to jury selection? . . . Bailiff, bring in the first twelve prospective jurors."

Banks walked a tightrope during the entire jury-selection process. At best, he hoped the jury would end up with at least one or two men who appeared to have a sense of justice and fair play. He watched as Roberts systematically used his peremptory challenges to exclude the few colored men called as prospective jurors. He knew he couldn't use his challenges as cavalierly as Roberts. All the white eyes in the courtroom were constantly cast on him with suspicion and hate.

In one exchange with a prospective juror, Banks said, "Sir, do you have any preconceived opinions about the defendant's guilt or innocence?"

The white man looked at Overton. "What's that darkie talkin' 'bout? I ain't used to no colored talkin' to me no way."

"He wants to know if you can give the colored boy a fair trial."

"Why don't he jus' say so," the man said. He turned to Banks. "Hell yes."

"Your Honor, I'd like to exercise a peremptory challenge and excuse this juror."

Overton peered at Banks over his reading glasses, amazed at what he just heard. "Are you sure, Alfred?"

"Yes, Your Honor."

"Sir, you are excused from the courtroom. Thank you for your cooperation," Overton said to the white man.

"Whaddya mean? Can't no colored boy 'cuse me. I jus' gonna leave." The prospective juror stomped out of the courtroom.

Jury selection took the remainder of the day. The last juror was selected at forty thirty. Overton swore the jury in and told the jury not to read newspaper accounts of the trial and not to discuss the trial with others, including family members.

Luke was shackled and brusquely removed from the courtroom, hardly given time to smile at his parents.

Roberts turned to Oliver. "Are McGrath and O'Connor going to cause us trouble?"

"I don't know. They've been told to keep their mouths shut. But under oath, I don't know what they'll say."

"Dick, you gotta talk to them. I don't want any surprises if they make it to the witness stand. Normally, police officers would be prosecution witnesses. I'm gonna have one of my assistants review case law and appeals. We'll try to find a legal basis for a stronger objection when the court convenes tomorrow."

"I'll talk to them."

"Yeah. Maybe you can hide them."

Dick Oliver sat down in front of Joe's desk. Brendan was out. "You and Brendan are gonna receive subpoenas requiring you to testify in Matthew's trial."

"I'm surprised Roberts wants us as witnesses."

"Roberts doesn't. Alfred Banks told Judge Overton that the prosecution was unable to provide him the transcript of your initial interrogation of Matthew. You're gonna be defense witnesses. How'd Banks know about the interrogation? You talk to him?"

Joe was miffed. "Hell no. I did as you told me and kept my mouth shut. C'mon, it's not too hard to figure out. Unless you also muzzled Matthew, you know he told Banks about the interrogation and the way he was beaten by Langford and Jackson until he signed the confession. Christ, it's the best defense Banks can offer."

"What are you going to do?"

"If you're asking me to lie on the witness stand, the answer is no."

"The chief and other important people are not gonna be happy," Dick said.

"So, we're gonna fry the wrong guy?"

"Goddammit, Joe. I've told you I don't buy your theories about the murders. I think we got the right guy."

"We'll see."

"Think long and hard about what you say on the stand." Dick left Joe's office.

A few minutes later Brendan returned to the office in his civvies, prepared to start his stakeout of Knight's house. "I'm ready to go boss. The car's ready."

"Did the carpool guys ask any questions?"

"No. When I told them I was doing an assignment for you, they were cooperative."

"Good. I've decided I'm gonna join you. That way we can spell each other on the watch and get some nap time. Also simplifies the communication issue. Tomorrow's gonna be a busy day."

Sally stuck her head in Joe's office. "Joe, there's someone from the courthouse who wants to see you and Brendan."

Joe smiled. He knew what was coming.

"Good afternoon, gentlemen. I'm Wilbur Thomas, a clerk in Judge Overton's Circuit Court. I have subpoenas for you." Thomas handed each man a document. "Thank you, gentlemen." Thomas left as abruptly as he arrived.

Brendan stared at the subpoena. "What the hell is this all about?"

"Luke's lawyer subpoenaed us as defense witnesses since the prosecution was unable to provide him a copy of our interrogation notes."

"Shit. What are we gonna do?"

"Answer his questions truthfully. Let's go get the car."

CHAPTER 53

THE NEW MOON

WEDNESDAY—NOVEMBER 12, 1947

J OE NUDGED BRENDAN AWAKE. It was his rotation on the lookout at
Weldon Knight's house. They had started the evening at Knight's
business and followed him when he left. He went directly to the
Downtown Club. He was in the club for two hours, then drove home.

Joe said, "Little activity. Did see a light go on and off. It looked like
a bathroom. Everybody has to take a piss at night including me. I'm
gonna slip out behind a tree, then turn in."

Joe got in the backseat and lay down for a restless hour. Brendan
woke him at three. The rotations continued until six. As Joe watched
Knight's house, the first hints of dawn crept into the overcast sky. He
reached into the back seat and shook Brendan.

"Wake up, sleepy head. It's dawn. No activity. Let's go. Drive back
to the office so I can get my car. Then return the car to the carpool
and go home, shower, and change clothes. Meet me in the office about
eight. We have to be in the courtroom by nine."

As soon as they were clear of Knight's house, Joe made a call at the
first phone booth.

"Birmingham Police Department, Sergeant Alison speaking."

"Joe McGrath, Dean. Just checking in on last night's activity.
Anything I should be interested in?"

"Nope. A burglary in Ensley. A couple of domestic dispute calls."

"Slow night. The kind I like," Joe said.

"Yep."

"Thanks, Dean."

Joe said to Brendan, "Nothing for us. Maybe our boy didn't show. And if Knight's our boy, we know why."

"Maybe he snuck out of his house in a way we didn't anticipate."

Joe nodded. "Hey, you're thinking like a detective. Could be. I guess we'll have to wait and see."

JOE GOT BACK TO THE OFFICE AT SEVEN THIRTY. Sally was already at her desk.

Joe was haggard, but couldn't resist. "Good morning, Sally. You got a kiss for me?"

She smiled, but looked at Joe with concern. "Good morning, Joe. I always have a kiss for you. Are you feeling all right?"

Joe took a Hershey's Kiss from the bowl. "Thanks for the kiss, Sally. I'm fine. Long night. Brendan and I did a stakeout to no avail."

"I'll get you a cup of coffee."

"Get two, please. Brendan's comin' in."

Ten minutes later, Brendan arrived looking as bleary eyed as Joe felt. Sally brought in two cups of steaming coffee.

"Sorry it took so long. I had to make a new pot."

"Thanks, Sally."

The two sat quietly, still in a daze, inhaling the aroma of the coffee and sipping. The phone rang, jarring the men from their coffee reverie.

"Joe McGrath here."

"Billy Donaldson, Joe. Got a call at seven fifteen reporting a dead woman's body in Third Alley South between Fourteenth Street South and Fifteenth Street South. Oliver told me to get you to cover it. He said he'd call the chief. I've already sent Jerry Howard and his patrol partner to the site. Told 'em to secure it for you and hold any witnesses."

"Who called it in, Billy?"

"Caller wouldn't identify himself. He just said there was a woman's body at that location and hung up."

"Brendan and I will get right over there. Call the coroner's office."

"Will do, Joe."

Brendan was ready to go when Joe hung up. At Sally's desk, Joe told her about the reported murder and added, "We're under subpoenas to be at the courthouse at nine. Dick Oliver knows. Call him and tell him we're on the way to the murder site. We'll drive separately. One of us will be at the courthouse on time."

Sally nodded.

It took Joe five minutes to reach the alleyway. He looked around the area. It was industrial with a mix of warehouses and small manufacturers and businesses. Howard and his partner had blocked off both ends of the alley. A handful of bystanders stood at each end of the alley, gawking at the scene.

Joe entered the alley and saw Howard. "Hey, Jerry."

"Joe, you're not gonna believe how much this looks like the murder scene in the alley behind the hotel." Jerry pointed to a loading dock between two warehouses.

Joe saw the body on the left side of the space. *Oh my God, we were right. He's done it again.* A young colored woman's nude body lay flat on the ground, face up, arranged in what was a Christian cross. Her legs were tight together, and her arms were perpendicular to her torso, completing the cross.

He knelt by the side of her body. He guessed she was in her twenties. A curvaceous figure complimented her mocha skin color. Most striking was her facial expression. Her face was sheathed in a rigid look of horror. Around her throat, he could see the telltale signs of a garrotte, and her lips were bruised. Her clothes were laid under her body like a blanket.

Joe stood up and saw Brendan looking over his shoulder. "It's the exact same MO as the other two murders. If Knight's our man, you were right. He somehow left his house and got back in without us seeing him."

"Maybe a guy this crazy has a tunnel entrance to his house."

"You've been reading too many *Batman* comics. But you could be right. We'll follow-up on Knight as soon as we can."

Frank Cutler and his two aides arrived. "Hi, Joe. What we got?"

"Hey, Frank. It's appears to be exactly like the September and October murders."

Cutler took one look at the body and whistled. "Goddamn! It's the same. We'll get right on it."

"I'm gonna look around the alley for a few moments, then I gotta get over to the courtroom before nine. Brendan will stay with you until you take the body. Can you get me a report by this afternoon?"

"Can do, Joe."

Joe motioned at Brendan to follow him. "You and Howard and his partner give the alley a careful going over. Talk to the folks behind the tape. I'm going to the courthouse in a few minutes. I need to talk to the DA and Banks and the judge. I don't know what they'll agree to do. After Cutler takes the body, you come to the courtroom. Howard can release the area if Cutler agrees. And tell Howard to talk to all the businesses on both sides of the alley. If I'm not in the courtroom or the area outside the courtroom where witnesses wait, come to the office."

JOE ARRIVED AT THE COURTROOM AT EIGHT FORTY. Lance Roberts and Alfred Banks were already at their respective tables. Matthew hadn't been brought to the courtroom yet.

Joe approached Roberts. "Mister District Attorney, I need to talk to you and Banks."

"What about, Joe? You're a defense witness. I'm sure you won't be called until after the lunch break. We've got opening statements. Then I'll present the prosecution's case. This trial won't last long."

"There was a murder early this morning similar to the murders Matthew's charged with. I think we should talk to Judge Overton."

"Another murder? What are you talking about?"

"Banks should be in on this conversation, Mr. Roberts."

Roberts called out to Banks. "Alfred, you better listen to this."

Banks joined the men and eyed Joe questionably.

Joe said, "Mr. Banks, I'm Homicide Detective Joe McGrath." He offered Banks his hand.

Banks shook Joe's hand. "I've heard a lot about you, Detective McGrath. Pleased to meet you."

Roberts watched, shaking his head, and said, "Joe says there's been another murder this morning similar to the murders your client is charged with. He wants us to talk to Judge Overton."

Dick Oliver entered the courtroom and saw the three men. Approaching them, he said, "Joe, Sally called and told me you were on the murder site. What's going on here?"

"Dick, I just left the murder scene. The MO is identical to the murders in September and October. We need to talk to Judge Overton."

"What do you want Overton to do?"

"Recess the trial until we have a better fix on what happened."

"What do you think, Lance?" Dick said.

"I don't like it one bit. We've got a confessed killer on trial. But Judge Overton needs to know what happened. I'll talk to the bailiff."

In a few minutes, the bailiff returned from the judge's chambers and told Roberts they could go in.

"Good morning, gentlemen. Good morning, Alfred. What brings the prosecution, defense, and BPD to my chambers?"

Roberts spoke up. "Your Honor, another colored girl was murdered last night on Third Alley South. Homicide Detective McGrath just left the crime scene. I'll let him describe the situation."

"Your Honor, the MO of the murder early this morning is identical to the two murders Luke Matthew is on trial for," Joe said.

"Detective McGrath, I take it you're implying that Matthew is not the murderer."

"I'm saying it raises serious doubts."

"You apparently didn't express any doubts before about Matthew."

"Your Honor, we had some doubts. He didn't match the profile we developed for the likely murderer. Of course, our profiles are seldom exact and frequently way off the mark. When Matthew signed the confession, we assumed we had the right man."

"What do you suggest, Detective McGrath?" Overton said.

"A two-day recess while we complete our investigation of this latest murder and the coroner completes his report."

"When will Frank Cutler have a report?"

"He said he'd have a report in my hands by this afternoon."

"What's your position on this, Lance?" Overton said.

"Your Honor, I think we're on sound legal grounds to continue the trial. However, I don't object to a two-day recess," Lance said.

With obvious reluctance, Overton turned to Banks. "And you, Alfred?"

Banks replied without hesitation. "Your Honor, I certainly agree with a two-day recess."

"Here's what I'll agree to do. After court is called to order, I'll announce that due to other court business, the trial will be in recess until ten o'clock tomorrow. I want all four of you in my chambers at nine tomorrow to brief me on the police investigation, the coroner's report, and any attendant legal issues. Is that clear?"

All four nodded.

"One other thing," Overton said, "You are all under a gag order. Don't talk to anyone, especially the press, about these discussions. You can acknowledge that a murder has taken place, but nothing else. Understand?"

Again, the men nodded.

"Your Honor," Joe said, "Jack Ritter with the *Birmingham News* will immediately smell a story. He has numerous sources in town including the BPD, city hall, the courthouse, and elsewhere. He'll be all over this looking for details. He may learn something that sounds as if it came from one of us."

Overton smiled. "I know Jack only too well. If he squeezes a story out of someone, I just hope I can't track it back to one of you. If I can, I'll hold that person in contempt of court." He looked at his watch. "It's after nine. Y'all get back in the courtroom. Let's get on with this, so we can do some more important work."

AFTER JUDGE OVERTON RECESSED THE COURT for the day, Dick Oliver pulled Joe aside. "Goddammit it, Joe. You've gone around me again. Why didn't you contact me before you came to the courtroom?"

"Dick, I wasn't trying to go around you. I had only a few minutes at the crime scene to size it up before I had to rush over here. I thought the court should know about the murder before the trial started."

"You didn't think I would tell them?"

"I'm sure you would have. But you didn't have the information I had. And I wasn't sure you'd be here this morning."

Jack Ritter came over and stepped between the two men. "Okay, Birmingham's top gumshoes, what's going on?"

"Judge Overton called a recess for other court business," Dick said.

"Oh c'mon. You and I know it has to do with Matthew's trial. The DA got a weak case or what? Maybe you can talk, Joe."

"Dick speaks for both of us. Chase your fantasy elsewhere."

Jack laughed at the two men. "I'll do just that." He walked toward the DA.

Dick said, "Joe, you and I gotta have a serious talk later. Right now, let's go tell the chief what's going on. Go straight to headquarters. I'll meet you at the chief's office."

WATSON GROWLED AT DICK AND JOE. "What the fuck's goin' on?"

"As I told you earlier today, Chief," Dick said, "there was another murder of a young colored girl. I sent Joe to the crime scene to check it out. He says the MO is the same as the two murders in September and October. He went—"

"How the fuck you know that, Professor? You clearvoyant?"

"No, Chief. I don't have any special powers. Just observation. The woman was strangled around the throat like the other two. Her body was arranged like a Christian symbol, a Christian cross this time, just like the other two. Her lips were bruised just like the other two. And early this morning was a new moon."

"So?" Watson said.

Joe wondered, *Is the chief really this slow or is he stringing me along?* "The same MO indicates the same murderer, Chief. That means Luke Matthew is not the murderer."

"Goddammit, Dick. We got a confession. What's McGrath up to?"

"Joe's trying to do his job, Chief. Judge Overton recessed the trial this morning until ten o'clock tomorrow. He wants Joe and me and the attorneys in his office at nine tomorrow to discuss the investigation and review the coroner's report."

"I don't give a shit about Joe's take on the murders: same MO, Christian cross, and all that dark moon jumbo mumbo."

Joe knew he should keep his mouth shut. "Chief, when I got to the crime scene, Jerry Howard told me it looked just like the September murder. Frank Cutler agreed."

The chief's face was bright red. "Jus' like. Jus' like. Goddammit, you ain't listenin' to me. Now both of you, listen up real good. You go in that courtroom tomorrow and tell Overton that the BPD stands behind the confession Matthew signed. And we want the trial to precede. You got it?"

They nodded.

"And if you don't, I'm gonna run both your sorry asses outta the department. Get outta here."

Joe and Dick stood, turned around in unison, and hurried into the hallway.

"What're we gonna do, Dick?"

"I'm going to follow orders. What about you?"

"I guess I will."

"Guess is not good enough, Joe."

"We've got the wrong man. You know we do."

"Maybe. But I'm going to follow orders."

BACK IN HIS OFFICE, Joe asked Brendan to step out while he made some calls.

"Stanford Ramsey's office."

"This is Homicide Detective Joe McGrath. I'd like to speak to Mr. Ramsey."

"I'll connect you."

"Hi, Joe. What's on your mind?" Stanford said.

"Another colored girl was killed this morning. Same MO as the other two."

"Yes, I've heard all that."

"Did you talk to Chief Watson?"

"Just hung up on a conversation with him."

"Well, you know everything I called to tell you."

"What are you going to say to Overton tomorrow, Joe?"

"I'm waiting on the coroner's report to verify my observations."

"You're ignoring my question."

"Stanford, we've got the wrong man."

"Joe, think long and hard about what you say tomorrow."

"The chief's about ready to throw me out the door."

"I'll take care of Watson for the time being. Anything else?"

"No."

CHAPTER 54

SAM'S VISITOR

WEDNESDAY—NOVEMBER 12, 1947

A FTER HIS PHONE CONVERSATION WITH RAMSEY, Joe sat quietly, fully realizing how precarious his position with the department had become. *I can't back down now. Hell, English teaching's not too bad.* He reached for the phone.

"Sam Rucker."

"Hey, Sam. Back in the office, huh?"

"Yep. First day back. The house's in pretty good shape except for some final touch-up work."

"Well, your dark moon theory was right. Another young colored woman was murdered early this morning. Same MO as the others, down to the bruised lips."

"The kiss of salvation. What was the body position?"

"A Christian cross."

"What about Luke Matthew?"

Joe explained the meeting with Judge Overton. He added, "The judge put us under a gag order, so don't talk to anyone about this."

"What can I do to help?"

"Lie low. I don't want your fingerprints on anything that's gone on recently. I'm in deep shit with Oliver, Watson, and Ramsey. I may be an ex-homicide detective soon. I always wanted to sell cars."

"I don't want you to martyr yourself on my behalf. I want to help. I'll take care of myself," Sam said.

"I guess this is my day to be lectured to."

"Joe, you know I didn't mean it that way."

"Yeah, I know. Just a little tense."

"Just remember, I'm here. Call me," Sam said.

"I'll keep you posted."

SAM DID SOME MORE WORK and was ready to go out for lunch when there was a knock. He opened the office door.

He was surprised to see Ethel Baker, a member of his church's congregation. "Mrs. Baker, what a surprise. Please come in."

"Sam, if it's not a bother, I'd like to talk to you for a few minutes."

"No bother, Mrs. Baker. Have a seat, please." He smiled at her. "I know, you want my support for a fundraising event."

She didn't smile. "No. I wish that was the case."

Sam had always admired Ethel Baker's spunk and intelligence. She was a diminutive woman, five feet at best. She was in her sixties, but looked younger with her smooth brown skin and black hair that had only a tinge of gray. As usual, she was well-dressed, as if she were going to church. Her dress was dark blue with matching gloves and a hat. She had a small purse, demurely hung over her left forearm.

"What can I do for you, Mrs. Baker?"

"Sam, at service three weeks ago, Reverend Stockton asked anyone who knew something related to those two murders to talk to the police or to him. Do you remember?"

"Yes, I certainly do."

"I saw something. I'm ashamed of myself. I was afraid to talk to anybody, especially the police. My son Herbert finally convinced me to talk to the reverend. I did yesterday. The reverend said I should tell you what I saw 'cause you'd know how to handle it. I don't want to get involved. The police and the white man's courts scare me."

"You have good reasons to be scared, Mrs. Baker. You can talk to me in complete confidence." Sam saw the tension in her face and tried to be calm and soothing. "Just relax and tell me what you saw. Then we can talk about how best to handle it."

Her face relaxed and a small smile formed at the edges of her mouth. "Reverend Stockton told me you'd be understanding. I live in a second floor apartment on Fourth Avenue North, a block from Ralston Park where that young woman was killed."

"Do you live east or west from the park, Mrs. Baker?"

"East."

"What's your address?"

"1325 Fourth Avenue North, Apartment 2C."

Sam nodded. "Go on."

"I'm an insomniac. I sleep a few hours, then wake up. I find it useless to lie in bed. I get up and read or knit until I'm drowsy. The night the woman was killed, I got up about three thirty. I have a habit of peeking though my drapes out my front window. I always think I'm gonna see something interesting. I never do. That is until that night."

"What did you see, Mrs. Baker?"

"Well, I musta been peeking out the window a few minutes, almost daydreaming, when I see this man walking on the sidewalk across the street. Now I don't know if he had been in the park, but he was coming from that direction."

"What did he look like?"

"He had on a long, black coat and wore a black hat with a big brim that came down over most of his face."

"Did you get a look at his face?"

"Not really. He turned around once to look back. Seemed like he thought someone was following him. His head lifted up a little bit. I could see some of his face. He was white. But I could never identify him. Didn't see enough of him, and most white men look alike to me. You know what I mean?"

Sam couldn't help chuckling. "Yes, ma'am. I sure do. What happened next?"

"He got to his car and drove off. It was parked near a streetlight. A new Buick Roadmaster. Two tone. Black roof and light green body."

"You seem to know cars pretty well, Mrs. Baker."

It was her turn to laugh. "Not really. But I know this car. Herbert's a top car salesman at Marcus Gilbert's Buick store. Every year they let him drive one of the new Buicks. I guess it's for advertising. He got this one in August. It's a 1948 model and the same color as the one I saw the night that girl was killed. He drives it all over town like some big shot. He also has been taking me on long drives on Sunday."

"You sure it's the latest model Buick?"

She sat up straight and looked at Sam as if he had been a naughty boy. "Sam, I know that car as well as I know my son. It's brand new," and she spoke even louder as she said, "It's a Buick. 1948."

Sam acted contrite although he wanted to smile lovingly at this delightful woman. "I'm sorry, Mrs. Baker. I meant no disrespect. In my business, one has to check important facts."

"Well, I hope it's useful."

"It's very useful. I know who to call immediately."

"Is he a policeman?"

"Yes, ma'am. But one we can trust. And don't worry, I will not mention your name to the man."

"Good. I'm pleased I came to see you. You've been understanding."

"One more thing, Mrs. Baker. Like I said, I won't mention your name to anyone. But if the murderer is apprehended and goes to trial, would you be willing to testify? We couldn't tell the court we heard about the car without producing a witness."

Mrs. Baker looked hard at Sam. "I'd prefer not to."

"I know. But if it proves necessary, I promise you I'll be at your side throughout the entire proceedings."

Sam could see the consternation on her face as she mulled the situation over. "All right, Sam, I'll testify, but only if absolutely necessary."

"Good. It may not come to pass. But if it does, I'll explain everything to you and be right there with you."

"I appreciate that. Is there anything else?"

"No. Thanks for all your help. I know it wasn't easy. And I will try to see that you don't have to testify. I was just getting ready to go to lunch. Would you like to join me or can I drive you home?"

"No thank you. I need to shop a bit. I'll catch the bus home."

Mrs. Baker left the office. Sam was glad she refused his offer as he picked up the phone.

JOE AND BRENDAN DISCUSSED THE MURDER. The phone rang.

"Joe McGrath here."

"We need to talk. Okay?"

"Just a sec." Turning to Brendan. "Close the door."

"Do you want me to leave?" Brendan said.

"No. It's Sam."

"What's up, Sam? You still mad at me because I told you I wanted no help right now?"

"No. But I got a lead that may help you. I had a visitor in my office a few minutes ago, an elderly colored woman. I can't tell you her name at this time. She's reluctant to go to the police or to court, but she said she would testify if it became necessary. I told her it would be necessary if an arrest and trial occurred. Anyway, she saw something interesting the night of the second murder on October fourteenth."

"Yeah, what?"

Sam explained to Joe what Ethel Baker had told him about the man she saw, including his coat, hat, and car. He added, "I think she's credible. We gotta follow-up on the car."

"You bet. I'll get Brendan on it right away. There are only two Buick dealers in Birmingham, Gilbert and Drennan. Shouldn't take long."

"Let me know what you find out," Sam said.

"Will do. This may be the break we've been looking for. Let's see where we are later today."

He told Brendan about the phone conversation. "You get your butt over to the Gilbert and Drennan dealerships and find out who purchased cars like this before October fourteenth. They weren't available until late August, so there can't be too many of that make, model, and color scheme out there. And change into your civvies so you look less cop. Get back here as soon as you can."

"Right boss."

CHAPTER 55

OLIVER'S EPIPHANY

WEDNESDAY—NOVEMBER 12, 1947

AFTER BRENDAN LEFT TO VISIT the Buick dealerships, Joe closed his office door. He felt overwhelmed with fatigue. He lay his head in his arms on his desk and fell asleep, waking with a start when someone knocked.

"Yes," he mumbled.

"Sorry to interrupt, Joe," Sally said. "This just came for you. It's from Judge Overton's court." She handed Joe the envelope.

"Thanks, Sally." She went back to her desk.

Joe opened the envelope. It was a formal notice of the gag order. Joe tossed it on his desk, suddenly realizing how hungry he was as he hadn't eaten today.

"Sally, I'm going over to the cops' diner. I'll be back soon."

"Okay, Joe. Have a nice lunch."

Joe sat at the counter. Helen swaggered up to him.

"Well, if it ain't Big Dick. Where you and Puppy Dog been? Chasin' perverts and murderers?"

Joe always cringed and smiled when she called him Big Dick. "I'm working on it, Helen. We've been busy boys. What's good today?"

"Yeah, too busy for me. We got a nice chowder. Goes good with a BLT and potato salad."

"Sounds good. And a Coke. And a piece of pecan pie."

"I'm still waiting to go for it with you," she smiled. "Comin' up."

Joe relaxed, enjoying his lunch. Helen always put him in a better mood.

He paid the bill and started for the door when Helen called out, "Thanks for the nice tip, Big Dick. Don't forget to call."

Joe doffed his hat and bowed to Helen and went back to his office.

JOE HAD BEEN SITTING AT HIS DESK FOR OVER AN HOUR mulling over the case and his future, when the phone rang.

"Joe McGrath here."

"Detective McGrath, it's Don over at the morgue."

"Hey, Don. How's the autopsy going?"

"Dr. Cutler finished it about thirty minutes ago. He's writing his report. He said it would be done in about an hour. He's asked me to bring it to you. Will you be in your office?"

"Yep. Can't wait to get my hands on it. Got any photos?"

"I'll check and see if they've been printed yet."

"If they have, bring me a set. If not, don't wait. I need the report as soon as possible."

"I'll check. I'll be over soon."

Don got to Joe's office just after two o'clock. "Hi, Detective McGrath. Here's the report and a few photos. They haven't all been printed yet. We'll get you copies as soon as they're done. Dr. Cutler told me to tell you that this murder is identical to the ones in September and October. He says it's highly likely that the same man did all three."

Joe was already scanning the report: garrotte-style strangling, bruised lips, a few body bruises, and time of death between two and three. "Yeah. I agree. Thanks for bringing these over, Don."

"Here's something else Dr. Cutler wanted me to give you." Don handed Joe a small envelope. "This button was found under the body after it was placed in a body bag. Dr. Cutler said it's silver in spite of its gold appearance. It's called gilt."

Joe opened the envelope and pulled out the button. He held it in his hand and stared at it.

"Something wrong?" Don said.

"I recognize this button. I've got to read the report and think about this. Thanks. I'll call if I need more."

Joe felt as if a carpet had been pulled out from underneath him. *Oh my God, this is like the buttons on Warren Abernathy's jacket.* Joe's mind kept racing with the many implications of the object he held in his hand. He continued staring at it as if he wished it would go away.

He finally looked at the button with some objectivity. It was about an inch in diameter. It was embossed with what appeared to be the coat of arms of the City of London, and with a magnifying glass, he could read the motto, *Domine Dirge Nos.* Joe smiled and thought about his mother. He was able to translate the Latin phrase, *Our Lord Direct Us.*

Joe was still fingering the button when Brendan returned to the office. "Hi, Puppy Dog. Have any luck?" Joe said.

"Puppy Dog?" Brendan said.

"I had lunch at the cops' diner. Helen asked about you."

"Nice. Yeah, both dealers cooperated. I went to Gilbert first. They've sold one Buick just like the one we're looking for. The buyer was a colored doctor, Eldridge Maxwell. He lives in Ensley. The manager told me we might see another one driving around town. Their top salesman, Herbert Baker, is allowed to drive the same car for his personal use for advertising purposes."

"And Drennan?" Joe said.

"Drennan sold two of this model and color to Birmingham residents. One was to an elderly gentleman named Drayton Cox. The other was sold to Warren Abernathy who—"

"Jesus Christ." Joe rubbed his head with his hands.

"You all right, Joe?"

"No. Yes. Shit, Brendan, this has to be the right guy."

"Abernathy?"

"Yep. But I wish he wasn't. He's the ex-husband of my new girlfriend."

"You're gonna go after him, aren't you, Joe?"

Joe's head snapped up as if someone had slapped him.

"Yes." Joe showed Brendan the button. "This was found under the body at the crime scene today. It came off a jacket owned by Abernathy." Joe explained how he came to know the button's source.

"What are we gonna do, Boss?"

"We can't just go out and arrest him or bring him in for questioning as we did Matthew. He'd demand to call his lawyer, someone like

Beauchamp, who would have him out in nothing flat. I gotta get a search warrant so we can search his home for the jacket," Joe said.

"How you gonna do that?"

"Good question. I know the chief will tell me to get lost. Did you get Abernathy's home address?"

Brendan nodded and handed Joe his notes. "He lives in the Forest Park area."

"That fits. It's one of the nicest residential neighborhoods in the city. Thanks. I'll be back soon." Joe put the button and notes in his pocket and rushed out of his office.

"Dick, I need to talk to you. We've got a prime suspect in the three murders."

"Oh, c'mon, Joe. We told Judge Overton we needed more time to investigate this last murder."

"I know, but two things just happened that point to one guy, Warren Abernathy."

"What? You must be kidding. He's the ex-husband of your lady friend. You jealous of him or something?"

Joe cringed at the word *jealous*. "People may react that way. I know the high society crowd, especially Stanford Ramsey, will be upset. Christ, the chief will probably crucify me."

"And what do you think I might do to you?"

"With the information we've got, you're the only person in the department I can turn to. Hear me out."

Dick nodded.

"A witness just came forward. The witness, a colored woman, would rather not be involved, but will testify if necessary." Joe explained her story and Brendan's visit to the Buick dealers.

"Maybe the colored guy that works at Gilbert Buick is the culprit. You said you had two things. What's the other one?"

Joe pulled the button out of his pocket and handed it to Dick.

"Interesting button. Where did this come from?" Dick said.

"Cutler found it under the body when they moved it this morning. I got his report and the button an hour ago. His report confirms that the three murders are identical. Last Monday, I met with a Shakespearean group. Warren was there."

Dick broke in, "Is that the group that includes Franklin Pierce?"

"Yes, and several others. They play a game where the participants try to identify Shakespearean quotes."

"I've heard of their game. Did you win?"

"Yes."

"Congratulations. The chief doesn't call you Professor for nothing."

Joe ignored the comment. "After the game, Warren and I talked for a few minutes. Earlier in the evening, I had noticed the beautifully tailored jacket he was wearing. As we stood talking, I saw the elegant buttons on it and complimented Warren on the jacket. Then Cutler finds the identical button under the body."

"Surely others in town have similar jackets with the same buttons."

"I seriously doubt it. Warren told me that he had traveled to London earlier this year and had two identical jackets handmade by a Savile Row tailor. And the button you're holding, which is silver gilt, has the coat of arms of the City of London on it. The Latin motto reads *Our Lord Direct Us.*"

"How do you know this about the button?"

Joe had to smile. "When I studied Shakespeare in high school and college, we also studied a lot of English history. And my mother tutored me in Latin, and I took four years in high school."

Dick handed the button back to Joe, and lifted his left hand to his chin and began rubbing it. Joe knew he was considering his options. "What is it you want to do?" Dick said.

"I need a search warrant. Before any more time passes, we need to search his home in hopes of finding the jacket with the missing button. If we find it, we'll have probable cause to arrest him," Joe said.

"And if you can't find the jacket or there's no button missing."

"There's still the car."

"That's much less persuasive than the button. What will you do if you can't get a warrant?"

"I don't know."

Dick's hand went back to his chin. "I thought your theories about the body positions and dark moon were bullshit. Warren was always a weird duck. He was a member of my Methodist church. But a few years ago, he left and joined a Pentecostal church on the north side. Now this is hearsay. I heard the preacher there was one of those fire and brimstone guys, talking about the need to punish all sinners and nonbelievers," Dick said.

"That matches our profile of the killer."

"Even so, I can't imagine Warren Abernathy committed these murders."

"With the evidence I now have and what you just told me, don't you think it's possible?" Joe said.

"Yeah, it's possible. Joe, I know you don't think much of me."

Joe thought carefully about what to say. "No. That's not it, Dick. You're an enigma to me. Sometimes you support what I want to do, like work with Sam Rucker. And then you're singing the chief's song."

Dick paused. He made a phone call.

"Lance Roberts."

"Lance, Dick Oliver, we've got a credible suspect in the murders of the three prostitutes, and it's not Luke Matthew. Joe McGrath and I want to go see Judge Taylor about issuing a search warrant for the suspect's house. We need you to join us."

"Who's the suspect?"

"Warren Abernathy."

"You must be joking."

"No. I'm gonna call Taylor right now. Can you join us? I'll call you back if he's not available."

"I'll be there in fifteen minutes."

Dick dialed the phone again.

"Judge Taylor's office."

CHAPTER 56

THE WARRANT

WEDNESDAY—NOVEMBER 12, 1947

"THIS IS HOMICIDE CAPTAIN RICHARD OLIVER. I'd like to speak to Judge Taylor."

"Just a moment, Captain Oliver."

"Hi, Dick. I haven't heard from you in a while. Am I in trouble?"

"Yeah, Robert. You were seen jaywalking. I've got a warrant for your arrest. Seriously, I need your help to issue a search warrant. It's very important. Lance Roberts, Homicide Detective Joe McGrath, and I need to talk to you about it."

"I thought you guys went to Judge Overton for warrants?"

"We usually do. However, in this case, we'd like to see you."

"Okay. Will there be a witness?"

"Yes, Detective McGrath."

"Can you come right over?"

"Yes."

"Good. I'll have my clerk hang around. He also serves as my steno."

"We'll be there in a few minutes."

"C'mon, Joe. This is the best judge in Birmingham to deal with something this sensitive."

"Aren't you gonna tell the chief about this?"

"You know better. We talk to the chief, he'll put the kibosh on it."

"Can I use your phone? I gotta call Brendan."

"Sure," Dick said.

"Joe McGrath's office. Brendan O'Connor speaking."

"Brendan. Joe. I'm going to a judge's office. You stay put until I return or call you."

"JUDGE TAYLOR, THIS IS DETECTIVE JOE MCGRATH," Dick said.

"Hello, Detective. Lance is already here. Sit down gentlemen. What brings you here so late in the day?"

"Robert, I'm sure you've heard of the murders in September and October of two colored prostitutes in Scratch Ankle," Dick said.

"Yes, I read about them."

Dick explained that a third murder had occurred this morning similar to the first two. He then went over the two pieces of evidence—the witness and the car, and the button—pointing to Warren Abernathy as the murderer.

"Lance, do you know of this," Taylor said.

"I know of the murder this morning, but the rest just occurred."

"I'll let Joe explain the details," Dick said.

"Joe, are you the source for the information to support the search warrant request?"

"Yes, Your Honor."

"Joe, we're not in a courtroom. Call me Robert. We need to transcribe your comments. I need to ask you some questions." Taylor called out to his clerk, "Vince, please come in here and bring your steno machine. I need your help."

As Vince set up his steno machine, Taylor motioned at the men in his office. "Vince, your know Lance Roberts. This is Homicide Captain Dick Oliver and Homicide Detective Joe McGrath. They've requested a search warrant for a man named Warren Abernathy. You need to transcribe Joe's testimony as his affidavit. Joe, I need to swear you in. You ready, Vince?"

"Yes sir."

After Joe was sworn in, Taylor said, "Tell me in your own words the justification you have for this search warrant request."

Joe explained the witness and the car, but kept Sam's name out of the story. He then showed Taylor the button and told him about his encounter with Warren Abernathy at the Shakespearean party.

Taylor listened intently to Joe and said, "I'm sure you both know that Warren is well-known in Birmingham. I'll admit he's something of a bon vivant, but this is a startling accusation. I have a few questions. Let's start with the button, as you're the direct witness. Do you know if anyone traveled with Warren on his London trip?"

"No, I don't know."

"Have you been able to determine if anyone else in Birmingham has a similar jacket?"

"No. We learned about the car and button just two hours ago. We certainly need to do the things you suggest, but time is of the essence now. If Warren is or becomes aware that a button is missing, he may hide or destroy the jacket," Joe said.

"Or have the button replaced. Jackets, especially expensive ones, come with replacements. I suspect Savile Row tailors do that."

"True enough. And if both jackets are not in his home, we'll immediately visit all the tailors and men's stores that might do a button replacement job. Warren doesn't strike me as being handy with a needle and thread."

Taylor smiled. "Let's talk about the car and the witness. You're in a position of hearsay with me. Do you think this witness is credible?"

"Yes. Very much so."

"Why? Who did she talk to?"

Joe didn't want to answer. "Is this conversation confidential?"

"A search warrant, if I decide to issue it, and this transcript will become part of an official court document."

Joe decided he had to proceed. "Sam Rucker. He's a colored private investigator. He's been assisting me with the investigation in the colored community. Colored people are reluctant to talk to the police. The witness came to Sam today and told him about the car."

"I know Sam Rucker. Good man. You don't remember me, do you?"

"No. You do look familiar."

"I was the presiding judge in the Davie Yarbo trial several years ago. You and Sam testified for the prosecution."

"My God. How could I have forgotten? I'm sorry."

"Not necessary. In fact, I prefer it that way. I think your testimonies, particularly Sam's, were responsible for the guilty verdict. When did Sam talk to the woman?"

"About noon today."

"Did Sam call you?" Taylor said.

"Yes," Joe said.

"What time?"

"Didn't look at my watch. But it was before one o'clock. My partner and I were on a stakeout all last night. I was beat and lay my head on my desk for a short nap at one."

"Back to the button. What time did you get it?"

"Two o'clock. Don, who works for Dr. Cutler, brought me the autopsy report on the latest murder and the button. Robert, I have to tell you something else. I'm separated from my wife. I have been dating Warren's ex-wife, Diane Lightfoot, for about three weeks."

"Dick, what do you make of all this?" Taylor said.

"Joe's love life is his own business. Some in the community might make an issue of it, but Diane and Warren have been divorced for years. The car is the least persuasive piece of evidence. The witness is not available at this time, and we don't have an affidavit of her comments. However, the button is persuasive since Joe was the witness. I think a search warrant is justified. If we can find the jacket with the missing button, we have probable cause to arrest him."

"Couldn't have summarized the situation better myself. Anything else, Dick?" Taylor said.

"Yes. The bodies of all three murder victims were left in arranged positions similar to Christian symbols. The murder early this morning was in a Christian cross. Also, all three murders occurred on the date of a dark moon. Joe and Sam developed a profile of the murderer based on these characteristics. I thought it was crap until Joe came to me with the evidence pointing at Warren. He left our Methodist church a few years ago and joined a conservative Pentecostal church. It's not compelling evidence at this time, but a pattern is emerging."

"Interesting, but not pertinent to your request. I do think the button is key at this point, and time is of the essence. Actually, I have such a high regard for Sam Rucker that I don't doubt what he told Joe is true. But that's not enough right now. One more question, Joe. What has been your contact and relationship with Warren Abernathy?"

"Robert, other than what Diane Lightfoot told me about her marriage and divorce, I've seen Warren only two times. First, at a party hosted by Stanford Ramsey. I was Diane's escort. She introduced me to Warren. I found him a bit pretentious. The second time I saw him was with the Shakespearean group at Franklin Pierce's house. That night I found him warmer and more friendly."

"No animosities toward him?" Taylor said.

"Absolutely not," Joe said.

"Lance, you've been quiet. What do you think? Do you agree that a search warrant is justified."

Lance paused. "First a murder this morning, and now all this out of the blue, but I won't say no. I hope Joe and Dick are right for their sake."

"Good. I'm satisfied we can proceed."

"If we find the jacket with the missing button, will you grant us permission to look for the car in his home?" Joe said.

"Yes, I'll go that far. Do you have Abernathy's home address?"

"Yes." Joe handed Taylor the paper Brendan had given him.

Taylor passed the address to Vince. "Prepare the search warrant for my signature, and the affidavit for Detective McGrath's signature."

ON THE WAY BACK TO HEADQUARTERS, Joe said to Dick, "He was sure the right judge to ask for this."

"The only judge. No one else on the bench in Birmingham would have given us the time of day. You going after Abernathy right away?"

"You bet. I'll grab Brendan as support, and we'll take off."

"I'll wait in my office until you return. With or without Warren, I want to be briefed. I may sit in on the interrogation if you bring him back."

"Okay."

"Joe, this better go well. If it blows up, it's not gonna be pretty. You heard what Lance said."

When they got to headquarters, each went to his office.

"Brendan, up and at 'em. We're in business. Got a search warrant. Let's go. I'll fill you in on the way."

CHAPTER 57

THE SEARCH

WEDNESDAY—NOVEMBER 12, 1947

I T WAS HALF PAST SEVEN when Joe and Brendan left headquarters. As they drove toward the Forest Park neighborhood on the Southside, Joe explained the proceedings at Judge Taylor's office and the significance of the search warrant.

Brendan said, "Are we gonna arrest Abernathy?"

"That's the tricky part. We can arrest him if we determine after our search that we have probable cause. Worst case, we don't find a jacket with a missing button. No arrest. He now knows he's a suspect. Best case, we find a jacket with a missing button. We arrest him."

Brendan's eyes were as wide open as a nocturnal lemur's. "Sounds like this might not be easy."

"A search or arrest is never easy. It's important how we conduct the search. During the entire search, we back each other up. You never know how a suspect will react when challenged with a search warrant or arrest. "

Brendan seemed uncomfortable. "Okay."

"Don't worry. It usually goes pretty smoothly."

Joe turned onto Crescent Road, drove to Abernathy's address, and parked the car to the right of his house. When Brendan reached to open the car door, Joe put his hand on Brendan's arm. "Stay put a minute. Let's size up the house before we go in."

Joe figured the one-story house had eight or ten rooms. All the drapes and shutters were closed, but most rooms appeared to be lit. There was a garage attached to the rear of the house.

"Okay, let's go." They walked up the steps of the porch. Joe knocked on the door and said loudly, "Police. Detective Joe McGrath. I'm here to serve a search warrant."

Almost immediately, they heard soft footsteps, and the door opened slowly. Initially, Warren saw only Joe. "What's this all about, Joe? Are you Shylock looking for another pound—" Warren saw Brendan. His demeanor turned dour. "I take it this is not a social call?"

"Warren, as I announced, I have a search warrant that grants us permission to search your home." Joe handed a copy of the warrant to Warren. While Warren read the warrant, Joe observed him. He appeared composed and was wearing a silk lounging jacket. He was also wearing silk house slippers with an embroidered emblem on the toes that looked like the City of London coat of arms.

Warren looked up angrily. "This is an affront, Joe. I was just preparing to sit down for a light supper."

"We need to come in."

"Who's your henchman?"

"Officer Brendan O'Connor. He's my partner." Warren's stance blocked the door entry. "We need to come in, Warren."

Joe was about to force his way in when Warren stepped aside.

"Come in, Joe, with your partner in crime. I'm going to call Robert Beauchamp right now. He'll put a stop to this. You don't realize the trouble he can cause you. He'll have you two in the slammer in short order," Warren said.

Joe and Brendan stepped into the hallway and closed the door. "You're not calling anyone right now, Warren. This search warrant has been legally issued by Judge Taylor." Joe scanned the interior of the house. The living room was to the right and the dining room was to the left. "Where's your bedroom, Warren?"

Warren didn't answer.

"Dammit it, Warren, where's your bedroom?"

Warren looked like he was ready to spit nails at Joe. "Down the hallway. First door on the left."

"Lead the way," Joe said.

When Warren hesitated, Joe and Brendan took him by the arms and pushed him forward. Warren shook their arms off and walked ahead. Joe saw the study located just opposite the bedroom door. The study had two large sliding doors and afforded a good view into part of the bedroom. "Let's go in the study," Joe said.

Warren went with no resistance. There was a chair in the study that could be seen from the bedroom door. "Warren, you sit here."

Warren sat down. "What's next. You going to work me over?"

"No, you sit here quietly. Officer O'Connor will watch you. I'm going into your bedroom to look around. Don't cause any trouble."

Warren growled at Joe, his face a sardonic scowl. "You're going to pay for this, McGrath."

Joe said to Brendan, "I'm going to search the bedroom. If Warren tries to move, handcuff him to the chair."

Joe went into the bedroom. Brendan stood in front of Warren, ready to respond to any movement.

After Joe disappeared into the bedroom, Warren said, "I'm going to call Robert Beauchamp now. I have a right to do so." He started to rise from the chair.

Brendan put his hand on the gun in his holster. "Move your ass one more time, I'll cuff you to the chair."

Warren hesitated, but sat down. "Your career is on the line."

A few minutes later, Joe came out of the bedroom with a jacket over each forearm.

Warren looked at Joe and laughed. "So you've come to take the jackets you admired at Franklin Pierce's."

Joe held up the light brown jacket. "Nice. I particularly admired the buttons at Franklin's." There were no buttons missing.

Turning to the dark blue jacket, Joe said, "Identical except for the color. You seem to have lost a button."

Warren appeared unconcerned. "So. I haven't worn that jacket in weeks. It must have worked its way loose."

"Could this be the button?" Joe pulled the button from his pocket and held it in front of Warren's face.

Warren's jaw sagged. "Where did you get that? Did you tear it off my jacket?"

"Frank Cutler, the coroner, found it underneath the body of a young colored women who was murdered early this morning at Third Alley South."

Warren's eyes darted around like a cornered animal, "It must be off someone else's jacket. Certainly, you don't think I committed such a crime."

"Brendan, go look in the garage and see if the Buick's there." Joe said.

Brendan returned in several minutes. "Yes, it's the car, Joe."

"Warren, I'm placing you under arrest. Suspicion of murder. We're taking you to headquarters for questioning."

Warren spoke in a voice teetering on the edge of panic. "I must call Beauchamp. I need my lawyer."

"In due course. Let's go."

Pleading even more, Warren said, "I need a coat," as he slipped off his lounging jacket. "And some shoes."

"Is there a coat in the hall closet?"

"Yes."

"We'll grab it on the way out. Where are your shoes?"

"By my bed." Warren pointed across the hallway into his bedroom. His shoes were visible on the floor at the foot of the bed.

"Brendan, go with Warren while he puts on his shoes. I'm gonna look around the study."

"Let's go, Warren," Brendan said.

When they entered the bedroom, Warren looked around as if he'd never been in the room.

"Sit down. Put your shoes on," Brendan said.

Warren turned facing Joe in the study and sat on the end of the bed. Brendan stood to Warren's right.

Joe started searching the study.

Warren took his time. Every time he lifted a shoe or finished tying one, he glanced into the study to check on Joe's whereabouts.

Brendan, getting impatient, said, "C'mon, let's go."

"I'm almost done," Warren said, as he glanced up and didn't see Joe in the study. Warren added, "I'm ready."

At exactly the same moment, Joe called out, "Brendan, how's it going?"

Brendan turned his head toward Joe's voice. "We're coming right—"

Warren timed it perfectly. He lunged at Brendan with his right shoulder, hitting him with a full body blow to the chest. Brendan stumbled back, then lost his balance and fell hard. The right side of his head hit a small table behind him. The table toppled with a crash, and Brendan lost consciousness. Warren darted to the opposite side of the room.

Joe heard the table crash to the floor and dashed toward the bedroom. He saw Brendan sprawled out to his left and to his right, he saw Warren standing by a chest of drawers, his back to Joe.

Joe reached for his gun and yelled, "Warren, put your hands up and turn around slowly."

Warren started lifting his arms.

There was a loud gunshot.

CHAPTER 58

THE GAROTTE

WEDNESDAY—NOVEMBER 12, 1947

J OE FOUND A PHONE and called Dick Oliver. "Dick, Warren Abernathy just shot himself. He's dead. He's our guy. The button's missing off his jacket, and the 1948 Buick's in the garage. We need the coroner and some support immediately. Brendan's banged up, but he's okay."

"Jesus Christ. What happened?"

"Just get out here with the coroner and support. I'll fill you in when you get here."

"I'll call them right now. Then I'm on my way."

Joe had left Brendan for a few moments to make the phone call. After the call, he went back to the study where he had put Brendan, who had gotten up right after Warren shot himself. Brendan was still feeling a little woozy and had a large welt on his right temple. By the time Dick and the support units arrived, Brendan was feeling better, walking around shaking it off.

Joe told the support units to tape off the house and keep neighbors and others, who were already gathering, behind the tape and barriers. He added, "If any press show up, come get Captain Oliver or me."

Joe explained to Dick everything that had transpired since he and Brendan entered Warren's home. Dick listened carefully. "Is Brendan going to be okay?"

"Yes, I think so. He took a pretty good hit to the head, but he's a tough kid. We'll watch him," Joe said.

"Rookie mistake, huh?"

"No. Homicide detective mistake. I failed in my support duties. I shouldn't have sent him into the bedroom alone with Warren. Especially since Warren now knew about the evidence we had."

"Why do you think Warren shot himself instead of taking a shot at you or Brendan?" Dick asked.

"Good question." Joe's face was perplexed. "I don't know."

"I'm going to call Lance Roberts. Maybe he'll call Judge Overton. We have to be in court tomorrow at ten," Dick said.

"They gotta release Luke Matthew."

"Only if Roberts drops the charges and Overton agrees. That's why we have to be there," Dick said.

Frank Cutler and his team arrived. Joe showed them the body and explained what happened. "Frank, take a look at Brendan. He took a bad whack to his head when Warren shoved him down."

"Where is he?" Frank said.

"In the study," Joe said, pointing the way.

"Okay. Then I'll check the body. Who'll identify the body?"

"His parents, I assume. It's going to be tough. He stuck the gun in his mouth. His face is a mess."

Frank sighed. "My God, this is unbelievable. I knew Warren. He seemed like a good guy."

"Yeah. I guess you can never tell. I'm going to search closets and desks in other rooms unless you think we need to do some fingerprints or other forensic work," Joe said.

"Unless there's something you want done, I don't see a need."

"Have your guys go over the Buick in the garage. Maybe they'll find something—dirt, a piece of clothing—that will prove the car was at the murder site this morning."

"Will do," Cutler said.

Joe found Dick in Warren's small office. "Did you talk to Lance Roberts?" Joe said.

"Yes and to the chief. Just hung up. Roberts is going to call Judge Overton tonight. Roberts wants you and me in court tomorrow."

"What did he say about Matthew?" Joe said.

"He said if everything is as it appears, he'll drop the charges."

"Good. What did the chief say?"

"Not much for the chief," Dick said.

"Did you tell him about your conversation with Roberts?" Joe said.

"Yes. He didn't object. But I suspect we'll get a blast tomorrow. He wants you and me in his office at seven thirty in the morning."

"Cutler and his guys are with the body. I asked Frank to have his guys check the Buick. I'm going to go through Warren's things carefully for anything that might give us a hint to his motives."

"Don't forget what I told you about his joining a conservative Pentecostal church," Dick said.

"Good idea. I'm going—"

"Oh, here y'all are," an officer working the front of the house said. "Jack Ritter and a couple of other press guys are out front. They're chomping at the bit. One of y'all better come talk to them."

"I'll go," Dick said.

Joe started going through Warren's desk. He found three things of interest. A 1947 calendar with a single day in each month circled. Joe knew the dates circled in September, October, and November were dark moon days. He suspected the other months were also. A recent Sunday program from the Hallelujah Pentecostal Church in North Birmingham. A Bible with a bookmark at Luke 7:37 and 7:38, the biblical passages that led to the phrase the "kiss of salvation." There were no notes or other pieces of information that gave any clues as to Warren's intentions or state of mind.

Brendan came into the office. "Dr. Cutler says I'll be fine. Just a bruise and maybe a mild concussion. Hell, I got a couple of those playing football. No big deal. He's almost finished. He just sent a guy to get a body bag and gurney."

"Good. I gotta talk to Frank. I want you to go through all the drawers and bookcases in all the other rooms including the kitchen and bathrooms. Anything that appears to be related to Warren and the murders, bag it and bring it to the office. We'll go over it later. If you're unsure whether or not an item's important, bag it. I'll search Warren's bedroom after Cutler removes his body. Are you up to it?" Joe said.

"Christ, Joe, I told you, I'm okay."

Joe shrugged his shoulders. "Go to it, tiger. I'll see you in a bit."

Joe went to Warren's bedroom. The bagged body was being loaded on the gurney. "Frank, what you got?"

"It's definitely a suicide." Frank paused and tried not to grin. "Unless you pulled the trigger. We'll check to make sure the fingerprints on the gun match Warren's."

Joe faked shock. "Very funny, Dr. Cutter. What's next here?"

"We'll take the body to the morgue and notify his parents. I hate to do this to them, but they'll have to arrange and pay for a clean up crew. I'll give them the names and phone numbers of a few people that do that work," Frank said.

"Goddamn, that's tough. After you leave, I'm gonna search around."

"Sure. I did see a bullet clip and holster in the open drawer of the chest. I assume that's where he kept the gun."

"I didn't see him pull it out of the drawer, but I'm pretty sure that's where it was."

"Okay, we're on our way. I'll have a formal report written sometime tomorrow."

"Say, you told Brendan he had a mild concussion. Is he gonna be okay?"

Frank grinned at Joe. "Why, papa bear, you're worried about your cub. That's nice. Yes, Joe. He's going to be fine. We'll talk tomorrow."

Joe searched the closet first. He wanted to be more thorough than he had been when he was looking for the jackets. None of the remaining clothing were of interest. There were several hats on the closet shelf and one large hat box. He opened the box. The hat in it was similar to the one described by Sam's witness. Using his handkerchief, he removed the hat from the box and saw a garotte wrapped like a small lasso. He placed the hat back in the box. He wanted Cutler to analyze the items.

Joe found Brendan and handed him the hat box. "Run this out to Cutler out front. Tell him I want the garotte analyzed. I think it's the murder weapon. If he's gone, take the box to his office when we get back to headquarters."

"Will do. I'll be right back."

Joe returned to the chest of drawers and found only clothing. He searched the two bookcases, a dresser, and one of two bedside tables and found nothing of interest.

The bottom and middle drawers of the other bedside table were equally uninteresting. He opened the top drawer and saw a large envelope. He picked it up and read on the envelope, "The Last Will and Testament of Warren Michael Abernathy, Jr." Joe added it to the other items he had. The only things remaining in the top drawer were pens and pencils, and pads of blank note paper.

Joe went into the living room. Brendan was back and searching the room. "Did you give the hat box to Cutler?"

"Yes," Brendan said.

"Have you found anything?"

"I bagged a few items. But I don't think they're pertinent."

"We'll check them back at the office. Go ahead and finish up. I found something I want to read."

Joe sat in a comfortable chair and opened the envelope. As he unfolded the will, Dick Oliver came back into the house. Joe put the will back in the envelope.

"Well. It's always fun with those newshounds," Dick said.

"What did you tell them?"

"As much as we know. They were shocked to hear that Warren Abernathy was a suspect in the murders."

Joe was surprised Dick had been so cooperative with the press. "The chief and Ramsey won't be happy."

"It's better to take the heat from those two now than later. We might as well set the record straight from the start. You know Ritter will dig out all the details."

Joe couldn't help smiling. "You're starting to sound like me, Dick."

"Heaven forbid. I'm going home. I'll see you in the morning before we meet with the chief."

"Okay. I'm going to have a few men stay around until we're sure the house is ready to be released to the family even if it takes all night and into tomorrow."

Dick nodded and left.

"I'm finished, boss," Brendan said.

"Good. Let's wrap up and go back to the office."

They gathered all their items and went out front. Joe scanned the three officers working the perimeter of the house and saw Steve Strickland.

"Hey, Steve. Over here. It's Joe McGrath."

"Hey, Detective McGrath. I saw you earlier but didn't have a chance to say hi."

"I want coverage here all night and tomorrow. If shifts run out, call the desk officer and get replacements. Don't stop the coverage until you get a call from headquarters telling you it's all right to take the tape and barriers down. I don't want any strangers or press getting into the house. Here's a set of keys I found. I checked them. This key locks the front door. You or your replacements lock the house up completely before you leave, and bring the keys back to headquarters. We'll give them to the family. Okay?"

Steve grinned at Joe's explicit instructions. "Yes, sir. We'll take good care of it."

Back at headquarters, Joe said, "Brendan, go home. I'll see you in the morning before we have to go to the courthouse."

Joe went to his office and sat in his chair. Actually, it was more of a sag. He was exhausted, mentally and physically, but he had to read the will. It was eight typed page dated January 22, 1947. He made a mental note: *Check if that's a new moon date.* He read through it quickly. It was standard legal language describing the disposition of his property and assets to his parents and siblings.

When he had briefly glanced at the will at Warren's home, he had noticed some handwriting on the back page. He turned the will over. It was written in black ink and was dated August 16, 1947. *Check that date.* He read the handwritten page. He shook his head and put the will back in the envelope.

But before he called it a day, he had to talk to Sam and Diane. He picked up the phone.

CHAPTER 59

WARREN'S WILL

THURSDAY—NOVEMBER 13, 1947

T HE ALARM WENT OFF AT SIX. Joe wanted to reread the will before he went to work. After he showered, shaved, and got dressed, he brewed a cup of coffee and sat in his large chair.

He reread the typed pages and turned to the handwritten page.

Dear Mom and Dad,

I hope you never have to see my will because that means something awful has come to light about me.

I know you're both disappointed in me. For reasons I don't comprehend, I have been unable to find and hold meaningful employment. I also know that many people call me the "Birmingham Playboy."

Dad, I appreciate all the doors you have opened for me over the years. Please forgive me for my lack of interest in the opportunities your efforts afforded me. I suppose I was born too close to money and never came to understand how precious other things can be. Perhaps you should have disowned me and cut off my monthly stipend to force me forward.

Mom, I know I broke your heart when I left the family church and joined Hallelujah Pentecostal. I was searching for some meaning and understanding in my self and life. I had been unable to find it elsewhere.

Someday, you may hear upsetting things about me, and actions I have taken.

Please know I love you and seek your understanding and forgiveness.

All my love,
Warren

Joe paused, still unsure of how to interpret what he had just read. A line was drawn across the page at this point. It was undated and written in pencil in the same hand.

I forgot to ask you to tell Byron and Abigail that I love them. I know the happiness they gave you as your normal children. Your three grandchildren are your gifts from God. I loved those kids as if they were mine. I melted when they called me Uncle Warren.

I wish my marriage to Diane had turned out as well. You must know that our breakup was all my fault. Diane never realized whom she was marrying. Please tell her I'm sorry and wish her well.

I am a shattered human being,
Demons prey upon my soul,
Have mercy dear God,
Pray for me—

Joe reread the handwritten page several times. Try as he might, he couldn't fight back the tears forming in his eyes. *Are these the pleadings of a tortured man seeking redemption? Is it a suicide note? Is it the ramblings of a madman? Probably a bit of each.*

He put the will back in the envelope. The only thing he was sure of was that he had to give it to the family.

JOE STOPPED AT THE COPS' DINER TO GET A QUICK BREAKFAST.

He slipped into a seat at the counter when Helen spotted him. "Hey, Big Dick. You're early. Where's Puppy Dog?"

"Hi, Helen. You know how young guys sleep to the last minute before they rush to work."

"I wish I had a bunk mate like that. What you having?"

"Two over easy, sausage, toast, and coffee. In a hurry."

"Comin' up, handsome."

Helen brought his breakfast, and Joe wolfed it down. When he saw Helen was busy in the back, he paid his bill at the cash register and left without saying goodbye.

At headquarters, Joe stopped by the desk officer to see if it was Billy Donaldson.

"Hey, Billy."

"Hi, Joe. Some night, huh?"

"An understatement, Billy. I got a question. You told me that the guy who called in the murder yesterday morning hung up without identifying himself."

"Correct."

"How would you describe his voice?"

"Umm, that's a tough one. Well, it probably wasn't a working man or a colored man. I guess it was a refined southern accent. I mean, maybe like a college professor. Oops, I don't mean you, Joe."

Joe laughed. "I know. Do you think the voice had the hint of a British accent?"

"I don't know much about British accents, but I suppose so. It sure was a bit different."

"Thanks, Billy."

"Do you think you know who it was?"

"Possibly, but could never prove it. See you around."

Joe got to his office just before seven thirty.

Dick Oliver came in soon after. "Well, Joe. Ready to go meet your Maker?"

Joe shrugged. "I guess now's as good a time as any."

When they got to the chief's office suite, his secretary was not at her desk.

The chief was sitting in his office, the door open. He called out in a calm voice, "Y'all c'mon in."

They both said good morning to the chief.

"Sit down, my two super sleuths. I kinda understand you, Joe. What I gonna call you Dick, a Turncoat? Look, you both on the front page of the *Post*." Watson threw the newspaper on his desk facing the two men. The headline was plastered across the top of the front page.

Prominent Birmingham Man Commits Suicide
Suspected as Murderer of Three Prostitutes

"Can't wait to see what Ritter has to say about you in the afternoon *News*," Watson said.

Neither man said a word.

"Why didn't y'all tell me what was going on?"

Dick spoke up. "Chief, after we talked to you yesterday about our meeting with Judge Overton, events started moving so fast that Joe and I hardly had time to talk to each other."

"You sure as shit had time to talk to Judge Taylor."

"Joe didn't learn about the button or the Buick until late Wednesday afternoon. We had to hustle to get to Judge Taylor's office. We needed to get the warrant so Joe and Brendan could go search Abernathy's home before he destroyed evidence or killed again," Dick said.

"Whaddya got to say, Joe?" Watson said.

"Dick's covered it well. The button Cutler found under the murder victim's body was missing from one of Abernathy's jackets that had identical buttons on it. Brendan verified the Buick was in Abernathy's garage. I also found the garot . . . I mean the small rope he used to strangle the women. Cutler's checking the rope to see if tissue or a blood sample on it matches the women killed last night."

Watson still appeared calm. "So now what?"

"Joe and I have to be in Judge Overton's court at ten. I think Lance Roberts is going to drop the charges against Luke Matthew. I assume Overton will release Matthew," Dick said.

Watson's voice got a bit more edgy. "We got a signed confession from that darkie. Now you tells me he goin' free and clear."

Joe knew he should keep his mouth shut but he couldn't take it. "Chief, you know the confession was beaten out of Matthew. I saw him the morning after his beating. It was vicious. Hell, most men would've signed."

Watson glowered at the men. "Goddammit, you two, get your butts outta here. I gotta think about this."

Outside the chief's office, Joe said, "Well, it could've been worse."

"I suppose, except I think he was just starting to emerge from the eye of the hurricane at the end," Dick said.

Back at his office, Joe said, "Hey, Sally. I'm sorry I didn't get my Hershey's Kiss this morning."

She smiled at Joe. "That's just the way it is some days, Joe. But I think you need one after what I just read in the morning paper."

"Tough night. I've got to go to the courthouse now. I need you to do two things for me. Type up the handwritten notes on the back of Warren Abernathy's will. Don't let the original out of your hands. It has to go back to the family. Put the typed notes in the top center drawer of my desk."

He handed Sally the envelope with the will.

"All right. What else?" Sally said.

"I need you to make a phone call for me. Let me get the number."

Joe went into his office, found the number for Dr. Theroux, and wrote it down on a piece of paper. He gave it to Sally. "Please tell his office I can't make my appointment today, but that I plan to be there next Thursday."

Sally recognized Dr. Theroux's name. She looked at Joe as he walked away, more as a mother than a secretary.

CHAPTER 60

DIANE'S DISBELIEF

THURSDAY—NOVEMBER 13, 1947

"I DON'T KNOW WHAT TO THINK, JOE. How could Warren do such things?" Joe had his arm around Diane as she leaned against his shoulder, weeping softly. It was Thursday night, the day after Warren's suicide. Joe had come over to her apartment and cooked supper.

"We'll never know a good answer to that question. But you gotta understand. You don't bear any responsibility for what happened."

"But I can't help wondering. Do you think he murdered other women when he was married to me?"

"There isn't a shred of evidence supporting any other similar murders. We checked back quite a ways. Nothing like this has happened in Birmingham or in all of Alabama." Joe pulled her tightly to him and stroked her hair.

"Remember. I told you he used to go out all night when we were married. He'd never talk about it. What do you suppose he was doing?"

"I have no idea. I'm just glad you divorced him for your sake." He pulled her head back and smiled. "And for my sake."

"I'm so glad you're here." She kissed him. "Take me to bed, Joe."

After making passionate love, they lay quietly thinking about the day's event. Diane finally said, "I read the newspapers today, but I couldn't focus. What happened?"

"Both good and irrational things," Joe said.

"Like what?"

"The good thing was that Lance Roberts dropped the charges against Luke Matthew. Judge Overton ordered him released immediately. My sidekick, Brendan O'Connor, took him home soon after court was dismissed."

"I know you thought he was innocent all along. Did the chief say anything after Matthew was released?"

"Not to me. I'm sure he will later. Before Dick Oliver and I went to Judge Overton's courtroom, we talked to Chief Watson. Actually, he was pretty calm at first. But when Matthew's name came up, he was his usual irrational self. In spite of what happened yesterday, I'm sure he'd just as soon seen Matthew tried for the murders. But the toughest thing was Warren's parents having to go to the morgue to identify the body. His brother and sister were with them. I wasn't there, but Frank Cutler said it was awful," Joe said

"God, I feel so sorry for them. Couldn't you have done it? You saw it happen," Diane said.

"The next of kin have to make the identification."

"I'll call them tomorrow and go see them if they wish," Diane said.

"I'm sure they'll appreciate that." Joe stared at the ceiling as if lost. He turned inward and said nothing for several minutes.

"What's on your mind? You look worried?" Diane said.

"Not worried. My mind's just spinning with all that's happened recently." He sat straight up in bed, turned to Diane and took her hand. "More good news though. The Wednesday before Thanksgiving I'm going to Huntsville to get my daughter, Jane. I can't wait. It's been almost a month since I've seen her. We'll spend Thanksgiving Day with my mother in Montevallo."

Diane's looked down. "Oh, that's nice."

Joe nudged his nose next to hers. "But we'll be back Thursday evening, and we can do something together on Friday and Saturday. I'll have to take Jane back to Huntsville on Sunday."

Diane smiled. "That's wonderful. Can I take her to Maxine's on Friday? We have some beautiful clothes for young girls."

"Of course. I know she'd love that. And then the three of us can go to Britling for lunch or an early dinner. We'll have a great time. It's Jane's favorite restaurant."

Joe turned out the bedside lamp. The two snuggled together, and he had his best night's sleep in a long time.

CHAPTER 61

RAMSEY'S RETREAT

FRIDAY—NOVEMBER 14, 1947

"S IT DOWN, JOE. THANKS FOR COMING," Stanford Ramsey said.

"Your secretary's call yesterday didn't sound like one that could be ignored," Joe said.

"Business, Joe. Quite a feather in your cap identifying Warren Abernathy as the murderer of those three prostitutes. The entire city's still abuzz with the story and Warren's suicide. And I heard Matthew was released after Roberts dropped the charges against him."

"Yes. About time."

"I suppose. As usual, Jack Ritter's column in the *News* trumped anything the morning *Post* could do. Ritter can't stop singing your praises. Did you feed him all the details?" Ramsey said.

"No. Dick Oliver talked to him and some other press guys the night Warren shot himself."

"Did anyone else talk to Ritter? He wrote about the unidentified person who saw Warren's car the night of the second murder and the button from his jacket found under the body of the third victim."

"Ritter has lots of contacts. Dick Oliver, the chief. Maybe even you."

Ramsey ignored the comment. "Big Bob Watson would like to can you and Dick. He said you two went behind his back with Judge Overton and then with Judge Taylor to get a search warrant."

"Yeah, that's true. We didn't clear things with the chief. But only because of timing. Events were moving so fast last Wednesday, we had little choice. We did explain things to the chief Thursday morning. He was pretty calm until he kicked us out of his office. Do you want us canned, Stanford?"

"I'll reel Dick in. He moves with the wind. Not my call on you."

"Oh, c'mon, Stanford. We all know the chief's your puppet."

"What do you want out of all this, Joe?"

"Two things. But certainly not the hero stuff Ritter's writing. I wish he'd turn it off. I'd like a six-month paid leave of absence. I want to spend most of my time in Montevallo, my hometown, trying to find the men who murdered my father twenty-four years ago." Joe told Stanford more about his father's murder.

"Now I remember that murder. Sounded awful. Do you really think you can find the murderer after so long a time?" Stanford said.

"I don't know, but I've got to try."

"Admirable. What's the second thing?"

"Stanford, I know about Mahogany Hall. I know what goes on there. The women, the white men in masks, the orgies. I know you own the place. I know prostitutes are sent up from New Orleans by your ex-mistress, who runs a brothel in the city. I know how they get from downtown Birmingham to Mahogany Hall. I've seen the place on a busy night."

Ramsey didn't so much as blink an eye. "Assuming anything you just said is true, what are you going to do with the information?"

"If all this gets out, somebody could face some stiff time for violating the Mann Act. I'd like you to stop having the girls transported over state lines from New Orleans."

"Are you trying to blackmail me, Joe? You may or may not know that I don't react too well to such threats."

"No. My first request is not conditioned on you doing anything about Mahogany Hall. But I do suggest you think long and hard about its continued operation. When I learned of it, I was surprised more people didn't know about it. Or maybe they do and keep their mouths shut because of your power and wealth. If Mahogany Hall becomes public knowledge, I don't think you'd appreciate the possible consequences. I'm not on a crusade to do away with prostitution in Birmingham. But I would like you and Marcus Gilbert to stop using the ladies from New Orleans."

"So Marcus is one of your sources for all this?"

"Nope. Marcus didn't say a word to me about Mahogany Hall or New Orleans," Joe said.

"Well, who are your sources?"

Joe couldn't help grinning. "Stanford, you know a good cop or reporter doesn't reveal his sources."

Joe felt Stanford's harsh gaze as he considered his options. "I'll tell Big Bob to approve your paid leave of absence. I'll think about the second item. Don't cross me, Joe."

"I won't, Stanford. But I do hope you take some action with Mahogany Hall."

As soon as Joe was out of his office, Stanford made a phone call. "It's time to implement the demo plan."

"All the way, Boss?"

"Yes. Get on it immediately. Start clearing it out today."

CHAPTER 62

JOE AND SAM'S CHOICES

SATURDAY—NOVEMBER 15, 1947

S AM WOKE EARLY ON SATURDAY MORNING FEELING ROTTEN. He had attended a dinner party at his mother's home last night. While nothing was said about Janice or his new lady friend, he sensed his mother and sisters' continued unhappiness with him.

Joe was coming over at nine to talk about the last few days. Sam put on his slippers and bathrobe and shuffled to the kitchen to make a pot of coffee.

A cup of hot coffee in hand, Sam went to his studio office and had the operator make a call.

"Hello, Miss Yolanda Chaisson's residence."

"Good morning, Frederick. It's Sam Rucker."

"Mr. Sam. Good to hear your voice."

"Is it too early to talk to Yolanda?"

"It's never too early or too late for you. Miss Yolanda would be angry at me if I didn't tell her you called. I'll go tell her."

"Sam, I've missed you. How are you?" Yolanda said.

"Lonely. I miss you too. I'd like to come to New Orleans soon."

"Oh, goody." Yolanda sounded like a child. "Can you come for Thanksgiving?"

"I wish. I'm committed to my mother and sisters on Thanksgiving. I was thinking about the first week in December."

"Wonderful. I can't wait. How's Mahogany Hall going?"

"The guy who murdered the prostitutes was found, a white guy from a prominent Birmingham family. He committed suicide when Joe McGrath tried to arrest him. Joe's the guy I've been working with. He's a homicide detective with the BPD."

"You've been working with a white cop?"

"Yeah. He's a good guy and my friend. We make a good team. You'd like him. "

"If you like him, I'm sure I would."

"There's a real twist in the case. Joe called me Wednesday night to tell me the news. He said the murderer, Warren Abernathy, is, or was I guess, the ex-husband of Diane Lightfoot, the lady he's seeing right now."

"My God. How awful for her. Maybe Joe and Diane would like to come to New Orleans to get away from it all. I have a nice guest room they could use. If they're uncomfortable staying here, there are lots of good hotels nearby. We could at least show them around New Orleans and some good restaurants."

"Joe will be here at nine. I'll talk to him about it. I'll let you know."

"Okay. Take the train. It's safer and more comfortable. I'll have Frederick pick you up at the Southern Railway Terminal."

"Good idea. I'll do it and suggest it to Joe also. I gotta go shower and get dressed. Can't wait to see you. My blood's boiling."

"Good. Keep it on boil. I love you."

JOE WAS TEMPTED TO PARK IN FRONT OF SAM'S HOME and knock on the front door. Instead he parked in the back as usual, realizing his rash impulse might lead to another bomb.

Sam, waiting at the back door, said, "C'mon in, conquering hero."

"Oh, stop that shit," Joe said. "I've been getting it from everyone, including Stanford Ramsey."

"Want a cup of coffee?" Sam said.

"You bet."

"Comin' up. Go sit down in the dining room."

Sam brought two cups of coffee to the table.

"Your house looks great." Joe said.

"Thanks. Don't tell the Klan. They might do a remodel. Hey, since you called me Wednesday night and told me the murderer was Warren

Abernathy, that's all I've read about in the newspapers. I was shocked when you told me that Abernathy was the ex-husband of your lady friend Diane Lightfoot. That's gotta be tough."

"Yeah, it's tough."

"You might not be a hero, but you did a good job, Joe."

"Strange. I don't feel that way. Of course, I'm glad we found the murderer and that Matthew is free. But it's wrapped around so much else. Diane, Chief Watson, Dick Oliver, Ramsey and Mahogany Hall, you, your lady Yolanda, me, and yes, Warren."

"You can't carry everybody's load," Sam said.

"I know. I keep telling Diane that. She's distraught over the whole situation. She's struggling to get a handle on things."

"Not surprising. Sounds like you are too. Do you have doubts that Warren is the murderer?"

Joe was surprised at the question. "No. Not for a minute. The car and the button are proof enough. And I found more in Warren's home. There was a large hat box in his closet. The hat looks similar to the one described by your witness."

"Her name is Mrs. Ethel Baker. Keep it to yourself. She a delightful and honest lady," Sam said.

Joe nodded. "Under the hat was a garotte, the type of weapon used to strangle the women. Cutler found blood and tissue samples in the rope that matched those of the woman killed early Wednesday morning. No doubt in my mind that Warren is the murderer."

"So what's eating at you?"

"Here, read this." He handed Sam the typed copy of Warren's handwritten notes. "It was written on the back of Warren's will. It's his handwriting, I had it verified. I had Brendan check the dates on the will and the notes. Both are dark moon days."

Sam read the typed notes, not once but several times. "It sure reads like a suicide note or, at least, an expression of the tormented soul of a man fighting demons."

"Maybe both. The phone call reporting the body and location came from a guy. The call was short. He didn't identify himself."

"Is that unusual?" Sam said.

"Nope. Happens a lot. After I read Warren's letter, I asked Billy Donaldson, who took the call, how he would describe the voice. He said it probably wasn't a colored man or a white working man, but more a refined southern voice. I had to lead him a bit by asking if the voice had any hint of a British accent. Billy said he didn't know much about British accents, but he supposed that was possible. I've talked to Warren several times and came to recognize he liked to mix a British accent into his southern speech," Joe said.

"I see where you're going," Sam said.

"Yep. Warren was the caller, and he put the button under the dead woman's body. I can never prove it so I want to keep it quiet. I thought about telling Diane and Warren's parents. Bad idea, just another thing for them to try and understand when there is little understanding."

"Do you think Warren set this up so he could commit suicide in your presence?" Sam said.

"I don't think so. He was surprised when we came to his home Wednesday night. I do think he was contemplating suicide. When he realized we had closed in on him so soon after the last murder, he decided to shoot himself that night. Just my theory, no proof."

"Plausible. Have you talked to the minister at that Pentecostal church Warren was attending? Might give you more insight into his state of mind," Sam said.

"How do you know about the Pentecostal church?"

"You called and told me Wednesday night right after Warren committed suicide."

Joe's face was blank. "Christ, I forgot. I'll get to the minister next week."

"I got two thoughts about why you're so bothered by this case and the outcome."

Joe was concerned. *Do I want to hear this?* But he said, "Yes?"

"You and Brendan were sent to look for probable cause in Warren's home and bring him in if you found any. You found the evidence you needed. You won't like this. You and Brendan fucked up the second part. You failed to bring him in alive," Sam said.

Joe grimaced as if he had been hit. "I know. It wasn't Brendan's fault. All mine. I failed to back him up properly when he was alone with Warren in the bedroom. Yeah, it's eating at me."

"Hard lesson, but you gotta get over it. You're still a good cop. You gotta know it doesn't always work out as planned."

"What else?" Joe said.

"I'm gonna sound like I'm preaching. We all wanna get the culprit. But in this case, I don't think it matters."

Joe was surprised. "Whaddya mean?"

"A white guy with money and social connections in this city could hire a good defense attorney like Robert Beauchamp. He would have gotten Warren off. Or at a minimum, with a light sentence," Sam said.

"You gotta be kidding. Even with all the evidence we found?"

"Christ, Joe, get real. You've forgotten where you live. This is Birmingham, not Boston."

Joe rubbed his head and relaxed a bit. "Right. The white man walks out the door. The colored man walks to the chair."

"Trite, but true. You gonna be all right?"

"Yeah. I'm seeing Dr. Theroux next Thursday. He'll want to know more about Warren. I'll ask him what he thinks about his suicide."

Sam was surprised, as he didn't know Joe was continuing to see Theroux. "That's a good idea. Lemme change the subject. I called Yolanda before you came over. I'm going to New Orleans the first week in December. She invited you and Diane to come along and enjoy her city. She said you could stay at her home or a nearby hotel."

Joe appeared confused. In spite of his several meetings at Sam's home, he had never been asked by a colored person to come to their home for a social visit. "Well, thanks. I'll have to talk to Diane."

Sam could sense Joe's reticence. "I'm sure Diane and Yolanda would get along. They have a lot in common. Diane's interested in dress design, and Yolanda's a successful interior decorator. New Orleans isn't perfect, Joe. But at least there are good restaurants and shops we could go to together."

"A getaway from Birmingham would be good. My daughter's with me over Thanksgiving. I have to take her back to Huntsville on November thirtieth. Lemme think about it and talk to Diane."

"Sure. It's okay to say no, Joe."

Joe smiled and nodded. "Thanks, you're a good friend. I also met with Stanford Ramsey yesterday."

"That musta been interesting. How'd it go?"

"Okay, I guess. I want to take a six-month paid leave of absence after the first of the year. I asked Stanford to support my request. He said he'd tell Chief Watson to approve it. Then I told him what we know about Mahogany Hall, but I didn't mention your name. I asked him to stop having the girls brought up here from New Orleans. He was not happy. Told me not to cross him, but said he'd think about it," Joe said.

"Watch your step with Ramsey. I'm told he doesn't like to be challenged," Sam said.

"Right. First of next week I'm going to take Brendan with me in a full dress police car to Mahogany Hall just to get a good look at the place in the daylight."

"Do you think that's a good idea?"

"If anybody gives us a hard time, I'll tell 'em we had a complaint from someone who drove in here by accident and was threatened."

"Ramsey won't like it if he hears you've been to Mahogany Hall again. He might nix your leave of absence."

"I've thought about that. If he does, I may resign from the force and become a private investigator."

Sam roared with laughter. "So now we're competitors. You probably should reconsider that. It's a tough racket, hard to make a living."

"Yeah, I know. But hear me out. Why don't we become partners?"

"You have lost your marbles. The Klan would be all over our asses and if we're lucky, that's all. The cops sure as hell wouldn't treat us like partners. Shit, no one would."

"Got a solution for that. I'd have to be the up-front owner and operator of the business. You'd work for me. Hell, many white businesses have colored staff in good positions. We'd sign a confidential business agreement making us equal partners."

Sam was unsure. "Why do you want the leave of absence?'

"I wanna spend time in Montevallo trying to find the men who murdered my father twenty-four years ago." Joe explained the background of the murder.

Sam's eyes brightened at the thought of being involved in another complex murder case. "What would I do while you're in Montevallo?"

"Leave of absence or new business, I'd like you to work with me on the case in Montevallo," Joe said.

Sam's face hardened.

Joe was sure Sam was going to say no.

Sam's expression softened to a warm smile. "When do we start?"

Acknowledgments

As with any new endeavor, there are more people to thank than memory, time, and space allow. Suffice it to say that this book, my first murder mystery, would have not been possible without them.

Four experts in their respective fields provided useful guidance and knowledge that I did not possess: Caryl Privett, a judge on the 10th Judicial Circuit Court in Birmingham, Jefferson County, Alabama, on local legal and jurisdictional issues; John Thornton, Professor Emeritus of Forensic Science at the University of California Berkeley, on forensic issues in 1947; Ron Welch, a retired Kaiser Hospital psychiatrist, on matters of the psyche; and Mike Worley, retired police officer, investigations commander, chief of police, and now a noted writer of murder mysteries, on police policies and procedures.

Writers and friends who read and commented on the manuscript include David Beckman, Armando Garcia-Dávila, Karen Hart, Tara Harvey, Dale Head, Liz Martin, and Linda McCabe.

Suzan Reed, an extraordinary graphic designer, developed and designed the gripping cover that encases *Kiss of Salvation*.

Arlene Miller and Jeanne Miller (not related) separately edited my manuscript with a keen eye for my grammar and punctuation mistakes. But they did have to restrain themselves to avoid correcting some of the Southern dialogue.

Any errors remaining in the book are mine, and mine alone.

As always, my lovely wife, Liz Martin, was my constant companion and staunchest supporter of my work.

About the Author

Waights Taylor Jr., born and raised in Birmingham, Alabama, lives in Santa Rosa, California. His professional career included twenty-four years in the aviation industry and then twenty-two years in management consulting. When his professional career was coming to an end, he turned to writing.

Made in the USA
San Bernardino, CA
30 August 2014